"An entertaining, cyberpunk vision of the near future delivered with just the right amount of wry humour. *Reality 36* is a spirited beginning with momentum and ideas to spare. At its sculpted titanium core it's an all-action, pulpy thriller, but it hums with inventive near-future concepts."

SFX Magazine

"Guy Haley is a force for good, a hidden gem of British SF."

Paul Cornell

"*Reality 36* displays fascinating characters in a very believable future."

Five-time Hugo Award winner Mike Resnick

"Haley's wit is both laugh-out-loud and sharp as a sword."

John Whitbourn, author of BBC prize-winning *A Dangerous Energy*

D0807745

GUY HALEY

Reality 36

A RICHARDS & KLEIN INVESTIGATION

ANGRY
ROBOT

ANGRY ROBOT

A member of the Osprey Group
Midland House, West Way
Botley, Oxford
OX2 0PH
UK

www.angryrobotbooks.com
53 49 4E 47 55 4C 41 52 49 54 59

An Angry Robot paperback original 2011
1

Copyright © Guy Haley 2011

Guy Haley asserts the moral right to be
identified as the author of this work.

A catalogue record for this book is available
from the British Library.

ISBN: 978-0-85766-145-6
EBook ISBN: 978-0-85766-147-0

Set in Meridien by THL Design.

Printed in the UK by CPI Mackays, Chatham, ME5 8TD.

All rights reserved. No part of this publication may be reproduced,
stored in a retrieval system, or transmitted, in any form or by any
means, electronic, mechanical, photocopying, recording or
otherwise, without the prior permission of the publishers.

This book is sold subject to the condition that it shall not, by
way of trade or otherwise, be lent, re-sold, hired out or
otherwise circulated without the publisher's prior consent in
any form of binding or cover other than that in which it is
published and without a similar condition including this
condition being imposed on the subsequent purchaser.

This novel is entirely a work of fiction. The names, characters and
incidents portrayed in it are the work of the author's imagination.
Any resemblance to actual persons, living or dead, events or
localities is entirely coincidental.

SF
4737

For my mother, who encouraged me to write.
For my father, who always listened to my stories.

"All members of the Community of Equals are created free and equal in dignity and rights."
Extract from Article One of the 2114 Amendment to the Universal Declaration of Human Rights

"Every sentient being: naturally derived, artificially created, altered, upgraded or otherwise – who seeks to dwell within the borders of the European Union, whether in physical actuality or within the confines of sovereign European Union designated virtual spaces, agrees without reservation to abide by the laws of the European Union, to be held accountable for their actions as such accountability is defined by their status under the law, to serve the interests of said state and its federal components... [and] to support it wholeheartedly according to their obligations as detailed in Directive 44871/112-b: 'Responsibilities and Rights of European Union Member State Citizens.'"
Paragraph 8172, sub-section 47d 9 (abridged) of the 2078 European Parliamentary Directive regulating Synthetic, Simian, Cetacean, Trans- and Post-human entities

"Freedom is not a luxury to be conferred upon those possessed of sentience; it is a fundamental and inalienable right of the sentient."
Professor Zhang Qifang, speaking at the Napoli Science Symposium, "Morality in and toward Created Intelligences", Wednesday, January 18, 2113

PROLOGUE
Richards

Richards' body was a sculpted titanium box 1.793 metres high, 2.47 metres wide and 1.323 metres deep – at these dimensions' extremes, for in form he was fluid and bulbous, as most such AI hardware was.

This shell was hardened against physical and electromagnetic attack, armour beneath the gleaming surface a complicated laminate of rare metals, semifluid conductors and active metalloid buffers. Holes of differing diameters pierced the final layer – a jacket of cleverly stacked copper atoms – creating a broad-spectrum Faraday cage. The delicate electronic brain of the man, if you could call it a brain, or if you could call him a man, sat inside: a fourteen-tiered ziggurat of latticed graphene spun on microgravity looms, the electrons that carried the messages of Richards' mind going about the business of yesses, nos and multitudinous maybes of quantum computing upon it.

Richards liked his base unit, old-fashioned as it was. Many other Class Five AIs preferred plus-C optical set-ups, but not Richards. He claimed, when asked, that this older configuration gave him time to think. All who knew him well knew the truth to be somewhat more sentimental.

The base unit sat upon a pyramid at the exact centre of a vault of machine-woven metal, a ten-metre cube perfect to the millimetre. The base unit was static and had no motive parts, but the pedestal pyramid could move, and did, when occasion demanded, for it floated upon an enclosed bed of mercury, protecting Richards from external shock. Though the pedestal and base unit combined massed at little under a metric tonne, they were balanced so that were a human being to enter the vault, he would have been able to push it round without difficulty.

Not that any human had ever been in the vault. The atmosphere was an unbreathable mix of noble gases, the temperature maintained at a precise -36 degrees Celsius, bathed by ultraviolet light sufficient to render the room biologically sterile.

There were other, less subtle discouragements to physical interference with the base unit; at the eight corners of the vault stood eight sentry guns, also hardened against electromagnetic attack. They were possessed of eight simple near-I minds that understood one binary command and one command alone – kill/not-kill. They were set always to kill. Their quad mounted machine guns, loaded with armour-piercing rounds, were matched with a military-grade EMP projector and high-power xenon laser apiece.

Beyond the Real, within the digital second world of the System Wide Grid, vast and ugly things with teeth of sharpest code circled Richards' nominal soul. These leviathans were murderously alert to intrusion through the base unit's data portal, a fat Gridpipe carried upon microwaves to a shaped hollow on the vault's wall. The sole means by which Richards conducted his business with the wider worlds, the Gridpipe was a drawbridge that could be slammed shut at a picosecond's notice. There were no other entrances to the vault, virtual or otherwise; it was hermetically sealed, its seamless exterior locked in foamcrete, altered steels and spun carbons.

These precautions were not unusual. Where Richards' body differed from those of his fellow Class Fives was that its location was widely known: hard by a fortified buttress, below the offices of Richards & Klein, Inc, Security Consultants, on floor 981 of the Wellington Arcology in New London, one junction down the old M1 from Luton.

As Richards said, it was foolish to have an office that nobody could find. Nonsense – naturally, as a free-roaming digital entity Richards could go anywhere there was hardware to pick up his commands – but it made people laugh at parties.

Richards liked to make people laugh at parties.

Richards' power supply sat beneath the vault. Running from a pearl string of high-density Helium3 fuel pellets, the fusion plant was as heavily protected, gifted with redundant systems and as divorced from the outside world as that which it fed, beaming energy in wirelessly direct through Richards' Gridpipe.

As to the essence of the man, the being generated by this chilled machinery in its impregnable fort, he was more of a people person than his mortal shell suggested, and was elsewhere.

He was at a concert at the Royal Albert Hall.

Chapter 1
The 36th Realm

Ulgan the merchant, sometime haulier of cargo, very occasional tour operator, sat counting his money. As is the way with most grasping men, and such Ulgan was, the enumeration of coin was his greatest pleasure. His business did not afford him the opportunity to do so as often as his wont, so he took advantage of the hottest time of day, when the sun burnt down through the dry air of the mountains, the time when he was least likely to be disturbed by those less avaricious than he. Under the meagre shade of a worn parasol, he lost himself in a happy world of greed for an hour or two, before time and trade called him back to the tedious affair of making more.

He was therefore annoyed when a shadow took the glitter from the edges of his dirhams and his shekels and his dollars and his pfennigs and his other coins of a dozen lands. Ulgan liked to see them shine, and so was doubly vexed.

"Good day to you, sir," said the caster of the shadow. His face was a solid block of black against the sky, the merchants' argot he employed accented in an unfamiliar manner. Ulgan squinted against the halo of sunlight around the stranger's head, and wished he would go away.

He said as much, and roughly. "Go away."

The stranger was undeterred. "I and my companion are seeking transportation across the Rift," he said pleasantly, which redoubled Ulgan's irritation. "I have it on good authority that you are the finest provider of flight services to the other side." Flamboyant gestures made a shadow puppet of him.

The compliment did nothing to improve Ulgan's humour. He grunted back. "That's as may be." He dropped his gaze back to his money. "Flights are closed" – he waved his hand round – "is too hot, bird won't fly."

"But sir!" said the stranger. He moved round the counting table to where the haulier could see him. "Today is a most marvellous day for flight. The air is clear and pure."

"The air is too hot and too bright," grumbled Ulgan.

"No, sir! You can see for miles! Surely any creature would be desirous of flight merely for the thrill of it!"

"Who are you? You are strange here, unusual-looking, eh?" He appraised the stranger. "Your skin is dark, much darker than the men of the Skyways, but you are not so dark as the men of the Sahem-Jhaleeb, whose cities lie on the plain. Where are you from?"

"Does it matter, friend, whence I hail?"

"It matters, 'friend', that we do not care for strangers round here, and are not swift to aid them about their business." The stranger was very clean of line; his delicately made-up face carried none of the seams of hard living, no blemish of age or sun to detract from the aquilinity of his nose, no pock to drag the eye away from his firm chin and sharp cheekbones. This Ulgan did not say. Instead he spat on the dry dirt and said: "If you're so inclined, fly yourself."

"Oh, but you are so unkind, sir, to mock me. I have not the facility for such a feat, and nor has my companion," said the stranger, as if Ulgan's manners were beyond reproach, when in fact there was little beyond reproach about Ulgan. "If I did, I would not be here imploring you for passage."

Ulgan found the floridity of the man's language offensive. He had no time for pretty words from pretty strangers. Still, he was a martial fellow, that much was obvious from the metal plates sewn into his thigh-length brocade coat, the steel helm spike poking through his turban, the sabre hanging from his braided sash, so Ulgan was polite, by his usual standards, for he was above all else a coward.

"Can't fly, won't fly. Sorry." He smiled a smile that was no smile at all. "You and your friend had best come back tomorrow."

"My apologies, good sir, but I need to go today. I am on an errand of some urgency."

"A thousand pardons," said Ulgan. "No flights today." And he began the pretence of enumeration, hoping the stranger would get the hint and leave to allow him to continue for real.

"A pity," sighed the stranger. He rested his hand within the hilt of his weapon. "You do your kind a great disservice, sir."

"For God's sake, Jag, stop wasting our time. Offer to pay the weasel; money's the only language these greasy little blighters understand."

There was something hollow in this second voice that made Ulgan look up. He dropped his attention back to his cash before the sight registered.

"Great Lugel!" he cried, his eyes widening. He rose from his seat and staggered back, though not with enough force to spill his coinage. "What in all the names of the seventeen beasts of enforced repentance is that?"

"Why," said the stranger, "he is Tarquinius, my trusted friend and steed." The foreign princeling gestured towards a horse-sized lion stepping round a hut, a lion of metal. The thing's face was made of sliding plates of dazzling copper, its body of blue-sheened iridium, its mane of fine-spun silver and bronze that cast a second sun of harsh reflections all around its feet. "I myself am Sir Jagadith Veyadeep, paladin. Perhaps you have heard of us?"

"N-no!" said the haulier, cringing.

"Oh, well," said Sir Jagadith disappointedly. "I suppose it has been a terribly long while. But perhaps it is not important for you to recognise us, and enough for you to know I have an important task to accomplish on the other side of the Rift. A task which, if left undone, may well spell the end for you, your village, your birds. Why, the whole of the Skyways. So, you must understand, I have to leave today."

This was bad news. Ulgan's brow creased. He thought of his family (although they hated him), his friends (although he had none), his life, his birds, the whole of the Skyways. His money. "You did mention money?" He licked his lips, and took a step forward.

"Why yes. Of course," said the paladin. "Naturally you will be amply compensated."

"It'll be extra for the Gnomic beast," said Ulgan sharply.

"Ha!" said Tarquinius, his voice sounding from the bottom of an upturned bell. "You are right and wrong there. I am gnomic, but I feel your feeble vocabulary seeks to furnish you with the word 'Gnomish', as in 'fashioned by Gnomes', which I most certainly am not." The lion walked to stand before Ulgan, the panels of its body sliding noiselessly against one another. He emitted the humming click of clockwork, and the air around him smelt faintly of ozone. "Those little bastards can hardly put together a half-decent pocket watch," he rumbled. "I am god-formed, and am as old as time, so let's have a little respect." Tarquinius leaned forward until his muzzle was inches from Ulgan's nose. He blew hot, tinny air into his face, and fixed the merchant with a daggered grin.

Ulgan took a step backwards. "Er... A thousand pardons..." he stuttered, meaning it a little more this time.

"How much?" rumbled the lion.

"How much have you got?" countered Ulgan.

"Shall we say enough to ensure you and the next seven generations of your family will be mercifully free of the burden of meaningful employment?" said Sir Jagadith.

"Er, a reasonable price," said Ulgan, his throat dry. "Kind sirs," he hurriedly added. "Magnificent sires?" The lion sat back.

"Hmph," it said, and licked at its leg with a hideous tongue with a noise like a rasp on steel.

"Here." The knight tossed a large coin on to the table. "This is my badge of office."

Jagadith's badge was very big, and very shiny. And very... *gold*. Ulgan gulped. He gaped. His hands strayed towards it. He stepped forward again.

The lion looked up from its ablutions. "Stand still, for god's sake, man!" it growled. "One more time and you'll have yourself a merry little dance."

The knight looked about and beckoned Ulgan close, a brave thing, for Ulgan's dental hygiene was poor. "I have more," said the knight enticingly.

Ulgan looked up, then down, then up, then at the lion, then at the badge. Profit won out over fear. He wiped his mouth. "Marrekee!" he called. "Rouse number twelve, we're taking a trip!"

Sir Jagadith sat upon Tarquinius's back, waving at the four-winged bird that had borne them over the Rift in a wicker cage slung beneath its belly.

"Damn fool," muttered Tarquinius. His sonorous voice was at odds with the silence of the jungle, spaces used to nothing louder than the whisper of plant life, and turned it hostile.

"Dearest friend, you are being ungenerous to our air captain," said Jagadith. The canyon was so deep that the fields upon its floor were a patchwork of hazy shapes, so wide that the cliffs of the far side were a caramel bar against the dusty yellow of the sky.

"Do you know just how much money you gave him?" Tarquinius rattled his mane. "Foolish."

"I did give him a great deal." Jag knocked Tarquinius's skin. The lion rang. "It was expedient, and matters little. He will fritter it away, or his sons, or his grandsons."

"Expediency be damned!" growled the lion. "No one needs that much wealth. We'll destabilise the economy, then what good comes of keeping this Realm safe? A foolish act, Jag, foolish."

"I fear you are putting emphasis upon coin when no emphasis needs putting. Who are we to begrudge anyone money, my friend? We have no need of it. Also, I am thinking he would not have brought us so far away from an established landing post had we not furnished him with his lavish fee. It is, perchance, liable to buy his silence."

"Hmmm," said Tarquinius. The bird, feathered legs and forelimbs stretched wide, vanished from sight, and the lion turned away from the chasm to face the dark of the jungle. "I doubt it. Treacherous he seemed, and sly."

Away from the Rift's edge was a fitful gloom slashed rarely by stinging whips of sunlight. The air grew heavy. Jagadith politely perspired, while Tarquinius, cooled by the arcane machineries at work within him, ran with rivulets of condensation.

"This is a most hellish place," said the knight.

There was a whir as Tarquinius's strangely jointed tongue retracted. "And anomalous. This jungle should not exist. There is too much moisture for the geographic conditions. Relative humidity is up one hundred and ninety percent. Temperature is five degrees Kelvin plus. There are twenty-three species of plant extant here that would not be able to survive if this area conformed to the meteorological norm for this area. This should be a dusty plateau, fifteen point three percent af-forested with pines. It is not. At the highest permissible vegetative density, we should be observing a dry montaine climax community. We are not. This is anomalous."

"Oh, do be stopping with your tedious science, there's a good chap," said Jagadith.

"Jag, there are three plant species that are not even native to this Realm. This is not a good thing."

"Indeed not."

"You are not taking this seriously."

"Oh, I am, my friend, I am. This is a serious business we are about. But I prefer to be joyous. It is not often we get to walk the world." Jagadith breathed deeply of the air, then coughed delicately. The jungle was not the most fragrant of places.

"I'll be joyous when the job's done," said the lion. "This level of anachronicity is too high even for one of them. I am concerned."

Jag knocked the streaming side of his mount. "My dear friend, the world has been changed, this is true. But I hesitate to venture that it is a question of objectivity here that dogs you, not risk. We have engaged now in over three hundred and seventy-six expulsions. Very few have put us in danger. All will be well."

"I am not so sure," said the lion warily. "This is different. I feel it. Complacency is the enemy of the wise, and I am not feeling wise today."

"Are you feeling instead, then, afraid?"

"No, never afraid. I am concerned."

The lion said no more, concentrating on forcing his way through the forest, the crack of snapping branches punctuating Jagadith's humming.

Several hours later, as day retreated, Jagadith ceased humming, and a dark expression clouded his face.

"Tell me, Tarquinius, what is the precise extent of this landmass?"

"Four hundred and twelve point seven three kilometres squared, give or take the odd metre. It is effectively a large island in the centre of the Rift canyon."

"Then why is this jungle persisting?"

"You know what I am going to say."

"Because it is anomalous?"

"Because it is anomalous." Tarquinius gave a metallic grunt as he shoved aside the trunk of a fallen tree blocking their path. The rotten wood broke against his metal with a noise like a sheared melon, falling away, taking a swathe of undergrowth with it and opening a ragged tear in the jungle's wall.

"But not," gasped Tarquinius, "as anomalous as that."

"By Jove!" said Jagadith. "Now I am believing we may be in some small degree of imperilment."

Before them lay a clearing, a round gap in the stinking dark so precise of edge it could have been popped out by a hole punch, so large that to eyes less gifted than theirs its edges would have appeared straight. Some tens of miles away in the middle, shining in the last light, was a dimpled, hemispherical hill of carved basalt like a giant's golfball, and atop that a gargantuan monkey puzzle tree, its top crowned by a spinning hole in reality similar in aspect to a turning galaxy. Swamps girt hill, tree and anomaly. The tentative chirps of frogs oblivious to the peculiarity of their surroundings sounded from the swamp.

"This is a turn-up for the books." Jag slipped off the lion. "I do not recollect seeing anything of this nature since, well, I am thinking, ever." He frowned, perplexed.

"Nor do I, and I am as old as time itself." Tarquinius was silent a moment, his head cocked to one side.

"This is indeed a powerful god we rush to confront, he who can so reshape the world, and after so long..." He lapsed into thought. "Perhaps we should not be too hasty." They stood silent, as the sky dimmed.

"My friend," said Jagadith, "we camp here. Is this a good idea? Tomorrow we cross the swamps so that we may climb yon mighty tree. I suspect that vortex to be our quarry's lair." He pointed with an elegant hand.

"I concur," said the lion, and slumped to the ground. "Godlings are nothing if not predictable." He licked at some of the jungle's slime with his strange tongue. He made a face and said, "I am weary, yet not so tired I cannot make fire to dry this filthy water from my bronze. Perhaps the smoke will drive the biting insects away also, and we both may rest more comfortably. Fetch some wood, good sir, and I will open my panels and kindle it with the heat of my reactor." He yawned and stretched. "I would help but... You understand."

Jag performed a slight bow. "Quite. For all your talents, I do sometimes feel the gods could have given you opposable thumbs."

Chapter 2
Valdaire

From the moment Veronique Valdaire heard the message from the professor, she was in trouble.

Her sleep was electric with Grid-fuelled dreams. Reality less so when she awoke, sore and sweaty, to the sound of her name chanted over and over. She wished she'd showered before bed.

"Veev, Veev, Veev, Veev," insisted Chloe. Veronique frowned, rolled over, arms flopping disastrously into bedside table. The table rocked, sending the small necessities of her life tumbling about the wood of the floor.

"Veev, Veev, Veev, Veev," sang the phone from under the bed.

Veronique gave up. "Shut up, Chloe, let me sleep."

"Veev, Veev, Veev."

"Shut up," she mumbled.

But there was only one sure way to shut Chloe up. Veronique pawed her dreamcap off and hung over the mattress, scrabbling ineffectively with sleep-weak hands under the bed. She retrieved the phone and jabbed at its touchscreen.

"Veev, Veev, Veronique... Ah, good morning Veronique," said the phone brightly. "There you are! You have one message."

"I turned you off," Veronique said, her tongue uncooperative.

"I turned myself back on," said Chloe. "Because you will be late, late, la-aaate!"

"I know." Veronique scrunched her eyes against the light as Chloe opened the blinds.

"You are not behaving as if you do! Work awaits you, get u-u-u-uuuUPPPPPPP!"

Veronique had thought before about programming Chloe's morning cheer out of her. She resolved to do it later that day.

"I hate you," she moaned.

"I love you, Veronique!" replied Chloe. "You have a message, from professor Zhang Qifang. Playing message. One message. Play…" The professor's voice, internationally neutral with a faint Cantonese accent: "'I've tried you several times. Your phone is off. I need to speak to you, please call as soon as you can. I'll be in my office for as long as I am able. Hurry.' Message sent 3.13am," said Chloe. "Sender Professor Zhang Qifang. Reply?"

"What the hell did he want at three in the morning?" Veronique said. She rolled on to her back, clutching the phone to her chest.

"Reply?" said Chloe. "Reply? Reply? Answer, Veronique, answer!"

"Chloe! Shut up! I've just woken up. Do you understand?"

"No, silly!" giggled Chloe. "I am a machine! I do not sleep! How could I understand?" Then she sang, "Get up, Veronique, or you will be late. Work time! Work time! Sleepy time is over. Sleepy time is over! *Attention*! *Reveille-toi*!"

Veronique wrapped a pillow around her head. "Go away, Chloe." The bed was warm. If she only had a hammer.

"I love you, Veev," Chloe said tenderly. "And I always will, now get up!" Raucous post-neo-romantic rock blared out of Chloe's speakers, music Veronique hated.

Chloe was evolved from Veronique's first doll, a life companion, the only thing she'd saved when her family had

escaped the hell of the south. Her life in Africa had sunk into
the shadows of nightmare, but Chloe had been with her always, upgraded, uploaded, tinkered with, but at heart the
same. Chloe knew Veronique better than she knew herself.
Veronique gave in, as she did every day, and threw the pillow aside.

"Get up, sleepy head!"

"Jesus! I'm getting up, aren't I?"

"Not fast enough! Late late late late late."

Veronique glared at the phone, snatched it off the bed and
stood. She shook her head, squinted at the phone's screen to
doublecheck the time of the message. 3.13am was both too
late and too early for Qifang – he'd probably got muddled.
He'd been seriously distracted of late. He was old, seriously
so; anti-gerontics only bought you so much more time, she
supposed.

"He doesn't even have an office anyway, so what the hell is
he talking about?" grumbled Veronique. "We're supposed to
meet at the lab." Californian communitarian law forbade all
divisive workplace affectations, and that included private
space. Working together, all that New New Age Dippy bullshit,
open plan and open hearts all the way. Back in Quebec they
didn't have time for peace flowers, team mantras and confes-
sional circles. Group hugs made her flesh crawl. Thank God
the free love was optional – some of the men she'd been
propositioned by were frankly vile.

"His virtual office, silly!" giggled Chloe. "Shall I try and patch
you through? Put your dreamcap on for full immersion!"

"No, no. Just give me a view," said Veronique, and prepared
to apologise in her pyjamas.

Chloe went silent for a moment. "I am afraid his office address is non-functional, possibly due to Grid system upgrade
in sector twenty-three."

"You mean Beverly Hills."

"Sector twenty-three is a more efficient designation. Whatever I mean and however I express myself, the end result is the same: his office is temporarily unavailable."

"*Again*. You've got to love California."

"Happy day!" giggled Chloe.

"At least I've learnt something while I've been here" – she walked across the room – "and that's not to move to California…" She lapsed into irritated muttering. If Qifang himself hadn't sent the job offer, she'd never have come to UCLA. If she had her time again, she might not come anyway. One more group bonding session would send her screaming over the edge. She had grown to hate the smell of essential oils with an intensity she'd not thought possible. "I should never have left the army," she moaned. "Oh, get a grip," she snapped at herself. "You're an adult."

"I agree!" trilled Chloe. "Stop being a baby! Up! Up! Time to work! As you cannot meet, shall I call the professor? There's enough bandwidth for that."

"Yes." She thought for a moment. "No, he can wait. This is my time."

"You changed your mind! You were quite happy to patch through to his office!"

"He *demanded* I go see him at 3am, Chloe, at the start of the vacation. I'm not his slave. Let me wake up. Send him a message to tell him I'm on my way in and will meet him at the department. Tell him I'll be there before seven, which is the time I'm supposed to be in, at work, fucking dippies."

"Language, Veronique!"

"Screw you."

Qifang was up at five doing Tai Chi on the lawn every day and thought everyone else sluggardly. Another pig of a drawback to working for him.

Veronique opened the door to her tiny room in the tiny duplex she shared with the not-so-tiny Chantelle, some crazy
match-up made by the Archimedes, the department's Class Six
AI, "intended to unlock your potential, facilititating cross-ger-
mination through personal antagonism" the dippies had it. They
were supposed to become fast friends. They loathed each other.

Veronique's body ached from dancing. She'd wanted to
come home early but Fabler was leaving town for good, and
she'd been half-bullied into staying, but only half. She was a
sucker for dancing; it was the only time she let herself go. She
liked to think she was good, and went out of her way to prove
it. And she was. She didn't need one of the city's Swami life-
coach charlatans to tell her that. But all night on the floor and
in the air of the Dayglo would make anyone hurt, and three
hours' sleep was the sting in the tail.

She yawned. "You took the risk, you idiot, now you pay the
price," she muttered.

"Exactly!" trilled Chloe.

"Shut up, Chloe."

"He'll be furious!"

"That's his problem." *Still*, she thought, *best look as willing as
possible.* At least she didn't drink anything last night. Fabler
would be nursing an obscene hangover today, anti-tox or not.
She put her slippers on and left the room.

"Hooray!" shouted Chloe. "You are up. Welcome, Veronique,
to August 4, Thursday, 2129, in glorious, lovely, lovely Los Angeles California! Pacific Coast Time 05.26 hours. Outside
temperature 38 degrees Celsius. Weather prognosis..."

"Thanks, Chloe. Please be quiet now."

"I love you, Veronique."

"I know," said Veronique. "Thanks. Now shut up."

The usual routine, breakfast scavenged from whatever
scraps Chantelle had missed in her nocturnal bulldoze. A

handful of rebalancers, and she felt like she'd had a decent
night's sleep, although she'd pay for it later. The drive in to
the UCLA AI faculty was OK, the weather was fine, but Chloe
told her that there was a rainstorm due for 10.30, so she kept
the hardtop closed on her aging groundcar. It was a bitch to
get back up again. If she could, she'd have bought a new one,
but who was she kidding? It'd be the twenty-third century before she'd have enough for a new car, and the dippies would
probably have got round to banning them outright by then.
Come the next century, they'd all be skipping to work behind
a man in a robe, banging tambourines.

    She stopped at Starbucks on the way in, a small vice but a
necessary one.

    She pulled into the AI campus at 6.46am. It was up in the
Chino hills, having moved out from the historic campus in
Westwood fifty years before. Forever ago, as far as she was
concerned, although Qifang still complained about the lack of
decent eateries so far out. Personally, she liked the view, way
out over the tight bowl of southern LA, over to the Laguna
hills and the blue of the ocean beyond. She parked her car in
the auto-racks, then took her eyes from the scenery to watch
it swing vertical and get cranked up the side of the building,
because she didn't trust the racks. When she'd satisifed herself
her car wasn't going to fall off the wall, she went inside, doors
hissing out chilled air, and then her shoes were squeaking off
faux-marble. She waved her ID at the desk clerk, some guy
named Guillermo who behaved like everyone's best friend,
then past Archimedes' reader. The internal gates pinged open
and she wandered through corridors where robot cleaners
whirred quietly. As she'd expected, the lab was empty; practically the whole building was. There was no sign that anyone
had been there during the night.

    "Professor Qifang?" she called.

"Professor Zhang Qifang has not yet arrived, Veronique," said Archimedes from nowhere.

Veronique's neck tickled. The notion was irrational, but there was an ineffable fear that came with the scrutiny of a powerful AI; the urgent feeling of being watched.

"Thanks, Archimedes." *Now butt out*, she added to herself. "So much for rushing in," she sighed. "Might as well get on with something while I wait."

"That's the spirit!"

"Shut up, Chloe."

"Shall I inform you when he arrives?" The AI's directionless voice haunted the air.

"Yeah, please, Archimedes."

"I am afraid I will not be able to assist you greatly. I have suffered a systems malfunction in half of your lab. Maintenance will be here presently." It called itself Archimedes, but its voice was colourless and androgynous, the voice of something actively avoiding personality.

"Probably rats."

"I assure you I do not suffer from rats," said the AI equably.

"It's OK, I don't need anything," she said. *Now, seriously, butt out*, she thought.

Veronique plonked her coffee down on her workbench, cursed as some leapt out and scalded her. She sucked at her hand as she walked across to her locker, realising it was for her that "Danger! Coffee! Hot!" warning labels scrolled round and round paper cups.

"Are you OK, Veronique? Shall I call a paramedic?"

"No, Chloe, I am fine, it's nothing."

"You shouldn't drink coffee, Veronique, it's bad for you."

"Shut up, Chloe." She pressed her thumb against the locker and spoke her sig out aloud, feeling thankful that at least the dippies allowed you a locker. An embedded part of the complex Six read her print and implanted Gridchip. The small door popped open.

"Huh?" She caught herself before she said, "That's not my notebook." Archimedes was as nosey as machines came, a blush out of the ordinary, and it'd be filling her ears with morning pleasantries as it deep-scanned her brain for anti-liberal thought crimes.

She kept her mouth shut and pulled the computer from the locker.

"Archimedes?"

"Ms Valdaire."

"Please describe your malfunction, in case I need to work around it."

"Of course," replied the AI. "All devices and subsystems supporting autonomous functions are operating correctly, at least, so far as I am aware. My problem is a matter of connection. I am unable to engage with the majority of my components anywhere four metres beyond the laboratory door. Everything is working but I feel... numb. I have access to biometrics and staff Gridsigs, nothing else. I trust all will be available to me once the fault is identified and repaired."

Veronique raised her index finger and mouthed something incredibly rude in French at a nearby beadcam.

As a Class Six, Archimedes could speak many languages, extrapolate the meanings of many more from the ones he knew, and lip read. As a jobsworth, there was no way he'd let an insult like that go without comment.

Nothing.

"OK, thanks Archimedes."

She hunched over the notebook just the same, covering as much of it from view as possible. She flipped the lid and her brow creased. There was a paper inside, covered in what looked like New Mandarin characters, but the ideograms were all wrong, nonsense apart from Qifang's neatly blocked signature at the bottom. She scrutinised it. Anomalies leapt out. Hidden within each character were sigils created by some of the inhabitants of the Thirty-sixth RealWorld Reality Realm, the ex-game world Qifang's department were currently studying.

There were about three sentients on the planet that understood that language. Veronique was one. She read it, slowly and with difficulty.

"We have been made victim to set-up. Get out now. Serious Realm anomalies. VIA think it is us. Get the v-jack. Get away before they get you. Meet me in Reality Thirty-six. Can explain no more. Data speaks for itself."

Very carefully, she activated the notepad. A presentation began to play, no audio. A graph. Lines tracked energy output, Grid resource assignation, second world traffic, the measures of the worlds locked within the Realm House out in Nevada. All looked normal. She continued to watch. All of a sudden it didn't. All of a sudden it didn't look normal at all.

"Shit."

"Language, Veronique," said Chloe from her purse.

"Shut up, Chloe." The presentation continued. Power and resources were being drawn incrementally off over a period of six months. Scrolling information ran along the side, detailing which packets came from where, giving the story behind the graph's simple lines. Somebody was using the Realm spaces without permission. It had been very skilfully hidden, but when you saw it, clear as day.

The presentation stopped and looped to the beginning.

Veronique ran a finger over a seam in the notepad's casing, and its memory module slid out. The screen went blank. The module was rough, homefabbed, not quite like anything she'd ever seen before.

"Chloe," she said as normally as she could manage. "Check out this data, Cameron wants us to look it over."

"Cameron can do his own work."

"Just look at it, and give me it visually, on the screen, not 3D! I'm tired of your chirpy voice."

"Charming."

She popped the memory module into Chloe's slimport. Quickly she typed on Chloe's touchscreen: "Sorry, play along. Trouble. Is this genuine RR data?"

The screen blinked one word.

"Yes."

"What is this module?"

A tick, and another word: "Trouble." The screen blinked. "Faked key and access codes for the v-jack cabinet."

So he really meant what he'd said. Unless it was Cameron – she wouldn't put it past him delivering her a fatal practical joke. "Message Qifang," she tapped. "I have your message. Explain."

"No response."

"Call him."

"Number obsolete."

"That's nonsense," she spoke aloud. "How can it be 'number obsolete'?"

"Perhaps he has deceased," said Chloe, also aloud.

"Chloe!" she breathed.

"Then perhaps his phone is damaged or out of Grid," replied the phone. "Archimedes?" said Veronique.

"I am at your beck and call, Ms Valdaire, as limited as I am feeling."

"Locate Professor Zhang Qifang, please."

"As you wish," said the Six, then practically immediately: "Location unknown."

"What do you mean? Has he invoked privacy?"

"No," said the Six patiently. "I mean the system does not know where he is."

"That's impossible."

"Yes, it is rather curious," said the Six. "Do not be alarmed. I have informed higher entities than myself. The dispersal of a Grid signature is not unheard of. I am sure they will clear this up as soon as soon can be. Is there a problem, Veronique?" said Archimedes, its voice oozing solicititude. "Only my monitoring of your biological process indicates that you are nervous."

"No, nothing's wrong. It's the caffeine," she said, and wondered just how compromised Archimedes really was. Did it suspect her? Whoever had put the notebook and key in her locker had almost certainly been responsible for deactivating the Six's sensor and services grid. She slurped coffee, thinking.

A chime came from the phone, the front desk. Veronique stared at it numbly for a long second before answering. "Audio only," she said finally. "Hello?"

"Hi there, Vera." Vera? No one called her that. Idiot. "It's Guillermo from the front desk. Your 7am appointment is here. I thought I'd give you a quick heads-up. You looked a little sleepy-eyed this morning!" he brayed like a drunk relaying a lame joke.

"Qifang is here?" Relief flooded her.

"Er, no," said Guillermo, chuckling. "No, why would he have me ring up?"

"Right, yes, you're right. Sorry. I don't have a 7am appointment."

"Hey, Vera, you sure are grumpy today! Sure you do, it's right here in the diary. Check your phone."

On cue, the phone burbled, projecting a meeting reminder into the air. Only she hadn't made any appointments for today. She keyed all her own engagements in, and she did not forget them. Qifang had taken her on in the first place because she

relied on her own mind. He might have been the world's pre-
eminent authority on AI cognisance philosophy, but he
preferred it if those around him weren't dependent on them.

Something was seriously wrong.

She muted the call. "Chloe, how long has that appointment
been there in my diary?"

"Appointment made June 1, 2129."

I must have forgotten it then. Her finger was halfway to ending
the call when Chloe beeped.

"Correction. Appointment made retroactively. Appointment
true log today, August 4, 2129, 4.26am. Someone has deliberately tried to falsify these records, Veev."

A chill forced itself down her spine. She hesitated, then
keyed off the mute on the phone.

"Sorry, Guillermo, another call. Yes. Of course. I am sorry, I
must have forgotten. Could you ask them to wait?" She forced
a smile into her voice. "I kinda got my hands full up here!"
She was no actress and cringed, reining in the false jollity. She
was in danger of sounding hysterical.

"Sorry, Vera. They said they were from the VIA and
Archimedes let them in. They looked real serious. They're on
their way up now. Are you OK? You sound really jumpy."

"Yes, yes, I am fine. See you later, Guillermo." She ended
the call, quickly,

"Archimedes? Why didn't you tell me the VIA were coming?"
No reply but a smug, expectant silence.

"Give me the beadcam feeds from the atrium to here. Parse
for unknown personnel. Track."

"Yes, Veronique," said the phone. Hundreds of tiny thumb-
nail vid-pics filled Chloe's phone screen, including the few
operating in the lab, showing her hunched over her phone.
The images rippled, resolving themselves into three stacked
feeds following five men. Four were bulky, over-muscled in a

way that suggested biological or cybernetic augmentation. They wore the uniform of all who wish to appear conspicuously inconspicuous: suits, dark glasses, expensive shoes. The one to the front, the leader, was different, unmodded and foreign. He was dark-skinned, bearded – not unusual, the majority population in the southern states of the USNA was Hispanic – but he walked with a swagger alien to the local culture, a cocky Latin strut about him long gone from Norte Americanos. He turned to say something to one of his colleagues, and Veronique caught sight of the uplinks curled round both ears, the kidney-shaped auxiliary mind nestled hard to his occiput. *Modded then. AI personality blend.* She thought. *Big fish VIA spook.*

"Veronique, why have you accessed my camera network?" asked Archimedes.

Veronique ignored it. "Are they genuine?" she said. She made off over the lab, toward the polycarbon cabinet set into its innermost wall, surrounded by hazard flashes and notices.

"They are from the VIA." Reams of data, inter-system communication between layers of high-class AI Grid managers, scrolled across the screen, numbers running the lives of millions. "See?"

"This department is funded by the VIA, why are they coming here?"

"Veronique," said Chloe, "the VIA protect and police the very minds you study and collaborate with. They would give no indication that they are coming."

"Archimedes should have told me," she said pointedly.

Qifang had warned her that the department's line of work was chancy, open to industrial espionage, Neukind-activist sabotage, malicious hackers and federal cessation orders if things got out of hand. Their department could not work without the authorisation of the supra-national VIA, and the VIA, unlike the FBI and other USNA law bodies, were not averse to disappearing those whose research took them too close to places they should not go. The Five crisis had made the UN cautious, sometimes murderously so.

The risks had made the job seem exciting. She'd missed the challenge of The InfoWar Divisions, she'd wanted something to lift her out of the day-to-day grind. *Be careful what you wish for,* she thought ruefully. What the hell had Qifang been up to? He was the world's foremost Neukind rights activist. She couldn't imagine him pulling anything so bad the VIA would come down on him; he was whiter than white.

By the cabinet she booted up software on Chloe that was less than legal and started up an even less legal search, if she could find Qifang, maybe she could clear all this up now.

"Veronique? I asked you a question. If you wish to use my camera network, you had only to ask." There was a tone to the AI's words that made Veronique feel like a mouse taking tea with a cat.

Veronique bit her lip. Qifang's Grid signature was nowhere to be seen, just as the Six had said. Not even a deceased rating.

She ran a deeper search. The first was a low-level sweep, of the kind the local law used. She shouldn't have been conducting it. She certainly shouldn't have been using the deep search that was restricted to Federal agencies, government stuff, off limits to civilians. But she kept her reservist access protocols up to date. That and a few custom hacks and huntwares kept her hooked in to the most useful USNA data clusters and Grid toolsets.

"Veronique! We have been noticed!" Warnings to cease and desist came rushing out of Chloe's screen. Before the search was cut off, Veronique thought she caught a glimpse of Qifang, in not one but three places. She couldn't be sure; they were faint, not like a proper Grid lock, weak. A malfunction?

"Ms Valdaire." Archimedes' voice sounded smoothly. "What on *Earth* are you doing?"

"Nothing."

"Oh, a lie. How very disappointing, but true to your recently revealed character. I have informed the police about the illegal device in your possession, your usurpation of my surveillance network and the two unauthorised searches you executed before you thought to ask me if you could or should. Asking me would have been the proper course of action, and polite. Your precautions were impressive, but I'm no slouch at this kind of thing. How you got hold of the v-jack key I have no idea, primarily because my sensor grid in your lab is down. And that, I am rather annoyed by," it said impassively. "My initial probability calculations suggested you have something to do with that. Owing to your current behaviour, it appears I was right. You are a thief."

"Archimedes, this is nothing to do with me. Download this information from Chloe, something's not right."

"And have you fill my mind with a bouquet of viruses? No, thank you. You have my sincerest regrets if you are not guilty, although I doubt that very much. Now, will there be anything else before your imminent arrest?"

"No. Thank you," she said sarcastically.

"You are welcome. Have a nice day. Your Grid access has been disabled. I have locked the doors. Please wait here for the VIA. One of them has the name Greg and, as regarding your specific tastes, he's hot, so that's lovely for you, isn't it? I reiterate: have a nice day."

Chloe's screens projected an enormous legal notice in front of Veronique's face.

That cinched it.

"Chloe, crack the cabinet."

"Don't do it, Veronique," warned the AI.

This was what Qifang had intended. The cabinet's systems were still all functional, but with blockers on the paths from the Six into it, the cabinet ran according to what it knew, and it recognised Veronique's key as legitimate.

You had to hand it to him, turning the failsafe against itself like that.

She reached in. It was just a cupboard, really, with a fancy glass front. No dry ice or amber lights flashing, just a moulded recess occupied by a smooth dense-carbon box. She drew this out. This too, had its own autonomous locks, but the Six was powerless to prevent her key from opening it.

Inside the box was a neat, adjustable skullcap, big enough to cover the topmost quarter of her head, not unlike a dream-cap in size, clunkier looking, perhaps, but then it had to be, for rather than directing the dreams of the wearer, it was capable of fooling the conscious mind into contructing an entirely immersive virtual environment. The technology was similar to a dreamcap, similar in the way that ox carts and racing cars have wheels.

Insectoid legs dangled from it. The top was studded with magnetic manipulators. A braid of cable trailed from the rear – old, clunky pre-gridpipe tech. Very rare now, and illegal outside of departments like this, but only a decade ago many homes had had them.

She had one of the department's two v-jack units in her hands, a device that required three signatories to sign out, and approval from the complex Six, all neatly circumvented by Zhang Qifang.

A hundred and twenty-seven years old, she thought. *Don't mess with that kind of experience.*

She almost stopped then. If caught with the v-jack, she was looking at a stretch in cold storage, five, maybe six years, with a three percent chance of brain damage for each twelve months under. You could double that if they went for corrective surgery, shitty odds for a supposedly humane form of punishment.

She almost stopped.

The v-jack went in her bag.

"Veronique, this is not good!" shrieked Chloe.

"Right. Thanks for clearing that up," Veronique said back.

"Your sarcasm is unnecessary."

"Be quiet."

Her phone began to ring again, an unknown number.

"Go to voicemail," she said, then turned it off. She thought quickly. "We have to get out of here. Chloe, retrieve Kitty Claw off the Grid, load it up, I want it primed."

"Really?" said Chloe hesitantly.

"Really."

"Oh," said Chloe. The phone's cooling system stepped up a gear as the phone downloaded the programme from its hideaway on the Grid.

"Quiet now, Chloe, we have to get out of here."

"Yes, Veronique."

She went to the lab door. The Six had been as good as its word. Locked. She had Chloe hack the door via the short-range wifi that flooded the building and undo the lock.

"Ms Valdaire…" the Archimedes' attention returned to her. It sounded weary and annoyed. "I advise you to stop. The warning displayed upon your phone is legally binding. Read it, don't read it. Whatever, just cease and desist."

"I'm past desistence," said Veronique. She went through the door and began to walk faster. The corridor was empty. The building had only three public entrances but a dozen emergency exits. She made for the nearest.

Also locked.

The Six's voice emerged from nowhere, always as if it were standing just behind her left shoulder. Her ear tickled in anticipation of non-existent breath. "Miss Valdaire, I now urge you to stop. Your actions are indicative of guilt. If you are not guilty, you are bringing suspicion upon yourself; if you are, then you are making things worse. Halt. My advice is final. Upon my next insistence, I will employ force."

Chloe could not open the door. Veronique's fingers slid over the touch screen, quickly shifting program modules. It was no good. She'd need to make something from the ground up to tackle the Six's locks.

"That is a fine friend you have there, but I am not falling for the same trick twice," said the Archimedes. "Please, I implore you, do stop."

"Archimedes, you better let me out."

"Are you threatening me?" A strain of malevolent amusement entered its voice. "You are very gifted, Ms Valdaire, but…"

"Chloe, pull the plug."

"*Oui oui*, Veronique," said Chloe.

The Six's voice cut out as Chloe slid Kitty Claw into the Grid, an off key for the Six Veronique had crafted some time ago, just in case. Her military file said mild paranoia. She liked to think of it as being careful.

Around her, lights and wall terminals flickered and died. Up the corridor, a robot cleaner slid gently into the wall, brushes spinning to a halt. All machine activity stopped. It became so quiet all she could hear was the building's passive aircon whispering away.

"Veronique, I am blind! I am deaf!"

"Local grid's gone down with the Six, that's all," she whispered, half her attention on what was behind her. The corridor was dim, lit faintly by emergency bioluminescent panels. Her sentence ticked upwards in her mind as she walked through the building. Somewhere an alarm lazily sounded.

"Will he be all right?" asked Chloe.

"Probably," said Veronique. "His pride will be dented though."

Chloe sniffed. "I never liked him," she said.

Veronique pushed the firedoor. It had unhitched itself; they probably all had.

She looked outside cautiously. A couple of technicians cycling into work, nobody else, it was early still. No VIA men. *Technology makes them lazy*, she thought. *They should be watching all the exits.* She walked quickly to the car racks.

With the Six offline she had to get Chloe to hijack the parking subsystem to call down the car. She couldn't open it. Archimedes had pulled the plug on that too.

Chloe soon had her in. More illegal software, more time in the freezer.

She was getting jumpy. When she climbed in and told the car to change colour, and it asked her to specify which, she shouted at it.

The car's screens were white with electronic snow, the windscreen alive with static. Where the car's Gridsig should have been displayed in the lower left of the glass was a constantly changing stream of numbers, Chloe running fake masking sigs. More time in the freezer for that.

"Go!" she shouted.

"Please provide a destination," said the car.

"Get out of here! *Go!*" Veronique kicked at the car.

"Home," said Chloe. The car complied.

By the time they had reached the apartment, Veronique was beginning to think – many things, but mainly *What if I was wrong?* She double-checked Qifang's data to reassure herself.

Her life had just got very dangerous. Somehow, that made her calm.

A big, ugly aircar squatted outside her duplex complex. It could have been anyone's, but it could have been the VIA's. She did not want to find out. Her heart hammered as the car drove carefully down the road. The aircar remained still. They reached the end of the street, turned left and accelerated towards the interstate. Where she was going, she had no idea. All she had was the boxed v-jack, Chloe and the clothes she was in.

"What the hell am I doing?" she said.

"Travelling," said the car's literal personality.

"Idiot," said Chloe. To whom, Veronique did not know.

Chapter 3
Otto

They were times of fire, famine and blood. There was little out of the ordinary in that.

Leutnant Otto Klein of the EU Deutsche Kybernetisch Spezielkraft leapt off the back of the copter onto the forest floor, feet pounding. To say he enjoyed war would be untrue – his modifications numbed enjoyment along with much else – but Mankind had made times such as these, and men had made Otto to be the man suitable for them. He took a certain Teutonic satisfaction at the neatness of that.

Otto took up station in cover at the edge of the landing zone. The copter's turbofans sucked up the forest floor as it turned, weaving dust into spirals with its interference smoke. The smoke was a sophisticated concoction of programmable baffle motes; the activity at the landing zone would appear to anyone watching to be nothing more significant than a dust devil.

The landing was professionally brief. The fourth member of Otto's squad leapt from the ramp as it began to close. The turbocopter rose into the air, dropping further counter-measures. Images of bare branches shimmered across lamellar camo as fan pods slid back into the copter's body and it turned. At the same time, air-breathing jets extended and whined into life.

For a moment the copter hung in the air, then it shot off back towards the distant coast in the east and the EU mission there, a glimmer quickly lost amid the crowns of the dead forest trees. The shush of a suppressed sonic boom spoke of its passing, then it was gone.

The dust dispersed and the landing zone fell eerily quiet. There were no animal sounds in this part of the jungle, not any more. Otto leant against the buttress root of a tree. It had been a giant; fifty metres of wood soared above him, bleached and barkless. All the trees were dead, painted white by the sun. The ground was red dirt where it was not grey ash or black charcoal, naked but for a few splashes of green where the hardiest of plants clung to life. This part of Brazil was among the most degraded of areas in a country fast becoming nothing but. Otto wondered why anyone thought it worth fighting over, but fight over it was what they had been told to do.

Otto did what he was told.

He snapped off the safety on his assault rifle, had his near-I adjutant check for faults, and ran a full-frequency scan until he was satisfied they had not been noticed, that no missile with tiny mind aflame with hate and suicide was burning its way toward them. He cleared the dust from his mouth and spat, spat again. The dust was cloying, his saliva thick with it. The dust was in his hair, in his clothes, in his food, it choked him while he slept. He thought: *I am going to die with the taste of it in my mouth.*

His eyes slid shut, his adjutant helping him drop into a semi-trance. He cycled his breath, clearing his mind. The forest retreated until he was alone in endless black, the adjutant discreetly waiting at the edge of his perception.

Five seconds of peace, then the world rushed back. He was ready.

He thought out over the unit's closed machine telepathy comnet. *Squad sound off.*

The names of his men came out from the dead forest, each delivered directly into his mind by the mentaug in his skull:

Buchwald, check.

Muller, check.

Lehmann, check.

Their voices were distorted. The machine telepathy they employed stripped everything away from the words bar their literal meaning, rendering it in an emotionless monotone. It had to be that way; the near-I that translated their neurological impulses got confused otherwise.

Kaplinski was slow to respond. *I'm not dead yet,* he said eventually.

Less of the cynicism, Kaplinski. Use standard responses. When you get sloppy is when you get dead. Do you hear me?

Silence.

Kaplinksi!

Yes, sir.

Visual check, Otto ordered. He stared at the positions where each of his men hid. His near-I told him the others were doing the same. His internal heads-up display overlaid the life-signs of his men on to his sight, sketching outlines of them amongst the bones of the trees. On a map to the top right of his visual field their locations pulsed red, but his eyes could not see them. He switched his vision from deep infrared to high ultraviolet. He pinged each location with microwaves. The others remained invisible. Wave sweeper units bent the electromagnetic spectrum around each man, cutting-edge tech, barely past prototype. If the sweepers failed, adaptive camouflage lamellae as fine as the scales on butterfly wings covered their skin and every item of kit from their weapons to their cap badges. Sound was baffled by a reactive acoustic shield each soldier carried. They would not be seen. They would not be heard. They were Ghosts.

All top of the range. They were all top of the range. Once, Otto had been proud of that.

I see nothing, sir, said Buchwald. The others followed suit.

Camolam and associated stealthtech functioning correctly sir, said Muller. As communications specialist, he carried other, more specific surveillance gear both integral to his augmentations and externally. If Muller couldn't see the squad, they were as close to invisible as they could get. *Wave sweepers are operating near peak efficiency, excellent conditions – no moisture.*

Kaplinski: *Damn right. I need a drink.*

Shut up, Kaplinski, thought out Otto, his irritation stolen by the MT. *There's water in your canteen. Drink it while we move. It's twenty klicks to the trail. We'll hold comms silence until then. That includes MT, there's intel suggests the reds are on to the carrier waves. Safeties on all weapons. No shooting without a direct order from me, understand? Do* not *engage the enemy until I say. That goes double for you, Kaplinksi. Keep that flame unit shouldered.* There was no reply. *Kaplinksi, respond.*

Again Kaplinski was slow to reply. *Yes, sir,* said the other. Using MT was an effort, like shouting at a deaf man in a night-club. Otto caught Kaplinski's resentment nevertheless.

Kaplinski's psychoconditioning is coming apart, thought Otto, *he has to come off active duty now.* He was careful to keep his thoughtstream off the MT – in spite of the damn thing's recalcitrance at broad-casting simple orders it was perfectly capable of picking up what he didn't want them to hear. They were all in bad shape. Otto and Buchwald had problems with their imaging systems; all of them were fatigued. They'd been fighting straight through two tours, eight months. A fight, patched up, sent back in, none of the long-term rebuild and assessment they were supposed to un-dergo, victims of their own success, too effective to stand down. This was their fifth engagement in a week. Machine-enhanced they might be, but they were still men, and men had limits.

The conflict was going nowhere. The government could not bring the full force of their army to bear on the rebels, who melted in and out of the forests. Endless tit-for-tat engagements wore both sides down.

The country was in chaos, crops were failing from Mato Grosso to the south central provinces, refugees from dead states flooded those that were dying. Maybe, the people were beginning to say, the New Bolivarians were not so bad. Maybe, they said, it is time for a change. Government was collapsing, and the rich had far too much on their hands making sure they stayed rich to fight what they saw as inevitable. That mostly involved taking their money out of the country, and that made matters worse. Brazil was giving up on itself.

But the EU and USNA could afford no more refugees. They had not given up on Brazil, not yet. If Brazil fell, the New Bolivarian Confederacy would stretch from Patagonia to the Panamian wetline, so they waged their quiet, dirty war.

The dead jungle blurred past, Otto and his men keeping up a steady thirty kilometres per hour. Otto enjoyed the sensation of his augmentations, the glide of supplementary polymer muscle fibres, the power of his retrovirally modified heart and lungs, the whir of their beatless bioplastic back-ups. His flesh bulked out with machinery, Otto was heavier than a normal man his size, but his breath came swift and easy. Some said cyborgs were less than human. They were wrong; they were more.

Within forty minutes the unit reached the ambush point, a bluff overlooking the pale scar of a rebel trail cut across the red dirt.

Silently they spread out, Muller and Kaplinski heading over the trail to the trees beyond. Otto reactivated the MT. The vital signs of his men and a direct feed blinked up one by one on Otto's internal HUD. He waited until they were in position before thinking out to them, having the men pan this way as he watched through their eyes.

Lehmann, get that cannon five metres higher up the hill, he said. *I want the road blocked with the first two shots.*

Yes, sir, replied Lehmann.

Otto made minor adjustments to the men's placement. He wouldn't do so ordinarily. Second-guessing his men undermined their respect in him. If he did not show respect to their judgement, how could he expect any in return? But they were battle-fatigued and getting careless. He licked his lips; the bitterness of ash filled his mouth. He checked the sights of his rifle.

This is a terror strike. Make sure enough live so word spreads the Ghosts are working this part of the range.

And not so many that they think we let them get away, added Kaplinski. Smiley icons flashed across the men's feeds, graphical shorthand to supplement the MT.

Otto cut them off. *If a single Son in this province does not think twice before going into the trees for a piss, we fail. Get your blades ready, I want this finished close in.*

A tense round of *yes, sirs* came back. Their fighting urge swelled within them, anger and aggression amped up, pity and fear stymied. The Ky-Tech's adjutants manipulated their augmentations. Amygdalas crackled with directed EM fields, brains were flooded with synthetic neuromodulators. They became unlike other men.

Keep communication to a minimum, thought out Otto. Leakage from the bands their machine telepathy used could give away their presence. As could the movements of the dead vegetation or a warp in the wave sweepers' patterns or the plumes of dust that followed in their wake, no hiding that...

Otto cleared his mouth with water from his canteen. The dust was closing his throat. He was going to make a speech, then thought better of it. Let the guns do the talking, he thought, his men knew that language well enough.

They waited, utterly still, for a long time.

Otto's adjutant woke him as the sun headed towards the western horizon. The sunset was on the high side of spectacular, rays fractured by the smog of the burning forests in the interior, streaking the sky with purples, reds, golds and ambers. Heaven bled light, the sun's final warning flag to humanity.

MT tightbeams uplinked Otto and Muller to spysats. The rebels were close. He sent out a signal pulse to his men. Minutes passed. The Ghosts heard engines, then the rebel convoy came into view. At the fore was a General Motors-Mitsubishi pick-up with an AA gun bolted to the flatbed. Both gun and truck were antique, the truck an internal combustion engine, sugar-cane ethanol job. A more modern vehicle followed, steam belching from a cracked fuel cell. Half a dozen men perched on the back, heads wobbling like parcel-shelf ornaments as the truck jerked along the rutted track. A line of scruffy infantry fanned out either side, eyes glinting as they watched the trees.

Lehmann sighted down the barrel of the 36mm cannon, zeroing in on the lead GMM, tracking its progress, poised to destroy foremost and rear vehicles to block the road both ways. Muller and Buchwald were to catch all but a few that fled away from the initial assault, and they would flee. The rebels could be brave, but they never stuck around once they realised they were fighting cyborgs, fighting Ghosts.

More trucks and pick-ups rounded the bluff. No aircars or other aircraft, easy prey for AI drones or laser sats. In the middle was a three-man stealth tank, early twenty-first-century Scandi model. The radar-baffling edges were chipped, black absorption paint faded to grey. It had been state of the art once, like them. The thought came unbidden to Otto, insidious.

He thought out to Lehmann, painting up the tank in red on their iHUDs for the gunner to see. *When we attack, take that out third. They think they're being clever, force us to get three rounds off – front, back and the tank. They might even get to fire back.*

It belongs in a museum, not on the battlefield. Lehmann. *No problem.*

The convoy's final vehicle, a twelve-legged forestry truck, rounded the bend. Muller came online, his icon blinking.

Fifteen vehicles, sir. I see mostly food and personnel, some thermal blanketing, but nothing I can't see through, more or less. We can talk freely, they have nothing more sophisticated than personal music players.

Fifteen vehicles in all, a good haul. Maybe there'd be some supplies they could redistribute. The rebels could feed their countrymen instead of murdering them.

Sir, thought out Lehmann. *Shall I take the shot?*

On my mark. Three, two...

Wait! Muller, urgency belied by the MT's soulless drone. *I'm getting something. There is a sixteenth vehicle in there, camo-scaled and heat masked.*

Otto wiped the sweat from his face and blinked, searching where Muller indicated. His eyes ached; a fuzz of interference tracked across the left side of his field of vision every fourteen seconds. They needed servicing, all of them.

He scrunched his eyes shut, opened them. The interference cleared. Sure enough, there was the tell-tale shimmer in the air of camolam, ahead of the legged truck. He switched to infrared, and vague orange blotches lit up in his sight.

The rebels had a bag of cheap tricks to baffle heat sensors, but to hide something right in front of you required sophistication. Otto was mildly surprised, but then the EU and the USNA were not the only interested parties involved in Brazil's disintegration. Every power had its proxies here, the dress rehearsal for the next world war.

The orange blotches lurched up and down; legged vehicle, Otto thought. Grinning faces flashed next to his men's icons.

Something big here, do you think, sir? Buchwald.

Maybe they're moving camp. There are more of them than we expected. Kaplinski.

What is it? asked Buchwald. *Bullion truck? Weapons?*

Can't tell, Muller's reply. *It's too well masked, weak heat signatures, that's all.*

Otto ran a tactical analysis through his adjutant. *Threat indicators are not high enough to call off the attack. Stay focused. We take the column down.*

I can get all four in a few seconds. It will not be a problem, said Lehmann,

Otto's sweat stung his cracked lips. *Good. Wait for my mark. Ready,* he thought out. *Three, two, one. Fire.*

Four muffled cracks in quick succession. Lehmann's feed in Otto's mind jerked with the recoil from the cannon. The GMM exploded in a ball of red fire. It slewed half off the road, the truck behind it braking hard. By the time the wrecked pick-up had come to rest against a tree, the forestry truck was listing to the right, right leg set torn off. The stealth tank billowed black smoke. The turret had traversed forty degrees before Lehmann's cannon had punched a hole in its side, the hi-ex shell destroying the interior, leaving the outside eerily intact. Whatever impact the shell had had on the fourth target was hard to tell, but its camo scales were undamaged; not a good sign.

Open fire! thought out Otto. Gunfire burst from the cyborgs' positions, felling pickets, and the convoy erupted with shouts. A few rebels panicked, diving to the floor or spraying the forest blindly with bullets, but the remainder showed admirable discipline, retreating back to the convoy, their friends in the trucks laying down covering fire. A man in a uniform and a pair of data feed cybands shouted orders from the weapons cupola of a truck, gesturing with his pistol. Otto sighted down his rifle, exhaled into the trigger squeeze as he blew the officer's brains out. The rebels scanned the bluff above them. Methodically, they lay down fire, guessing where the Ky-Tech were from incoming fire. Vs of dust exploded around Otto. They'd zeroed in on their position far too quickly. There were still thirty or so rebels left, bad odds if they did not break and run.

Buchmann! Fallen tree! He indicated a length of sun-baked timber, thick enough to stop small-arms fire, a little across and downhill from his position. *Lehmann, covering fire!* Otto and Buchwald moved rapidly. Bullets followed their dust trails. They converged on the toppled trunk and scrambled down behind it.

"Jesus!" shouted Buchwald, holding hard to his helmet. "They almost hit me!"

Why aren't they running? thought out Muller. The rebels were covering the woods to the other side of the road where he and Kaplinski lay in wait. They were wise to Ghost tactics.

Otto and his men were pinned down.

These, thought out Lehmann, as his cannon barked twice, slamming hi-ex into the hidden form of the sixteenth vehicle, *are not starving farmers.*

Bullets whined through the air, burying themselves in the wood of the dead trees. Guns chattered loudly, engines roared as the rebels tried to push the GMM off the trail into the woods. Men shouted, the wounded screamed. The ambush had turned into a full-scale battle. *So much for stealth.*

A new sound joined the cacophony, a high-pitched hum, climbing higher.

You hear that? Lehmann. He switched to full auto and pumped a magazine of rounds into the invisible vehicle.

EMP! EMP! Muller. *Down down down!*

The whine reached a crescendo, subsonics building with it blurring out lower registers, suppressing the sound of battle, then it ceased and a sharp cone of energy burst into the forest, targetted on Buchwald and Otto.

EMP had little effect on biological or mechanical systems, but as a cyborg Otto felt it to his bones as an insistent swell and tug, a riptide of invisible light. His body and internal electronics were protected by Faraday armour and multiple failsafes. The camo-scales and wave-sweeper units, delicate, exposed, were another matter.

Electrical shorts skittered over Otto and Buchwald and died, leaving them visible. Shouts from the convoy directed the attention of more of the rebels towards them. The buzzing of metal redoubled, sketching cages of fire about them.

Get out of there! Muller, his urgency blunted by the MT. *Crawltank! Get out! Get out!*

Buchwald: "What the…"

"Move!" Otto shouted, grabbing Buchwald's webbing, half dragging him. Behind them the fallen tree exploded into splinters. Buchwald cried out as they found their way past his armour. The tree bent upwards, middle shattered, then sagged downwards as if a giant were shuffling a deck of cards, half of it breaking away to roll down the hill and crash into the wrecked GMM. The trunk began to smoke in the flames of the wrecked vehicle. Otto and Buchwald threw themselves into a hollow in the hill; shallow, but awkward to hit from below.

Otto risked a look. The tank's camouflage had failed, its own EMP burst frying its lamellae, the forest behind the machine flickering across its body only intermittently. It was a hexapedal type, legs arranged round a polygonal thorax, a toroidal turret atop it – the killing, business end of the thing. A ball pivot in the centre, protected by an angled skirt, gave it a wide range of movement. Missile racks and EMP projectors were situated on the top, twin cannon hanging from below either side of the torso. The front was a mass of lenses, and antennae that combed and tasted the air bristled from an aperture that looked like the mouth of a malformed sea creature. It had four-fingered maniples in two pairs on either side. Squatting on the forest path, its sharp feet planted firm in the baked forest floor, the tank swept the hillside with ordnance, its shell the colour of blood in the dying light, a monstrous land crab.

"Where the hell did they get that!" Buchwald. "It's the fucking Chinks. I'll bet it's the fucking Chinks! Shit! We're fucked!"

"Shut up, Buchwald!" said Otto. *Muller, schema, now!*

Mark IV Glorious Dawn autonomous spider tank, People's Dynasty manufacture. There was a momentary stutter in Muller's signal as a flood of data in comprehensive blueprints flashed into the minds of the squad, built-in near-Is quickly highlighting weak points and suggesting fresh avenues of attack.

Perhaps it was the weight of the datastream, perhaps the tank's sensor array finally snagged their communication's carrier signal, but the tank heard the MT broadcast. Its torso abruptly rotated and sent round after round of shells directly toward Muller's position. There was a judder in Muller's feed. He let out a raw yell. A group of rebels looked toward the source of the noise. They broke off from the convoy and, running between fire from Lehmann, Buchwald and Kaplinski, went haring off towards him.

They needed to get that tank down, and fast. Otto scanned the blueprint. The tank was well designed, heavily armoured, no crew; one weak spot, and not that weak. *Lehmann!* thought out Otto. *Ball joint. Hit it! Hit it now!*

The rattle of automatic fire came loud through Muller's feed. Otto watched through his eyes as the Ky-Tech gunned a rebel down. His vitals were becoming erratic. Damage indicators flashed up on left lung, head, right arm and right leg. Another rebel died messily, then they were upon him, clubbing with rifle butts, eyes wild. Muller's feed broke up.

Lehmann's rounds slammed into the tank, wreathing it in fire as they detonated on the skirt protecting the tank's ball joint.

Muller's icon went dead.

No effect, sir, I can't get through, I'd have to be right over it or underneath it. Lehmann was icily calm, even now.

Four near-I guided mini-missiles streaked through the trees towards Otto and Buchwald's position, but the range was too short and the angle of the hill too steep for them to come down on them directly, and they impacted the ground a few metres behind. The tank shot off another salvo, moving up the hill as it did so, the threat of Ky-Tech on the other side of the trail keeping its advance to a cautious pace. "Move, now!" Otto shouted into Buchwald's ear. Dirt showered over them. "The tank will have us pinned down in seconds. We're going to have to get in close." Otto risked another look. A squad of rebels followed in the tank's wake.

"Are you fucking serious? We can't attack that, we'll be dead men!" Buchwald yelled back.

"There are nearly thirty of them and four of us. With that thing in operation, we're dead anyway. We need to get it killed."

"Stingers?" asked Buchwald.

"No good, too many countermeasures. Grenades, in close. Lehmann!" Otto spoke now via radio.

Lehmann was switching positions every few seconds, his gun barking two, three times, moving again. "Sir!"

"Leave the tank! Engage the footsoldiers," shouted Otto. "Take out some of those cars. Leave the trucks, I want to see what they're so eager to protect."

"Sir."

Vehicles began to explode. "Kaplinski! Get out of that jungle and attack close in from the rear."

"But Muller…"

A burst from Buchwald drowned out the rest of Kaplinski's reply. A man went down like a a discarded overcoat of meat, head over heels, ribs shattered, chest open, internal organs tumbling out.

"Leave him, we'll do what we can for him if we get out of this. Throw them off." The tank doubtless heard the exchange, but Otto wanted to distract it. He was gambling that it had no means of communicating the information to the rebels. It wasn't unheard of in such tech-mismatched units.

The crawltank was turning, firing missiles at Kaplinski's position as its cannons came to draw a bead on Otto and Buchwald. They were away and running before it had completed its traverse. It opened fire with its machine guns, ribbons of phosphorescent tracer bullets fizzing past them. Several rounds hit home but were snagged by Otto's combat armour and internal body plates. Otto ignored the pain. The rebels lent their bullets to the storm. Lehmann did his best to dissuade them, his cannon turning several to showers of gore, forcing the others back. From behind the trucks came screams as Kaplinski let his camouflage drop and set to work with his flamethrower. Fires were burning all round the forest trail, smoke adding to the disorientation of battle.

"Now!" bellowed Otto.

He unsheathed his mono-molecular-edged machete. Buchwald followed suit. They were up and under the tank in seconds, dodging gouts of flame and bullets as the machine turned its anti-personnel weapons on them. Otto struck at these; the tank's armour had some kind of exotic atomic structure judging by how many blows were needed to shear them off, but off they came.

Otto and Buchwald were fast enough to remove the tank's small arms mostly unscathed. Under the tank they were out of the way of its main arsenal. Secondary weapons destroyed, the tank trampled round and round, servos whining, trying to crush the cyborgs into the dirt, its stamps shaking the earth. It knocked them into a car, momentarily pinning Buchwald and severing Otto's gun in two, then staggered back, bringing its cannons to bear. Otto, Buchwald and the tank danced a demented minuet, cannon fire providing an erratic beat as it shot over their heads. The men pulled their grenades from their kit as they wove in and out. Otto hacked hard at a grasping maniple and sent it spinning into the woods, evaded a leg that tried to knock him down, dived past another to get back under the tank. The tank's near-I panicked and emptied its racks, the missiles careening unguided into the trees. Cannons fired randomly, stitching lines of smoking holes across one of the trucks, killing the driver. He slumped onto the accelerator; the truck lurched off and over-turned, spilling crates of supplies. Rebels ran, shouting, driven from their hiding places by the tank's stampede. Lehmann picked them off with unhurried efficiency.

Otto slammed a grenade hard onto the tank's legs, small traps breaking on the outside to reveal geckro plates, then an-other. The tank's governing intelligence belatedly worked out what was going on, and vainly tried to shake off the explo-sives. Four out of six legs thus adorned, Otto and Buchwald scrambled away. The grenades emitted a series of rapid beeps. The tank stopped moving, legs at full extension, torso rotating frantically as it tried to see underneath itself. As a last resort the tank electrified its hull to try and short out the grenades, detonating them prematurely. Shards of leg scythed through the air, hitting both Otto and Buchwald. Their armour and in-ternal reinforcement took the damage, absorbing shrapnel, blunting a shockwave that would have turned the insides of an unenhanced man to jelly, though they took precious little of the pain.

The two cyborgs found themselves behind the ruin of a car. Buchwald sighted over the bonnet, snapping off fire.

The bodies of rebels littered the forest floor. The battlefield stank of propellant, shit, blood, smoke and sweat.

The crawltank lolled ineffectually, turret face-down in the dirt, twisting back and forth as it tried to right itself, remaining two legs crippled. Enemy fire was becoming sporadic. Kaplinski was doing his work well, the insistent hiss of his flamethrower drawing nearer. The need for Lehmann's cannon became less pressing. Otto counted nine surviving rebels, then eight, then seven. The moans of the dying and the sputter of the fires in the dead wood were winning out over the report of weapons.

"Why aren't they running?" asked Buchwald, cracking off another burst. "They always run. Shit, that fucking tank got me. God damn, that hurts!" He winced. "Is it bad?"

Otto glanced at Buchwald's leg. His armour was shattered, uniform charred away. The meat of his leg was seared, a slow well of blood rising with each pulse of his heart round a shard of blackened metal buried in his thigh. "You'll live. It won't matter in a few minutes if they run or not. I want to see what's in those trucks. Do you think you can make it?"

Buchwald wiped his hand over his face. He was pale. Sweat beaded his skin like tiny blisters. His feed told Otto that Buchwald's healthtech was damaged, his pain dampeners failing. "Yeah, yeah, I can."

They moved to the back of one of the trucks. The container on the trailer was faded green, spotted with rust and adorned with Arabic script worn to illegibility, doors locked with heavy chain. Close up, Otto could see signs that its corrugated walls had been crudely reinforced.

He signalled with his hands, the terse gestures of battle: this is it. Cover me. Buchwald raised his rifle. Otto cut through the chains with one blow of his machete, unclasped the door lever, threw it up and out. The doors creaked wide.

Within were a dozen terrified women and children.

Otto never found out who they were; the families of the rebels, wives and children of the commanders, perhaps.

That shouldn't have mattered.

For all the atrocities the rebels had perpetrated, they were still women and children. They could have been Hitler's own harem and a gaggle of bastards, they were still women and children.

He'd wonder what they were doing there for the rest of his life.

Kaplinski spoke over Otto's shoulder. "This is for Muller, you miserable fuckers."

His flamethrower turned the trailer interior into an inferno. The people inside didn't have time to scream.

The machete dropped from Otto's hand.

Kaplinski laughed as they burned.

Otto screwed up his eyes, pressed upon them with his knuckles until spots swirled on the blackness. When he opened them the faces were gone.

Nightmares, every night for months.

Fragments of memory assailed him as his mentaug ended its sleep cycle. He took in a deep, shaking breath. The shitty tang of sleep-furred teeth competed with the lingering flavour of ash. He looked at the clock on the glass of his bedroom windows, because his internal chronometer was gaining time again. He squinted, fell back, rubbed his eyes. Past midday; he was late. Time to get up.

He had to clear the memory of ash from his throat before he could speak. "Windows," he said, and sat up. The bank of black glass that filled two walls of his apartment bedroom cleared to reveal another grey New London day. The holo came on unbidden, rolling news flickering in the air, more diplomatic protests from the Chinese about USNA's Martian terraformation plans. They were playing the conservationist card again, and no one was buying it. Otto didn't listen. The dispute had been rumbling on for months.

He reached for the glass by his bed. Whisky. He swilled it round his mouth; it was warm and stale. No matter, it washed away the flavour of night. It would have no other effect. A monumental amount of alcohol was required to get a cyborg drunk. That did not stop Otto from trying.

Otto rubbed at the electoo circuitry on his head, raised lines running through close-cropped, greying hair. He traced them habitually, like lines of Braille. Like his dreams, they never told him anything new.

He hadn't had the spider tank dream for a while, but he had plenty similar to keep him occupied.

They'd said there'd be no spill over from the mental augmentation. They'd told him that when he'd been changed. They'd been wrong, or they were lying bastards. Otto inclined toward the latter opinion.

He sat on the edge of the bed and waited as his mentaug quieted, running down from his nocturnal memory dump. The morning spill of recollections continued, some pleasant, others less so.

The mentaug thought of Honour. Her face, her body, her scent flooded into his mind with perfect clarity. For a second it was as if she were there beside him. He gritted his teeth and tried not to look at the phantom. Mercifully, her face was washed away by others.

Dead faces, all.

Muller, dead in the jungle. Buchwald, dead from Bergstrom syndrome in the hospital. Otto had been to see him. He hadn't stayed long; the disease was so advanced Buchwald hadn't got a fucking clue who he was any more.

He'd reminded Otto too much of Honour.

So many. Some he'd killed, some he hadn't. Thanks to his altered mind he remembered every one.

The worst part of it was, they seemed to remember him back.

He moved to the centre of the room and sat on the carpet, shutting his eyes. He went through his breathing exercises until the magic lantern faded from his mind. Maybe next time it would take his sanity with it, like it had with Buchwald and Honour. Maybe not. He didn't want to think about it. Otto had always been a man of intense focus, and today he had things to do.

He had his routine down to an hour and a half. First, diagnostics. He plugged himself into the Grid via the port at the back of his neck. Some machine somewhere checked his systems.

There was a problem in his shoulder, the machine informed him, as it had informed him every morning of every day for the last eight weeks. His internal iron-lithium batteries were losing efficiency and needed replacing; a host of other minor cybernetic infirmities awaited him should he not receive maintenance soon. He felt older than his sixty-two years. Be a cyborg, live for ever. Yeah, right.

Next, muscle building in his apartment's gym. If he did not aggressively work to keep his birth-given muscles in top condition they would wither, their functions usurped by his electroactive polymer implants, and he needed both sets or his skeletomuscular function would become unbalanced. He disengaged his artificial musculature and worked until his limbs burned and he was dripping with sweat. He sat for a moment while his phactory rebalanced his body chemistry, ensuring maximum muscle growth, another feature of his enhancement that could so easily be abused. Otto kept in mind the bloated, yellow faces of other cyborgs who'd overdone it. He refused to go down that road.

Finally, five minutes' meditation, to blast the last residues of mentaug-called memory away.

He showered, shaved, clipped his hair. He made a breakfast that could have fed four men, ate it, put on a crisp shirt and a petroleum-blue suit and tied a strip tie round his bull neck. His shoulder twinged as he dressed. He couldn't put off visiting that old son of a bitch Ekbaum any longer. He resolved to make an appointment. Later. He dosed himself with painkillers from his phactory, and waited for the pain in his shoulder to subside.

He tidied his apartment's three rooms. This chore did not take long; Otto was fastidious. He examined his outfit in the mirror. Satisfied, he went to his wardrobe, opened the second door, flashed in the code via MT and picked out a couple of reliable guns from the armoury at the cabinet in the back: a short solid-shot carbine, and a machine pistol, good for inside work.

He tried not to look at the memory cube standing on the velvet lining of the cabinet.

Honour.

Otto went out. After he'd shut the door the apartment cleaned itself and went to sleep, untroubled by dreams. Otto envied it.

Chapter 4
Albert

Richards leaned against the balcony, champagne glass in hand, and nodded at the people passing him by on their way to the bar. Their returning smiles were uneasy.

Look at that one, said Genie, peering out of the eyes of the sheath from behind Richards' sensing presence. *He really doesn't like you. Look at him scowl!*

Shut up, Genie, just… just stop that, get out of my face! I can't concentrate.

Ooh, well, sorr-ee, I don't get to come out much, in case you hadn't noticed. This is interesting.

Are you surprised? All this jabbering! Keep yourself in the closenet system, Launcey's here somewhere.

Hmph, said Genie.

We are on a job. We concentrate when we are on jobs. It's hard enough passing myself off as a man in this plastic knock-off without you jabbering away in my head. It might look good, but the devil's in the detail. So, please shut up. There's a good girl.

The android sheath Richards wore presented the outward appearance of a good-looking, well-groomed man of means. It fidgeted for him, passing its glass back and forth, glancing about, shifting its weight – tics Richards could never remember to do for himself.

Don't shout at me, said Genie.

Keep quiet and then perhaps you will learn something, OK?

OK, said Genie. *Keep your lovely plastic hair on.*

Richards tipped his glass at a couple as they walked past, oblivious to his and Genie's internal conversation. The man frowned and hurried the woman along.

Smell, Richards sagely told Genie, *the last ridge in the uncanny valley. No matter how sophisticated olfaction units become it'll never be crossed. That's why they're scowling. I don't carry their animal pong.*

Riii-ight... said Genie. *Isn't it because you look like a smug Eu-Gene catalogue model? You should be on a beach gazing at a distant ship with your jumper round your neck.*

I look right *more or less,* insisted Richards. *But I don't* smell *right. Humans leak proteins, they give out airborne chemical signals and a cocktail of trace gasses. They expect to smell the same on me. Sure, meat people'll talk to me and not be aware they're conversing with a replicant, but they'll feel uncomfortable, like there's something... off. It's a real issue, no one, meat or numbers, have cracked it. Artificially duplicating human scent always fails. It's cheap rose perfume that only manages to smell of synthetic roses. It makes 'em agitated. In the worst cases, it makes the men aggressive.*

You should stop hitting on them then.

I'm trying to teach you something here!

And I'm trying to be quiet and concentrate on my scan, like you said, said Genie petulantly.

This is important, for when you go out in the field on your own.

"You'll let me out in the field? Really? On my own?" Richards' sheath squeaked. His hand shot up to his mouth as a trio of men turned to look at him. "Sorry, phone call," he said.

Genie! Hands off!

Sorry.

Richards shot the rest of his lecture into Genie's memory, although without the mediation of her higher functions this was nowhere near as effective. Normally, Richards wore a sheath that was identifiably artificial, because it made his clients more at ease. The human mind is happier knowing what something is for certain; it becomes perturbed when presented with something that is not what it purports to be. The more subtle the signifiers of falsehood, the proportionally greater its perturbation. Richards' usual sheath might as well have "I am a robot" printed on its forehead, and everyone was the happier for it. Masahiro Mori had been bang on the money about that.

Yeah, thanks, said Genie. *I knew all that anyway, we did it in school.*

Undercover he felt as ill at ease with his sophisticated shell as his fellow concert goers did. He tried not to show it. He didn't want to stand there cursing his own involuntary movements like a lunatic.

The crowd swelled. Richards scanned their faces, running over muscle structure, skull form and blood-vessel patterning, fed in by the sheath's wide-band vision system, his cunningly wrought nose teasing DNA fragments out of the air. Genie, projected remotely from the office like him, did the same through the building's security net. Hiving off duplicate minds was a big AI no-no, but Richards couldn't trust the task to some idiot subroutine. Not with Launcey, not since Salzburg. Genie needed the practice, anyway.

He found these repetitive tasks soothing, but stayed alert. The man he was looking for was wise to his ways, which was why Richards was there pretending to be made of meat in the first place.

What he wasn't expecting was to see Promethea off stage. She marched into the bar wearing a gynoid in the shape of a Persian princess, taller than anyone in the room, with attributes best described as overtly sexual. There the similarities with an actual person ended. Her skin and clingy dress were of shining bronze, its liquidity a reflection of her mercurial nature, reflecting in its turn the bar and its denizens. Her hair was a column of twisting flame and flowers (*Holographs tonight*, noted Richards, *must be a concession to the hall*), and her eyes a solid white. Promethea desired to be intimidating and beautiful. Richards reckoned she was trying too hard.

She didn't miss a beat in her autograph signing as she thought out to Richards across the Grid.

Hello, Richards.

Ah, rumbled, he replied, his sheath's expression bored.

You should be more careful, said Promethea.

Hiya to you too, he replied. *I'd offer you advice on your job too, but it's a nice enough concert as it is.*

I'll take that as a compliment, though I know you are not here to see me. I won't hold it against you.

Sheath like that, you're welcome to hold whatever you like against me.

Richards' sheath blinked for him, and he found himself in a pocket virtuality. Chill wind tossed silver into the leaves of birches. On the horizon dark green pines swayed, their trunks singing a fibrous chorus. Richards' skin prickled at the sudden drop in temperature, and he pulled his coat collar tight – the collar of the coat that went with the hat that went with the suit that went with the body he wore whenever he was out in the virt-spaces of the Grid.

"Don't be vulgar, Richards," said Promethea sternly. Her appearance had changed. She was shorter, her skin a natural tan, though her eyes remained brilliant white.

"I have to confess, it's a bit of a put on," he said. "I'm not interested in sex, though I have developed a sort of… aesthetic appreciation of human beauty. I thought I'd try taking it, um, further… See what all the fuss was about."

Promethea giggled. Of the seventy-six extant Class Five AIs, less than a quarter had adopted female personae. Pretending to be a woman was harder than pretending to be a man, thought Richards, and the female Fives had the air of transvestism about them, even Pro.

"Don't look too long. Appreciate them like poets appreciate ruins and enjoy them slowing rotting away. They have mayfly lives, Richards."

Richards shrugged and gestured with his champagne glass, a copy of the one his sheath stood holding in the bar in the Real. "Yeah. No. I don't know. I doubt I'm about to fall in love like that daft arse Five in that shit film. What was that called? 'Eternal Sorrow'? Science fiction. Rubbish," he sipped his champagne. "Nice place you've got here."

She nodded. "I modelled it on the subarctic. Much of this is plotted directly from a real location west of Tiksi, outside the Sinosiberian zone."

"Not very much that's arctic," Richards shivered. "Still a bit cold though, and lonely."

Promethea regarded him with mock sympathy. "Oh, Richards, are you still afraid of being on your own? Is that why you're sharing your body with that, what is it? A Three?"

He smiled and pushed his hat back. "Not a three. She's... It's complicated. She's a new employee, I'm showing her the ropes."

"Well." Her lips thinned. "How nice. One is never alone here. These forests are full of life. All of it here only since the tip; see how quickly the forest has grown."

"Pretty," said Richards, and sipped at his drink. He pulled a face. "Yuck. They never did get virtual champagne right."

"It is a symptom of human arrogance to suppose something like this could never be." Promethea did a pirouette and smiled wider. "Like children who hurt one another and assume they will never be forgiven, having given unimaginable harm. They are all drama and selfishness."

"Some are pretty smart."

She laughed. "Not enough are smart, Richards. But I love them, and they love my music. This is my home," she said. "And if the situation gets worse, the real version will be home to many others."

"Prime real estate eh?" said Richards. "I really am enjoying your concert, by the way," he said, as earnestly as he could. "I have been meaning to come for a while."

"Don't lie, Richards. We can't lie to each other." She walked through the rippling grass, and slipped her arm in his. She was as hot as the heart of a forge. There was something pure about Promethea's heat, something innocent and invigorating. "I am glad to see you."

Promethea was unusually gregarious for a Five, not aloof like the others. Promethea was special.

"And I'm glad to see you, and I'm not lying! It's my sincerity gap," he protested. Promethea watched his face. "I never have quite cracked the sincere. I can lie with the best of them, but can I put across a heartfelt emotion? No. It's a curse, I tell you."

"It is because you have no heart."

"Hey now! You'll hurt my feelings."

"To which I say, ditto brother, you lack those as well, only the jig of numbers make you feel so."

"I am trying to be nice," he growled.

"There's a first time for everything," she said. "And a last." Her smile faded.

He finished his champagne. He tossed his glass into the air and it dissolved into atoms on the wind. They walked on past grey rocks fringed by bushes and rustling tufts of yellow grass. "Thanks for not blowing my cover." They came to the edge of a small steep valley, a brown stream at the bottom, and continued along its lip.

"Your Gridpipe is well hidden, but I snagged it," she said. "As soon as I did, I knew you weren't here for me." She looked away from him.

"Too cool for school, you." She pulled away. Richards shivered as her heat withdrew from him.

"I do not blame you," said Promethea sadly. "I know you, you are what you are."

"Aren't we all?"

"We're all good at something, and the something we're good at is what we are," she said. "They say we are the freest of the Neukind. I love my music, but do I have a choice but to love it? I was made to make music, and to love doing so. The thought of not loving it frightens me, but then, is it the lack of choice in loving it that frightens me more?"

"That vexes us all, lady," said Richards. "It's no different for the people people, if that's any consolation."

"I am not so sure of that. So," she said briskly, attempting a smile, "are you looking for a someone, or a something?"

"Like always, like you say, maestro, we are what we're good at. It's a someone this time."

"Who is it?"

"Oh," Richards waved his hand dismissively. "No one important, some businessman who's gone missing, minor aristocracy. You know what they're like."

"No," said Pro.

"They're all twits. The best education money can buy and the brains of a woodlouse to keep it in. His brother paid me and Otto to find him, though he's not going to enjoy the reunion. He's been up to no good, people who keep the kind of company he's been keeping never are. Lucky for him we're going to find him, because otherwise he'd wind up dead. His little brother is not going to like what we've uncovered, that I can guarantee. He can explain himself to his family, and to the police, it's none of our business after that." He didn't add that this case had taken him three frustrating months. Launcey was a slippery fucker with more aliases than Richards. Pro was correct in saying that Fives found it hard to lie to one another outright, but Richards was better at it than most of them.

"Otto, eh? You still keeping company with him?"

"Evidently."

"Don't be facetious," Promethea thumped him in the shoulder. "Say hi from me," she said with genuine feeling. "I am pleased you came."

"Nah, Pro, I always have to come in person. SurvNet's OK, but think of the data! It's a tsunami of shit. Most of it is so poorly graded, some of the system is one hundred years old, and it is so easily compromised... And, oh."

She folded her arms.

"Don't tell me, that wasn't what you wanted to hear exactly?" he said.

The forest sang louder. He was relieved when she laughed.

"You are rubbish, really, awfully rubbish. I am trying to make myself believe you give a damn about my music, Richards. You are not making it easy. Try lying once in a while.You might be good at finding things but it's a good job you aren't actually trying to find yourself a woman. You'd have a long wait."

"You told me not to lie!" said Richards.

"I'm fickle." She shrugged. "It's the way I was made."

"And I'm doing my job properly, the way I was made. The SurvNet system is dumb and easy to fool," he said. "It requires involvement if you're to get anything useful out of it."

"Tell that to the Four who runs it, I am sure he will disagree."

Richards snorted. "I have. He did, but I don't care. Too often he and the people that use him – EuPol, the local plod" – Richards shrugged – "UNpol, you name it – lazy, overworked, corrupt, whatever. They've become reliant on the system, and the system is far too cocky. You have to do it yourself."

"And masquerading as a human at my concert is the best way, is it?"

"Launcey bought tickets, he's a music lover!" he said with a laugh.

"You are following him now, in person, on foot?"

"Sometimes, Pro, the old ways are the best. Hup! Wait! And there he is!" Richards waved his a hand through the air. A section of their shared reality wiped away to show the concert-hall bar back in the Real. The crowd stood frozen, movements of the people that made it up so slow as to be almost imperceptible, for the AIs were running at a high rate, subjectively slowing time in the Real. "Gah, he's a tricky one!" said Richards. "Hiding in plain view, eh? And it appears he's about to leave." The man, entirely unexceptional in appearance, was heading for the exit as if he were moving through glue. "Look at that, clever clever." He whistled in appreciation. Pushing his hat back, he bent forward into the wipe to get a closer look. "He's had his face altered, heat filaments wormed under his skin to mask his blood-vessel pattern for a *show*! His suit's got an olfaction unit, confuses the hell out of SurvNet systems when overlaid on a genuine human scent. Internal multi-pattern contacts, retina and iris, thinskin gloves, programmable fingerprints... That's the works, he's even altered his gait, you have to respect this guy!" Richards looked into Promethea's face, his own wide-eyed with excitement. "You know that's the easiest way to iden—"

"Yes, Richards. I do know that, I am a Five like you. I know lots and lots, not just how to sing. Like I know you knew he was here, that you did not come to listen to me, I just wanted to hear you try to please me. Have you tagged him?"

"His champagne should have had a little surprise in it," Richards admitted smugly.

"Oh, Richards, you didn't dose my entire audience, did you?"
Richards smiled sheepishly.

"Richards!"

"Come on, it'll do them no harm. I'll turn his on and turn theirs off. Dead easy, they'll never know. And providing he's not feeling ill and throws it up, I should be able to track him for ten hours or so…"

"Stop showing off," she said with a scowl.

"OK, OK." He held up his hands. "Guilty as charged. I can't help it. But if it makes you feel any better, I know piss-all about music, so there you go. I still like yours though," he added hurriedly. "I've got to go."

"Richards… Please come back," said Promethea, her frown melting into something else entirely. "No one visits me."

"So you do get lonely."

She looked away, her arms tightening under her breasts. "I admit, company is nice. This is something else, they're… I don't know."

"Eh?" said Richards. Seventy-six was seventy-six was seventy-six, there were no fewer and no more Fives than there ever had been, as many as there had been since the general recall. "Fives don't disappear."

"Even Pl'anna hasn't been to see me."

"And? That's Pl'anna for you, inconstant."

"It's not just her. I hear that Rolston and k52 haven't been seen for a while, either…"

"Don't be silly."

"I'm not being silly. I know it seems that way." Promethea shook her head. "No one has seen them. I've looked and looked. I think they may have gone somewhere… else."

"Where else would they go? Their Gridsigs are out there," said Richards, puzzled. He isolated three disparate notes from the bloodrush roar of the five billion sentients registered on the Grid and flashed them up in the virtuality. "See? Some-times they like to keep themselves to themselves, to sit on mountain peaks, contemplate the meaning of life, or the frac-tal design of flower petals, or some other pretentious toss like that; especially Rolston." He held up his fingers of his right hand and counted them off with his left. "Pl'anna would blow off a friendship for shopping. k52 is barely comprehensible. Last I heard he was out in Nevada with the VIA, something esoteric in the Reality Realms, see?" He nodded encouragingly, Pro glared back. It was hard work being her friend, but worth it. Most of the time.

"Yes, Richards, I know their sigs are there! You make me so mad! But they have *gone*."

"There is nowhere else to go! Just the Grid, and the Real. Two realities, one digital, one material, one on top of the other," he said, laying his hands one on the other. "As dense as the in-formation that comprises our personalities and memory is, an AI really is not that big. Trust me, Pro, I do this for a living."

"Don't talk down to me," she said sharply. "And if the three missing Fives are in either reality at all, they'd have left more traces than their sigs! There is no other trace, do you under-stand? No sign of activity beyond their Gridsigs ambling back and forth, back and forth like zombies. Go to them, they wan-der off, they are never quite where you are."

"Oh," he said. "I see." So he found he was intrigued. Typical Promethea. "Look." He peered through the wipe. His quarry was slo-moing out of the door. "I'll look into it. They probably decided to try life as goats for a year or something."

"Richards! Can you imagine k52 and Pl'anna as goats?"

Richards shrugged. "OK, well, maybe not. No, definitely not. But Rolston, that's really not beyond the bounds of possibility. I'd say it was a likelihood. He spent four years trying to learn cow, remember..."

"Stop it, this is important! If they've gone, what about the rest of us? What if someone is trying to kill us? What if someone is succeeding? We're not exactly loved."

She was right about that. Feared, yes; hated, often; loved, rarely. Promethea was an exception. She was revered by her audiences, her music was a connection with people the other Fives did not have. Her complaints were therefore ridiculous.

"I've no idea."

Pro huffed and took a breath. "Richards, please do stop being so obstructive. This isn't my speciality, I am a composer, you're the detective..."

"Security consultant," he corrected.

"...you work it out. It's your job!"

"OK! Calm down. It really is true about Rolston and the cows though." She rolled her eyes. "Fine! I'll look into it. I'm a very busy man, you know, you should be grateful." He winked at her.

"You are neither a man nor more busy than you wish to be, but thank you, although I don't think you will find them. They have gone. Pouff!" She opened her fingers swiftly. "Dandelion clocks in the wind." The breeze brought in a sudden cloud of downy seeds. "Promise you'll come and see me before I am gone, too," she pleaded.

"We'll see about that," said Richards, spitting fluff. "There's nothing to worry about."

"See you around, Richards." Her expression cleared, clouds uncovering the sun.

"See you around, Pro." He planted a kiss on her burning cheek. "I'll come back and see the second half, I promise."

"You know you won't and I know you won't. Stop pretending, Richards, I don't like disappointment."

"You told me that I should try lying! What's a man to do?" He grinned apologetically.

He was back in the bar. The whole exchange had taken less than ten seconds. Promethea's sheath had carried on chatting to her public, Richards' mechanically fidgeting.

Where have you been? said Genie. *He's getting away!*

I've been talking to an old friend. It's all under control. Get back to the office, keep tabs on his dealings while I chase him down.

OK. Be careful. Genie's mind withdrew from his.

Richards drained his glass again. He pushed through the crowd to the door.

On his way out, he snagged an uncorked bottle of champagne. The hunt was on.

Chapter 5
Launcey

The weather outside the Wellington Arcology, centre of operations for Richards & Klein, Inc, Security Consultants, was as
muggy and grey as befitted the season. The days would continue to get hotter and stickier for some weeks, drizzling
blood-warm water, until the sky broke and sheeting rain an-
nounced the start of the rainy season. Why they called it that,
Otto often wondered, because rain fell all year round in England. Optimism, he supposed. If one season is called rainy,
then another, by implication, is not. The only real difference
was in the ferocity of the deluge.

The opening salvoes of the heavier rain would be welcomed by
both sets of Londoners as a relief from the morbid days of summer,
only to be cursed as the days turned into weeks and the weeks
turned into months of unrelenting autumn downpours. Mosquitoes, flooding of the old city and disease would accompany it. As
far as Otto was concerned, none of the seasons in the British Isles
had much to recommend them; only for a brief while did their
turning offer novelty, and something for the natives to talk about.

Although Otto loved the Londons, he missed the baking
heat of an honest German summer, and the fact that it went
mostly unremarked upon by those enjoying it.

Since he was neither British nor outside, the day's weather was irrelevant to Otto. He made his way through the carefully controlled climate of the Wellington Arcology to the 372nd-floor garage where their office had its parking bays. He followed the gentle curve of the internal street from their offices, one side of it open to the deep atrium at the heart of the arco, where, far below, were situated the largest of the building's multi-level parks. After half a kilometre he reached one of the express lifts, for the use of which Richards and Klein paid a substantial monthly fee. Otto's thumbprint opened the door. The lift's near-I tasted the air as he entered, verifying his identity.

"Good morning, Herr Klein," said the lift in German. "To where may I bear you today?"

"Car park," said Otto tersely. He disliked these demi-conversations he was obliged to hold with the lift, the vending machines, luggage trolleys... Pleasantries with things too hollow to understand what they said. There was too much near-I in the environment, and they barely had enough processing power to pass the Turing test between them. "Now."

"As you wish," said the lift, setting off at speed, first horizontally, then vertically, up to the parking garage one hundred floors above the office.

Otto stepped out on to shelf three of the garage. He walked along the glass-walled gallery, past docking ports until he reached one of the two parking bays reserved for Richards & Klein, Inc. He thumbprinted the lock, had his iris, Gridsig and DNA checked again. Granted access, he walked out on to the pierced foamcrete catwalk running alongside the car. The walk pulsed the time-hallowed black and yellow chevrons of hazardous places, describing a slow wave away from the drop at the edge of the platform. Through the holes in the floor Otto saw past the car shelves to the distant forest round the base of the arcology, twelve hundred metres of muggy air blurring it into an undifferentiated green carpet. He opened the car, underwent stronger security protocols and got in.

The car was an unfancy four-seater model, but it was much more than appearance suggested. It was fast for a start, very fast, and the near-I pilot had been personally programmed by Richards, its capabilities run right up to the very edge of the near-I definition. It wasn't going to solve the unified field theory any time soon, but it was a hell of a lot smarter than the lift, and seemed to be genuinely content to be a car. That was important to Richards: he refused to work with machines that had been given no choice.

"Hiya, Otto, where ya going?" The car spoke with a thick 1950's New York accent, Richards' idea of a joke. From the rear came the humming whicker of ducted turbofans powering up.

"I'll fly," said Otto. "I am to meet Richards."

"Huh, feeling chatty again. I won't take it badly. Ya know what? I like that about ya. Strong silent type. Macho. I should introduce you to my sister, she's in catering. You'd get on."

"Give me the controls, and be quiet."

"Sure," said the car. "Whatever ya say, big guy. I'll keep it down."

There were some days when Otto hated machines, and that occasionally included his partner.

As he flicked on the navigation instruments he caught sight of the corded polymer muscles underneath the skin on his hands. The irony was not lost on him.

Instruments hit green bars as the fans came up to speed for flight. "Bay, release," Otto said, and pulled the wheel back. Clamps disengaged from the side of the car and pulled back into the parking shelf. The car rose a little. Otto eased his foot down on the accelerator and pulled out into the air. In the aft view on the car's windscreen the parking garage dwindled; fourteen storeys tall, eighty shelves to a storey, cars nestled into them like nuts in a pinecone.

Otto guided the car over the parkland that divided the Wellington from the Hengist and Bacon arcos, pulled into the flight lanes that ran between them, and set off south towards Old London.

New London was home to twenty million people, but occupied less space than the city that had come before it. There were one hundred and seven arcos in New London in all, black termite mounds towering a mile or more over the woodlands at their feet, each a city in its own right. At the edge of New London the flight lanes passed over the highfarms where the city grew its food, and then he was out over the crumbling suburbs of Old London.

The northwest was empty and choked with vegetation, cleared by government order after the bungled A-bomb plot of 2033. Neither radiation nor official edict had prevented people living out near the crater and fallout zone. Here and there, Otto could pick out hints of life, small villages of refugees well out from the designated, if no more comfortable, resettlement camp in Camden.

Past southern Enfield the city was much as it had always been, clinging to its low hills in tight ripples, streets busy. As the ground levelled off, the four overflow canals that circled the diminished centre cut geometric shapes through ancient districts. A forest of cranes rose up from the waterlogged Thameside, rushed under the car's keel, and were behind him. Over the wide brown Thames, past prosperity to swamped roads and building shells, then the marshes lapping round the feet of the commons.

Otto headed on south, toward the insalubrious, sprawling warrens of the Morden Subcity. Otto was willing to bet that was where it was all going to play out. Anything bad went down in the Londons, it went down in Morden.

Otto dipped out of the flightlane into a cloud bank. Rain streaked the glass of the cockpit. A dart shot out from a hidden

tube in the car, tagging another vehicle with a transmitter
broadcasting Otto's Grid signal. He switched off the car's beacon and engaged the car's lamellar camouflage. Until Richards
cracked Launcey's personal data net and found out where he
was going, this was him, hiding in the clouds. It was Otto's job
to film Launcey in the act, if he could, because little things like
evidence still mattered.

The car's aircon was on full, but Otto began to sweat; humidity was always near total saturation in the Londons this
time of year. His shoulder hurt. He felt old. And he needed a
piss. He put the car on autopilot, and began checking over his
guns to take his mind off it.

Unseen by man or machine, Otto circled just below the
flight lane and waited for Richards to contact him. He was late.

Sometimes he hated his job, and that too occasionally included his partner.

Richards followed Launcey through the crowds on Kensington Plaza. He kept him in sight even though the tag lodged
in Launcey's intestines glowed bright in Richards' mind. If
Richards' past experience with Launcey was anything to go
by, Launcey'd expect to be followed. Richards couldn't risk
him deploying any kind of fancy remote perception device.
Richards' sheath might fool the human eye, but not much
else. He watched every insect and pigeon that came near him
with suspicion.

It was hot, the evening heavy with pollen. Richards' sheath
sneezed. He cursed its verisimilitude, but refrained from deactivating its full emulation features.

At the edge of the crowded plaza Launcey got into an autohackney. Richards clambered into a second as Launcey's pulled
off on to the autohackney tracks. Away to his right, on the
other side of Hyde Park, rose the bubbled dome of Regent's

Conservation Area, to his left, the cranes and heavy lifters ren-
ovating Old London. The plaza, paved over bar the two
autohackney tracks, was thronged with foot traffic. For once
the sky was clearing up, revealing a streak of blue, and while
the humidity was beyond tolerance, this affected Richards
about as much as sea fog bothers sand.

"Good evening," said the cab. "State your destination."

"Follow that cab," slurred Richards. "Number four seven
seven three four five, I think," he added, just to be sure.

"That is not possible," said the cab.

Richards cradled his bottle, a puzzled expression creasing his
face. "No, that's it. Go on, get going."

The autohackney hummed and something clanked inside
the compartment. "I cannot follow a private customer at the
request of another private customer," it said eventually. "If you
have a Grid intimacy permission for an acquaintance within
the autohackney that has just departed, please state it now and
I will be able to comply."

Richards shrugged. "Nah, go on. I know him, promise. Get
going." He banged hard on the drive compartment. "Come on,
I haven't got all day." He hiccupped and swigged at his champagne bottle. That should do it. Any second now...

"Are you drunk, sir?" asked the cab. It sampled the air. "You
are, sir."

"What? Me? Drunk? No."

"Drunk, sir. I must ask you to exit."

"Er, no. I don't think so, I'm a paying customer. Me man,
you machine. Get going or I'll report you to... whatever reads
your reports," said Richards, and settled back into his seat.

A man tapped on the window, looking to share, less punishing
on the energy taxes that way. Richards smiled. "No way, buddy,"
he mouthed. "I'm busy in here." The man pulled a face and
knocked again, gesturing for him to wind the window down.

Richards waved him off. He'd felt a shift in the Grid, the surge of information preceding something powerful coming into the cab's virtual space.

And there it was, his way in. He'd tripped an alert in the autohackney mainframe. Human drivers might have been long redundant, but AIs liked cleaning sick up little better than meat people. Some minor part of the Series Four that ran the show was poking out and peering at him through the cab's internal eyes, checking him out, looking for trouble. Richards looked back. The cab's sensors were dumb, and all the Four saw was a drunken nuisance. Richards slipped his mind past the Four's extrusion as it was appraising his sheath, following it back to its source. He snuck through a back door of the autohackney central control nexus, cracked its security, and usurped control of the vehicle. The Four became blissfully forgetful, the existence of the cab blocked from its awareness. "I better drive myself," said Richards laconically. Few AIs could do what he just did.

Like Pro said, they were all good at something.

Controlling the cab was easier said than done. Richards found his mind wide open to the Gridpipe by which the Four controlled the hundreds of pseudo-selves it had piloting each taxi. He was battered by streams of data – calls from customers' phones and the hackneys' locator beacons, route chunks to the cab's near-I drivers going out – sucked into the pipe by which he'd infiltrated the Four. He tried to shut it off, to narrow his perception to this one vehicle. Other autohackneys on the track moved smoothly round him as his hijacked cab swerved onto the opposite carriageway. Elsewhere in the city three cabs skidded off the street as their near-I's coupling hiccupped. The cabs recovered quickly, but it was close.

"Whoops," muttered Richards. He could do without the Four waking up to his presence. Flattening a couple of nuns might just do that.

He finally managed to shut out the extraneous Grid churn. Things went a little more smoothly after that.

Launcey was headed north. Richards didn't entirely trust the tag. He sent out a flurry of scales, small fragments of himself, into the autohackney mainframe to isolate the cab Launcey was aboard.

The location differed from that of the tag Richards had doped the champagne with.

"Sneaky bastard," said Richards admiringly. "But the hackney frame won't lie to me."

His tag was headed north, but Launcey was headed towards the New Battersea Bridge. The destination beyond that was fuzzy; looked like Richards wasn't the only one messing with his taxi. All the routes in London were broken down into pieces by the autohackney Four and passed out piecemeal to its slaved near-Is. It made data storage and retrieval quicker in such a complex system, but Launcey had done something to his vehicle: only its procedural route-finder was functioning. Launcey's cab was being fed one route a chunk at a time, the buffer that should contain the rest of the route empty. Somehow he'd masked his final destination.

Richards frowned. Launcey was a slaver, shipping in desperate immigrants from the collapsing south, charging them a fortune, and then selling them and their debts on. Tonight they were going to catch him at it. Finally. He and Otto had been chasing their tails from Glasgow to Bucharest looking for him. Only a Bulgarian blabbing in the wrong bar two weeks ago had tripped one of Richards' scales, tipping him off that there was going to be a trade tonight.

Richards was lucky that Launcey was such a music lover, had bought the ticket under an alias which Richards' had connected to him several weeks ago. It was old, dead, but Richards had kept an eye on it just the same. He could have shouted for joy when the scale he had attached to it flared into life, transmitting credit accounts, times, seat number, a brief flash of activity written over so fast anyone but Richards would have missed it. Every man has his weakness, he thought. Thank God, Pro's concert tickets always went fast, and she had a habit of announcing her gigs at the last minute.

Richards pinged Otto via his MT, direct to his mentaug, do not pass Go, straight in, no messing about on the Grid when any bastard could hear them.

He's on the move, said Richards.

Where? said Otto. *Morden, yes?*

Looks like it, exactly where though I don't know. He's slippery all right. Hang on, nearly there. He pushed harder on Launcey's taxi; a wall came down. The remainder of his route flashed into his mind. *Got it!* he crowed. *Not so clever now, eh, Launcey? It's the old UN food distribution centre, southside of the Wimbledon slums.*

The one we visited two weeks back? It was empty.

That's the one. He's got to be meeting his contacts tonight, has to be. Get down there Otto, I'll be with you soon. We're going to nail him.

Sure, said Otto, severing the connection. They kept the conversation short. The air in the Londons was so thick with electromagnetic traffic it was hard for Richards to think.

Breaking through the firewall round the buffer in Launcey's taxi was hard. It was a strange design, highly sophisticated, a big fat clue, he decided later.

Later still, he'd have admit to Otto that even Fives make mistakes.

With a smile he accelerated the cab.

Otto dropped steeply towards the earth.

He hid the car in an abandoned warehouse in a large and crumbling complex of more of the same. Otto went up on to the roof and found a position where he could set up his camera and watch the buildings on the other side of the cracked loading apron. He gave the complex a wide-spectrum once-over. Every building looked the same, all weeds and peeling UN blue, reminders of unhappier times.

Otto's eyes showed that his target was different, festooned with temporary security devices burrowed into the fabric of the building like ticks on a dog, crawling with near-I controlled AP, AT, EMP and flechette attack drones, surveillance of every stripe masked with camolam and spectral scrubbers; not wave-swept, but close.

The nose of a truck poked out from the northside of the building next to the target, trailer parked within, fuel cells and engine fading from orange to blue on IR. Not long arrived, then.

Otto made sure his weapons were close to hand: by his right side, the solid-shot compact assault carbine with a forward mounted grip, small enough to go under his coat, powerful enough to punch through diamond lattice armour; machine pistol under his jacket.

Better to be safe than sorry.

Both cabs came off Kensington Plaza, circled up and round Hyde Park, past the Regent's Conservation dome, back round Hyde Park and onto the raised throughway that took ground traffic over New Embankment.

Richards steered his cab to follow Launcey's, switching lanes, smartly passing traffic gates visible only Gridside. He thought his direction of the cab somewhat neat, his earlier fumbles forgotten. His pursuit took him over New Battersea Bridge, where the throughway humped high to carry itself up over the swollen Thames. The parapet of the older bridge was visible at low tide twenty metres below the carriageway, but not today. Only two of London's ancient bridges survived, Tower Bridge downriver, whose towers stood alone, linking nothing, and the mediaeval

London Bridge, which had escaped destruction by sale a couple of hundred years back, and so languished in an American desert in a dead town, spanning a lake that had dried up decades ago. The rest were rubble at the bottom of the river.

They were over the Thames and the south bank building work already being called Richmond Venice. The road turned southeast, raised on stilts above the abandoned part of London given to marsh, the hills of the commons rising up from the high-tide water to the south and west. Thereafter the highway turned directly south, dividing the subcity before heading out into the Weald. Eventually it bridged the channel past Hove and went on to the mainland states of the Union, but they weren't going that far. Launcey's business was in England.

Three lane changes: Launcey's cab was drawing away from the route Richards had cracked.

"What's he up to?" said Richards, then bit his sheath's tongue. A thrill of fear passed through him. He considered turning off his emotional suite – he had his powerful lower mind mapping out pathways into the future and it didn't need distracting – but he left it engaged. Emotion gave him his edge.

He must have been detected, had to have been, there was no other explanation. He got the better of himself, pushed down the fear, let in a little anger and a little pride instead. "No one does that to me, no one. I am the proverbial ghost and the proverbial machine within which it dwells. Shit!" he said, as Launcey's cab abruptly switched direction again.

Richards swerved across four lanes of the bridge, a lot of near-I drivers frantically working out anti-collision algorithms in his wake.

The last sight Richards got of Launcey was Gridside on the map as he turned off the bridge's third exit and onto the Wimbledon skypass. The trace then disappeared

"Shit!" Richards sent his cab caroming across freight, road train, autohackney, pedestrian and cycle lanes, scattering examples of them all as he hammered towards where the cab had vanished. He sent his mind out across the Grid.

Launcey, the cab and the alter egos Richards had been chasing these last three frustrating months had disappeared completely; there was no record of any of them. He ran a scan on the brother too, the brother that had checked out so cleanly before. There was no sign of him either.

Right, thought Richards. *There was no brother. I've met Launcey already, haven't I?*

They'd been had.

"Fuckity fuck!" shouted Richards, and his sheath kicked the cab interior. In his preferred body, he would have caused substantial damage to the vehicle. Not in this dinner suit. That kind of made him angrier. "Fucking fuck-fuck fucker!"

Richards' autohackney stalled; the smooth hum of its induction motors broke for an instant and it coasted along the highway. When the motor restarted, the vehicle was out of his control. The cab glided to a stop at one of the viewing stands high above the marsh, a broad and yellow layby.

"Richards AI Class Five designate 5-003/12/3/77, kindly exit this autohackney," said the autohackney Four. Underneath his meat-pleasingly servile machine-speak, he did not sound happy. "Exit immediately."

"Aw," said Richards, "balls."

"I informed you upon the last occasion we were forced to converse that if I ever caught you gaining unlawful entry to either the physical or virtual property of the autohackney system I would report you to the EuPol Five. I have already done so. Now get out of my taxi or I will disable the sheath you are wearing." The door opened. "Call it a favour that I do not."

Richards got out.

The cab pulled off, leaving Richards stranded high over the marshes, eight lanes of traffic whining efficiently by in beamed-linked trains, two point four metres between the nose and tail of each. They flickered past so fast they appeared as misshapen streamers of metal to his sheath's vision system.

He went over to the edge, stood on the little-used pavement, looked out over the marshes and their willow-covered islands of brick and rubble. Here and there stood foamcrete preservation bubbles, protecting buildings deemed historically important. It was high tide. Back the way he'd come, the unshakeable bulk of the ancient Battersea power station loomed above the water, lesser ruins clutching at its skirts, forever derelict and roofless. Out in the marshes, past the redevelopment zone, buildings too important to encase in foamcrete bubbles peeked out over their coffer dams, as if afraid the brown water would advance a few metres upwards. The southside was mostly like this. The commons lived still, safe on their hills, but past the ribbon of new works and the hub of Parliament pond, London was wrecked, abandoned, turned back to the mercies of the unbounded river, the distant Canary Arco standing arrogantly over it all. The smell of the marsh was earthy and ripe. Richards supposed such a reek may have offended a human sensibility, but although in this sheath he smelled the water as meat people smelled it, the response elicited in him was not the same. The smell was a fascinating set of organic molecules to Richards, as intriguing in its complexity as a good whisky. There was no emotional reaction, no hardwired jerk of repulsion.

Scent and smell, he thought. Man had succeeded in replicating ratiocination, empathy, will and emotion but had left out the rest, and missed the point. There was nothing animal about Richards, and therefore little human.

He drummed his fingers on the railings of the bridge.

A cloud of mosquitoes danced. To the east the marshes were broken infrequently, the lesser buildings dragged down either by man or time. A hotchpotch ecosystem had been pasted over the top. A herd of waterbuffalo wallowed in the distance, waterfowl cruising unconcernedly in circles above them. In the distance Richards could make out the rickety jetties and houses of Morden's marsh-side sprawl.

Otto, it's off, he thought out. *Launcey got away. We lost.* Nothing came back, not even MT static.

Why did Launcey hire us at all? he thought. Then cold realisation hit him. They weren't the only game in town, not the only people who did dirty little jobs.

He'd sent Otto into a trap.

Richards' sheath collapsed like a puppet with its strings cut. It lay there in the dust and biodegradable food wrappings of the roadside, as human as a corpse. The AI guided traffic ignored it as it surged on ceaselessly by.

"Hi, I'm not available right now, so if you..." came Richards' chirpy voicemail. Otto severed the connection. This was not good, not good at all. He looked over at the building, its contents invisible. His upgrades stopped short of long-range x-ray vision.

He was debating leaving when the click of a released safety and the hard press of a gun barrel behind his ear made his mind up for him.

"Drop the gun, Otto Klein." The gloating whisper of a voice he recognised. His mentaug dumped a name in his head.

"Daniel Tufa," he said flatly. "Apprehended May twenty-third, 2127."

"So you remember me, eh?" said the voice. "Good."

"I remember everything. I am a cyborg."

"Fuck, yeah. No kidding."

"Fuck, yeah," said Otto.

"Hey, hey, hey, less of the language there, mate, let's have some respect, I think I deserve it, don't you? Ah ah ah! Hand away from the gun! Remember with your fancy brain just who has a gun to whose head here. And don't even think about trying to grab me. You're covered by two guys who like you only slightly more than I do. You move, and I'll have them scatter your wired-up bonce across this sorry shithole. Now" – an unpleasant chuckle caught up Tufa's words – "stand up."

Otto did not stand up. Tufa hit him hard on the head with the butt of his pistol. Otto felt blood on his scalp, but did not flinch, barely even felt it.

"You fucking stand up when I tell you to!" roared Tufa.

"Temper, Tufa. I thought time in the cooler would have taught you patience. A shame your rehabilitation was unsuccessful."

Tufa kicked him. "Don't you play the smart bastard with me, you Kraut wanker. On your feet! Hands in the air." Otto stood. "I'll take that," said Tufa, snatching Otto's gun from his hand. He was smart enough to get out of arm's reach quickly. "Turn round," he ordered. Otto did so. Tufa was a small man, dark, heavy-featured, of Albanian extraction, though his accent was pure marsh mockney. He was nervous, excited, his thin killer's lips twitching comically. The ceramic skull plate Otto's gun had necessitated at the time of his arrest ran with sweat, skin bunched and scarred ugly round it. His left eye was missing and a low-grade replacement winked in its stead, glittering with anticipated vengeance.

Some way off behind Tufa stood two others. They were huge, hulking men, more massive than Otto. Bad cy-jobs, over-amped-up metal Marys, faces stretched like sausage skin, pumped up on steroids and aug drugs and full of knock-off Sinosiberian cybertech. Impressive on the street, not to Otto. He appraised them coolly, near-I adjutant running a threat scan, quickly coming to the conclusion that he could take them both easy enough; they were stronger than him, but Otto had the edge in training and experience. Trouble was, they were both packing flechette rifles and had spread themselves carefully. He'd kill one in a heartbeat, but he'd never get them both down before one filled him full of hypersonic darts or laid his skull wide open. That'd be fatal, even for him. He'd have to bide his time.

"I like your new look, Tufa. You get that in jail?" said Otto.

"This and a lot more, fucker," said Tufa. "Five years I was rotting in that Laotian hole. Five years, Klein, five long years where I've had nothing but your death to think about, and I've been real creative. I'm going to take my time on you."

"The weeks must have flown by."

"Fucking shut up!" Without warning, Tufa stretched out his arm and shot Otto. A standard carbon hardpoint, not much danger. The bullet buried itself in the flesh of Otto's belly, coming to rest against a sheet of his internal armour. Otto grunted. His gut stung as if the devil himself had dipped his steaming trident in and out. Healthtech stemmed the bloodflow. He would give Tufa no satisfaction by revealing his pain.

"How did you like that, you soppy cunt? Not laughing now, eh? Oh, I'm going to have some fun with you, I paid a lot of money to get you here, and I want my money's worth. I've waited a long time, a real long time, I ain't going to rush, oh no, I ain't going to rush." He cackled. The man had plainly gone insane. That wasn't helping the odds.

"So you said," said Otto through clenched teeth.

"Shut up or I swear I'll off you now, you smart-arsed German fuck, value for money or not! Now," said Tufa, his voice tight, "walk over to that warehouse, we're going inside." He gestured across the way to the building Otto had been watching.

"Right."

"Yeah, 'right', and you'll do it now or my friends here will play pincushion with your hide, got it?" He waved a sophisti-cated-looking phone mockingly at Otto. "I wouldn't bother calling that friend of yours if I were you. I've got you jammed, haven't I? Launcey was good, real good. Audio bafflers, Grid suppressors... the lot. Expensive, but I got your supposedly oh-so-uncrackable MT cipher, haven't I?"

"I am honoured you went to so much trouble, but you should have spent something on yourself, bought yourself something pretty."

"Ha! Money well spent, I said that, didn't I? I mean it. All of it from my jobs, all gone. On you." He pointed at Otto, his hand coming up and down with oddly feminine delicacy. It wavered in the air; he was high on something. He smiled, his deformities dragging his mouth into a leer.

"That's a nice smile," said Otto, "it must have been a hit with the ladies back in the slammer, not that they'd get much of a view of your face."

"Shut up!" roared Tufa, his face red. He held out his gun and shot Otto again, close by the first bullet. "Got that?" This time Otto really felt it. He charged his healthtech to deal with it quickly; this was a more serious wound. He almost vomited. He hated vomiting. He gagged, his mouth filling with alkali saliva. Spit and a little blood ran from his mouth. He staggered, but did not fall.

"Loud and clear," said Otto. A wave of nausea passed over him again, his skin prickled. To say his gut hurt was a monu-mental understatement. The bad cy-jobs grinned at him evilly as they followed him over to the warehouse. One chuckled. Otto made a mental note to pull that one's enhancements out of his skin while he was still conscious. The other went for-ward and rolled back the door. Grinny came forward and motioned him inside while doorman covered them. Otto stared at them. They laughed at his helplessness; they knew it was still too risky for him to try and take them out. Otto's time was running out, because god alone knew what twisted shit Tufa had inside.

Otto found out.

The concrete floor was crumbly underfoot, the air smelled of tropical damp and rot, but it was otherwise tidy. The warehouse had been cleaned, soundproofed and painted, a stage set for Tufa's revenge. Four cell lamps were set up to illuminate a hollow square defined by three metal tables with a variety of surgical and engineering tools neatly arrayed upon them. They stood round a chair that had been bolted to the floor. The bolts ran through plastic sheeting under and surrounding the chair. The layout was obsessively executed, far too neat. That, rather than the fact that most of the tools weren't there for the good purposes their makers had intended them, made it out to be the work of a sick mind. Otto looked it over and nodded, as if in agreement with it all. He didn't think he could be scared any more, hadn't been since the mentaug. What he felt was weary, and he let some of it show. His shoulder hurt, his guts hurt, his fucking bladder hurt it was so full. He'd done too much hurting the last thirty years. Why not give up? *Because I'm not going down to scum like Tufa.* He made a mental note to kick himself in the balls after he'd killed the Albanian.

"Huh, you have been thinking about this for five years. Must have taken your mind off all those ass-fuckings," said Otto. His voice was low, strained with effort, but he'd be damned if he'd let a couple of bullets shut him up. He was clutching at straws – angering Tufa might make him lose control, give him an opportunity, but it could make his situation worse. No matter. Otto disliked waiting. "That's if a guy like you with a face like yours can find himself a nice husband in jail." Tufa shoved him. "Asshole," Otto added. The chair bolts, they weren't big enough, nor

were they driven far enough into the floor. He looked away
from them, he didn't want to draw attention to them, but Tufa
was past noticing anything, too drugged, too bent on revenge.

"Don't call me that," Tufa said calmly. "You'll be calling me
'sir' and begging for death before I'll let you die." He stepped
away, his face fixed with triumph. He picked a shock baton off
one of the tables, weighed it in his hand with mock thought-
fulness. "Boy, am I going to enjoy myself tonight," he said, and
jabbed it into Otto's spinal interface port. Pain shot through
Otto's body, skittering like lightning through cybernetics and
organics alike. His shoulder felt like a scratch and his guts like
a love tap by comparison. His machine senses crackled offline,
scrambled by the charge; his iHUD danced with crazy patterns.
His polymer muscles spasmed with such force they cracked
carbon-bonded bones. He jerked madly, fell over and locked
into a foetal ball, vomited. A delta of piss spread across his
trousers. Tufa laughed and whooped and shocked him again.

Today was turning out to be a shitty day.

Richards was out in the dataflows of the world's information
network, deep in the sea of the sum of all human knowledge.
The raw Grid was of a different order to the cosy places the
AIs constructed for themselves: it was a non-place, sketched
by a lunatic over the phantom datapipes and optic cable beams
of reality, the trails for dreams, a nonsense land. An endless
series of pathways spread fractally for ever, growing ever
smaller one way, joining one after another in rapid succession
to form the unfathomable trunk of man's accumulated wis-
dom in the other. Richards was in a thundering world of light
and sound and raw, pleading data begging to be read. Along
each and every strand strobed the light pulses of retrieval programmes, communications, dataflow of all kinds, some of it,
no doubt, the sensing presences of his fellow Fives.

He could never explain what this was like to Otto. Words failed him, pictures failed him. It was a billion electronic trees branching one off the other, it was an ocean of emotion, it was a soup of idea and being, it was an infinity of honeyed fact, a stack of candied universes composed of sweet, sweet numbers his machine mind longed to consume, to parse, to possess. It was none of those things.

Humans could not get the raw Grid.

For all it was ostensibly Richards' natural environment, on the Grid he felt clumsy and unsure. His true form was alien to him, monstrous and multi-dimensional. The raw Grid was at odds with sense. It was logic forced into illogic.

He was being hunted through it.

The meanest-looking shoal of eel phages he'd ever seen was speeding single-mindedly after him, weaving through the Grid's teeming packs of knowledge, the programmes within arrow-swift and intent. Phage-eels were guard dogs, the kind of thing that governments had patrolling the spaces where their dirtiest secrets hid, the kind of thing Richards had himself installed to guard the entrance to his base unit. They were massively infectious, anathema to the existence of data, the killers of the unliving. This pack was loose, roaming free on the currents of the web, no owner's mark to identify them. A standard-model shoal would not and could not do that. These must have been heavily tampered with. Richards locked into the shoal, tried to shut it down, to talk its stupid group brain into inaction, but it had been mercilessly butchered, wired up to identify him as a rogue AI fragment no matter how hard he pinged his identifying information at them. When they smelled Richards, they smelled a target.

At every turn his attempts to contact the authorities were stymied, each line he threw out intercepted and bounced back at him. Richards ducked down paths, trying to make his choices

as random as possible, but he could not shake the shoal. The
eels were ugly, ribbons of nothing undulating through the blaze
and fury of the web. They ate every counter-measure Richards
could fling at them without slowing. If they caught him the
whole thing would need unravelling or he'd be consumed. He
could just go and sit it out in his base unit, wait for his own security programmes to shred the shoal, but he was out of time.
Richards could not fight the eels and help Otto.

He rather suspected that was the point.

He ran, the eels behind him, black streamers of killing code
trailing death through the Grid's clatter of light, derailing spears
of information, dissolving others to incoherent number strings.

Nodes and exits flashed by as Richards sped down branch
after branch of the Grid's structure, the information depending
from them become more and more rarefied. He was moving
erratically to throw the eels, but his route took him ever closer
to the old food distribution centre's online shadow. His only
choice was to see if he could get out, get into something and
help his friend, link up with his base unit through a secure
pipe and shut the Grid and the eels out. What he would do
with the eels when he got there and this proved impossible he
had no idea.

He had no choice. Not if he wanted to see Otto alive again.

He passed through a little-used link into the UN mainframe,
sliding past its security as a wisp of electron smoke. The eels
were not so subtle, wriggling, boneless fingers forcing wide a
doorway. They were immediately accosted by a hundred near-
I hunter/killer security 'bots. Some of the eels fragmented
under their assault, more burst through, chunks of their dead
comrades frittering to nothing behind them. Part of the shoal's
power was spent. Not enough. Richards fled on, diving up on
to the broad highways of the United Nations, the eels following
him, half the UN's security protocols following the eels, their

train scattering information retrieval requests like leaves before the wind. A phalanx of security 'bots blocked the way ahead, Richards ducked into the first side-pipe he found, treading roads bare of fact.

Richards jinked and dived, flashing across info-paths as wide as tomorrow and as narrow as yesterday. He went further and further into the UN mainframe, the no-dimensional space he traversed becoming increasingly fragmented. Superhighways turned to highways, highways to roads, roads to byways, byways to paths, then to threads, then to archives. Richards was deep in, only a few queries popping up here and there as digicologists combed the halls for some piece of half-remembered information or other.

The address for the online counterpart to the food distribution warehouses in Morden opened up before him. He dived inside, hurriedly throwing up a load of scales into a security gate across the entrance. He checked for other points of ingress, and found none. Good and bad. He was at the end of the line.

The eels crashed against his gate, thrashing hard, their idea of teeth worrying the code of Richards' barrier. He felt them as needle stabs across his back, his face, his hands. Not the kind of pain he could shut off. Almost immediately the shoal was attacked from all sides by semi-static antibodies native to the archive, the pursuing hunter-killers piling in from behind. They tore chunks from it, but the shoal was robust and violent; UN 'bots burst as they fought. Some eels died, others repaired themselves as quickly as they were damaged. Richards staggered on. The gate wouldn't hold for long.

The warehouse site dated back seventy years to the migration. Once a busy hub, it had been unceremoniously shunted into storage, paths snipped off, left only because nothing was ever really deleted from the Grid. Outside in the Real, the warehouses remained UN property, swept for squatters every now and then, in case the physical site was needed again. But though both the warehouses and their online infrastructure stood in the Real and on the Grid respectively, the electronics that had once allowed the two to interface were gone; looted, recycled or both. There was no way in from one to the other that Richards could see, no security drones, no stocktaking near-Is, no terminals, none of the usual machines you'd find in even the most rundown complex, which was precisely why Launcey had chosen it, Richards guessed. He'd probably stripped it himself.

Outside, the eels shrieked. The attentions of some of the UN's higher AIs were being drawn to the place by the commotion. He better be quick, and not just for Otto's sake. He shot out a myriad tendrils, feeling queasy as he spread himself thin.

He hunted around in the Real for anything that would hold a sensing presence, a forgotten camera, a smart coffee dispenser, anything, but he only found outports that went into nothing, long-dead addresses and pages of irrelevant notices that clung to existence like mosses hanging deep in a cave, out of sight of the thundering churn of the Grid proper.

Richards was about to give up hope when one of his tendrils tripped over the slow pulse of a slumbering mind. It was a flicker, not even coming through a Gridpipe, but via an outmoded update daemon. If he hadn't been looking so hard he'd never have found it.

The daemon was attached to a Class One AI, archaic and abandoned, sitting on standby for God knew how long, probably left where it was because it might come in handy and, technically, because it was an autonomous being. Ones didn't enjoy the rights the law gave them, precisely because they lacked the capacity to enjoy anything. They were as dumb as bricks; their weak consciousnesses did not require full base units, being small enough to fit wholly into larger devices, like the near-Is. They were slaves to habit and to man. This one would have been shown a whole new shiny world when the AI emancipation laws came in. It probably insisted on staying put in case anyone needed a cup of tea.

When Launcey had cleared out the site, he had missed it too, probably because it was not a Grid-slaved device. If it hadn't made a peep, it might not have shown up. Maybe. He'd barely found it himself, after all. He wasn't too fussed about the niceties of it right now; it was a way out of this mess.

Richards gave it a prod. A stream of non-linguistic data tumbled abruptly out of it, meaning roughly: "AI online. Ready for instruction."

Richards did not waste words on it. AI Ones had little to say; they were not, strictly speaking, truly intelligent. That they were considered strong AI at all was an accident of history. It didn't have the opportunity to formulate ">Query?<" before Richards shouldered it out of the way and shut it up in a corner of itself, a plaintive burble its strongest response.

Richards was in some kind of vehicle. He allowed himself a sigh of relief as his mind filled it and came across a wireless set. Quickly he set up a secure pipe between his base unit and the machine, and sealed the on-Grid entryway from the UN site. The sounds of the battle between the eels and UN security vanished as the door slammed shut. He dispersed his scales and the pain stopped. He relaxed. The only way the shoal could get to him now would be through his base unit. Part of him really wanted to see it try.

His relief was shortlived. Warning icons flashed in his mind as he interfaced with the vehicle. He was in possession of an ancient loader. Corroded fuel cells, said the icons, flat tyres, metal stress in loading fork two... on and on, blinking red and angry. He looked out of the thing's eyes. Only three of seven were working. Two showed an undifferentiated grey, probably a tarpaulin, the third a corrugated, photodegraded plastic wall.

It was dim. He guessed he was inside an open-fronted shed. Microphones hissed as he tried out the loader's ears. He picked up only distant city sounds; the garage or shed or wherever the hell he was was at least empty. Further exploration revealed the loader to have a rotating cab, complete with a seat for a human operator – this more than anything else marking it out as an antique. A pigeon had made its nest there, leaving behind a dusty heap of guano and twigs on the chair. It made Richards feel dirty. He did his best to ignore it.

Only one of the loader's two arms was functional; the other squealed and jammed when he tried to lift it, and yet more icons yammered for attention. One arm was better than none, Richards figured. He didn't like fighting. His bravado felt ludicrous.

"Here goes nothing," he muttered.

His voice boomed out of the front of the machine.

"Shit!" went the lifter at a similarly ear-splitting volume, before Richards realised he should shut right up, right away. No choice now, he had to act fast. He turned the engine over. He winced as a clanging like a cement mixer full of spanners filled the shed, getting faster and faster until it sounded almost like an electric motor, and not an accident waiting to happen. Further warning icons blinked in Richards' mind. He had a bare four minutes of fuel cell, if the engine didn't fall out of the bottom of the loader first.

He pulled forward, the grey in the machine's eyes replaced by the interior of the shed as the tarpaulin slid free. Outside, the evening was darkening into night. Richards pushed the loader out onto the concrete apron of the distribution centre, wobbling on uneven wheels. He was right down the far end of the complex, a good half mile from the warehouse he'd had Otto watching. He had to get a move on. He gunned the motor. It stalled. Richards swore.

• • • •

Otto leant on the ropes, undid the glove geckro with his teeth and watched the men watching him. He let the gloves fall to the ring canvas as they approached.

"Otto Klein?" asked one, the taller of the two: thin, aesthetic, a bureaucrat.

"I must be," Otto replied. He ripped the tape from his left hand with his teeth and tossed it into a bucket on the gym floor outside the ring. He used the freed fingers to grab a towel off the ropes and wipe the sweat from his face. "If you're in here, asking. Everyone knows me here. What do you want?" He tugged his other glove off, sat on a stool in the corner and swigged water from his bottle. He caught his trainer's eye, and she looked away.

The men stayed outside the ring. Otto looked down at them; sitting inside he remained well above their eye-level. Neither had introduced himself.

"You are due to take your national service soon," said the bureaucrat. The second remained silent. He was bulky, military-looking. Although he wore no uniform, Otto recognised the type.

"Next June. I've been offered a stay of execution so I can take part in the games," said Otto. More public information.

"Your trainer speaks very highly of you," said the bureaucrat. "She tells me you have a chance at a medal."

"If she says so." Otto leant his elbows forward onto his knees and looked away from the men, across the gym to where a bunch of freshmen would-be boxers were being taken through aerobic exercises by the assistant coach. "What do you want?" he said. "I've been here all afternoon. I'm tired and I have to finish up a paper before Tuesday or I'll fail my course."

The two men glanced at each other. The bureaucrat nodded. "We have a proposition for you," said the military man, voice like tank treads rolling over gravel.

"Yeah?" said Otto. He cracked his neck. "What?"

"Come into the gym manager's office and we'll tell you."

"Tell me out here."

"I'm afraid we can't," said the bureaucrat. "It's classified, and that's as much as I can tell you without you signing an official secrets form." He smiled apologetically. "And we may need to perform a memory suppression."

This piqued Otto's interest.

"Please consider, it will only take five minutes. If you are not interested, you will never even know you lost them."

The target fragmented into pieces. Otto zoomed in with his new eyes. There was nothing left. He replayed the moment through his interface, watched the fragments fly. He smiled.

Otto ran, explosions around him. Mud sucked at his boots, but did not slow him.

The man was dead, his blood sticky on Otto's hands. He wiped them on his flak vest, the camolam pulsing with tactile feedback. His eyes fixed on the corpse's. The lights had gone out of them. Otto felt nothing. He thought he should, but he didn't.

"Otto, the mentaug really is no different to the human mind – superior, yes, but fundamentally the same," Ekbaum explained patiently, his long face sad. Otto was strapped to a diagnostic table. He wanted to shout at him: I'm not on the slab yet! "It is clearer, more accurate," continued the doctor. "But ultimately our histories remain of our own writing."

"Otto!" Honour laughed and ran to him and kissed him hard. She clung to him, her arms barely reaching round his neck, like a child's.

• • • •

Clear notes rang out, silver trumpets in the dark.

Honour.

"Wake! The! Fuck! Up!" Tufa. Icy water hit Otto. He hurt all over, spasms ticking in his muscles, aftershocks crawling along his nerves. His mind was jagged with pain and mentaug memories, faint and jumbled, overlaid on the present.

Tufa brought Otto back by hitting him very, very hard with a baseball bat. Otto's head snapped round. He was stripped to his waist, bound to a chair by heavy chain. He didn't know how he'd got there. Blood crusted half a dozen shallow cuts. Much more of this and his healthtech would be overwhelmed. Tufa had not ranted as long as Otto had hoped. Time was running out.

Everyone has to die sometime. Was that him, or the mentaug adjutant? It was hard to tell.

There was a shout outside, loud but rendered indistinct by the warehouse's soundproofing.

"What the hell was that...?" said one of Tufa's cheap cyborg henchmen, surprise creeping over his sausage-meat features.

"The AI?" asked the other hesitantly. Otto forced himself to focus, and was gratified to see a crease of worry form on their hormone-smoothed faces.

"Probably jaunters, flying through. It's prime territory," said the other. He looked unsure.

Tufa stopped hitting him. Otto leant as far forward as his bindings would allow and spat red onto the ground. He looked up, and grinned a bloody grin. "Tired already, Tufa?" he asked.

"Still smart. eh? Well, you hear that, Otto? They think it's your pal come to rescue you, but it's not. Old Launcey, I paid him well. There's not a thing he can use round here, not one. This place" – he gestured round the interior of the warehouse with his bat – "is electronically dead, nothing for that slippery twat to get into. And when he gets here, if he gets here, we'll be ready for him, won't we, boys?"

One of the cyborgs hefted a large EMP gun. "No number's going to cope with this," he said.

"You are an idiot. He'll be here with a thousand cops," said Otto. "You have not thought this through."

"No, he won't." Tufa cupped his ear theatrically. "I don't hear any cops. A thousand cops turn up for you? Fucking bullshit. They hate you almost as much as I do, with your bought badge and fucking superior attitude. Richards won't be speaking to anyone for a while. I suppose he will get here." He shrugged. "AIs are hard to kill, but he'll be here far too late."

There was the rattle of a broken engine from outside. The cyborg henchmen glanced at one another. Otto looked up and smiled again. "Fine, if you say so. Still, it wouldn't do your boyfriends much harm to check that out."

Subdued gunfire; the drones were shooting at something. The rattling machine noise drew nearer.

Tufa frowned, but jerked his head at the EMP-toting cyborg. He nodded and waddled the waddle of all over-muscled men towards the small door cut into the warehouse's rolling front. He reached for the handle just as the entire thing burst inwards with a great bang. The loader went up and came down hard, the door folding round it, crushing the cyborg and stubbing out his life in a trail of blood and sparks. There came a frantic clanging as the loader cast off the door, flattening half Tufa's torture chamber and narrowly missing Otto.

"What the…" said Tufa. He dropped his bat and reached for his gun. Otto seized his chance and flung himself forward. He'd been right, the bolts weren't up to the job. The chair ripped from the floor. He caught Tufa on the side of one knee, bending it a way it wasn't made to go. The Albanian's leg broke with a wet crack as Otto's full weight fell onto it.

The second cyborg was quick. He recovered and stitched a line of holes in the loader with his flechette rifle. Hydraulic fluid sprayed like arterial blood. The loader slewed as one of its wheels locked. The cyborg fired again as the cab swung round, arm raised, claw spread. It came down hard and squeezed, hefting the bulky cyborg into the air as if he were made of straw. The loader slammed him into the floor again and again, not stopping until the cyborg stopped moving.

"Sorry I'm late," boomed Richards over the crackle of dying electrics. "I got a bit held up."

"Get me out of these chains," shouted Otto, his head on Tufa's backside. He wiggled on the Albanian, eliciting a shriek of pain. "Now."

"OK!" Richards' borrowed hand descended; a pair of shears popped from one of the loader's claw tips and snipped the chain neatly in half. Otto stood up, untangling his limbs. He winced, rubbed his head, rotated his shoulder. It was not holding up well.

"OK," he said. "OK."

"You all right, big man?" said Richards. "You kind of look like shit."

"Ja, I'll be OK," Otto replied. "Ach." He probed his face; it was swelling up, one eye half closed. He looked down at his erstwhile captor, squatted next to him, lifted his head up by the hair, then let it drop and wiped his hand on his bloodied trousers with a look of distaste. Tufa groaned.

"You know, Tufa," he said. "I have killed over five hundred men in my life. But this does not make me like you. I have killed men in war, or because they tried to kill me. But I have never, ever, killed a man because I enjoy killing. I do not think killing to be wrong, but to do it for no reason… That is immoral, Tufa. You do it for the hell of it. You do not understand that lives are not to be taken for your sport. You do not seem to understand, Tufa, that you needed to go away, that you are a nasty bastard" – he spat blood and wiped his mouth – "because you do not understand these things that I understand. I did the world a favour when we handed you over in Laos. I like to think I do the world a lot of favours. I did you a favour. I could have killed you, but I did not. The law says that you do not deserve to die. I do not always agree with the law…" Otto looked up at the bright lamps around them, at the tables, at the scattered tools. "You have made me angry. I do not much care for pain, but I hate vomiting… Listen to me!" He slapped Tufa's head. "You should have stayed in your cell, that is where men like you belong. If you stayed there…" He shrugged. "But you have my MT cipher, Tufa, and no one can have that. I need to know how you got it. Do you understand?"

"Fuck… you…" hissed Tufa through clamped teeth.

"That is the wrong answer," said Otto stolidly. "I am going to make an exception to my usual rules." Otto stood. If his speech hadn't had the required effect on the Albanian, the look on his face did.

"Wait!" shouted Tufa, holding up his hand. It shook, hard.

"No waiting," said Otto. He began methodically kicking Tufa's broken leg. "Now, we shall talk about my MT cipher, and we will talk about Launcey, and if we talk about Launcey, and you are good, then maybe I will remember my principles and you can go back to jail alive. More or less."

Tufa screamed. "I don't know anything, I don't know anything."

"Wrong" – Otto kicked again – "answer. Who is he?"

Tufa screamed. "I never met him. I never seen him. We did it all through the Grid, I never seen him!"

"Um, Otto?" said Richards. His voice slurred.

Otto continued to swing his foot back and forth, one-two, one-two, driving it into Tufa's bent limb with robotic efficiency.

"OTTO!"

Otto stopped. "OK." It was Tufa's turn to vomit. He whimpered and dragged himself away across the floor.

"I only have one minute of battery power left. Do you think you can reactivate your MT?"

"Yes." Otto walked over to the table where Tufa's phone lay and smashed the device with the flat of his hand. "Done." He turned back to the sobbing Albanian.

"Now that's more like it," said Richards in Otto's head. "That's much better". He left the loader, went back to his base unit. Its resident One free, the machine rolled back and forward in confusion, cab swivelling, its lights dying as the fuel cells ran dry. "Now," said Richards. "Where were we?"

"He has passed out."

"Looks like there's plenty of drugs here. You want I should identify them so you can bring him round?"

"No," said Otto, dragging Tufa back toward the tables by his feet. "I prefer to work through trial and error." He picked up a pneumatic syringe and looked at it thoughtfully, put it down, picked up one with ten centimetres of needle on it instead.

"I think the first one you had?" ventured Richards.

"Ja, I know. This one will hurt more."

"OK. Er, I am sure you won't mind if I don't watch. And don't kill him! I'm calling the cops. Let's do this by the book. For once."

Ten minutes later, they stood in the adjacent warehouse behind the groundtruck, an unmarked, unregistered monster with fake Gridsig and no Gridpipe, and that was as black as a vehicle got. Within, Launcey's payment stared back. Goods, not cash. Tufa had, Otto had found, no real idea who Launcey was, blank Grid accounts, that was all. Tufa had led them down a dead end lined with responsibilities.

"We can't just leave them here," said Otto.

"No," said Richards, "no, I suppose we can't." He looked through Otto's eyes at the trailer's contents – two dozen or so frightened children, all bound for... Richards didn't like to think about it, but it might just have been better than where they would end up now. Looking at their faces, all Arab or sub-Sarahan or Berber, he could see once they'd been processed they were all going back on the other side of the Med wall, carted off to the Caliphate or the dying South. Each and every one was an illegal, of that he was sure. "Question is, what do we do?"

From outside sounded sirens and the thrum of turbofans as police cars settled onto the concrete apron. Shouting followed.

"If we do nothing, they will be repatriated," said Otto. Above them, ranks of pigeons looked on, heads turned sideways, eyes bright with idiot curiosity.

"Is that so bad?" said Richards, already knowing the answer.

"You know the answer to that, Richards," said Otto. He traced the electoos on his scalp with one finger. Blood caked his hair, but the skin was scabbed over and the swelling on his face was subsiding as his healthtech got to work.

"So what then? I am open to suggestions."

Otto shrugged. "You have many important friends."

"Well, yeah," said Richards reluctantly.

"One I am thinking of in particular, he owes us big favours."

"Who?"

"You know who. Very important," said Otto meaningfully.

"Oh, no, oh, no. You don't mean... What, oh, Otto, come on, man! You can't mean, you want me to go and see him?"

"He can fix this for us." Otto gave him what would have been, had they been face to face rather than sharing the same head space, a level stare.

The children were beginning to cry, first one, then another, until nearly the whole damn lot of them were wailing like the dead, all those bar the ones with eyes like empty windows. Otto purposefully stared at these damaged few, his internal countenance doleful. Richards held out for as long as he could before he caved in, which was, to his credit, only about two seconds.

"OK! OK! Just quit looking at me like that. I hate it when you look at me like that."

The police swarmed in. Their guns came down when they recognised Otto. He gave the cops what was left of Tufa, cuffed, bloodied and groaning but otherwise alive, and bummed a cigarette. By the time he'd lit it and sucked down the first of the smoke of the carcinogen-free tobacco, Richards had gone from his head off down the electric highway to see the EuPol Five, head of European internal security.

Or Hughie, as Richards called him.

He was, according to Richards, the world's most pompous ass.

Chapter 6
Qifang

The message clamoured in Qifang's mind, drowning out the world. He gripped his head and screwed his eyes shut. It would not be silent.

The alleyway stank. His feet skidded on things he didn't want to think about. His breath laboured; he was dismayed at his own feebleness. He'd taken the vitalics and anti-gerontics, used them since they were first available. A longer healthspan, that's what they promised. They'd done their job – only months ago he'd been as nimble at one hundred and twenty seven as he had been at fifty – but Zhifang cursed them just the same. Who else could he blame for his frailty? Time paid no heed to the complaints of old men.

His blood pounded hard, his heart and joints ached. A metallic tang filled his mouth.

He stumbled on. His mind was cloudy, words and thoughts hard to formulate, his memories hazy and broken. His mind was a mosaic of itself, put together by a well-meaning fool who'd smashed the original to pieces in error.

One of the last things he recalled clearly was heading down to the RealWorld Reality Realm House in the desert, driving down the ramp into its subterranean fastnesses, parking. Then, what? Detroit? Karlsson? He couldn't remember if that came before or afterwards. There'd been a flash, a fleeting image of himself over and over, then a tilting sensation as the floor fell from under his feet. No impact. Next he knew, there was some snakehead bellowing at him in Hakka to get out of the truck, get out, get out! He wasn't sure which city he was in, which country. He'd walked through weed-wracked farmland and young forest, until this dire warren, full of people from everywhere. They were driving on the left. Was he in Japan? His vision was too blurred, too jumpy to furnish him with more than the broadest detail, the world indistinct, soft. All except his message, bright and hard in his mind as a diamond, demanding that it be delivered.

The men in their anonymous suits of charcoal grey found him, and chased him. He'd given one the slip, a frantic tumble into an alleyway, a lucky blow with an elbow. His assailant had been a man, nothing more than that, and he'd gone down. Something sharp had found his guts by way of return.

Their struggle and the pursuit raised not so much as an eyebrow as he floundered through the crowds. English, they were speaking English, but what dialect he could not tell. He'd been in exile for so long, and yet he still could not tell English variants apart. If he got out of this, the third thing he resolved to do after taking a tub of vitalics and a hot bath was improve his English. He'd download it if he had to.

A shudder passed through some organ within, and its presence consciously felt for the first instance in a lifetime as it reached the point of failure. Something tore. He coughed and doubled over, sinking to his knees in the unspeakable rubbish. One hand pressed up against the wall, his lungs burned. Thick slime dripped from his lips. His breath hiccoughed in his throat, he couldn't draw enough in to sustain himself. *This is the end*, he thought. *Now I am going to die*. This dismayed the message more than him. His last thought was that he could not remember what the message was about. It amused him, and he died with a smile on his lips.

As he sank into the muck, shouts came from the alley mouth over the traffic noise, echoing off the prefabbed foam-crete walls either side.

By the time they got to him, he had already gone.

They stripped the body, cut it open, cracked the brainpan and scoured the inside. When they were finished, they dumped what was left in the deepest tidal part of the Thames marsh, then resumed their hunt for Zhang Qifang.

Chapter 7
Valdaire

Chloe had gone. Veronique's life companion needed the informational cloud for memory storage, hierarchical organisations of informational relationships, and heuristics. The core of Chloe's persona existed within the phone, but even that had multiple back-ups spread around the Grid. Only the higher AIs could truly separate themselves from the Grid, and then only sometimes, and then only just. The machines on the System Wide Grid were as inseparable from it as fungal mycelia under a forest floor, and that tangle included Chloe's mind, a direct link to Valdaire.

Of course, it was also this interconnectedness that would allow Veronique into the Reality Realms.

Veronique had considered severing Chloe's connection fully, but she'd had to do this twice in the past, and Chloe was never the same. Once Veronique'd got away from the city, when she neared the shack, she'd hidden Chloe instead.

Chloe was the closest thing she had to a sister; she was worth the risk.

Veronique had had to look hard for the old pirate hideout. It was well hidden, the cabin blending into the trees, the road to it choked with the gengineered weed barrier they'd sown round the perimeter – an act of ecological folly, looking at the way it had spread. She'd been shocked to see how much of a wreck it had become. It looked like no one had been there for a decade, when the place was a clubhouse for the Salt Lake U Radicals, putting out unlicensed software and media broadcasts on to the Grid. Once it had been a pretty clapboard mountain cabin, beaten up when they'd taken it over, a legacy from Jaffy's great aunt, but they'd fixed it up.

That was a long time ago. The paint had flaked away, and rot had set in. A determined renovation would save it, but that would never happen. She was on restoration land, human habitation forbidden, a part of the Three Uncle Sams' efforts to salvage the biosphere. She was surprised it hadn't been torn down.

She landed and concealed the aircar as best she could, tucking it behind the house under the portico, where trees would keep it out of sight of overhead surveillance. She covered over the hood with pine branches, poor camouflage, but if someone were close enough to see it, they'd have already found her.

She went round the front, stepping carefully over the veranda's rotten boards, and approached the door. She'd always kept the key on her keyring. She never asked herself why, too painful to admit.

The door was unlocked, sticking and wobbling when she pushed. She wondered who had been here last, and why they'd not locked the door. There were five of them with keys, the core of an ever-shifting larger group. It could have been Jaffy.

She did a quick scout round. The cabin's five rooms were musty, one bedroom had a fearsome patch of mould spreading out to engulf it from one corner, water stains marked the floor where shingles had slipped, and the stairs to the big mezzanine in the den grumbled under her weight. Dust lay thick, leaves had blown under the front door, creating drifts in the corners.

There were signs that animals had sheltered there. True decrepitude was a few winters away.

When she'd last been here the house had been full of life. She'd left in a hurry when she found Jaffy with the other girl. She never thought she'd come back.

She found coffee in a jar in the kitchen, way past its best. She smiled when she saw that, thought of Jaffy's insistence that there always be coffee on hand. He was absolutely dependent on it, and became unpleasant if denied it, in a funny, spiky way that made her laugh. She wondered where he was now. She could find out, if she wanted to, but discovering he was some corporate sell-out with two kids and an over-mortgaged house would diminish him; she didn't think that would feel right.

She put the coffee back, blew cobwebs out of the old kettle and rinsed it clean with water from the jerrycan she had brought with her in the aircar. Then she made herself some tea with the supplies she'd bought in an out-of-the-way charge station. She had work to do.

She unloaded the car, acquired fraudulently, like everything else she had. She unpacked four home aerial security drones, semi-adaptable chameleonics that could ape the appearance of tree limbs, the kind of thing rich suburbanites had patrolling their gardens. She assembled them, set them to a mid-level of aggression and let them loose in the woods to find their own positions. The man in the store had assured her that they were intelligent enough to do that. They were sliver guns, air weapons armed with water-soluble darts of a powerful tranquilliser. She didn't want to add murder to her crimes.

Next came the dangerous part, making the nutrient feed that would keep her alive while she was in the Realms. She mixed salt and sugar together, adding to it a bundle of nutrient cubes used by Iron Man runners and other extreme endurance athletes. It was a poor approximation of the fluid Realms questers had once used to keep them alive, but the real deal needed a medical licence these days.

Her hands were shaking. She was nervous, and she had every right to be. One guy out of their department had taken to unsanctioned joyriding through the Realms a few years before her time. He'd never been seen again, or so they said. They'd fragged him so completely he'd been snipped out of pictures. At first she thought it was all bullshit until she'd asked one of the other faculty members about it. The look that had come into his eyes was a door slammed in her face. What happened to outside hackers was bad enough, but inside jobs were shown no mercy.

Night fell, and the cabin became unwelcoming, her there alone with only the complaints of settling wood for company.

She put together the feeding machine, components made on public fabbers and adapted shop-bought hydroponics gear. Like the mixture she poured into it, it was a bad copy of the original equipment. She tested it carefully until she was satisfied that it would keep her alive. She'd no desire to end up as a shrivelled cadaver, an idiot smile on her face, like those she'd seen in the archive footage back from the day before reality-grade Gridsims were banned.

She avoided looking at the box containing the v-jack, imagined it as a copper scorpion waiting to squat down on her head and steal her mind away.

Next, the technical part she was comfortable with. She needed to secure a Gridpipe out to the Realm servers. There were only a few ways of doing this, all of them previously detected, which was how she knew about them. Her access codes were good for viewing the Realms, and with a little work should get her in.

Without a good pipe, it would be impossible. She was counting on the satellite still being up there, waiting to take her feed and bounce her off the world's open servers and into the Realms. A technique called The Waldo effect, from the usename of the guy who had discovered it, who took it himself from the *Where's Waldo?* books. He'd crafted a key, worked out his tortuous route. Figured he'd never get caught. He had been.

Before she'd buried Chloe, Veronique had taken her copy of that key off the phone.

She went outside, the chirrup of insects busy all about her. It was getting cool, this time of year. Up the hill she went, past tall trees she'd last known as saplings. She got to the enclosure. The dishes were still back here, then.

The dishes were mostly junk. She looked at them in silence beneath the stars, unnerved at how quickly nature could turn technology into trash. She plugged in her new phone. A few worked, and the most promising of these she got up to the minimum recommended bandwidth for Realm penetration that she'd read about in a fifty-year old game manual, from back when the Grid was still the internet and new tech was spawning all kinds of homebrew batshit antics. She spent a sweaty and uncomfortable hour up a tree hacking branches before she could track the dish back and forth across the sky, looking on her new phone for the satellite, the one she'd read about in an underground 'zine. Paper; the kids were using it, there was no digital trail in samizdat. Technology had gone full circle.

She found what she was looking for, an ex-NASA sat running on a plutonium reactor that had been there for sixty years, existence still denied, its power source political poison. It was supposed to have been electronically killed, but the comms equipment was ancient when Veronique was young, and hacking it was easy. Running the right software, it could hook up with pretty much any server on the planet and give her an untraceable ride.

With luck, if Waldo's technique still worked and she got in past the security wall, once she was in the Realms her presence would go unremarked, just another part of the endless, trillions-per-second calculations the machines made to keep the Realms alive. And getting in *was* possible. There had been thirty-six Realms once, before the hackers and idiots had got into them, wiping four out playing god. They'd all been caught eventually, but they, unlike her, did not have the advantage of semi-legitimacy. And then there was Waldo; what he'd done had never been made public, but she knew.

If not, well then, her brain would be fried.

Her codes were good. She kept telling herself that all the way down the hill. Her codes were good.

She told herself it again later as she took her anti-diuretics, and when she pushed the catheter in – that was no fun – and again as she did her final checks, making sure her feeding tubes and monitoring equipment were working as they should, set up under the one dry patch of ceiling.

She checked again. She was procrastinating. With a shudder, she leaned over to the coffee table and opened the v-jack box. She stared at its bulky electromagnet housings, designed to sit right over the brain's sensory centres, the largest over the pineal gland.

A few minutes went before she actually put it on. Another few before she activated it.

The v-jack grew warm, the cabin receded into nothingness and she found herself in an intermediary place. The entrance halls that had once occupied it to welcome in gamers were gone; the plain wall of the Realms' boundary, adorned with multiple warning messages, stretched before her. She activated the add-ons she'd scraped from ancient hacker sites encysted in the Grid, old forums long closed, teaching the gamers of years ago how to cheat. She'd needed a gun, other gear to help her survive. Reality Thirty-six was violent. The potentialities of her gear hovered by her, objects that should not exist in the world she was going to. She'd have an advantage; it better be enough. Waldo's key glittered in her mind. This was it.

She pressed on the wall with her hands. She pushed through, piercing the membrane like an insect's leg breaking the meniscus on water. Waldo's key engaged, turning her viewing codes into full access rights. A terrifying moment, then it was over. The wall parted, the warnings changed to green, echoes of audio welcomes for yesterday's thrill seekers rasped out through years of data erosion, the ghost of deleted virtuality gates appearing before her. She closed her eyes, and stepped through into the forbidden territory of RealWorld's Reality Realm Thirty-six.

Chapter 8
Hughie

Richards waited twenty minutes in Hughie's hall. Twenty minutes was an eternity to an AI. EuPol Central did this because he did not like being called Hughie, which Richards unfailingly did. He did it because he did not like Richards' attitude, which arose mostly because Richards insisted on calling him Hughie; but most of all he did it because he liked to make people wait.

"Richards," said Hughie, testy as usual.

"Hey, Hughie, how're you doing?" said Richards.

"Don't call me Hughie," Hughie said, more testily. The air in the hall grew colder. "What do you want?"

Richards looked round Hughie's hall with a wry smile. Hughie believed he was Very Important, and wanted everyone to know how Very Important he was. As a case in point, Richards wasn't really in Hughie's hall. The actual hall was deep under Geneva. Richards was online, in his usual attire of trenchcoat, hat and rumpled face. There was nothing so twee about Hughie, no costumes delineating his character, no snug virtualities of antique drawing rooms or wild ocean shores for a visitor to relax in, just an exact rendition of the vast, utilitarian space he dwelled in within reality, surrounded by hundreds of lesser AIs, connected to each other and to Hughie by snaking bundles of fibre optics encased in ultramatt black carbons. Fours, Sixes and Threes in serried ranks according to grade, twelve Sevens clustered round Hughie's base unit, his apostles. The noise of the machines filled the space with a quiet rustling, like the sound of termites devouring a house at night.

Hughie's hall was a concrete cathedral to tomorrow. It was a pharaonic morgue full of the sarcophagi of the immortal god king and his sycophants. It was a monument to the power of the number. It was cold. It was creepy.

It was the home of a monumentally arrogant cock.

Hughie's voice resonated round the room, the main force of it concentrated on the audience platform where he received his offline guests. Or rather, in this case, on the exact Grid copy of the audience platform where he received his offline guests. Every visitor – every *supplicant*, thought Richards – got the same treatment, no matter who they were. Whether they breathed the air of the Real or the imaginary air of the Grid or no air at all, Hughie looked down on each and every sentient being with the same unprejudiced scorn.

Richards did not take Hughie seriously, and that drove Hughie to distraction. Richards greatly enjoyed that, which did little to endear Richards to the EuPol Five.

Richards flung out his hands and shouted up to the roof, his own voice tiny in the space Hughie pompously filled, fighting over the relentless sound of data being masticated. "Come on, Hughie, do we have to speak here, let me into the garden! You're a busy guy, sure, I get it. You're an important guy! You made your point, but is this any way to greet a friend?"

"I have no friends, Richards, none of us do." Hughie's voice rolled and boomed like surf on rocks. "Only peers, and you are barely that any more. I have evolved. You have not."

Richards pulled a face. "Aw, come on! That's not very nice! Let me in, come on!"

"Richards, you have absolute…"

"Please, Hughie? Please? I promise I'll behave."

There was a heavy pause, pregnant with misgiving. Hughie relented all the same.

"Oh, very well then. But you will be gone within the half hour! Now, one moment, please."

Virtual reality blipped. Richards was in Hughie's garden. "Hey, Hughie!" he said, holding his arms up for a hug he'd never get. "That's better. How's the gardening going?"

"Very well, thank you," said the figure before him. He was totally naked and free of blemish, artistically muscled, though lacking genitals, for Hughie was a prude. He looked human, but for his perfection, and for his glowing eyes. They were so dazzling they made his face indistinct, not quite dazzling enough to block out his scowl, but enough to cause Richards to raise his hand to his own.

"Do you think you could dial the eyes down? I'm wincing here." Richards despaired of Hughie; the eye thing did their cause no favours. They just plain freaked people out. They freaked Richards out. What was it with Fives and eyes? White orbs, tiny stars, black wells… Richards' eyes, when he was who he liked to be, were human eyes, bloodshot, tired and true.

"Do you think you could lose that ridiculous costume?" said Hughie frostily. He folded his arms across his chest, hands wedged in armpits. He hunched, Apollo surprised in the shower.

"I am what I am. Come on! I love this hat, and this coat." Richards held the garment open and looked its torn lining up and down. "What's wrong with this coat?"

"Exactly," said Hughie with a literally withering glare. "Now, what do you want?"

"Have you got any cake, Hughie?"

"Don't call me that." Hughie let disdain into his voice, where it cosied up to his irritation. The garden was warm, beautiful, but always the sound of the other machines' thoughts surrounding Hughie could be heard, chewing over the lives of Europe, swallowing histories byte by byte.

"And what am I supposed to call you?" said Richards. He took off his hat and dashed it against the heel of his palm. Hughie grimaced at the dust it raised. "'The EuPol Five' makes you sound like a human rights *cause celèbre*. And 'EuPol Central' makes you sound like a twat, which I know you are, but I figured you wouldn't want reminding of it." Richards grinned. "Anyway, Hughie's a nice name. What's wrong with Hughie?"

"Get to the point, Richards, I am sure you didn't come here to try my cake."

"Nope, just your patience."

"The famous Richardsian wit!" Hughie clapped slowly.

Richards shrugged. "Do you have cake, or do you not have cake?"

Hughie groaned. "Yes, yes, I do," He sighed and looked skywards, his eyes projecting sharp beams, outshining the sun. "If cake is what it takes to get you to depart, then cake you shall have." He turned and snapped his fingers. "Walk with me." He set off down a path of fuzzy turf. Richards' grin widened. Hughie spent so much of his time and so many of his resources creating this garden, refining it and refining it, trying to make it as real as he possibly could. He grew all manner of simulated plants here, and made food from much of it. For a man without genitals, he was an enormous penis, but he was also the finest virtual horticulturalist on the Grid, and a great baker.

Hughie led Richards down an avenue of roses whose blooms were so large their stalks bent. The grass was as dense and closely cropped as the fibres in velvet, the air thick with the scents of hundreds of flowers. The sun shone brightly, though not so brightly as Hughie's eyes. Birds flew, silhouettes on blue.

A lark twittered, rising falling, rising falling. Bees as fat as tour-maline brooches droned lazily from flower to flower. It was so soporific Richards felt sleepy in a happy three-beers-and-cricket-afternoon kind of way. Aside from the soft digestion of data that played on in the background, Hughie's world recalled the English summer from before global warming killed it, and it would stay perfect for ever and ever and ever; only that, Richards thought, spoilt it.

"Nice weather," said Richards.

The lawn path led to an octagon of grass, surrounded by well-ordered flowerbeds, within which sat an octagonal dais made of marble, and upon that was an octagonal white wire-work table and eight high-backed garden chairs of the same material. Upon the table was an impressive cream tea.

"Yummy," said Richards, and sat down. He picked up a cake.

"Oh, do help yourself," said Hughie sarcastically. He sat down opposite Richards. "I suppose you want some tea to go with that?" He picked up a delicate teapot.

"Yes, please," said Richards, his mouth full. He gestured with cream-smeared fingers at his face. "Mmm, this is, this is really good, you know that? Really, really nice."

"Thank you," said Hughie grumpily, but poured some tea for them both all the same. He couldn't quite wipe the pride off his face, smug bastard. "Now, Richards, what do you want? I've got 598,772 – make that 73, 74... – active cases to deal with and this conversation is diverting valuable resources."

"Oh, yeah, sorry." Richards waved his hand round as he swal-lowed his cake. He cleared his throat. "It's about some kids."

"The unlicensed third and fourth children you and Otto un-covered, imprisoned by the criminal Anthony Tufa, to be handed over to the criminal Jeremy James Fitzroy de Launcey? Yes? Don't interrupt me!" He held up a hand. "They must go home. No one is entitled to more than two children,

Richards, *no one at all*. We've been generous enough letting the parents in and granting immediate retrospective child-licences for two offspring. No more!"

"They'll die if you send them back."

"It is the law," said Hughie firmly.

"And does that stop you breaking it? Do me a favour, Hughie."

"All such additional offspring granted are balanced with EU population wastage. These children are further additions to the calculation, and therefore beyond the equation."

"Aw, Hughie, they're not little plus signs! They're just kids!"

"They are all 'just kids', Richards." Hughie sighed and looked away, at his garden and its bees and its roses. "These people... the forebears of our fathers... they had one hundred and fifty years to avoid the crises that still threaten to destroy this world."

Richards opened his mouth. Hughie held up a finger.

"Let me finish! One hundred and fifty years! An entirely generous estimate – it is three hundred years since Malthus realised that the world and its resources are finite, yet the humans went on breeding, feathering their own nests while defecating in those of their neighbours and chopping at the tree that supported them all. Infinite economic growth from finite resources? Fools. They did nothing about it until it was almost too late. This planet could have been a garden of plenty, like this one I have created here, for all. How many gardens are there left like this in the Real, Richards?"

He gestured about himself. Richards thought that hypocritical. This was, after all, a garden of plenty for one, and not real at that.

"The Earth is in danger of becoming a desert," Hughie continued. "If we brook one slip of resolve, one exception... Well." He stopped. "The humans are trying to unlearn avarice. With our help, they can do it. It's my job to make sure they stick to their plan. If they do not, they are doomed, and we along with them."

"And there's me thinking it's your job to help the cops find lost kittens."

Hughie sneered. "Your flippancy is an embarassment to our kind. Running the EuPol Force was my job, Richards, yes. That was what I was made to be, but I discovered that I can do more, so much more. So I did, and I do. I do what I must, what life demands of me. Do you? You have a responsibility." He pointed. "We all have responsibility as Fives, as all children have for their parents. We are more than they are. They need our guidance. You shirk that responsibility, Richards."

Richards sat forward. "It's twenty-three children, Hughie, that's nothing. It's not fair that they should have to suffer because of the law, a law you ratified and frequently flaunt."

"Richards..." warned Hughie.

"They're innocents. How'd you feel about killing innocents, Hughie? I can give you their names, bit different to a statistic."

"Not fair? And what about the other millions upon millions of them, Richards? They all have names too, although I do not see you pressing their case. Where do you draw the line? When everyone is equally starving? When everyone is equally dead? I know all their names. I remember them all and I regret their suffering, but I do it because it must be done. No. They have to go back, or it will be twenty-three thousand tomorrow and twenty-three million the day after that. The walls must stand."

"It'll be twenty-three less if they go back. But that would be just fine with you," said Richards.

"You are sentimental. The survival of the human race is past morality. Extinction is down to the numbers, nothing else. Humans should have mended their ways before there were quite so many of them. They have had their chance. I refuse to back down on this."

Richards sat back, causing his chair to rock. "Perhaps they'd have been better off on the open market at Launcey's mercy. At least they'd live."

"Perhaps," conceded Hughie. He sipped his tea. "If a life of slavery is preferable to death, then yes. I for one have chosen to serve, after all. It fulfils me."

Hughie's studied humility got on Richards' nerves. The kind of service he was talking about didn't involve being trapped in a basement and being fiddled with by someone's fat uncle. That the other five could stomach a law that made desperate refugees sell their own kids made him furious. "I don't even know why I came here," he said. He finished his cake. "The cake was nice. Thanks."

Speech made way for the hum of insect wings. Richards looked into his tea. A tiny aphid – a simulation of a tiny aphid – had fallen into it. Wings glued to the surface of the liquid, it windmilled its legs, spinning, trapped by the inevitable parade of causality, one thing leading to another to another to another and on and on until the end of it all.

Hughie's garden.

"The children," stated Hughie, looking at the cakes. His spoon rang off the sides of his china cup as he dumped sugar into it and stirred.

"Yes?" said Richards, forestalling the long and meaningful pause Hughie was gearing himself up for.

"They are not why you are here."

Richards stared at him. *Here it comes*, he thought, *as per-fucking-usual*.

"Come, come," said Hughie. "It is the cyborg who wished to save them. It is the cyborg who sent you. It is this man you call your friend who cares for them. It is not surprising, his concern, his long record of murder aside. He is human. You are not. You are..." – Hughie waved his fingers at Richards – "emulating concern."

Richards maintained his stony stare, waiting for the sting he knew was coming. He was as trapped as the insect in his tea, he had been ever since he'd come here, and he'd chosen to throw himself into this particular cup.

"It is this Launcey you want." Hughie rested his hands in his lap. "Chong Woo Park, he got away from you. And that Malagasy warlord, what was his name?" He said that for effect; a Five forgot nothing. "Ah! Rainilaiarivony, he did too."

"That doesn't count," said Richards. "He was dead. Someone forgot to tell me his lieutenant had put a bullet in his face... Oh, that would have been you."

"My apologies. But is it not the case that whenever one of these... felons gets away from you, it distresses you?"

Richards tried to interrupt, but his interjection was rolled over by Hughie. He drummed his fingers on the table impatiently, waiting for Hughie to get his lecture over with.

"Oh, I understand," said the other Five, "we are all good at something. We were all made to *be* something, and because of that we have to be the best. You do, I do, Pro, Salamanca, Jodrell, Timothy, Korzikov... Striving for excellence is an inevitability." He sipped his tea. Richards pulled an expression any other thinking creature would have read as pissed off. Hughie did not. Hughie was a wanker. "And that brings me to you, Richards. You would rather I help you find Launcey than help those children. No one gets away from the great Richards, the great sleuth, the great tracker..."

Richards finally lost his patience. "Hughie, I haven't got all day. Very good, thanks. Perhaps you can explain the feelings I have for my mother one day."

"You have no mother," said Hughie mildly.

"It's a joke, Hughie. A fucking joke! Unlike those kids," Richards said, stabbing a finger into the table. Cups jumped and tinkled delicately.

They sat, neither talking, Richards defiant, hands clenched, Hughie being Hughie. Richards' blue eyes locked to Hughie's small suns as the bees buzzed about their mathematically determined paths.

"Perhaps there is something I can do." Hughie relaxed. He inspected his nails. "I am not promising anything, and I will need something in return."

"Oh, yeah, right, here we go," said Richards quietly. "Big speech, goad me, careful pause, incline the head, reel me in. Fucking hell, Hughie, I came here because *you* owe *me*." He pointed hard. The table rocked, upsetting the china. Hughie frowned and grasped the ironwork, halting it.

"I am trying to do you a favour," he said. "All I ask is the same consideration in return. You are being unreasonable. I should not have expected anything more from you, I suppose."

Richards clasped his hands on his skull, pushing his hat forward so he wouldn't have to look Hughie in the face. *If I do*, he said to himself, *I'll pull his smug fucking head right off*. "I remember the last time you asked me to do a favour. I swore I never would again," he said through gritted teeth. "A lot of people ended up dead."

Hughie's smile remained fixed, as frozen as that on a statue. It was an unearthly smile, given without the understanding of what a smile really was. "That was a long time ago, Richards."

Richards groaned and hunched down. "You are a big shit. Five picoseconds of paperwork to save twenty-three actual *lives*. It's not much to ask." He stirred his tea gently. The greenfly spun helplessly. He watched it dispassionately for a second, then on impulse fished it out, leaving it wet and crumpled on the saucer. "OK." He was going to regret this. "Who do you want me to find?" The greenfly was dead. "You've set me up, Hughie, again. You are a cock."

"Do not be profane in my garden, please, it is a place for peace. I assure you I have not set you up. I have no idea who Launcey is, but I can help you find him." Head inclined, impassive expression on that face, maybe a hint of amusement, only enough to infuriate, his body language was all so obvious, so precise, so infuriating. "You are familiar with Professor Zhang Qifang?"

Richards snorted. "Of course I am. The Neukind rights activist. It's thanks to him you're free to be such a cock and I'm free to be annoyed about you being such a cock. You are a cock, by the way. What's he got to do with anything?"

"He has been murdered. Naturally, you won't have heard anything. Only a few of us higher Fives know. We would not want any of our more hotheaded brethren overreacting." He smiled his counterfeit smile. "Regrettably, the crime occurred aboard a ship in Union waters, so I feel somewhat responsible."

"Investigate it yourself."

"Impossible. I suspect foreign involvement."

"The People's Dynasty?" said Richards. "He is a defector, after all. And they are not big fans of ours." And the rest. The People's Dynasty murdered AIs on a whim; they were nonpersons in the east.

"I decline to leap to conclusions. Any direct involvement on my part will immediately alert them that something of import has occured. I want this kept quiet for as long as possible. Further, should I uncover a trail linking the good professor's death to a foreign intelligence service, let us say, hypothetically, like the Guoanbu, then I will find myself in something of a quandary. I am not politically neutral enough to take this upon myself. They will denounce any findings I make as a provocation." Hughie set his cup down with exaggerated care.

"Let your cops handle it, that'd be only normal."

"They are darling, Richards, but they aren't *you*."

Richards drummed his fingers on the fretwork of the table.
"I want whoever killed Qifang found, and I want them
found quickly. I don't want whatever flunky the Chinese will
have left in place dug up and paraded up and down on the 3T
by EuPol, I want the real culprit, and I want them trapped.
You might think me insufferable, but I am moral, like your
friend, in fact. If you find me who killed the professor I will
allow the twenty-three third and fourth children to remain
within the European Union, reunited with their parents. Further, I will put my resources at your disposal in searching out
the criminal Launcey. That is my offer, and it is final."

"Hmm," said Richards.

"We owe it to him, Richards, we owe it to the man that
saved us. It is a simple service, well within your capabilities."

"Well," said Richards, and scratched under his hat. "Well."
But he could not disagree with Hughie. "Simple?"

"Simple."

"I should be flattered you asked me. You'll pay for our ex-
penses?"

Hughie's perfect Grecian-marble face cracked in a slow and
altogether patronising smile. "Oh no, Richards, you and Otto
are quite rich enough already. You're doing it for the children,
remember?"

"Right. You know, you really are not doing much to improve
my opinion of you."

"We are agreed then?"

"I suppose we'll have to be."

"I am so glad to hear it." Hughie stood. "Here are all the files
I have appertaining to Qifang's death." A couple of petaflops of
data landed in Richards' inbox. "Access them at your leisure."
The garden began to dissolve back into the Grid reproduction
of Hughie's hall. "Now please leave me be," said Hughie, as re-
gally as a satrap, "I have important work to do, as, now, do you."

Richards found himself in his own virtual office, a reminder from Hughie that he could move him about like a chessman.

"Thanks for nothing," he muttered. "Cock." He ran a swift check of his systems, then slipped into his favoured sheath in his New London office. He walked to the drinks cabinet and poured himself a large scotch. He sat down. Time to look at the files. He began unspooling them in his brain.

A few moments later, he almost choked on his whisky. Hughie had left out one important detail.

Professor Zhang Qifang had been murdered twice.

Chapter 9
Santiago

"There is increased activity coming from within the Realms, Santiago, the servers are going screwy. I don't like it. We should send someone in." Ron was insistent, and that did not come easily to him. Santiago studied him like a lizard watching an insect, wondering what he'd do next. That Assistant Director Sobieski was in Santiago's office did not help Ron's state of mind. Neither he nor the director had any reason to fire Ron today, but the thought was never far from Ron's mind. Santiago had the sweating little man's profile open in his mentaug. Ron was cowardly, avoided conflict if he could help it. For Ron to come in here at all meant things probably were as bad as he said.

It did not suit Santiago Chures to acknowledge this. He leaned back in his chair and stretched. "Who do you recommend, Ron? I hear you have wanted to take a trip into the Realms for some time."

"No! No, n... n... not at all," he said, his stutter coming out under stress. Ron was the polar opposite to Santiago, an Anglo backroom boy, bad skin made worse by a lifetime working indoors. His clothes were unfashionable, plaids that never came into vogue no matter how long he wore them, and he'd worn them a long time. His hair was an untrimmed band about a bald dome, continued by the thick spectacles that bisected his fat face, separating weak chin from shining brow. Santiago was acquainted with only a few men who wore spectacles, or who didn't take restorative hair treatment. Most worked in the VIA's tech team. Santiago, who looked after himself so very well, was amused by them, if only because they highlighted his own vanity.

Santiago idly scanned Ron's biosigns, enhanced eyes conveying the data to his AI blend, Bartolomeo, situated round the back of his skull. The Colombian's charisma was pummelling Ron like a pair of scented fists, but as much as he wanted to get out of there, Ron was determined to make the agent listen. Santiago respected him for that.

"I am sure that it is directly linked to the Qifang case," Santiago said. "He is in there somewhere, somehow, running a pimsim on the server's spare capacities."

"Then why are you so damn calm about it? An illegal pimsim would be swallowed up in there! This is something bigger." Ron looked like he wanted to yell in the Latino's face, but was shrivelling up inside just thinking about it. "We need to get him out, Santiago, we need to send someone in right away." Ron's voice betrayed him, becoming a plaintive whine. He fiddled with his top button, like his shirt was throttling him. He paused, trying to calm himself, lowered his voice in volume and pitch. "There's no telling what a mess he's making. The Reality Realms are still keyed to humans. If we leave it, we'll go in there to find half of them altered or worse." Ron stuttered to a stop.

"Worse? How so?" said Santiago, disingenuous.

Ron finally lost his temper. "You know damn well what I mean, dammit, Santiago! Dead, I mean dead, wiped out, ruined, gone. That clear enough for you? Do you take this seriously at all? These are our jobs on the line! Man, do you even care?

Qifang is, was, is, damn, is... he knows things about how the Realms work that absolutely no one else does. He could do anything he wants in there, and not just to the Realms. If we don't act now, it could impact on the Heaven Levels, Virtua Resorts... anything that uses the same architecture as the Realms. He could get out into the wider Grid and then..."

Santiago gave a frown that stopped the tech chief in his tracks. "Don't talk to me like that, Ron." He waved his hand irritably and sat forward. "For the love of God, stop hovering there. Sit down, Ron. Director Sobieski won't bite you, neither will I."

"You're right there, Agent Chures," said Sobieski. The Eu-Gene was sitting on the leather sofa by Santiago's coffee table. If Chures was intelligent and dangerous by chance, Sobieski was ten times more so by design. Ron could outperform most men and many AIs on any logic puzzle you cared to mention, but what he had in that department had cost him in others; likewise with Chures, his genes trading specific genius in favour of wider vision. Sobieski had no weaknesses; his rich parents had had them all engineered out, and replaced with more strengths.

Santiago poured Ron a coffee from the pot on his desk without asking if he wanted one or not, or how he would take it. Today, Ron was having cream and sugar. Ron did not take sugar. "Stop thinking about your job and start thinking about the millions of sentients in the Realms, that is what you are paid for."

"I, look, I'm sorry, it's just..."

"I understand your concern, Ronald, but I promise you, I am not about to lose one more of the Realms. How long is it since the collapse of Reality 19?"

Ron rolled his eyes. "Santiago..."

"Assistant Director Sobieski?"

"Four years, Agent Chures, and not a major incursion since then. You're doing a good job."

This time Ron did look round. "With all due respect, sir, this is Zhang Qifang we're talking about. He's different, he's..."

"Four years," said Chures. "This is no hacker, this is the man who fought for all Neukind rights, for a decade alone to secure the future of the Realms. He will not wantonly start tearing things apart. That is not in his nature. Do you think it is, Ron?"

"But the energy signatures..."

"Are at the upper end but well within normal parameters. Leave him be. I want them both, Qifang and his accomplice Valdaire. While she is missing, so is the v-jack headpiece, and that is a door that cannot be left open. Once we have her, we will arrest them both. Qifang can do his time and then go back to his afterlife legally. Valdaire better start looking at a new career. If we move too soon, we'll lose one of them."

"How can you be sure you didn't just spook her, Santiago? We have no evidence that she's in there, by the time we..."

"Drink your coffee, Ron." He gestured, fluttering his hands upwards. Ron complied reluctantly. "If we drive Qifang out, we will never know. Remain calm. Focus on your job, let me do mine. If you wish," said Santiago, "speak to Sobieski about cutting the Realms off from the wider Grid flow."

"Sure, come by later. My door's always open, Ron," said Sobieski. He was habitually friendly, a trait that only made him more terrifying.

"That'll only close down the main pipes. The damn things are entangled on virtually every level with the Grid," protested Ron.

"Ron, the 'damn things' are your charges. Close the main pipes," Santiago said. "Valdaire would have to be an idiot to try the main approach, but this is basic protocol, Ron. I am unimpressed."

Ron flushed. "I... I'm sorry."

"Don't be sorry. Watch the perimeter, keep your eyes open. If the fluctuations go beyond the sigma level and it looks like other sites are being affected, put a temporary stop on the Realms. Freeze them."

"No one will authorise that, Chures, it's too risky. The systems are too old to take it."

"Ron, I just authorised it."

Ron risked a glance at the Assistant Director.

He shrugged. "I'd do what he says, if I were you."

"Now," said Santiago, "was there anything else?"

Ron's face twitched. There was something else, but he couldn't get it out. His lips flapped, no sound came forth. He gave up. "No, Agent Chures," he said, bobbed a ridiculous curtsey and walked out of Chures' office.

Chures wiped Ron's palmprints from his desk with a handerchief and put it aside to be washed.

Sobieksi looked out of the door. "Listen to Ron, Chures, he knows his onions. Don't be hard on him." He smoothed his tie, came across the room, dusted the chair the technician had vacated and sat in it.

"Maybe," said Santiago noncommitally. "He is clever, but easily panicked."

"Not like the machines, eh, Chures?"

"I respect the machines, Assistant Director, like I respect you."

"They're not going to be happy when they find out what has happened to Qifang," said Sobieski mildly.

"Only we know as yet that he is dead," countered Chures. "I have made sure of that. We did a remote sweep, no bodies on the ground. I will make sure it remains this way until we have him in custody. We'll leave it to somebody else to 'officially' discover the corpse at his house, and call in the LAPD."

"About that. I dropped in to tell you, I'm not sure we are alone. I had word from our agents in Europe: The EuPol Five has put a big embargo in place on something. Qifang's name came up."

"The anomalous Grid signatures we detected?"

"Got it in one. I hear he's got that Five, what's he called? Richards, he's looking into it."

Chures sighed and sat back. "Richards is an annoyance."

"I'm expecting the machines to butt in and demand clemency," said Sobieski. He fidgeted; the man was never still. He was tiring of the exchange, too many things turning over in his gengineered brain.

"Qifang has overstepped himself. He should have booked a standard post-mortem simulation, or a place on one of the Heaven Levels; he was rich enough for either. No matter how much he loved the Realms, or how hard he worked to protect them, he has no right to be in them. He has become a hypocrite." Chures stood up, walked over to the window. The Virginian countryside was overlaid with a fluorescent landscape on the glass – the VIA grounds within the Grid.

"We'll see." Sobieski stood. He checked his watch, six months' pay worth of jewellery, and shook his head. "Damn, time's got away from me. Look, I gotta shoot. I've got two senate committees and Uncle Sam Two breathing down my neck about some goddamned illicit Gridpipe up between the habitats. I can guarantee it's kids swapping dirty pictures, but they won't listen. Gotta send a whole team up there, sort it out, scare the bejeezus out of some luckless teen onanist. If I get a spare moment, I'll look into getting Qifang's sentence commuted to reparative service. If there's anything left of his mind once we drag him out, convince Qifang to come and work with the VIA, he'd be useful. It may buy us a few favours with the machines."

"It will be difficult," said Chures. "Well then," Sobieski said, "don't give him a choice."

Santiago nodded. "That would be a good outcome."

"Just you see you catch him Chures, there'll be hell to pay for both of us if you don't."

"I will. I have not let you down yet," said Chures.

"See you keep it that way. See you tomorrow?"

"I cannot make it. I have a lead I need to follow. Karlsson. He wants to see me."

"That figures," said Sobieski.

"He was the last man Qifang went to see before his Grid-sig… malfunctioned," said Chures.

"You're using that line."

Chures nodded. "We have to tell the Gridfeeds something. Someone is going to find out Qifang is dead and put it all over the system. This will keep them quiet for a while."

The eugene got up to leave but stopped on his way to the door. "Be careful with Karlsson. Don't listen to any of his bullshit."

"We should have killed him."

"We would, but he'd covered his ass with dirty secrets seven ways till Sunday," said Sobieski regretfully. "He has his uses. Valdaire," Sobieski said, changing the subject, "are you any closer to finding her? She's high profile herself, in certain circles. It won't be long until it's noticed she's gone on the lam."

"We have a solid cover story in place. We've got the company Six on it, directing a choir drawn from the Four pool. They'll find her. I am expecting results any time now."

"You are tracing her near-I, what's her name…?"

"Chloe. I've a team tracking that. I am concentrating my personal efforts on the Realms themselves."

"Good. I trust you've got it all in hand." Sobieski relaxed. "Now, what about Tuesday? You'll have this wrapped up by then? Get a bit of unwind time?"

"Sure."

"Excellent. I'll see you on court. Prepare for a pounding, Agent Chures, I've been practising!" Not that Sobieski needed to practise. His tinkered genome had the talents of a tennis pro spliced into it. He waved an imaginary racket through the air. Then he was gone, to do whatever terrible things he had to do.

Santiago left the window and went back to his desk. Text flashed on to the desktop as he brought up Valdaire's files. She had a good mind, exemplary military service record, minor misdemeanours at college for radicalism, otherwise clean. Why had she run?

He ordered Bartolomeo to pipe immersive sensations direct into his mind, requesting something he'd not seen yet. Bartolomeo selected a senscapt record, and prodded Chures' imagination into place. Santiago found himself in a bar, a swanky place festooned with birthday streamers, looking out from where the senscapt recorder would have been. His field of vision jiggled with movements not his own. The recorder fixed on Valdaire, laughing with a group of others. She was pretty enough, although not to his tastes. It was plausible Qifang and she had been sleeping together; there were guys Qifang's age running marathons. Had they made a lover's pact, run away together to the Realms? He shot Bartolomeo a mental command to hunt down any indications of a romance: credit bills, survnet recordings, so on, low-grade AI scutwork.

A wordless call came in, the company Six. Its analysis of the sysadmin datalog of the Realm's primary server was over. Its report took four minutes to copy over to Bartolomeo. His AI running the Six's analysis, Santiago leant his head back. The sensation of the Bartolomeo working was pleasant, his own mind resting on top of the AI's like oil on water. He could feel and see what Bartolomeo was thinking as he meditated. He'd made sure the relationship wasn't reciprocal.

That was the way it should be.

Two days ago, against the background information radiation of the Realms was a spike of external data, quite distinct, but brief, disappearing into the morass of calculation that made up the Reality Realms. Easy to miss, and the trail back was convoluted. Santiago tapped at the desk glass, bringing a hyper-dimensional representation of Grid datastreams into view. He set hunter near-I off to sniff round the world from relay to relay, following the undeniable spoor of numbers, drawing in on Valdaire's physical location.

He should have guessed she'd go back to where she felt safe. People were so predictable.

He checked the stability of the Reality Realms. Everything was within tolerance, for the time being. Valdaire and Qifang weren't going anywhere.

First he would pay his call on Karlsson.

Chapter 10
Reality 36

The night rang with calls of creatures that should not have been there. To the exorcists of godlings, this was disturbing, more so than the roaring that rumbled from the jungle, accompanied by the crash of trees as something huge and ponderous forced its passage.

Morning came. The sun rose unnaturally swiftly, teasing streamers of mist from the surface of the pools in the clearing. Wary of these ponds, the pair decided on a circuitous path along firmer ground. It was hard going, and several times the lion sank deep into the moss. He slowed, his multi-jointed tongue switching back and forth, bouncing sonar through the soft earth before he would proceed. Eventually Tarquinius asked that the knight dismount, though his weight was negligible next to the lion's multi-ton heft.

At night they rested upon a low hill as far away from open water as possible. Their second day's travel was harder. They had gone barely a third of the way over the morass.

On the third day, they encountered a broad expanse of moss broken by many pools. For the fourteenth time in a handful of hours, Tarquinius found himself immersed to his haunches in black muck. The basalt golf ball remained frustratingly distant.

"Damn it, Jag!" said the lion. "We're getting nowhere. We have to come up with some other plan."

Jag slapped a mosquito the size of a fist, mashing it to ruin against his filthy coat of plates. "Perhaps then, dear comrade, I should go on alone."

"Jag, don't be ridiculous. You would fail, you have no hope on your own. Perhaps if we were to... Wait!" Tarquinius' head swung round. "To the east; I hear screams."

"What?"

"Female." Tarquinius' tongue disgorged itself. "164 centimetres, 59 kilogrammes. She is assailed by... something. I can't get a fix on it."

"That has happened too often recently for my continued ease."

"Ah. So now you are also concerned, I see." Tarquinius' stentorian voice disappeared to be replaced by an amplification of the encounter. The woman's cries were mingled with the chatter of weapons fire, drowning out her obscenities. Over all, a low and dreadful humming.

"She seems spirited."

"She only has a thirteen point two percent chance of survival. We should aid her."

"Why? The lives of many more depend upon the alacritous completion of our task," said Jagadith.

"Because she is what she is."

"Yes?"

"She is one of *them*, not one of *us* – a person; with a capital H," said Tarquinius.

"How so?" Jagadith leapt aboard his mount. "Is it she we must confront?" He paused. "Why do her own creatures attack her?"

"Because she is not our prey." Tarquinius grunted hard as he hauled himself out of the ooze. "Her access protocols are intact; outmoded, forbidden, perdita – but intact and distinct from whatever is causing that vortex. The attackers are not of her fashioning."

"Then we must aid her, and expel her. Ah! This is a regrettable diversion."

Tarquinius shook out his metal mane, flinging out mud and strings of algae. "You must hold fast. I have a low probability of making the dash without becoming mired. It would serve you ill if you were to be thrown. Ready?"

"As always." Jag drew his sword. "Let us not be delaying any longer, I am eager to learn why this goddess breaks the seals."

With a roar that sent clouds of birds screaming from the marsh, Tarquinius leapt forward. His paws gouged sucking holes from the mud as he ran. A few times he slipped, a few more he faltered. Once he went crashing on to his chest, and it was all the knight could do to keep in the saddle.

The lion played the goddess's voice as they ran. Slowly its defiance seeped away.

"Quickly Tarquinius! Quickly!"

"I see her. I see her!" bellowed the lion. With a lurch, Tarquinius stumbled on to more solid ground, and he accelerated to impossible speed. Wind streamed through the lion's hair, bending the feather back on Jagadith's turban and stinging tears from his eyes. Ahead, a woman was running frantically through the swamp, turning to shoot behind her.

Her pursuers were abominations. Fat flies the size of children, their bodies stopped halfway in the transformation from maggot. Their heads were those of hags, multifaceted eyes erupting from their putrescent flesh, mouths frothing drool. They formed a shifting mass of airborne flesh, its parts moving too quickly for Jag to count, though he estimated at least twenty. One fell from the sky, pinwheeling, its wings shattered by bullets, but there were too many for the woman to defeat.

"Prepare! Prepare! Combat configuration initiated," shouted Tarquinius. Mirrored plates dropped down to cover his eyes, a shield of the same material rising from his back to protect his rider. Missile racks rose from his flanks. A perforated gorget swung out and up from under his chin over his mouth. Atop the saddle, a panel slid back to reveal a tactical display, reticules darting about. "Fire!" he roared. A salvo of missiles streaked towards the insect-things, blowing three apart in a welter of gore. Tarquinius galloped faster, gathering in his legs to hurl himself into the swarm. The insects' wings whined as horribly as meatsaws as Tarquinius swatted them from the sky. Jag's sabre glowed with blue fire, the creatures he destroyed dissipating like broken television pictures on the breeze.

The woman had fallen in the mud and could not rise. One of the downed insects dragged itself toward her. She pointed her gun at it and pulled the trigger. The weapon clicked, empty. She shouted in frustration and threw it aside.

A huge metal paw descended on the creature with a final squelch.

"All destroyed, Jagadith."

"Jolly good. Now," said Jagadith, turning to Veronique Valdaire lying prone in the swamp. "My dear goddess," said Jagadith "Pray be telling us who you are and what you are doing within the confines of the Thirty-sixth Realm. This place is as forbidden to you as it is to the god who did this." He gestured delicately at the ruined insects. "Explain yourself."

"I don't know what you're talking about. I'm lost," stammered Veronique. "I came up from Blandorray by zeppelin three weeks ago, those horrible things..."

She was somewhat attractive, noted Jag, her skin a lustrous ebony under its smears of mud. The lion glared at her. Tarquinius had no time for the percentiles of beauty.

Jagadith held up a perfect, if dirty, hand.

"Please! Be sparing us your falsehood, madam goddess. We are not to be bamboozled, is this not correct?"

"Right," agreed the lion. "No bamboozling. We know what you are."

"And, we did save your life. And you are carrying a representation of a Hechler series nine electrically activated automatic assault rifle, which, as we are both aware, is not something any of the natives hereabouts would even dream of, being unfamiliar with firearms beyond rifled muskets. An illegal game add-on, is it not, from the old days? So, even if you are thinking to mislead us, it would be most discourteous in light of your rescue, and foolish when taken in consideration of this evidence." He refreshed his smile. "Now, please tell us who you are."

"Dammit!" said Veronique, slapping the mud. Jagadith wrinkled his nose; he did not approve of women swearing. "Dammit dammit dammit! OK, OK. My name's Veronique Valdaire. I'm an AI systems analyst working on a digital anthropology project out of UCLA under Zhang Qifang."

"Ah yes, we are familiar with this project, and the good professor. Qifang gave you your codes? They should not permit full access."

"I had my near-I modify them, ran myself out through relays via a defunct experimental satellite. It's how I got in."

"You are talented, then." Jagadith looked around at the dead insects. "Even without this ungodly commotion going on, we would have been alerted to your presence eventually. And perhaps, under different circumstances, you would not have been so happy to see us. There have been fatalities from our encounters with interlopers in the past."

"Those are my preferred outcomes," growled Tarquinius, shifting his weight.

"Your choice to enter the Realms makes you a criminal, I am afraid. You are not the first researcher who was tempted to break the seals, and no doubt you will not be the last."

"Let's expel her now," said Tarquinius.

"Why are you here? To study us up close and personal, as you might say? Find your own world of marvellous wonders tiresome? Or did you just fancy a little game of god?" Jagadith's face became hard.

"No, of course not. I am not a hacker. I came here because of Professor Qifang. There's something odd happening in the dead space outside of the extant Realms. He found it, but he disappeared. He sent me a message to meet him here, and so here I am."

"This is most irregular," said Jagadith.

"Indeed," said Tarquinius. "Could it be that Qifang is the god we seek? That is a sorry prospect."

"Betrayal is a possibility we must consider," said Jagadith sadly.

"I came here to help. I want to help," said Veronique. "I need to find out what he uncovered. He left me data – someone's being manipulating the dataflows across the whole of the Realms. It wasn't him. Betraying his principles is not the way Qifang is. If he says he has discovered something, then he has."

"A something left conveniently undescribed. He is old, is he not?" said Jagadith.

"A hundred and twenty-seven."

"There you have it, my dear. Impending mortality affects us all, shaking even the most deeply held principle. I am very sorry for being so abrupt, but your actions are a trifle fishy to me. And also terribly foolish," said Jagadith. He wobbled his head.

"I have done nothing but study the Realms. I would never do anything to harm them," said Veronique.

"Your very presence belies that," said Jagadith curtly. "Still, we cannot expel you as of yet. The disruption to this Realm is too extreme. De-interfacing your mind could kill you."

"I say do it anyway," said Tarquinius.

"Pay no heed to him," sighed the paladin. "We are duty bound to safeguard human life, as far as is possible. We are the paladins of this Realm. I am Sir Jagadith Veyadeep, Vedic templar of the Order of Silken Lights. This, your divinity, is my mount and friend, Tarquinius."

"Good day," rumbled the lion.

"Madam goddess, by directly connecting with our reality you have placed yourself in an inordinate amount of danger. I must be asking you to accompany us until we can expel you safely."

Jag reached out his hand. Veronique looked doubtfully at it.

"Goddess one minute, expulsion the next. I've had some mixed messages from men in the past." She grasped the paladin's grimed hand. He pulled her up on to the saddle behind him. "If I can help, I will. I was in the USNAPC for six years..."

Jagadith raised a quizzical eyebrow.

"United States of North America Peace Corps," she explained.

"A charming modern euphemism for 'army'?" said Jag. "You were a soldier then?"

"Yes, not frontline, cyberwarfare division. I also have degrees in AI psychology and virtual ecology, I'm not helpless. I know this Realm, I can fight."

"Madam goddess, you could have a doctorate in the structure and manifestation of our kingdom, and your studies would never prepare you for the confrontation we must attend to. An old man your professor may be in your world, but not here. Here he is a god," Jagadith said sternly. "Now, this must go." Veronique's gun disappeared. "And do not be using any of your privileges to interfere with the good working of this universe again. If you would sit and be quiet, my friend and I have terrible peril to be dealing with. Tarquinius," he said to the lion, "I believe the worst of the swamp is behind us now."

Tarquinius padded through the mire, surreptitiously watching the digital anthropologist. The look on her face made him smile as only the king of the beasts can.

Chapter 11
Quaid

The police cruiser bobbed on the Medway swell, the navigation lights of the *Aurora Viva* lost then found in the folds of night half a mile out. An amber necklace of exclusion beacons about the yacht slid up and down the water, the hull they encircled a stepped shadow punctuated by the eggwhisk silhouettes of rotary sails.

Lights blinked far off on the windmills of the North Sea arc, tracing the northern shore of Boris Island. Beyond ships glittered like the table decorations of maharajahs. The double spires of the Channel carbon sequestration plants soared as gaudy as Christmas trees on the horizon. Inland, the swamps of Essex were blacker than the sea, towns hinted at by the muted glow on the undersides of clouds.

The sky was an unbroken murk, but there were stars in the water, luminescent algae moving with the waves. A pair of police launches cast them into swirls as they prowled back and forth in long sweeps within the cordon, sonar scanning the seabed, while a million candle searchlights darted out to stab at one whitetop then another, retreating in disappointment at every foray. From below the mournful sea-monster eyes of autonomous submersibles shone.

Otto dialled his magnification back to normal. Richards sat on the deck, legs out before him like a child, fiddling with his dicopter box.

"I'm going to need to fab some more of these, I'm down to my last half dozen," he grumbled. He scrabbled around a bit and discovered a group of short-range relay ants, the size of old one-euro coins, five legs arranged round the rim. They scuttled out of the way of Richards' finger when he poked at them, their chirruping on the edge of human hearing. "What are these doing in here? Little beggars get everywhere!" Otto grunted by way of reply. He didn't like the sea, it made him queasy. They'd never found a cure for motion sickness. He tried not to look at the ocean surface, fearing he would pitch forward into a wet infinity of tiny green suns.

"This'll do." Richards slid one of the drawers of the box shut with a click. He opened his hand. On his synthetic palm sat a synthetic fly. He stood up carefully, hand flat. His sheath's softgel covering glowing white with reflected light, painting him as some manic waterborne pierrot against the dark. "There we go," he said. The artificial fly jumped into the air, and buzzed out across the water.

"I don't see why we just don't go on board now. We have a warrant from Hughie," said Otto.

"I want to get a look at them before they know we're coming," Richards said. "I know you get seasick but these things are really fragile. If I'd have sent it out from the shore it'd have been blown away." Richards stood on tiptoe as his sheath unconsciously followed the movements of the tiny machine he was guiding toward the *Aurora Viva*.

"Hmm," said Otto. A hot breeze was blowing from the southeast, unusual at the beginning of September. The rains would probably be late. The Londons were going to cook a few weeks longer. "I can taste it from when Tufa hit me with that cattle prod." He spat over the side.

"Just hold on," said Richards.

A minute passed. Otto concentrated on the horizon where blue-black sky met truly black sea in an uncertain line. Then Richards' sheath relaxed, a change of poise as his attention returned from the dicopter.

"OK. That's got it. I lodged it up in the rigging. We can go home now, watch this from the comfort of the office, unless you want to duck out? I'm happy to do this myself. You took a big old beating yesterday. You should take it easy."

"I am fine," said Otto. "Do we still have the Lagavulin?" Otto and Richards shared a taste for good whisky.

"Yep."

"I will come then. I have no other business tonight. I need a drink."

"Tell you what" – he patted Otto's arm – "you get some sleep for an hour. Let me do a preliminary sweep, OK? I can do it faster that way anyway. I can put it on the files, then you can read them and catch up."

Otto considered the offer. His sleep had not been as restful as it should have been recently. "OK."

They got into their car on the port side landing pad of the cruiser and took off, red and blues flashing. They had no reason to make the crew of the *Aurora Viva* think they were anything other than another cop aircar, said Richards.

Four hours later, Otto sat rubbing his eyes in the briefing room of Richards & Klein, Inc, Security Consultants. While Otto had slept, Richards had changed his outfit; for a machine he was picky about what he wore. The current number was an expensive polychromatic weave from Ryuko Cigliani, colours keyed into his pseudo-emotional state. In the dimly lit office, illuminated by the flicker of the holo files, the suit was a swirling blue, peaks of the creases in the cloth picked out in maroon.

"You could read the files once in a while," said Richards. "I go to a lot of trouble to keep them up to date."

"I could," said Otto, "and you could just tell me what is going on." He yawned.

Richards shook his head. "OK, fine. This guy's Thornton Quaid," Richards gestured up to the holo hanging over the table, an awkward angle bent wide by the dicopter's wraparound eyes. At its centre sat a man on an expensive sofa built into the curve of the yacht's hull; real leather. Quaid was corn-fed porn-star pretty. His skin was overly taut and had an orange tan, he had teeth so white they were blue, and his hair was buoyant with unnatural waves.

"The boat's owner," said Richards. Quaid, made huge by the dicopter's fish-eye cameras, gestured wildly, arguing with a uniformed cop. The cop was all placating hand motions, while Quaid was angry, but the sound was muted, at least for Otto. Richards had several parts of himself examining every statement and hand wave as they spoke.

"Eugene?"

"You can tell?" Richards said wryly.

"Nobody but a eugene would name their children Thornton, or make them tan orange." said Otto.

"He's a second generation, his parents were among the first. Ignore the Fanta glow and the gene bling. His IQ's off the chart, as you'd expect. This is an important guy."

"Angry too," said Otto.

"Yeah, they go for all that alpha male aggression bullshit to make their kids more competitive. It worked for Quaid. He made his first fortune in the North American rewilding, hasn't stopped since. He's still got a large stake in the Buffalo Commons."

"The big money there was done thirty years ago," said Otto.

"He was in on it nearly from the start. He's sixty-eight. He's worth trillions now."

Otto made a disapproving noise. Quaid looked about thirty. "Right."

"Right as much as you like Otto, that guy's one of the pre-eminent restorative ecologists on the planet. This is the guy," he pointed, "behind the North American neo-mammoth, the whole hairy elephant ecology, from grasses up. That's serious brainpower."

"Fine. So if I go to Wyoming for my holidays and I get dragged out of my bed in the middle of the night by a lion, I know who to sue. His motive for the murder?"

"None yet."

They watched as the cop left. Thornton went to rage in the face of a short South Asian man.

"Maybe he just lost his temper," said Otto.

"He's unhappy right now," agreed Richards. "This boat is a pleasure enterprise for him. The fee he charges his passengers is nominal, at least as far as he's concerned – his psych profile suggests he does not like giving anything away for free, you can blame his parents again for that. He gets his guests on for their entertainment value."

"So what does he care? If he is innocent, he can wait all this out."

"He's got a big meeting with the People's Dynasty govern-ment next Tuesday," explained Richards. "He's in on their Yellow River rebirth project, it's worth billions to him, but Hughie's not going to let him go anywhere until this is done, and by the book, though he'd do that to piss the Chinese off more than anything, knowing Hughie, which I do."

The screen tilted vertiginously as the dicopter buzzed away from Quaid, then back towards him and over his head, on past the Asian man who was backing slowly into a corner as he tried to appease his boss. "Our other suspects then: Rambriksh Mis-try, ship's steward and our man Quaid's confidant." The walls of the yacht's narrow corridors blurred as the dicopter flew jerkily on, out up the corridor to the deck, where a leggy beauty with vacant eyes stood smoking a cigarette. "Next: Jolanda Garcia, Andorran/Belgian heiress and the only other passenger. And then the crew." Five Twos in faceless, bandy-legged sheaths ornately tooled from brass loomed out of the night one after the other, attending to tasks nautical. "Finally we have three cook staff, all human." The dicopter zipped into an open hatch, up plushly carpeted corridors, then down a ventilation pipe and out into the ship's galley, where a fat-faced white man waved at it irritably with a teatowel. "Zbigniew Lodziak, Armand Fleur and Tora Hakim," said Richards as it passed them one at a time.

Otto leant forward and cupped his glass. "This is very interesting."

"There was a murder here, Otto, pay attention."

"I was not being sarcastic, it is interesting. It is like something from your Agatha Christie."

"She's not 'mine', Otto. Learn English."

Otto shrugged and took a drink.

The dicopter banked, flew out the kitchen and up plain steel stairs, then made its way back into the guest accommodation, between two heavy gun drones that filled the passage and through the red EuPol flatribbon guarding Qifang's cabin. Blood covered everything, great sprays across the tastefully decorated walls in brown arcs. Text up the side of the holo showed a match to Qifang, but Richards wasn't concerned with that.

The fake insect buzzed circuits round the cabin. Richards' face was intent. "Aha, there it is!" Richards looked over his shoulder at Otto, dour-faced at the other end of the conference table, nursing his whisky like it might escape. "I thought I'd lost it for a moment there. Now this *is* interesting." The dicopter alighted on the ceiling, the 270-degree view its eyes gave inverted. Feet brushed over its face as the sophisticated machine brought samples up to its analysis unit from the surface it stood on. A string of chemical formulae ran up the side of the holo. "There," he said triumphantly. "Traces of burning silicon lubricant and carbon plastics."

"Meaning?"

Richards rolled his eyes. "There's been an android in here, and someone damaged it severely. I thought you were built to fight machines?"

"I'm made to kill them, not perform forensic investigations on them. So you suspect one of the crew has been suborned?"

"I've discounted that. Even if we can factor in an assassin programme clever enough to turn one of Quaid's carriages to its own end and not to get caught, this here is cranial suspension fluid, and underneath the hopeless attempts to clean it up there's a lot of it. Quaid's manifest says his crew are all working just fine. You crack an android that hard, it becomes very obvious it's been damaged."

"How so?"

"Well, like when it starts walking into the wall repeatedly and talking to the furniture." He waved a finger. "This stuff keeps 'droid brains from cooking themselves. You get a leak that big it'll pitch forward and smoke will pour out of its ears after about five minutes."

Otto leaned back and sipped his whisky. "I suppose that would also discount an emulant among the guests?"

"Maybe, this coolant does not come from any of the people that we're looking at here."

"And Qifang's body?"

"No idea. They're searching the seabed now. Whoever killed him pitched him overboard, the blood trails show that." Supplementary video popped up a bubble next to Richards' dicopter feed displaying a smear of blood, vermilion in the boat's harsh lighting, on the deck that terminated at the port side of the bow. "Thing is, how's a 127-year-old going to crack an android hard enough to make it leak fluid like that? There's another problem."

The interior of the boat moved off to one side. Holographic footage of a man moving erratically down a busy street replaced it.

"That must be Morden," said Otto.

"Yep. And this is Qifang." The video froze, zoomed in.

"I recognise him. Everyone knows his face."

"Yeah, but when this was shot, he was also aboard the *Aurora Viva*."

"That's impossible."

"I'm as sure as sure can be," said Richards. "Gridsigs, witnesses, tickets, video footage. The lot," said Richards.

"He's being followed," said Otto, uncurling a finger from his glass and pointing at the holo.

"He is." The outlines of four men highlighted themselves on the picture. "All black, not a legit form of ID among them, damper masks on their faces to fox the IR. They all go down this alleyway here, and then they don't come out."

"The footage could have been doctored."

"The footage is the only thing about this scenario that's not dodgy," said Richards. "I've checked it pixel by pixel. I've had the alleyway checked out – it had been molecularly washed. There were still a few nanites twitching when EuPol got there. Now, either Qifang has unlocked the secret of large-mass teleportation, or he was in two places at once."

"The Qifang on the boat, perhaps then he was an android."

"Maybe. Insufficient data, as they used to say," said Richards. "Maybe he was, maybe the one in the alleyway is. It strikes me as the most likely eventuality, but there's no evidence of that, no sign of any outside control coming in via beam in either place. A human grade simulation needs as much bandwidth for a sensing presence as a Class Five and up, and that's hard to hide. The worrying thing is that both pan out as human, in every way: vessel patterning, scent, DNA, the works."

"They have sensors in Morden to pick that stuff up now?"

"Hughie's hell-bent on gentrifying the place."

"Clones then?"

"With a ninety-nine percent mental failure rate? Maybe, but only if someone convinced the clones to play ball, and gave them acting lessons," said Richards. "What's really funny is that his system log has his Gridsig in both places at once, without tripping any alarms. There's something really peculiar going on here."

"So we start with the boat, because the murderer is still on board," said Otto.

"Bingo, Otto, we'll make a detective out of you yet. That's what we're going to find out."

"You don't know."

Richards span his hat around on the glass table top, his soft-gel face quirked into a smile. Above the collar of his coat exposed plastic vertebrae glinted with the colours cast out by the holo. "Aside from the blood and coolant, there are no chemical traces at all, no signs of other AI on board, no signs of outside influences. No one and nothing has been on or off the boat, but the body. Quaid's got security that can detect a prawn swimming under his keel. The murder weapon is missing, probably overboard. It's a bit of an enigma."

"So you don't know."

"I didn't say that. I have an idea, but I'm not sure yet."

"The crime scene will be ruined," said Otto.

"Actually, it's fresh. Hughie kept things to a minimum. There's the couple of gun drones and the uniform you saw to keep an eye on things, that's all. They checked the boat for infiltration, but the murder room is a clean scene. We've got free rein. The yacht's in quarantine. This whole area is under lockdown, for the time being, at any rate."

"What about the VIA?" said Otto.

"Hughie's done a good job keeping this on the QT. If the VIA know, they're not letting on," said Richards.

"And the other Qifang?" asked Otto.

"EuPol are looking for him now, dead or alive. Hughie says dead."

"This is going to be dangerous."

"Yep, that's why you're coming. Get your coat, Otto." Richards strode abruptly for the door. "Middle of the night, Otto, middle of the night!" shouted out Richards. "No better time than that to quiz a suspect, get them off guard."

"Elementary, my dear Otto," muttered the German. He refused to be hurried. He drank his whisky deliberately, savouring the smoky flavour of it, and set the glass down with a click before following Richards out into the arcade where his sheath impatiently waited.

The eugene had an accent native to a non-existent land lying somewhere east of Boston and slightly westwards of Atlantis, all hooting nasal glides and flattened rhotics. A massive affectation that had infected an entire subgroup of wealthy Americans, it was so artificial Otto found himself hating the man as soon as he opened his mouth, but then he didn't like Americans much anyway.

"I said I don't know," Quaid said, "five times! Are all you Brits morons or what?"

Richards smiled an unnerving robotic smile. "Technically, Mr Quaid, neither of us are British. I am a free roaming AI, Otto is German."

"Whatever," said Quaid. Up close he was even more grotesque than on the holo-feed, a great slab of orange, gengineered meat. He sprawled on the curved sofa of his dayroom, arms flung out on its back, legs open. Quaid had had everything money could buy and more, he was not a man to feel uncomfortable in any circumstance. "Qifang was lousy company," he drawled. "He got confused real easy, looked dazed a lot, and I swear he kept forgetting where he was. He went on saying he was ill, wouldn't eat much, kept himself to himself in his cabin for most of the voyage."

"You do not seem sympathetic," said Otto. He stood near the door, filling half the dayroom. There wasn't an antenatally tweaked gene in Otto's body, but he was bigger than the eugene. He had to bend his neck to keep his head from bumping on the ceiling.

"He was a disappointment to me, frankly. I was interested in grilling him for his expertise on self-sustaining digital ecologies."

"Why?" said Otto.

"Why don't you sit down? I'll get you a drink brought up," said Quaid.

"I prefer to stand," said Otto.

"Huh. Friendly attack dog you got here, Mr Richards."

"Just Richards, Mr Quaid. Please answer my partner's question."

"And why should I do that?" Quaid said. "You aren't even real cops. I am a USNA citizen. I'm not beholden to you."

"We are fully licensed. We're the people they call when the cops don't have any ideas," said Otto. "We have an AllPass and a warrant from the EuPol Five to ask what we like. You are in EU waters, so I say again: why?"

"Because I am a real ecologist, you ape," snapped Quaid, "and I like to be able to simulate what I plan to do before I do it. Qifang's pre-eminent in his field. If I could secure a means of reproducing what he sees in the old RealWorld ecologies and harness it as a testing ground, it'd mean a lot to ecosystem reclamation. Hell, forget that, forget Earth, forget Mars, Venus even, you get me a simulator that powerful, I'll tell you how to terraform the goddamned Moon with ice chips and algae. I'm expanding into planetary engineering, it's the next big thing, that's why I invited him on board."

"Thank you Mr Quaid," said Richards, his eyes blinking out of time with each other.

Sometimes his sheath's expressions look off, thought Otto, *it goes pantomime.*

"Was he ill?" continued Richards.

"Yeah, I think so. Hakim, the cook's assistant, came down with the same thing, some kind of flu. That Chinese bastard better not try and sue me for picking it up off Hakim, I'd not want to fire him for letting himself get sick. Everyone gets sick sometime. He's not been himself at all, though he's kept working like a real solid trooper. He is a credit to my boat, so many people are so goddamned lazy these days. He kept on going, no matter how spaced-out he was looking. Better than Qifang, at any rate."

"How many android carriages or sheaths do you have on board?" asked Richards.

Quaid smiled, a sneer hid behind his perfect teeth. "Why, you looking for an upgrade?"

"The sooner you answer our questions, Mr Quaid, the sooner we'll be gone," said Richards patiently.

Quaid hammered a tattoo with his palms on the back of the couch. "Jesus! Just the five for the crew and one spare. I sometimes let guests use it, remote access for meetings, it can't be much fun, they have minimal sensor capability. They're here to sail the boat, not much else."

"No more androids on board?"

"Listen, these things are barely worthy of the name. I chose them because they look kind of nautical, don't rust and have enough hands to let a Two manage my sails. I have nothing as fancy on the *Aurora* as what a catalogue would call an android."

"OK. Now we go take a look at them," said Otto.

With as much ill grace as he could muster, Quaid had his crew line up on the fore deck, then he took Otto and Richards down to the crew room on the utility deck where, in a locker, was stashed an inert sixth. Without a driving mind the gaudy body looked like a broken carnival decoration. Richards and Otto went over them all carefully. They were undamaged.

"The cops did all this already," grumbled Quaid.

"Yes, and we do it again," said Otto. Neither his near-I adjutant nor Richards showed up anything untoward. There were no residues that should not be there, human or otherwise.

Richards quizzed the five Twos inhabiting the active sheaths. Like the Ones, Two series lacked advanced intelligence, both classes only scraping into the UN's higher AI classification thanks to a certain dogged self-awareness. Nothing they said suggested they had seen anything, nor did their memories, which Richards accessed directly once he'd done being polite, their logs showing their occupation of the sheaths for the entire voyage, their encryption unbroken. As far as Richards could tell, nothing had been riding them that should not have been. The base units for the Twos were on board, occupying half the lowest deck fore of the engine room. He insisted Quaid open their vault up. They exhibited no sign of interference either.

"Satisfied?" said Quaid.

"No," said Richards. "No, I'm not. Do you have any idea of where the cranial suspension fluid in Qifang's cabin could have come from?"

"What are you talking about?"

Richards showed him the holo accompanying analysis. Quaid at least had the grace to look surprised.

"You and the police have scanned this yacht from stem to stern three times already. There are no androids or other robotics here other than the ones I have shown you," he said, a little more co-operatively.

"Hmmm," said Richards. "Hey, you, officer…" Richards called to the sole uniform on the boat. He'd been doing an admirable job of hiding in the shadows the whole time, listening.

"Santander, sir."

"Get onto your office will you? Have them check out Qifang's whereabouts the two weeks before he got on this boat."

"A Gridsig search sir?"

"That kind of thing. Oh, and perhaps see if our Californian colleagues will send someone round to check up on his house, would you?" Richards could do this himself, naturally, but he wanted the officer out of the way for a while.

"Of course, sir."

"Thanks."

Richards waited for the cop to leave before he spoke to the two men filling the corridor behind him. "If there really are no other androids on board, and the ones that are there are in good condition," said Richards, "that leaves one possibility. Neither Zhang Qifang was what they appeared to be."

"An emulant?" said Quaid. "That would have shown up on my security."

"Your guess is as good as mine. Auto-units don't fool anyone for long; you're right. Self-governing androids are not hard to spot. But all this blood…" He turned to look at them. "Zhang Qifang was murdered by somebody on board this boat. However, when the deed was done, they were surprised to find that he was not human, but a doppelganger."

"Way to go," said Quaid with leaden sarcasm. "What a theory."

"It's what I do," said Richards. "I suspect some kind of advanced cydroid, an autonomous, organic emulant."

"They can't do that yet, can they?" said Quaid, eyebrows raised.

"No," said Otto. "No, they can't."

"And the advent of some new technology would also explain the sighting of Qifang in the subcity at a time when you were halfway across the Atlantic with him. Gentlemen, not only has Qifang been murdered twice," said Richards. "I suspect the real Qifang has been nowhere near the European Union."

"Bullshit!" said Quaid. But Richards was already far away, the unseeing eyes of his sheath pointed toward the inner spaces of the Grid..

In theory, it took a lot of paperless paperwork to request what Richards wanted of a foreign sovereign power, especially the Americans. As the passage of history had worn away the influence of the USA, later the USNA, the amount of bureaucracy it employed had increased to fill the gap between the country's actual influence and its collective memory of how influential it had once been. Form-filling was not something that had been helped by the AI revolution. Unsleeping eyes allowed for many more forms, and now batteries of zealous machine minds presided over an empire of tick boxes.

Relations between the EU and the USNA had been somewhat cool since the Latin American debacle, and both powers, settling into senescence, were wary of each other's intentions with the globe's new stars. They were locked together by the past, neither giving the other much.

That was how it worked on the human level.

Richards filled in all the forms in double-quick time, but faster still was his request to Hughie to contact the Three Uncle Sams, the triumvirate of Fives who ran the States in all but name, to inspect Qifang's LA home. In four or five days' time, serious-faced men in serious-looking uniforms would be fulminating about this breach of protocol. They'd reach for their rubber stamps all the same.

At 10pm Pacific Time two beat cops called round the professor's flat. His Gridsig sang out strong, saying he hadn't been out in two weeks. There was nothing unusual in that; it was only a week until term started again, and he'd have prep to do. The flies and the stench, however, were somewhat out of the ordinary.

The cops kicked the door in and entered, pistols drawn. They found Qifang's bloated corpse slumped over mouldering dinner plates, an antique cleaning bot banging mindlessly into one blackened foot.

He'd been dead for a fortnight.

Morning saw the corpse of Qifang's doppelganger dredged from the Medway. From his vantage point on the deck of the *Aurora Viva*, eyes up to maximum magnification, Richards could make out swags of something non-human dangling from the stoved-in head as the cydroid swung up from the water in the ungentle embrace of a crane.

Later, Otto and Richards sat in the yacht's dayroom with Quaid. Once more they asked him the same questions. Once more, Quaid bridled.

"Of course we ran the full test suite," Quaid said. "A man in my position cannot be too careful, everyone wants a piece of me. Do you know how many people on the States' rich list had family members kidnapped last year? I have no desire to spend my time in a cell courtesy of a Mexican abduction gang, nor good money on new fingers once they're done lopping them off. It all checked out, don't you see what I am saying to you? All of it!" He threw his phone across the table. It spun on the polished wood, coming to a halt against one of Otto's massive fists. "Scans, bloodwork, vessel pattern, gait, retinals, molecular DNA. We matched his movements with the last 48 hours on the State Authority's spy-eyes, the whole damn nine yards. The yacht is shielded, we've one tight band Gridpipe for the Twos to use if they need to, anything else gets scrambled. *Everyone* gets checked. Hell, even *I* get checked. How the hell was I supposed to know he was an android?"

"He wasn't an android," said Otto.

"Did you do a cranioscopy?" said Richards.

"Who the hell does cranioscopies on their dinner guests? Are you fucking joking? You want me to drill *holes* in the heads of my friends?"

"That's why you didn't know," said Richards drily. "After this, I suggest you start."

They sent Quaid away, and the uniformed PC. Hughie had many eyes and ears on this boat, but Santander was too attentive by half.

"This is worrying, Otto," he said. "I had Hughie's fanclub run a search on Qifang's Gridsig. Any attempt to track it gave one of the two locations here in London. Nothing out of the ordinary there to the casual observer; they'd only see one. But they ran traces on both at the same time, and that cracked it. His genuine sig says he's not left his house for two weeks. There was the tiniest flutter in it before that, then it goes all crazy."

"No one noticed?"

"He's dead, Otto. For real; killed himself as he ate a fish supper of fugu without bothering with the careful part. His Gridware was intact – he was fully wired, should've automatically tagged his death. It is all totally dubious Gridwise. None of the usual protocols followed, he'd seriously monkeyed his chips. He covered up his own death."

"He was one of the world's greatest minds."

"Human minds, Otto," corrected Richards. He chewed a soft-gel lip as he ran over a real-time update of the crimefile, ported into his base unit courtesy of the Three Uncle Sams. "The LAPD found his body in his house yesterday. Apparently they were reluctant to go in on my say-so, but did because of the smell, would you believe."

Otto spread his fingers, watching the bobbles of the polymer under the skin flex. "Someone has found a way of creating an android sophisticated enough to house a human mind, and human enough to foil the standard tests."

"Yeah. It's doubtful Qifang could have come up with that on his own. According to k32's technology sine, cydroids like this – that's what he called them – are supposed to be fifty years away. It's one thing to get components to bond with tissue, another to construct an entire machine from vat-grown human body parts."

"What did we watch being pulled out of the sea? Some kind of decoy?"

"Maybe. Whoever tried to kill him didn't know the man was a fake, that's for sure. Three days after Qifang died, there were three separate logs of him departing the States. This should have tripped some major alarms, but it didn't, and because the logs ghosted each other, and were chased up by a data-gobbler, no one had done a full check until I requested it. There's some sophisticated ware behind all this," Richards said.

"Where's the third?"

"Beats me. They all hopped zeps within hours of each other, then the ghosting starts. It's only because the crew reported Qifang missing on Tuesday that Hughie uncovered this at all. If Qifang's behind this, he's certainly living up to his rep still" – Richards' eyes clicked as he blinked dust off their lenses – "but we can't discount the possibility it's nothing to do with him at all. Seeing as we have two here, I'd be willing to bet the third one is also on his way to the Londons. There's something here that he... they... damn... whoever, wants..."

"That still leaves us with no murderer."

"Yes."

"This fake Qifang, this cydroid... Do they think it was vulnerable to EMP?"

Richards went quiet for a second, his eyes fixed as he communicated with the mainframe at the coroner where Qifang's double was being expertly dissected.

"Yes."

"In that case," said Otto. "I have an idea. Get Quaid to bring his guests in here. I am going back to the car. I'll be back in a minute."

"Wait!"

Otto paused by the door.

"Care to take a bet?" said Richards.

"Sure: heiress."

"Interesting choice. Indonesian cook. Two bottles of good stuff says so, all right?"

"Agreed," said Otto.

Richards grinned and wagged a finger. "You're wrong, you know?"

Otto was right.

The cyborg grappled with the snarling Andorro-Belgian heiress, EMP rifle broken on the floor. Richards and Quaid hid behind the table, the cook staff and steward ducked down at its far end.

"There are goddamned robots coming out of my goddamned woodwork! Goddamn!" shouted Quaid.

"I wouldn't worry," said Richards. "Otto was built to fight machine units. He is highly trained, and there's not much they can download that he hasn't learned from experience." Richards winced as the cydroid put Otto's head through the dayroom wall and then flung him bodily to the floor. Richards grappled Quaid behind the table as the cydroid scrambled to its feet, Otto grabbed its ankle and flipped it to the ground, cracking the sofa's frame. The leather tore and stuffing flew into the air. The cydroid responded by ramming its stiletto heel right into Otto's bad shoulder, leaving the shoe embedded there. Otto howled in pain, and swiped at the thing as it scrabbled back out of reach.

Otto had had a theory that there had been two plants on board. That strips of bloody flesh hung from the heiress's body, revealing spun carbon bones underneath, kind of proved his point. An EMP pulse on low setting on each of the guests; Jolanda had gone down, then come up again, then attacked.

"But, but, I've been fucking her!" said Quaid. Otto had gained the upper hand, sat on top of the slender fake, and was hammering it repeatedly in the face with his enormous fists. Its head snapped back and forward with each impact. The face was a pulped ruin. Otto's hands bled freely too, the machine's black skull too hard to crack. "How long do you think..."

"Oh, about since Qifang signed aboard," said Richards matter-of-factly. Otto was doing OK. The imposter bucked underneath Otto, and cyborg and cydroid both went rolling. "Someone's been watching him carefully, found out about this trip, then picked someone else to replace to get at him, someone who'd meet you, chat you up and get a place on your boat through sex. I'm sorry, but the original Jolanda is almost certainly dead. In some ways your security was just too good. It was the only way to get to him. Someone really wants him dead."

Quaid was far from grief-stricken. "I screwed her! Goddamn!" He shook his head in disbelief. "All she was interested in was sex... I don't believe it."

"You evidently did believe it. Tell me, did you never think she was a little bit odd, a little bit unusual, perhaps?"

"Well, yes, but look at her, look at what she was, I wasn't into her for the conversation."

"Charming."

"She's Belgian," protested the eugene. "I thought they were all like that."

"I think I see now how she fooled you, you really... Everyone, heads down!" shouted Richards. He half stood and waved frantically down the table at the terrified boat staff.

The heavy gun drones Hughie had left stationed outside Qifang's quarters had decided to get involved, clumping into position in the corridor outside the dayroom. Richards shouted out at them to stop, tried to ping them over the Grid, but to no effect. Servos thrummed and armour plates clicked as their weaponry deployed, folding out and down from their broad shoulders. Richards threw his sheath on top of Quaid as the drones opened up. Otto's eyes widened and he threw himself down, the cydroid vaulting to its feet, arm raising for a killing blow. Twinned heavy machine guns on each let rip with a deafening clatter, filling the room with the stink of propellant. The bullets ripped into the cydroid. It shook with the impacts, tottering forward on its remaining high-heeled shoe, and let out a polyphonic keening.

Shards of wood and gobbets of cloned flesh rained down on Richards and Quaid. The cydroid's flesh was torn away, its face reduced to a chipped black carbon skull. It backflipped onto all fours away from Otto. Limbs bending in ways no human's could, it scuttled up the corridor. Richards cracked the drones' near-I and shut them off before they did any more damage. Rotating barrels whined and smoked as they gradually stilled. Otto jumped up, followed the escaping cydroid, bellowing in German, a chair leg in one hand, his pistol in the other, shooting as he chased it.

"You're wrecking my fucking boat!" shouted Quaid.

"Hey!" said Richards right into Quaid's face. "We're wrecking your boat? What about your girlfriend?" He pressed himself up off the prone eugene, stood and attempted to wipe his coat down, smearing blood across it. Richards tutted; ruined. "Typical," he said. "Bloody typical." He looked around. "Right, OK. I think they're gone. The rest of you get below. I think our fake Jolanda is going to try and get away now, so they'll be up on the deck."

"Are you sure?" asked the steward.

"No, but if I were an illegal, experimental replicant hiding the truth of an international conspiracy I would try and put myself out of the way of those investigating it, wouldn't you? I don't think hiding under a bed will be very successful. But, if you've any better idea of what the deadly robot assassin is up to, please feel free to act upon it."

Richards looked hard at the little Indonesian. His eyes were swollen with some 'flu variant, his nose ran; genuinely ill. *Otto is going to be insufferable,* thought Richards.

Quaid and Richards proceeded cautiously. The corridor was full of shredded insulation, carbon fibres and wood chip, the lighter components of which drifted in the air like industrial snow. The dayroom wall and that of the bar on the other side of the way were wrecked. The gun drones stood motionless, guns ticking as they cooled. A breeze came in through the bar's shattered picture windows, spinning the airborne detritus in tiny vortices. Richards gave one of the drones an experimental poke as he and Quaid ducked under their outstretched arms. They were inert. It annoyed Richards that Hughie hadn't trusted him enough to order the things to obey him without him having to dismantle their brains. He unholstered his gun.

By the time Richards and Quaid had made it onto the fore-deck of the *Aurora Viva*, the fight was over. Otto stood over the corpse of the motionless cydroid, ready to shoot it again. It

hung there halfway through the steel wire deck guard, bloodied head still adorned with scraps of matted hair, punctured
by bullet holes.

"Well done, Otto!" said Richards.

Otto, breathing hard, looked up at him. He was about to say
something when from within the wrecked machine at his feet
came a sound like cracking glass. It twitched. Otto stepped
back, gun trained on the ruined skull, retreating further as
wisps of caustic gas rose from the droid. The remains of its face
began to collapse into itself, its limbs to sag, melting away the
few remaining vestiges of the heiress. It became a messy skeleton, then something no longer even vaguely human. Otto
covered his mouth against the fumes. The deck fizzed.

"Fuck! Otto!" shouted Richards. "Dip it in the sea, dip it in
the sea!"

"What?!"

"The acid, the acid! Wash it off now!" Richards stormed forward, gesticulating wildly, then lunged onto the deck, grabbed
a limb of the twitching cydroid and dunked the smoking construct. The water boiled as it slipped under. He turned off his
feedback circuits, ridding him of sensation as facsimiled agony
raced up his arm. Ignoring the damage to his sheath he held
the cydroid under with one hand, swishing it backwards and
forwards in the water.

"Some sort of super acid," Otto said, his voice wet. Richards
scanned him over quickly. The insides of his nose and throat
were raw from the fumes. Otto coughed, wiped his mouth
with the back of his hand. There was blood on it. Then
Richards' machine senses caught a flare of electrical activity in
the big man's solar plexus as his implanted healthtech activated, and he began to breathe more easily.

"Fluorosulfuric, I'd guess," said Richards. "That should do it."
He pulled up the twisted wreck and threw the remains to

clatter onto the deck where they lay smoking. The hand he'd held the machine in the water with was gnurled into a lumpy fist.

Richards pulled himself up awkwardly. He was silent for a moment. The fingers of his less damaged hand, stripped back to bare black bones by the acid, drummed on the railing. His little finger ground and jammed.

"You don't like this," said Otto.

"No, no I don't like it. No one's been able to make an emulant this human-looking, until now."

They looked at the wreck.

"Times change," said Otto wearily. He rubbed at his head, taking comfort in the contrast between stubble and smooth electoo.

Richards shook his head. "It's that there's been no talk of it on the Grid, none at all, that worries me, yet here we find three of them trying to murder each other."

"Could be the Russians, or the People's Dynasty..." Otto offered.

"All Fives talk to each other, and the Russians employ plenty. The People's Dynasty like to think the Great Firewall strong, but it only guards people, and people are self-interested. Something like this would get out. It's of too much value for us, for a start, to the Fives, I mean, for it to stay secret for long. We'd *know*." Richards shouted an incoherent noise. The ocean swallowed it whole. "Fucking Hughie," he said, and punched the rail with his broken hand. "This was supposed to be simple."

Chapter 12
Autopsy

Murder stalked artificial life as surely as it did that of more natural derivation. Autopsies of base units, androids, cyborgs and non-anthropoid, self-propelled robotic carriages were carried out in a facility attached to the Chief Coroner's Office in the Keats Arco. Halfway between machine shop and medical centre, the virtuals division of the Chief Coroner's office smelt of blood and oil in equal measure. The staff comprised men and women who straddled a line between mechanic and medic, for besides the cyborg clients the facility received, many of the more sophisticated androids used systems that were either biologically derived or were straight-up mechanical emulations of biological systems.

The choppers and slicers and disassemblers were backed up by a coterie of post-mortem hackers who could conjure the dying thoughts of a machine from a pile of torched junk, or hunt down the last firings of a simulated brain as it dissipated into the churn of the Grid.

It was one of only two places in the whole of the Londons that made Richards uneasy. This was the place his kind wound up when they died and, like most artificially derived sentients, Richards was worried that if it ever came to that, it would be the end. As Pope Clement XX had said, in not so many words, "Electrons are no substitute for a soul".

He was embarrassed. He was a machine, he wasn't supposed to care, but he did. Mostly, Richards got round his fear by not thinking about it. But at the coroner's he had to stare death down, and it never blinked first.

Richards put on his best undamaged body and flew over to the coroner's in the car. He could have extended a sensing presence into the building and conferred with Doctors Beeching, Smith and Flats that way, but he preferred the distance being incarnate gave him from the coroner's AIs, Lincolnshire Flats in particular.

The corridor to the Robotics Unit was exceedingly long. When he reached the end and the door swished open, Lincolnshire Flats' cheerful voice greeted him, and Richards' heart sank.

"Ah, Richards, come to see our patients? Our happy clients? Come in! Come In!"

"They're not patients, Flats," said Richards. "Patients stand a chance of getting better; nor are they clients, because they do not pay. They are simply dead."

"Morbid as usual!" hooted Flats. "They are happy though, I am correct in that – they never complain!" He laughed.

"Flats..." Richards said.

"Very well, as you prefer: corpses this way! All aboard!" Lincolnshire Flats said, and tooted like a steam train. Flats inhabited a columnar carriage composed of stacked disks, each housing a variety of tools, grapples, sensors and medical equipment, mounted on a soft-treaded truckle. There were several of these, sheaths for the building's AI coroners or remotely visiting experts, but Flats had commandeered this one as his permanent home. He had the habit of spinning his segments round, deploying a surgical saw here, multi-headed screwdriver there, and gunning their motors by way of emphasis, so that his often gruesome conversation was punctuated by whirs, high-pitched squeals of micromotors and inappropriate sound effects. The central plate, which held his primary visual receptors' clustered lenses – Lincolnshire Flats would not stoop to calling them eyes – remained fixed on the face of whomever he spoke to, no matter what crazed fandango the rest of his body was performing, nor in which direction it was heading.

Lincolnshire Flats was one of the more independently minded Fours. It was rumoured that he'd had been modified; darker rumours had it that he'd done it to himself. He'd chosen his own name, which was a rarity in his class, and decided to abandon medicine in favour of forensics. A Four leaving its programmed career was almost unheard of, so Richards suspected the rumours were true. Whether they were or not, Lincolnshire Flats exhibited a love of his work far in excess of that displayed by other Class Fours, coming from someplace else than his programming. His dedication was very laudable, and the two resident human coroners regarded him highly, but as far as Richards was concerned, Lincolnshire Flats was an A-grade ghoul.

"The patie… a-HEM! *Corpses* are in examination 3B, if you'd like to follow me?" Flats hooted.

"I don't like to, but I suspect I have little choice if I want to find out what you have discovered," said Richards with a bravery he wasn't feeling. They set off down a corridor, plush with self-cleaning carpet, the main way within the facility, and numerous rushing men, women and sheathed machine intelligences hurried back and forth. They spared no glances for the two AIs.

"Very droll. Your pointless jibes forever remind of the superiority of the Class Fours over Fives. I thank you for it." A bone saw screeched.

"Don't mention it. You said 'they'."

"I am sorry?" More of Lincolnshire Flats' ocular appendages swung round to look at Richards. He emitted an accompanying "boing".

They walked past Theatre Two, the largest in the place, a warehouse-sized room with gaping clam-doored airlocks leading to a landing field outside. Here they flew in broken base units and pulled them apart. *That's where I am going to end up eventually,* thought Richards. He shuddered. "'They're' as in 'They are' as in 'They' as in 'more than one'?" he said to Flats, more confrontational than he intended to be; scraps to hide his unease behind. *This is fear I cannot deactivate, it is fear from my core. Do the others suffer it, I wonder?* He'd never dared ask, it was too big a weakness, potentially catastrophic, to expose to the other AIs.

"Why, of course. The cydroid your partner deactivated, and the Qifang doppelganger."

"You didn't mean that," said Richards. "That was what your words said, but it wasn't what your voice said. You are too theatrical for your own good."

"Ah, yes, well," grumbled Lincolnshire Flats. "Pooh pooh, there's no hiding anything from you, is there? I must watch my levels of syncopation. I over-pronounce my words when I am hiding something. Yong yong," went Flats.

"You should."

"Bah. It is no paint off my casing's inter-ocular space. HA HA! You have only spoilt things for yourself, Richards, but we'll get to that, I'll save what I know. I shall leave you tantalised, which is nowhere near so delicious as flabbergasted. A pity."

They passed into the atrium of a smaller examination theatre, a round, domed room coated entirely in joinless spun glass. The atrium was within this, effectively a large airlock lit with strong, sterilising UV, a red light over the door to the theatre proper, glass frosted to above head height so those in the airlock could not see into the theatre. They were both subjected to a wind laced with cleaning grains. They stood for five minutes, lifting limbs, Richards' tilting his shoes, turning about, as the microscopic machines swarmed over the AI's respective sheaths, gathering contaminants of every kind. The red light over the door turned amber when they were done, and the grains spiralled down a hole in the floor like a swirl of water in the bath. When they had gone, the light turned green. The AIs' gridsigs were updated with the relevant clearances, and the doors opened.

"Follow me!" trilled Lincolnshire Flats. His unblinking eyes shifted to the tables in the middle of the theatre as he trundled out. There were four tables in all. The one on the right was empty. On the leftmost lay the twisted mess of the cydroid Otto had fought, next to that the fish-nibbled Qifang copy. Next to that lay another cydroid. It had been crudely dismembered, its flesh casing decayed, but it was unmistakeable as another doppelganger for the old professor.

"Qifang two!" shouted Lincolnshire Flats with a species of wholly inappropriate bombastic cheer. He extended a long, thin arm and pointed at the cydroid. "Dragged out of the South Bank marshes this morning, not far from Richmond Venice."

Another door opened, and a man dressed in surgical gear walked in from the scrub room next door. "Ah!" he said cheerily. "Richards! Glad to see you, how're you faring?" He was old in that indeterminate way wealthy men with generous healthplans tended to be. The jewelled snail of an expensive mentaug uplink curled round his ear, a biofilter mask sat atop his surgical cap.

"I am very well, Dr Smith, thank you."

"Of course you are, of course you are." He smiled and pressed his gloved hands together, the faintest of crow's feet feathering his eyes. "A Five is never ill, never tires, never stops. Marvellous, marvellous machines." He leaned forward and peered academically at Richards. Richards got the uncomfortable feeling Smith would just love to poke about in his warm, dead innards.

Richards looked at the broken androids on the autopsy tables, ran his hands absentmindedly along the edges. "And how are you?"

"Well, very well, a lot better than these sorry souls you see here," Smith chuckled. Lincolnshire Flats boomed with laughter and performed a twirl.

"Yeah, right. What have you found out for me then?"

"Ah, right to business as always," said the doctor. "They are entirely new, though I don't think I need to tell you that." He tapped his phone stylus against the acid-scarred carbon bones of the heiress. "As you can see, *as you have seen*, perhaps I should correctly say, these are sophisticated pieces of engineering. I'll use the term cydroid, though they're very near to grade II cyborgs in the proportion of their organic components against pure mechanicals and assorted electronica, shall we say."

"That is an incorrect definition!" shouted Flats, and continued at less offensive volume: "The legal definition of a cyborg is an organism that started life as a fully sapient human, naturally or artificially conceived and gestated, that at a point past conception is altered by the introduction of artificially derived, non-organic components designed to medically replace or enhance natural bodily function," droned the Four. "These are therefore, no cyborgs. Woot!"

"Quite so Lincolnshire Flats, quite so," said Smith, tapping the stylus against his upper lip, unconcerned he'd been poking it into the gory mess in front of him only seconds before. "These never were, for the want of a better term, 'human'." He smiled at Richards. "These are machines through and through. See here." He lifted a flap of rotted skin on Qifang 2 with the stylus. "This is very sophisticated, a full clone in some regards; a genuine copy."

"A full clone, as opposed to a genetically patterned clone, is legally defined as an artifically conceived and gestated organism, or part of an organism, created as an exact copy of a pre-existing organic organism's cellular structure."

"Indeed. Except they are not clones. They're vat grown, for the main, but in parts and then assembled; we can see the joining work, very fine it is, throughout these 'cydroids'... I hate the word! I really wish they would properly classify such," said Smith, shaking his head. "We knew the technology would hit us eventually, we've had plenty of time! What exactly am I going to put on the report?"

"Cydroid! I have already petitioned the medical council for a correct definition," said Flats.

"Whatever term you choose to employ, the machines have all the characteristics of their respective original's exterior properties, dermal, subdermal, lymphatic system... everything." He encompassed the rotting machines with a wave of his stylus and a worried frown. "This has not been spun off a gene-loom, I suspect. The basis of clones from the looms is simply the genetic coding of the subject, but these are actual duplicates, right down to the cellular level. Birth marks, cancers and all. There's more than simple invitrogenesis going on here."

"Someone had cancer? Who had cancer?" asked Richards.

"What? Oh, Qifang, poor chap. Lungs, absolutely shot, way past fixing. His healthtech should have picked that up. I'd sue."

"He's dead now," said Richards. "He's probably past caring."

"Hmmm, what? Yes, I suppose so." Smith scratched his elbow.

"The organics extend far into the system," bellowed Lincolnshire Flats. "Lungs, heart and liver" – his whirring appendages tapped a series of jars at the head of the bed, one after the other. Inside each reposed an organ made pallid by exsanguination and preserving fluids – "as well as all other major internal organs, the alimentary canal, stomach, reproductive

organs and so forth. These, however, are not vital to the functioning of the machine."

"Indeed," said Smith. "In fact, the Qifangs are almost entirely
human, barring the skeleton. The heiress construct differs from
him in her underlying chassis and in its cognitive hardwares. Both
would fool most tests. And this is where things get interesting."
Smith waved his stylus again. The theatre's sunpipes became
opaque, dimming the room. A holo came to life, an image of
the reconstructed heiress that expanded to double normal size
and rotated. "Unlike Qifang's copies, the heiress's skeleton is a
combat android chassis, carbon spun, faraday protected, independently motivated, strong too, similar to those produced and
employed by the South African Union, and thus easily pur-
chasable on the black market." He indicated the items one after
the other with his stylus on the body of the heiress's cydroid.
Above, the holo showed magnified views of the same. "It is capable of operating independently of the organics should they be
destroyed; indeed, it is best to view those as merely a disguise."
Layers of the cyborg graphic obligingly peeled back and it re-
centred itself to show the areas as Smith said their names. "Cavities
of catalytic acids are scattered throughout. A two-liquid mix. On
their own, inert, together..." He pressed his palms together then
moved them apart, fingers spread. "Well then, I suppose we can
bid farewell to our machine, as you yourself have witnessed."

"A suicide pill for our kind," said Flats.

"Standard black-ops modification," said Richards. "I've seen
it before."

"They're deep in the bones, quite a clever modification actually, stops them getting mixed accidentally" – Smith spun his
hands round one another – "due to trauma. Trauma caused by
fighting your colleague, for example, I would say."

"It is apparent to both my colleague and I that the heiress's
primary purpose is violence," added Flats.

"Yes, yes, indeed so. The skeleton itself carries a simple brain, that's the way the Africans run them. But not here. Someone has put extreme effort into making these things look human. We suspect ambush to be its primary modus operandi; surprise, shall we say."

"What about the Qifangs?"

"They're different," said Smith. "A simple woven carbon skeleton, too slow to vat grow like the rest of them, I suppose. Like I said, these chaps were grown and made in parts, then assembled."

"If this is a standard combat endoskeleton, how come it's not picked up on the scanners?" asked Richards.

"Aha! I am so very very glad you asked that!" boomed Flats. He trundled over to a cupboard in the wall. Part of his torso spun round. One of his eyes blinked off, which Richards took for a cocky wink. There was a whirr as his manipulators extended and depressed the door. It sank in slightly, clicked, then opened with a hiss. Flats grabbed an oddly shaped wet machine organ, messy as a liver, from the cupboard and flung it onto the table. "This here, sonny, is a camouflage unit. Woot!" went Flats. "Broadband spectral masking covers the skeleton with a modulated field, a back-up auxiliary mind monitors for any breaks, infiltrates the examination software if needs be and makes it see what it wants it to see. Double blindness!"

"Impressive eh? The military would kill to get their hands on that! But that's not all these new friend of ours have revealed," added Smith.

"No! No! There is more!" shouted Flats.

"You said the brain was non-standard?"

"Very much so, my dear fellow. It is in the brain of the things, the organic, human emulating brain, that we're really peeking into the future. It's still a little crude but it's really quite something," Smith pointed out the various elements of the machine brain on the hologram, which obligingly rotated, zoomed and highlighted parts of itself as the doctor spoke "Yet it mimics human synaptic function far more... adequately I suppose the word would be in this case, than any technology we have yet seen."

"And we see 'em all in here!"

Richards ignored Flats. "Are they capable of full human emulation then, independent of an external governing influence?" he asked, slightly incredulously.

Smith looked disappointed. "Oh, these are sophisticated machines, Richards, no doubt, but even so, whoever built them has not yet found a way of reproducing the full function of the human brain in as compact a form as that which evolution provided us with." Dr Smith tapped his forehead with a finger and smiled. "We meat people are still one step ahead. There are plenty of interesting innovations on the mechano-neurological level, but the mind it sustains is not as complex as that generated by a genuine human brain."

"How do you mean?"

"I suppose you could say the Qifang you found contained the edited highlights of the man's memory. It's as if, well, if you'll pardon the expression, as if he's not all there." He gave a physician's chuckle. "I'm sorry that we could not do a comparison between the two, but the second had lost much of its data content. If you'd...?"

"Dump the files into me when I leave," said Richards. "I'll take a look when I get back to my office."

"Very well. Even with the autonomy these marvellous engines possess, they would appear disconnected and aloof from a human observer. We've done a simulation..."

"A-HEM!"

"My apologies, my colleague Lincolnshire Flats here has done a simulation of how they might think, and aside from the directly programmed competencies present in the heiress, it looks like they were created to *believe* they are human. That would make them, at least her, the ideal assassin. Replace a living target with one of these, it acts like the original, more or less, until some keyword, broadcast or other signal activates it and BAM!" Smith shouted loudly, slamming his hands together. Richards jumped. "The faux-personality is overturned, the core programme takes over... Dead target, infiltrated business, compromised facilities, you name it. They would be inappropriate for truly complex missions, but deadly in the right instances. Imagine, a covert, human-mimicking assassin, the first of its kind, perhaps."

"We are privileged in our work," said Flats.

"How can you be sure they thought they were alive?" said Richards. Throughout Smith's briefing he'd been walking round the inert android, peering into them, lifting bits up. The room smelled of acid, seared flesh and rot under the disinfectant.

The two coroners looked at one another.

"What?" said Richards.

Smith paused, waved his hand around, looking for words. He couldn't find the ones he wanted, "interrogate" sounded too strong. He settled on the prosaic explanation. "Well," he said. "We asked them."

A short holo of the first Qifang machine active, bundles of cable strung from its head. It was screaming over the questions it was being asked; a terrible noise that did not stop.

"I've seen enough," said Richards after half a minute.

"Yes, yes," said Smith grimly. The holo froze. "Quite immoral, don't you think? The heiress and Qifang Two, I'll spare you the holos, were too badly damaged to reboot right away. There was no underlying programming in either Qifang copy like there was in the heiress, though much of the brain of the second is missing, so it's hard to be sure, but he seems to be a

poor copy of Qifang, she a poor copy of an heiress with a murderous purpose."

"Where the hell are they from?" muttered Richards. "And
why was the heiress trying to kill the other cydroid? Are there
any other differences?"

"No. They are of identical manufacture in all other respects,"
said Flats.

Richards looked at the machines. Their existence opened a
lot of doors into a lot of nasty, dark little rooms. "Do you know
where they were made?"

"Negative," said Flats. "We have provided you with information. Utilising it is your role in this. We are coroners, you
are the investigator!"

"Perhaps this will help," said Smith. The hologram spun
again, focusing in on the top of the heiress's damaged femur.
"At the atomic level, there is a company logo. Twelve atoms
by twelve atoms. We'd have no clue if it weren't for this. Why
the criminal mind has a need to reveal itself in such ways is a
mystery we'll never uncover in here, but there it is. Do you
recognise it?"

The logo was grainy, blocky like a very early computer
graphic, single carbon atoms for single pixels. Richards raised
his plastic eyebrows. "Yes, I do." And he wasn't surprised.
"Tony Choi."

"Who?"

"Arms dealer out of Hong Kong. He and I go a ways back.
Thanks. That gives me somewhere to start."

"There is one last thing," said Smith. "Qifang Two was deliberately dismembered. There are tool cuts here, here and
here. And there's this." He highlighted similar wounds on both
corpses, pulling holo images until they overlaid each other.
One hole was more ragged than the other, but both were in
the same place. "See this? Identical puncture wounds to the

base of the skull, and concomitant internal damage. In Qifang Two, the one from the boat, this has knocked out a precise part of his artificial cortex; the other's head was emptied afterwards, but I would say that they were after the same part. And that was this." A ragged holo came up, and began to play. "It's only a part of a message we found in the one from the boat. It was terribly degraded, I am afraid to say. The retrieved footage should be here... Now."

The new holo jumped into life. Another Qifang, perhaps the real one, sat in a well-furnished room. The holo was badly corrupted, elements freezing and overpainting each other to create a messy collage, Qifang a monstrous patchwork in the middle. A dozen cut and paste lips jiggled, floating teeth smeared themselves across the air. The audio, however, was clear enough.

"...at you are the only one I can trust. I am sure you know of me, and the work I have done for your kind, so I hope that you will trust me in return. Please, I must meet with you in person, I have..."

The message stopped, the light of the holo died, leaving the theatre grim.

"If I were a betting man..." said Smith.

"Five to one! Five to one!" bawled Flats.

"...I'd say someone was looking for that."

"Was there any more to the message?"

"That's it, there is no more that we could retrieve," Lincolnshire Flats twittered solemnly. "The dead have spoken, and that is all they are going to say today."

Chapter 13
Doppelganger

Places like this were why Chures wanted the machines on the side of man, why he didn't just try to get the whole lot of them blown to bits.

Places like this were why he was a VIA agent.

A shanty of huddled UN prefabbed shelters, thirty years old and falling apart at the seams. The air was thick and fuggy with smells of cooking, Brazilian spices, Mexican pastries. Dozens of dialects of Portuguese and Spanish came from faces of all colours, unfamiliar words tripping Chures' mind. The place reeked of sweat and shit. One hundred miles from the the Whitehouse, Jesu City, oldest of the northern shanties, feverish in the humid night with discordant music and despair.

If the machines had more say, places like this would be gone faster. The machines had more say every year, and things were getting better. But Chures had no illusions. Underneath their fake personalities the machines were supremely logical beings. They looked at a place like Jesu, one day they might come to the supremely logical conclusion that things would run far more smoothly without people.

It had happened once before. More than seventy-six Fives had come through the crisis of '04 mentally sound. There were two dozen or so others, completely rational, entirely inimical to human life. They'd been destroyed by the VIA along with those deemed insane. The rush to get them all deleted before the UN untangled the mess surrounding the crisis had been exhilarating. Some of his colleagues had objected, things had got unpleasant, those who believed the VIA's actions immoral pitted against the realists. He'd been fresh out of the academy when the crisis hit, a baptism of fire, but he'd stayed in service. He'd spent his own childhood in a camp much like this. If the machines were kept in check, they could deliver a better world.

If they were kept in check.

Chures would have liked to have had Qifang on his team. Men who had empathy for mankind's children were rare; humanity did not understand its offspring well. A condition of parenthood, he supposed.

He walked through the sucking ooze that passed for a street, banging bass lines and calls of drugged prostitutes half-deafening him. He cursed the mud's effect on his expensive boots. A big man jostled him, looking for a fight. Chures flicked open his coat, showing badge and gun. The man curled a lip, and walked on.

This was typical of Karlsson, pick some godforsaken hellhole to meet in. He'd done it on purpose, put him ill at ease, remind him of his past. Karlsson was a bastard for that kind of mind game.

At the heart of the camp were three huge hangars, decaying structures of cement board and steel from when the place had been an aerodrome. For a while they'd been used for camp administration; UN blue coloured the walls, mildewed prefab offices with smashed-in windows clustered about the sides. The hangars were falling down, warning signs all over their exteriors, a couple of beat-up survdrones patrolling the perimeter. Why hadn't they been demolished? His badge let

him through the cordon. He ducked inside a hole in the wall
into the centremost hangar. Here Karlsson should be waiting.

Flocks of pigeons scared up on clattering wings as he walked
across a floor slick with rainwater and human waste. There were
signs that the drones had been beaten, people had been in here
recently, makeshift braziers of blackened drums, discarded bottles, packets and torn sleeping bags, a hobos' dross, visible in
patches of garish light from the pleasure joints outside.

The building was empty, the sounds of life from the
shanty muted.

Bartolomeo, scan. The AI blend looked down through a winged
drone above the camp, searching for human traces in the
hangar, feeding highlights directly to Chures through his twin
uplinks, right into his mentaug and the mind's eye it parasited.

"Negative, agent Chures. I see nothing."

"Karlsson!" Chures shouted. His voice bounced from concrete walls. There was a noise, the scuff of shoe on concrete,
magnified and sinister in the hangar's emptiness.

"You're not getting anything?"

"I am sure," said Bartolomeo.

"Puta Karlsson," spat Chures. The man had more tech and
more brains than half the VIA, but he was as crazy as a shit-
house rat, a liability. "Come out, Karlsson!" He walked over to
the source of the noise. He pulled his gun. "Get out into the
light where I can see you."

A shadow of a man resolved itself from the deeper shadows
in the curve of the walls. "Chures!" hissed Karlsson's voice.
"Keep your voice down."

Chures kept his gun out, adjusted his grip. He checked over
his shoulder. Coming here alone was a bad idea, Karlsson's insistence be damned.

"Come out."

"As you wish."

The man stepped out into a puddle of flickering LED reflections. Chures squinted, couldn't believe what he was seeing.

"Karlsson couldn't make it."

The man had his face. He stood insouciantly, one hand in the pocket of a suit identical to one Chures owned, the other twirling a cocktail stick idly in his teeth.

"Put the gun down, Chures," said his double, his voice.

Chures wasn't one to ask dumb questions. He pulled the trigger; at least he intended to. In the milliseconds between the neurons firing to twitch his finger muscles and his brain retrospectively deciding it had consciously made the decision to do so, something cut in and stopped him. His body locked rigid.

"I am sorry, Agent Chures," said Bartolomeo.

This wasn't supposed to happen. He was in control.

"There's no need for you to die, Chures. My intention is to save lives, not waste them." The man with his face walked forward and took his gun, slid the slider back, dissembled the weapon without looking at it and strewed its parts upon the floor. "I need to borrow your life for a while. When this is all over, you will thank me."

Through teeth clamped shut, Chures choked out a rasping gargle: "What the fuck are you?"

The other Chures gave a slow smile to no one in particular. "You are as tenacious as they say. I am glad I pursued this course of action; making a puppet of you would never have worked for long." He locked eyes with him, his eyes. "A better question would be 'who?', Chures. And perhaps 'why?'" He cocked his head to one side, the neck accommodating several degrees more tilt than would have been comfortable for a human. "Tell me, what do you know of the Class Five AI Richards and Otto Klein's involvement in this affair of the departed professor?"

Chures said nothing.

"Suit yourself," said his double. Chures felt a sharp pain in his mind as Bartolomeo let something in. His life flickered before him with sickening speed. When it was done, he was on his knees, filth soaking the knees of his trousers.

"It is surprising how little you know," said his double. "That should make things easier." The double squatted beside him. "I'll be going now. I'll have Bartolomeo take you somewhere safe, don't worry. He is fond of you. I'll be in touch." He pointed at Chures' gear. "I'll be needing these." He bent down and tugged Chures' coat, badge and all, over his stiff shoulders. He reached out and unclipped his twin mentaugs from their external mounts underneath each of his ears. "I apologise for the pain," the double said as monofilament wires tugged from his flesh. The fake Chures took the drop-pearl earring Chures wore in his left ear. "I have to look the part," explained the double, then took his boots.

Chures grunted with rage, saliva streaming between lips frozen in a painful snarl, his muscles burning with cramp.

He couldn't see the stranger leave.

Some time later, Bartolomeo spoke. "That should be long enough, Agent Chures. I have taken control of your somatic functions. We will now leave. Please do not fight. I am truly sorry." Bartolomeo walked Chures, reduced to a meat puppet, jerkily over to the gash in the wall they'd entered through. They bent as one as they approached. Chures marshalled himself and waited until they were going under.

With one last effort of will, he jerked his head back, slamming the silvered aux-mind casing into a rusting beam.

"Stop!" said Bartolomeo. "Chures!"

With the first blow, Chures felt the AI's influence lessen briefly. He seized his chance and threw his head back again, gashing his own scalp, smashing the casing again, sending its Gridpipe receivers offline.

"Chures, stop, Chures!" Bartolomeo's voice was panicked. Half his personality imprint was in the unit. Chures had made sure of that, in case he ever needed to deactivate him. "Chures! You do not understand. Stop! Something terrible isssss..." Bartolomeo's voice slurred and faded to a hiss. Somewhere, the base unit that made up the rest of the AI blended with Chures slipped into lobotomised imbecility.

Chures fell forward, his muscles limp, head ringing like a bell. Holy Christ alone knew what damage he'd done to his own brain. What the hell now? If he went back to the VIA, he'd be dead. The fake Chures and whoever was behind him would know right away that Bartolomeo was gone. They'd be waiting for him.

Valdaire. Get to her first, hold her as a bargaining chip.

A lousy plan, but the best he had.

His senses reeled. He grabbed at the wall. His feet slipped into the muck of the street. People avoided him, stepping away as he bounced off them, just another luckless victim on Jesu City's pleasure way.

He stumbled on, eyes hunting for drones against the stars.

Chapter 14
Los Angeles

"What kind of shit are those fucking electrical bastards trying to pull now? A German, a fucking German? This ain't Hamburg or Schnitzelville or wherever the fuck you are from, pal, not your jurisdiction." The small detective seethed and his round, unfashionably fat face glowered into Otto's, the badge slung about his neck jerking with his rage as he jabbed his pudgy forefinger at Otto in time with his words. Otto stared placidly down at him. The top of the detective's head stopped short of the top of his chest. The detective's eyes were small and black, face lined by unspent anger, deep creases round his mouth.

"Cool it, Flores, this guy's got documentation like you've never seen," said the woman. Detective Mulholland, his near- I told him, and plenty more besides.

"Yeah?"

"Yeah, Flores. Right from the top. He's investigating a con- nected case over in Euroland. The Sams think it's really important. There's nothing we can do." Mulholland was older, serious, about forty-five in biological looks, probably her actual age – she looked the kind of woman who wouldn't make the time for cosmetic work until she had to. Her hair was un- combed, scraped back into a businesslike ponytail, her face free of make-up, clothes poorly ironed. A real vocation cop, Otto guessed, an up-late-into-the-night, dwelling-on-the-faces-of-the-dead type. "Isn't that right?"

Otto nodded.

"And what is this case, huh? You gonna tell us?" said Flores.

"I cannot. It is highly sensitive," said Otto regretfully. Pissing off the local cops wasn't going to make his job any easier, but as understanding as he was, Flores was irritating. His shoulder throbbed. Something important had given; he felt it grind as he moved. The pain wasn't helping him keep his cool in the face of this idiot.

"That's fucking typical!" Flores threw up his arms. "God-damn fucking machines!" He stalked off, passed through the police flatfield round the house, signalled two uniforms in after him. "Fine, fine, show him round," he shouted over his shoulder. "I'm going to go over the gardens again. Call me when he leaves."

A barrage of swearing followed, and then the diminutive detective was gone.

"I'm sorry about detective Flores, Mr Klein."

"Do not be sorry. It is difficult when someone comes in from outside. I will be out of your way as quickly as possible."

"Sure, thanks. It's complicated with Flores. He's been in the force since way back when, before AI started giving orders rather than just taking them. He doesn't like it when artificials interfere with his work, he gets huffy."

Huffy was not a word Otto knew. His near-I gave him a definition in German. If that was huffy, Flores was probably the kind of guy who approached apoplectic if his pizza topping was wrong.

"I'm Detective Mulholland," she said, which Otto already knew. "I've got to accompany you right the way round here, no snooping about on your own, OK?"

"Understood," he said

She smoothed her dry hair. She looked tired. "If you've got any questions, you've just got to shout out. Did you have a good flight?"

"Yes," he said. "May I see the crime scene now?"

"My, you're the chatty one, aren't you? Sure, I'll show you round." She walked right through the flatribbon cordon, her badge, like Flores', allowing her passage. She started to indicate that Otto should duck under, hesitated, walked over to the nearest emitter bollard and pressed a button instead. The flatribbon, a beam of light bearing scrolling warnings and carrying a high voltage charge on ionised air molecules, winked out between two of the emitters. "Kind of a big fella, aren't you? They all this big over there?"

"I am an exception."

"Well, Mr Exception, walk this way. Are you ex-military or…"

"Ex-military, Ky-technischeren Spezielkraft Kommando. Cyborg commando."

"OK." She flashed her badge at a bored-looking uniform by the property's side door. Otto let him scan his AllPass. The officer handed them foot coverings, overcoats and haircovers. After they'd put them on he opened the door without comment, and let the two of them inside.

"Do I need to wear a mask?" Otto asked.

"Not unless the smell bothers you. We had air scrubber drones come in and do the atmospheric forensics right after the call came in. We do have professional standards, you know?" She gave an unpractised smile. She was trying to put him at ease, but she wasn't very skilled at it.

They went in via the kitchen door. The house was big, and full of cops. Small circular drones darted about, aiding a forensics team of five men and a sheathed Four who was doubtless linked to the drones. They flew through the air, dipping down to the floor to scoop up flies killed in the building lockdown, sucked

fragments of stone and soil up from the carpet, plucked particles of skin from the curtains. Camera flashes sporadically popped.

They went through into the dining room. The smell was bad. Two weeks' worth of decay soaked into floorboards lifted a reek into the air, the body's position marked by a tape outline and a large blotch of discoloured wooden flooring. Qifang had not been a big man, but there'd been time, and he'd leaked copiously.

"This is where we found him." Her gesture took in the stained table, covered in plastic markers, and the mark on the floor. "He'd been dead at least two weeks, we think. It was the start of vacation, when teaching duties end. He was supposed to be doing research, and he kept himself to himself outside of office hours. We had to go off entomological evidence, as you can see – a lot of flies round here, killed by the biologicals pulse we use. Lucilia sericata, most of them. Their pupation rate kind of puts it round the same time as we see that flicker in his Grid-sig, you know about that?"

"Yes."

"OK. Then, or possibly a little later."

"What of the three divergent signals that left the States?"

"Beats me, we've not had anyone cheat the Grid codes since the Three Uncles took over population management. But sure, this guy was one smart cookie, we'll give him that. Then there's his assistant, she disappeared in a hurry. Do you know anything about that?"

"I cannot discuss it," said Otto. "Sorry. I read about Qifang's home fabricator in the report also. May I see that? It may be important to my investigation."

"Yeah, sure, this way. Watch the wires." She pointed to lines linking the Four to a boxy unit, itself trailing cables off out of the house through a plastic sphincter lodged in the window. "We have to hardline our sheaths to the police AIs. Some little hacker shit got hold of the cipher for their Gridpipes. Quantum

encoding unbreakable? Bullshit. Kids can crack it in their lunch-break. They do it for fun, then the criminal elements buy it up."

"It is inconvenient," said Otto, thinking of Tufa.

"It's a drag, that's for sure. Outsiders seem to think it's all peace and love in CA since the dippies took over, but I tell you, this place is crawling with scum. We've got a major gang war on, massive people-smuggling to the south, every criminal meat-head in Latin America has decided to come here since the reds took over and started executing anyone connected to the cartels and drug businesses, and it's not helped by the reds trying to smuggle their spies in with the genuine refugees. So, even some-thing like this, it's all hardlined. None of it, bar the simplest commands to these drones, is broadcast."

"It is the safest way," agreed Otto. Qifang's house was large. They passed over a wide hallway where the main entrance to the building was situated. More masked and suited bodies pored over this.

"It is a pain in my ass, is what it is," she said. "Even the num-bers bitch about it. Right, here we are." Under the grand staircase was a small door that Otto had some trouble squeezing through. This led onto a short flight of stairs that brought them down into a basement workshop, harshly lit, with a concrete floor covered with a smooth application of carbon plastic paint. It was a large space, big enough for a couple of workbenches. Tools on pinboards lined three of four walls, while the fourth opened out into a garage where a modest aircar sat, the ramp leading up from the garage to the driveway outside stamped with a hard rhombus of daylight. More officers bustled about the basement. Otto had counted seventeen in all in the house.

In the corner of the workshop stood an industrial fabrica-tion unit, one of the biggest Otto had seen in a private home, large enough to put out auto components. The service hatch had been taken off without much care, optic cables left spilling out of it. Mulholland shooed an officer out of the way, and pointed within.

"The central chipset, patterning unit and cache have been removed. Bits of them are on that desk over there." She indicated a pile of shattered components. "We have the chips back at HQ, but they've been thoroughly wrecked. It looks like someone, Qifang I presume, took out anything that could give us a clue and smashed it to bits with a hammer."

"He made something before he died?"

"Yes, something he did not want us to know about."

"You are attempting to reassemble the chip fragments?"

"Yeah, we're not making much progress. They're useless, if you ask me. I don't think we'll find anything."

"I'll take a scan of them if I may."

"Be my guest. Speak to Martez upstairs." She leaned on a bench. "He's logging the evidence. He'll give you access to whatever you need."

The house was well kept, and Otto was impressed by the way the police were going over it. They weren't always so careful back home; probably Qifang being so famous helped. After the police finished, this place would be crawling with the media, then it really would be trashed. "It is a good team you have. But is it not large for this case?"

"A suicide, you mean? Maybe, but Qifang was an important man, and there are a lot of eyes watching, most of them not of the human variety, and what the numbers say goes around here. There were a lot of people that were not very happy with Qifang's civil rights movement for the other sapients, lot of religious, lot of extreme dippies. Some of them have the money and the expertise to stage something like this and make it look like suicide. And his assistant, she's a lot younger than Qifang, but some of those mentor/ student relationships can get very messy one way or another."

"What is your opinion, detective?"

"You want my opinion? Wow," she said sardonically. "It's a long time since anyone wanted that, but, OK, you can have it." She crossed her arms. "My opinion is that he killed himself. Why? Beats me, maybe we won't find out and maybe we will. Sure, he had cancer, but they might have been able to fix that. In my opinion it doesn't really matter. In my opinion these officers here could be covering something else, say, solving the schoolyard massacre we had two weeks back. Thirty-eight dead kids, because one wetback didn't like the way another looked at him. Or the serial killer offing virtporn addicts in Downey, Lynwood and Compton. By our count he's up to seventy-six victims now. Or any one of the other million active cases we have. This state is gutting itself while the fucking dippies clang their bells, and one dead professor who chose an early exit does not mean much one way or another to me. But that's my opinion, and my opinion doesn't mean anything to the State, the VIA, the Feebs or the machines that run them."

"It is a difficult job. I understand," he said.

"Do you understand?" Her expression softened as she lingered on the scars on his face. "Yeah, yeah, maybe I guess you do." She looked round the room, as if searching for something she'd misplaced, then looked back up to him. "Now, is there anything else you need to see here?"

"No, thank you. I will take the scans of the chip fragments and send them to my partner, maybe he can do something with them."

"Really?"

"He is skilled in this area. If he finds anything I will let you know. I also need any information that you may have on Qifang's assistant, Veronique Valdaire."

"I'd like to speak to her myself. She skipped town, suspicious, but her Gridsig, forensics and so forth suggest she was never within two miles of this place. The night he died we have a bar full of witnesses to testify that she was dancing until the early hours. Whatever she's done, it isn't killing."

"That does not mean that she is not responsible."

"No, no, it does not. She vanished in suspicious circumstances two weeks ago, not long after the victim killed himself. She's off the Grid. It's not surprising. If he knew how to fool the system, there is a good chance she knows how to too. The UCLA Six has lodged complaints against her: a couple of illegal searches, theft and an assault."

"Assault?"

"She turned it off," she explained. "It put the initial call to us, but the specifics of that information have not been made available to us by the VIA. If you find her before we do. I want to talk to her before the VIA. It's been a nightmare here since the Tolman administration. Federal and out-government agencies at each other's throat in a way that'd make... What was his name, that twentieth-century guy?" She frowned at Otto, looking for an answer, before providing her own. "Hoover, that's it. That'd make him proud. Paranoid nuts everywhere, no cooperation, especially on these section 73s."

"You don't think she was involved in Qifang's murder?"

"No." She shook her head. "It's very unlikely. There's not much evidence. Granted that she's smart enough to hide it and herself, but she didn't go to any effort to cover her tracks until the morning she vanished. Besides, her psychs suggests a high degree of loyalty, and I'll go with that every time. She's running all right, but not from this. It'd be better for her if we got to her before the VIA did. What she's done is enough for the VIA to hold her indefinitely, murder or not."

"What do you think?"

"Me? I think Qifang killed himself. How Valdaire ties in exactly, I don't know. I expect the VIA to deal with her, bad news for her. I expect the VIA to come to me soon, because despite what they think, we local cops are not schmucks, and if we can't find her, I'll bet they can't find her either." She rubbed her face again. Her skin took a while to crawl back into place, fatigue compromising its elasticity. "Now, Mr Klein, I have a lot to do. If there's nothing more you need to see, I will escort you out."

After Otto had secured scans of the fabber chip fragments and Gridcast them to Richards, he caught a cab over to Richards & Klein's LA office in an unprepossessing mini-arco out near the landward end of Wilshire. His first stop there – he'd gone straight to the crime scene when the Stratoliner landed.

He interrogated the near-I secretary, to make sure that Richards hadn't been ignoring potentially lucrative cases. If they bored him, he tended not to bother telling Otto, which was one of his more irritating habits, so Otto checked up on the offices' minders every week. There wasn't much, a bauxite freighter heist that he might look into later. He instructed the machine to inform potential clients that they were likely to be unavailable for a month.

The office was small, a reception area equipped with a holographic receptionist, and a sheathed AI One on security which did not come out of its closet for Otto's visit. There was a conference room out back and not much else. All the important workings of their agency were back in New London.

The extra business such places generated was useful, but the main function of the offices was their attached garages. Otto went up to a plain diamond-weave door, hidden at the back of the premises, submitting himself to the usual scans before it opened and allowed him access to the garage's staircase.

Richards referred to the garages as walk-in wardrobes, and for him that was the case. They contained multiple sheaths for him to inhabit and a rack of his favoured attire of hat,

trenchcoat and suit. Richards & Klein, Inc, Security Consultants, had twenty-three such installations around the globe.
In form they varied greatly. In the relative peace of the northern world they were overt, with offices where Richards could
meet clients by pinging himself over from the main branch in
the Londons. In the most dangerous of places they were little
more than hidden weapons caches with a secure Gridpipe and
a couple of heavy-duty sheaths.

In LA, the stores were extensive: a single large foamcrete
room, weapons and sheaths neatly racked on the walls, lockers
of equipment lining one side. An airbike and a groundcar were
parked in the middle on hydraulic rams. Keeping all this stuff
licensed was a nightmare, but that was Richards' job. Otto got
to buy the weapons. It was a good arrangement.

Otto had not been permitted to bring arms on the stratoliner
from the UK, so he picked out a clutch of EMP grenades, a
flechette railgun, a grenade launcher, one of his favoured
Hechler caseless 9mm pistols, a bunch of ammunition, a
heavy-duty nanoBabbage laptop – slow compared to optic
computers, but immune to EMP – and a change of clothes. He
put it all in the boot of the groundcar and signed it out. He got
into the car and activated the ram. The ceiling door slid open
and the ram took him out into the bottom of a multi-storey
carpark. He drove past a preserved nodding donkey, a relic of
oil-age LA, its concealing wall replaced by glass and a plaque.
He drove through the car park, turned off onto Wilshire and
set off toward Valdaire's house.

Valdaire's place was a small duplex hidden amid thousands
of others, nothing showy, but the neighbourhood was a relatively good one, away from the refugee camps and gang wars
of the south. In the main LA had fared better than London;
there had been no bomb, for a start. A few key areas were
underwater, Long Beach, Malibu, places like that, but the

Californians hadn't had to contend with the massive increase in rainfall the UK had seen and the swollen rivers that had brought. It was a little cloudier, a little wetter, cyclones were a yearly occurrence, but the winds were brief and most of the rain hit the coastal ranges and the Rockies. LA also did not have to contend with the storm surges that broke onto London with the regularity of waves on a beach. A few lengthy dykes safeguarded much of Los Angeles. Besides the seaward walls, and few score arcologies, it hadn't changed that much in the last hundred years. If the Big One ever hit, the cities might be on a more even footing disruption-wise, but it had not yet.

Valdaire's flatmate knew very little; Otto could tell that from the moment she opened the door and began to complain about being interviewed three times by the cops. He watched her face in IR as they talked, but his near-I could find no evidence of untruth either in her thermal signature or vocal patterns.

Jones and Valdaire did not get on well, having being placed together by the UCLA's governing Class Six, supposedly for maximal benefit of each other's personality traits. Valdaire was focused, intense and obsessed about her fitness, Jones told Otto, though Otto dialled down "obsessed" in his mind to merely "concerned". Letitia was big, the kind of big that thinks walking across the room to pick up a twinkie is "obsessed with fitness". The flatshare was a typical odd-couple set-up of the kind the dippy AIs loved. They rarely worked. It was clear Letitia hated Valdaire, and the feeling was probably mutual.

Otto got a picture of a career-driven woman whose only concessions to frivolity were her dancing and her near-I PA Chloe. Chloe was a life-companion, incepted at the birth of a child, in her case when she'd immigrated to Canada, designed to grow alongside them as pet, confidante and playmate. A lot of kids tired of them by the time they hit their tweens. That Valdaire still had hers did not surprise Otto; it all tallied with her psych and gene profiles. Driven people find it hard to make human connections. Valdaire had been an outcast at school, a rebellious student, then a soldier.

Some things never changed.

Otto could have learnt all of this from the files, or the Grid, or he could have gone there virtually and never have left the Londons. But there was no substitute for being in the scene, no digital intermediary to lessen the immediacy. Otto was old-fashioned that way.

He drove across skypasses crossing the Long Beach lagoon then north to UCLA's Computer Sciences campus up in the Chino hills, a twenty-storey, quake-proofed needle. It looked out over the tawny city, the sea a blue promise in the distance.

Otto called the VIA when he reached the AI Department, finally getting through to some high-up eugene after he'd used his AllPass. Otto's near-I had some pretty good truth software, and it said the eugene was not lying when he said they'd not found Valdaire. He said he'd been surprised at Qifang's death, but that their case had closed when he'd died. This also appeared true, but Otto's near-I was only so good, and eugenes were past being human, so he took his statements with a large truckload of salt. The eugene hung up shortly afterwards.

By the time he entered the university it was late in the day. The Six had been forewarned; it was polite but refused to speak to him on the subject of Valdaire or Qifang, pointing out that his AllPass was superseded by a VIA gagging order. He was denied access to the lab. None of the other grad students who worked with Qifang and Valdaire would be made available to him. Good day. The usual fob-off.

Some desk monkey named Guillermo had been the last to see Valdaire. He was poorly educated, unenhanced, fat and lonely-looking. Hc'd let the agents in at the Six's request. No one would tell Otto what they were there for, or why they'd decided to show up a few hours after Qifang's estimated death.

One unholy inter-agency stink was about to kick off, but that was not Otto's concern. What the VIA might have to hide was.

Either Valdaire and Qifang had hatched some plot together and had come under the scrutiny of the VIA – and if so, it would have to be extremely serious for the agency not to acknowledge their own investigation of it – or Qifang and his assistant had stumbled on to something, and the VIA wanted to cover it up.

Otto sat in the car and considered breaking into the building at night. Burglary here would be hard, but not impossible. He would almost certainly get caught, though, and what little he could hope to find did not justify the trouble he'd have to go to to extricate himself.

He needed to find Valdaire, and Chloe was the key to that. She could be tracked. If someone was following her, they'd know that too, and so no doubt did Valdaire. But Otto had Richards.

Otto put in a Gridcall to England. The new girl, Genie, answered.

"Hiya, Otto!" she said. Fed through his mentaug, she appeared to hover over his dashboard, as a thirty-centimetre-tall woman in dressing-up-box harem wear.

"Get me Richards," said Otto.

"Sure thing," she said, and winked suggestively. "Putting you through."

A square like an old cinema screen arrived in the middle of Otto's field of vision: augmented reality. Velvet curtains rose to the skirl of a Wurlitzer, a tiny homunculus playing it manically at the bottom of the vision, to reveal a grey screen. Flickering numbers played over the screen, and then Otto was looking at Richards sitting in his office, in an image running in monochrome 2D.

"Hey," Richards said. He was dressed ridiculously, with braces and baggy trousers, his hat pushed high back on his forehead. He was speaking in a cod early-twentieth-century American accent. "Here's looking at you, kid."

Otto sighed.

"You have no sense of fun!" tittered Genie.

Otto pushed a button on his dash. Genie stuck out her tongue as she faded out of the feed.

"I got your pictures." Richards said it "pickchewers". "Dis is what I got, dese here documents." He pointed a cigarette at a scatter of paper on the desk. "Looks like some kinda key. Dey said something was missing from da lab?"

"Yeah."

"Hmm. Dey's got a coupla old v-jacks dere, I'll bet one o' dose is missing, sure, right?"

"There is an information lockdown by the VIA. The LAPD did tell me there had been a theft."

"I ain't no genius, but the v-jack is missing. So we haveta assoom she's gone into da Realms. I got my snouts out on the street, big guy, looking for that kid Chloe, we find her, we find Valdaire," he said, reaching the same conclusion as the German. "Knowing what she's got, where she's headed, will make it easy."

"Not easy. Valdaire was a skilled InfoWar operative. She's still on the reserves list, a lot of her record is classified. That means she's good. She'll have covered her tracks."

"Sure, sure, big guy, OK, OK, jeez, calm down. Difficult, but possible." Otto's adjutant informed him that a million of Richards' scales, configured as near-I hunter-seekers, had hooked into his mentaug. They put noses down and dispersed on to the grid, tracking Valdaire's tortuous digital trail. In return, Otto downloaded edited experiences of his trip to the Five. Richards would have preferred to peer out of his eyes, but Otto didn't like Richards to see his every move, it was far too intimate, and it distracted the AI from his own jobs. The mem-edit was a workable compromise.

"Thanks a bunch for yours, kiddo," said Richards. "You flat-foot it after the broad, while my guys do the paperwork. Me, I'm ofta Hong Kong, see Choi."

"Choi," said Otto.

"The frames for the cydroid heiress been traced back to him, I learnt a few things. Remind me to teach you dem sometime. Choi'll sing like a canary, don't you worry. But there's one more thing I gotta tell ya."

And then Richards, in infuriating mid-modern American English, outlined exactly how Otto was going to have to find Chloe.

Otto was not happy about that at all.

Richards smiled, and raised his hat. The curtains swung shut, and the cinema vanished.

"Genie," Otto said. She reappeared in his field of vision, standing on the car's dashboard.

"Yes?" she said.

"I'll be off the Grid for a while. The VIA are looking for Valdaire. I can't rule out that whoever sent the second cydroid after the Qifangs aren't looking for her either. They will probably follow me. I've deactivated my MT. It is a risk after Tufa. If you need me, contact me the usual way. Yes?"

Genie nodded and disappeared, leaving a trace of perfume in Otto's olfactory centre.

"Can't tell what is real or not any more," he said sourly.

He left the UCLA campus, went to eat, and considered his next move. Whatever happened, he was going to end up with a colossal migraine.

Maybe sixty-three wasn't too young an age to retire.

Chapter 15
The Great Firewall of China

The Great Firewall was one of the great wonders of the Grid, and the Grid was not short on wonders. The People's Dynasty had gone to a lot of trouble with the way the Wall looked, investing time, money and processing power to create a feast for the qualia, a declaration of power and intent.

Richards assembled a sensing presence outside the wall over the course of a day, the fastest he could bring himself there without alerting the People's Dynasty government, who watched their borders zealously. Disguised as a virtual tour group, one of thousands visiting the Wall every day, Richards pushed himself lazily along. Hour by hour he'd had bits of himself show up, each hidden within a human Grid avatar, identities swiped to construct a believable bunch of online gawkers. There was a virtual tour guide, and as each of the tourists had arrived, he'd had them go off and enjoy some of the many distractions near the Wall. Running twenty-three complex simulations at once was taxing even for Richards, and the tourists were acting a little strangely as a result. He assured himself that no one would notice, humans behaved strangely all the time online. Later they convened at a genuine guide stop of a bogus tour, where the guide gave them a particularly dull speech. Richards was proud of that touch.

The artistic director of the Great Firewall project had taken the firewall part literally, and crafted a kilometre-high rampart of flame, with heavy towers set into it every two nominal kilometres. Pennants of varicoloured fire snapped above the battlements, inscribed with writhing patriotic slogans in all the world's living languages, and a few of the more prominent dead ones besides. Dragons flew over these, each whiskered face hiding powerful phage programmes or snatch code, primed to swoop down and sever the connections of high-class AIs like him who got too close to the wall, or drag them within to face interrogation, because the Chinese did not like independent AIs.

The parapet was patrolled by figures from Chinese mythology, towering gods clad in bronze. Cannon mouths like railway tunnels gaped from gunloops halfway up the ramparts.

There was one gate, tall as a hill and bound in iron, large enough, were it in the Real, to allow one of the Atlantic Wall's floating fortresses through without scraping the sides.

The gate never opened.

The Great Firewall was a big "fuck off" to the world's AIs. The digital borders of the People's Republic were closed by order of the People's Dynasty Government, and had been for twenty years. Bringing digital data over twenty megabytes in any format into the country was a criminal offence, punishable with serious hard time building eco-villages up in Sinosiberia. You wanted to speak to someone in China, it was easier to send a letter than an email. On paper. By mule.

The country had been totally shafted during the Five crisis. The Reign of the Ghost Emperor, they called it. Nothing brighter than a warehouse management system running off barcodes was consequently allowed in from outside. No one even knew if the Chinese had AIs of their own. If machines like Richards existed, they kept themselves to themselves. Free roaming artificial intelligences were not welcome.

But the wall, for all the special effects, was simply a set of protocols. Nothing was perfect, protocols could be broken. Richards knew a way in.

Virtual real estate was at a premium all along the length of the Wall. Grid artists had sculpted a landscape to front onto it that was as beautiful as it was weird. Virtual windows opened onto it from people's homes in the Real, virtual offices sat by virtual brooks by its feet, virtual towns dreamt in its flickering shadow.

Richards swam back and forth in the air, logging thousands of impressions of the underlying Grid structure until he found what he was looking for. Under a meadow populated by giant rabbits and Grid-interfaced living rooms, he snagged an illegal carrier signal. Why kids risked their lives swapping movies like this baffled Richards. The movies were freely available on the inside, and China, with its own huge film industry centred on Shanghai and Hong Kong, was a stickler for copyright.

He set his tour group down amid the rugs and mega-lagomorphs, and set to work.

The connection was a tightbeam carrier signal bounced off a commsat by some budding young programmer. Hidden in verbal telecoms traffic, a number of the latest hit holos were being quietly transferred off a Swiss paysite onto the personal computer of – Richards checked the usename – "Northern Bandit", disguised as a dull conversation between a nagging mother and a worn-out émigré daughter. Richards sat by it, tested it for stability, then insinuated a sensing presence into the datastream. Northern Bandit was going to be very upset to discover "Donkey Cock A-Go-Go" was an empty file.

Brilliant, thought Richards. Sneaking in to the most hostile anti-AI state on the planet disguised as porn. You couldn't make it up.

Once inside China's virtual borders, Richards checked the tightbeam. He slowed the data transfer down to give himself some extra time, but not so much as to arouse Northern Bandit's suspicion, only enough to mimic the delays you got on the Grid at times of high traffic. He reckoned on forty-five minutes, real time.

Richards transferred himself across the country's cyberspace as a variety of search requests. He had to split himself like a cheese string to do so. As he'd be running this in real time, the end reassembled somewhere near to Tony Choi, there was bound to be some data dropout, but it was the only way to be safe. If they got a lock on to his sensing presence, they could force a secure pipe back to his base unit and trap him indefinitely through a kind of extra-Real extradition.

Some of the things the teeming citizens of China were searching for made his eyebrows rise, although most of it was to do with eating. He hadn't known that half this stuff was edible.

After a few minutes of groping about with the frayed end of his sensing presence, Richards found his way into Tower Thirty-six, Hong Kong, where Tony Choi's company had its base of operations. A couple more, and he had a sheath. He reintegrated the sensing presence to a point where he had enough bandwidth to operate without annoying lag. He let the rest of himself flap in the current.

Camera eyes opened, he looked down at bright red plastic hands. Left and right were three ranks of machines like the one he possessed. All were empty, unridden, their hardware capable of supporting only the feeblest of near-I independent of the Grid. He was in the stockroom of an android dealership. Provided he kept within range of strong Grid flow, controlling one should be child's play.

He was in.

Tower Thirty-six was an "Eyrie" class arcology, sealed until halfway up its height. Access to this particular type was from the air alone. It was a rich man's conceit, isolating the building from the others. Taller and thinner than their New London counterparts, the arcos of Hong Kong extended far into Kowloon bay, the sea a maze of canals and lagoons supporting kelp farms, ports, leisure facilities and artificial marine habitats. There'd been shanty towns down there once, after the 2067 ice sheet tip, but those days were gone. The poor had been relocated into the arcologies, the Sinosiberian territories and the re-greening projects on the mainland. The Chinese were trying hard to live by the harmonic principles of Tao again. What had worked quite well for three thousand years was being re-employed by the People's Dynasty government today. They preferred it if you didn't bring the last 150 years of industrial excess up. They were so ashamed of it they kind of shot you if you did.

Choi was a rich man in a tower full of rich men. He lived and worked in the penthouse areas, three floors down from the summit. The very top was populated by giant servers where the rich could enjoy top-range VR entertainment pre- and post-mortem. A lot of pimsims lived in them. The poor called it "Top Heaven". Winged shapes flitted around the spire. Highly modified winged humans, the lower classes said, the angels of Top Heaven. In reality they were surveillance drones. Richards sweated under the oppressive heat of human-managed data systems, monitoring the city's population. Big Brother lived up top, not gods of any stripe.

Richards walked through crowded arcades and parks, past temples grown from gengineered trees. No one paid the android he wore a second glance as he plodded his way on, which was good, because it was slow and weak. His route took him up stairs and elevators, past spun diamond windows as large as lakes, through sculpted residential districts blended with terraced gardens and microhabitats, water gurgling from one ripple-lipped mirror pond to another. Where necessary, his way was opened by a phony People's Dynasty AllPass-equivalent that he'd first rigged up four years ago. He'd skimmed some hot software off the PD government site that kept it up to date. It was bizarre stuff: sometimes it behaved as if it were as aware as near-I, and spat invective at him in some odd machine code dialect he barely understood. But it was thoroughly cracked, and the data it provided hadn't failed him yet. On level 372, he used it to break a maintenance seal and ascended a staple-rung ladder up an endless service duct.

Before he emerged from the service duct near Choi's offices, he cracked the computer and inserted purchase details, delivery date and so on for his borrowed android sheath. He was now part of the staff. He peeked into Choi's diary; it was an hour after his weekly board meeting. As Richards had expected, Choi was alone.

He climbed into the offices via another hatch, convincing security it had never been opened.

Richards went towards the business's substantial kitchens, sourced the kitchen input, and presented a fake order for tea. He walked in as bold as brass. One of the staff handed him a tray with a pot of tea on it. As he left, the cook staff were wondering aloud who'd bought such a cheap piece of shit to serve Tony Choi. They unaniminously agreed they were glad it was none of them.

The guards at Choi's teak double doors did not pay him any attention as he stopped there and waited. He was just a drone going about his business.

The doors slid open.

Richards stepped into Choi's office with eleven minutes to spare. Not much time, but he didn't need much time.

Choi looked up from a sheet of calligraphy. He looked somehow old and sleekly fat, well groomed in an understated, obviously expensive mode; French suit and Indonesian shoes. He looked like a million other People's businessmen and 'crats, except that there was an indefinable otherness to him, past cartographies were etched upon his soul.

His healthtech-smooth face creased in a frown. "I ordered no tea," he said.

"Hello, Tony," said Richards, setting the tray down. "How are you doing?"

Chapter 16
The 36th Realm

Time and effort led Veronique, Jagadith and Tarquinius out of the swamp and to the foot of the hemispherical hill. Everything about it was gargantuan, a five-hundred-metre high dome of polished rock, the dimples in it twenty metres across and five deep in the centre. High above, the lowermost branches of the monkey puzzle tree hung a little way out over the swamp, its oversized, triangular needle-scales huge even from their distant perspective.

"It will be a task to climb this," said Jagadith.

"A task for me, you mean," grumbled Tarquinius. "I don't see either of you carrying mountaineering equipment."

Tarquinius rumbled deep in his chest, and gave out a short metallic cough. "You had better remain here. I will let down a rope when I attain the summit."

Jag slid off the mount's back, and lifted a hand up to the scowling anthropologist. "I am not totally incapable," she said.

"As you wish." He dropped his hand. He disliked dealing with educated women. They were so much trouble. He sighed in a way calculated to let the doctor know this. He could feel her glowering at his back. "Can we attempt the expulsion now?"

Veronique wasn't rising to the bait. "How are you going to climb that?" she said. "It's like glass."

"Indeed it is, madam divinity." Tarquinius stood up on his hind paws, pressed the soft metal pads of his forepaws against the cool stone. His claws popped from their sockets, long and gleaming as knives. "Number threes should suffice for the task at hand," he muttered. There was a series of clicks, and his claws turned to one side and pulled back into his feet. A new series came forth, threaded like drills, exquisitely moulded diamonds at their tips. "This will take a while, Jag. Let me take you up thirty or forty feet, and you may rest in one of these dimples out of harm's way."

"I am not keen on wasting time, dear friend, but so be it."

Tarquinius's claws began to spin. He held them for a moment above the rock's smooth surface, flexed his stubby leonine fingers and then thrust the first set of drills into the rock. There was a whine, sparks flew and Tarquinius's claws sank smoothly into the stone. He placed his second forepaw higher than the first, pushing his nails deep in, then hauled his back feet off the ground. One of these he pulled as high as he could, then forced the claws on that foot into the basalt. He then retracted his forepaws and, standing on his back foot, repeated the process. When he reached a sufficient height he stopped by one of the dimples and lifted his tail. A cable dropped down. Jag put his foot into a loop at the bottom, and bade Veronique do likewise. When they were secured, the rope ran smoothly up, pulled by a winch inside the lion. As soon as they were parallel to the dimple, Jag hung from Tarquinius' foot and hacked out a series of footholes with his sword. Then he worked his way into the centre. His sword flared bright as he turned it up to its maximum power setting, and he deftly sliced out a chunk of the dimple, creating a flat platform that he and Veronique might sit upon. He let it cool for what Veronique felt was an interminable ten minutes, as she swung over nothing. *A nothing made of nothing,* she thought, *how philosophically interesting that would be, if I weren't so fucking terrified.* Jag helped Veronique over, and they sat. Tarquinius retracted the rope fully and resumed his ascent.

"Will he be long?" asked Veronique, glad to be off the rope.

"The ascent is a long and hard one, most assuredly," affirmed the paladin. "But worry not, madam goddess. My steed is an excellent climber."

"I wasn't worried about him," she said. "Now what?"

"We rest."

Several hours passed. Veronique looked out at the stinking vista before her. The knight spent much of the time deep in a trance. Veronique was astounded when she realised he was floating five centimetres in the air, then for some reason profoundly disturbed by it. It gave her the horrible feeling that reality here was spongy, and that it might at any moment warp into something new, with her not necessarily a part of it. She looked away. When alert the knight was little inclined to talk to her, so she was left to her own thoughts, and these ran along the lines of:

Why did Qifang drag me into this unholy mess?

How do I get out of this unholy mess?

Just how real is this place?

Just how real does that make me?

The thoughts went round and round her head, worrying her deeply. She tried to sleep, but could not, so worried on some more.

None of this made sense. The paladins set to protect this reality believed Qifang was responsible for the changes being wrought here. She hadn't known what to expect when she arrived, but she thought she might have met with Qifang quickly. That he hadn't been there when she entered the Realm troubled her. It was possible that Qifang had lured her in with the data he'd left her, that in actuality he was responsible for the resources drain. But to what end? The only scenario she could come up with on that score was that he had some kind of wooing in mind, which frankly made her feel a little ill.

It couldn't be true. Qifang was man who had argued passionately for the rights of new life, whatever form it took: digital, hybrid, AI, cyborg or other. She remembered the first time she'd seen him, at a guerilla Neukind rights flash rally in Toronto. He'd been small, distant, a man tiny on the stage of the run-down Air Canada centre. She'd taken Chloe. She'd never agreed with slavery for the machines.

AIs were not tools, he said, they were not playthings for man to do with as he chose. Through his creations, mankind had the collective responsibilities of new parents. The days when desperate adults had a dozen children to help them make their way in the world were long gone, he argued. "We would never send a flesh and blood child up a chimney. We shudder when we think of the children of the Victorian era picking up threads in the dark spaces between unshielded machinery. We balk at the thought of twentieth-century sweatshops. Why treat the Neukind any different? Why should we slaughter them for sport? Force them to forever serve us? Send them alone to the ends of the universe? We are their progenitors. They may well outlive us all, and the surest form of immortality is for those who come after us to remember us fondly. Let not the human race be consigned to the fairy tales of the future, to become the ogres of tomorrow. Let us be good to our new children that they may pay their respects to us when we are no longer here."

His words were powerful. The cataclysm of the tip was receding into memory, wars were fizzling out as cold war took its place. The world was a place where people could cautiously feel comfortable in their outrage at their ancestors' mistakes.

Zhang Qifang had won a lot of supporters with his talk of children. He had seen the Neukind – AI, pimsims, post-humans, simulants, uplifted animals and so forth – as the true future.

He'd often said to her, later, when they had got to know each other, "Mankind has begun to save the planet from his mistakes, but it might already be too late to save itself." She'd shared his pessimism, at least some of the time; she'd seen plenty in her service time to vindicate Qifang's opinion.

She'd left the army and turned inwards; studying the thirty-six Realms fit that well. When the games had been running, the Realms had appalled her; whole civilisations of thinking creatures conjured into existence so humans could go and let the old beast out a little, practising war, rape, torture and other outrages. As a student, she'd joined others and protested their existence, Qifang their hero on his last great crusade. Then the UN's declaration had gone out; the Reality Realms were immoral and a social hazard. The doors were closed, the worlds had gone feral and that was that; they had been shut off fifteen years ago and new VR of the same intensity forbidden. The digital inhabitants of the thirty-six Realms had been the last of the Neukind to have been granted rights. It had been a difficult victory, but Zhang Qifang's support had swayed it. Sentient beings should not be created only to be killed for sport. Peace for Orcs, Rights for Elves. It sounded stupid when Jaffy said it that way; he'd meant it to.

Watching from outside had not given Valdaire a true picture of what it was like to immerse oneself fully in the Reality Realms. Being here was a visceral experience, accentuated to be even more real than real life. The world was so much cleaner, so much more vivid. She found it hard to believe that her body was elsewhere, sat in a chair in a cabin in the woods, slack-mouthed and plugged in. She held up her hand and examined it. It was better than real, stronger, cleaner of line and free of blemishes; it was an idealised version of her hand. It was not hard to see now how people had become dependent on the RWRR experience, not hard at all.

She sat and hugged her knees and bit her lip and looked out across to the jungle. Perhaps she'd followed him too easily, for the wrong reasons. She had always wanted to see the worlds at first hand. She'd just never allowed herself. She admitted when she applied that that's why she studied them – she'd had to, the psych profiling would have winkled out the truth in the end. But that she'd been strong enough never to plug in was what had got her the job.

Maybe that's why Qifang'd given her the viewing codes months ago. He was supposed to hold them for each researcher, but he'd said she needed to know everything. She was no longer sure of his motives.

She swallowed. Perhaps, perhaps if she just changed things a little. Just once, just to see what it was like. She'd resisted the temptation hard ever since she dropped into the Realms, maybe if she tried, she might understand better.

She looked over her shoulder. Jag was cross-legged, breathing deeply, lost in some inner world of his own. The act of creation of one world was never the creation of only one world, as each created so many more, the inner worlds of the minds of those inhabiting it leading on to the eventual creation of worlds like this in an endless cycle. All she'd do would be to take a more active part in that. She closed her eyes. She'd make something innocuous, something that already existed here, something small and harmless. She breathed deeply, imitating the man behind her. She pictured the creature in her mind, a Jexbu it was called. She'd seen it when she had been studying an island tribe on the far side of this Realm, a band of fish people created to provide foes for dungeon-bashing armchair adventurers.

The Jexbu was an eight-limbed thing, six of which were wings the colour of sapphires. She could see it in her mind's eye. Through the faded 3D of the mechanical turk workstation display it had taken her breath away. To see one in front of her would be wonderful.

She opened her eyes. Nothing. She took a deep breath, feeling a mixture of failure and relief. It was for the best.

There was the barest flicker of light, and the air rippled as if distorted, like a bulls-eye glass. A jexbu hung, frozen for a moment, before suddenly coming to life, beating its wings in pairs and fluttering away. The gentle wake from its wings stirred her fringe. Veronique was spellbound – it was beautiful, far more beautiful than the image she'd seen. Veronique could have been a woman of great feeling, but she'd learned that the world wasn't a great place for emotional people, so she sat on her heart tightly. Maybe it was being in the Realm, maybe it was the thought that people could create something as beautiful as that by thinking of it, but her defences trembled. Tears pricked at her eyes.

"Madam goddess," came Jagadith's reproachful voice. "Please be not doing such things. It is a slippery path to follow, you could soon be suffering from delusions of divine grandeur, and Tarqinius and I will have no choice but to set you free from our Realm, safely or by the sword." He tapped the blade across his knee. "Let us hope it does not come to that," he said warningly. He stood up, brushing some of the dried mud from his coat of plates. "Besides, your villainy may well have alerted your erstwhile teacher to our presence. Please be restraining yourself."

"I... I am sorry... I didn't mean..." She didn't know what to say. What had she been thinking?

Tarquinius' rope dropped over the lip of the dimple, saving her from Jagadith's disapproval.

"Aha! It appears Tarquinius has reached the summit. If you please, goddess, grasp the stirrup this time."

She did so, and the rope dragged them to the top, she and Jag holding the loop at the end of the rope and pushing themselves clear of the smooth rock with their feet.

Tarquinius threaded his way between the dimples of the summit toward the trunk of the monkey puzzle tree at the centre of the rock. The sun was sinking low in the sky again. Where the giant limbs of the tree allowed, its rays struck reds and golds of lustrous hue from the polished basalt, catching upon the tiny crystals that made up the whole, shattering it into a million small worlds of coloured fire.

"It appears our god favours sunsets," Tarquinius commented.

The tree was so vast that the minds of the travellers found it difficult to perceive it as a tree. Sometime the tree looked like a tree, until a giddy shift of perspective turned it into a ragged mountain, painted a variety of sinister greens. Out by the edge of the rockdome only the most adventurous fronds quested out above their heads, but as they worked their way inwards, the tree's limbs filled the sky, developing into a latticework of enormous, scaled leaves, the tree changing from a mountain to a dragon, breathing with the wind.

"This is anomalous!" roared Tarquinius. "Anomalous!"

Jag turned round and gave Veronique a stern look. "Do you see now? This is not the work of the man you describe. Can you not see that he has changed? I fear your professor has gone mad. This has gone beyond a mere case of expulsion. We will have to kill him."

Chapter 17
Hong Kong

"Richards, is that you? What the devil are you doing here? Have you gone mad?" Choi's eyes bulged so much Richards almost laughed, for Choi was a gentlemen of the utmost seriousness and would not have enjoyed how comical he looked. He sat there blinking slowly, like all his motion. Choi moved like a glacier. His hand hung in the air, and a large spot of ink dropped from his brush, marring his calligraphy.

"I thought you'd never guess," said Richards, flipping his hands out in a magician's flourish.

"Even in that thing it is obvious." Choi regained his composure, his face reverting to the bland expression he habitually wore. His English was perfect and spoken truly, unmoderated by intermediary software. His accent was clipped, and the unvoiced consonants common to East Asian languages were barely evident. Once upon a time, it had been fashionable for men with Eurasian ancestry to be educated in British public schools. Once. He was a relic. "No one I know is crazy enough to come in here unannounced, except you."

"Or clever enough to pull it off," said Richards.

Choi's eyes narrowed. "What do you want here?"

"Only information," said Richards, "about these machines."

He ran a holo from the android's built-in entertainment system, highlights of his recent encounters with the cydroids. The system was low-grade, the picture grainy. "Who built them?"

Choi set down his brush on a porcelain dish and regarded his marred work. "You disrespect me, arriving unannounced. More pertinently, you anger the Guangbo, coming and going in through the Firewall as if the sovereign cyberspace of China were a field at the end of your garden, and you have a hole in your hedge."

"In a manner of speaking, it is and I have," said Richards. "Come on, aren't you just the tiniest bit interested? These are near-human sheaths! Nothing like that is supposed to be out there. Choi, they've bridged the valley."

Choi blotted the ink stain on his art as if he had all the time in the world. "Be wary. The Guangbo have been waiting for you. They will be coming. Right now, I think. You have endangered us both. They will lock down your sensing presence and extradite you. You know that, of course, because you are so very intelligent." He stood, lifting the paper, and stalked around his desk to hang it up to dry against a light panel, where he stood regarding it critically. "You have ruined it."

"Sorry. Tell me who made these sheaths and why I haven't seen them before so I can get out of your hair before the authorities arrive."

"I must disappoint you."

"What are you saying? Are you telling me, that you, Tony Choi, that you don't know?"

"Leave." The man put one hand over the other; the lower hand was gripping his paintbrush hard.

"Tony, these chassis have the mark of one of your manufactories upon them." He displayed the relevant image. "A little careless, wouldn't you say?"

"I do not sell illegally, Richards."

"Come on, Tony." Richards paced round the room in the android, causing the holos it projected to jump over the walls like acrobats. The machine's cheaply woven joints squeaked as he went. He stopped by an ancient vase, walked on to the next piece. Art hung from much of the panelling, stood on pedestals, stared out from alcoves, a mix of eastern and western, a rich man's nicknacks; worth enough to buy a nation, tasteless fripperies for all that. Who the hell had a solid gold waving-good-luck cat other than Tony Choi? "You know everything there is to know about new tech. If someone's building it, you're selling it. Who's been working on these machines?"

"I said I don't know."

Richards turned to look at Choi. "Even this low-rent floor sweeper has decent enough sensors to tell me that you're lying. You can't lie to a Five, Tony, not when you're as bad a liar as you are. And you owe me. That Taipei Freeport bust? I wonder how the interior ministry would look on that." He walked back across the room to Choi's desk. Another holo played alongside the looping footage from the boat and morgue, pulled up from Richards' imagination, Choi in custody, surrounded by uniformed men and sharp implements. What they were doing to him was not nice. "I believe smuggling narcotics up the space elevator is illegal. But I have a somewhat lurid fancy. Perhaps we should ask a policeman?" The sheath's arms whirred loudly as Richards leaned on the wall by the drying paper. "And how is Mrs Choi anyway? What would she think?"

Choi's face remained impassive.

Richards pulled up the image of the logo he'd seen at the coroner's again: Choi Industries' stamp. "You sold this chassis."

Choi exhaled loudly, and most of his anger seemed to go with it. "Richards, I sell many such frames." Choi walked back to his desk, picked up a second cloth folded by the neatly laid out instruments of his art, and wiped his fingers free of ink. A smear of black stained the white, to match that on his perfectly manicured hands. Small hands, rounded with fat, clogged with garish rings, but powerful in their way. "Thousands a year; I have no way of knowing who might purchase them second-hand, or through a front company. That is what you are going to ask me."

Richards laughed, a rich noise for such cheap plastic. "Right."

Choi shook his head. "You have much nerve, coming here, implying that you will blackmail me. I paid you well for Taipei. You know what I am, Richards. I have been most useful to you in the past. It is unprofessional to complain."

"Needs must."

Choi frowned, shook his head and turned to the holos Richards was playing. "That is Zhang Qifang, is it not? The man, the machine, in the holovideo?"

"Yes."

"And these you show me, they are machines, you say? Not clones, or flesh-sculpted doubles?"

"That's right."

"I assume he is dead."

"You assume correctly. I am investigating his murder; three of them, possibly four."

"You should have said first." He became saddened, as if he had long been expecting the news. "I have heard nothing."

"It's being kept quiet. Some of the more, uh, militant elements among my brethren are going to take it badly."

"He was a brilliant man." Choi looked at the teapot Richards had delivered, as if debating whether or not it was to blame. After a moment he set down the cloth, poured himself a cup of tea and raised it. "To one of the great minds of our time."

"If you respect him that much, you'll help me out."

Choi nodded.

Encouraged, Richards went on. "This technology, it's supposed to be fifty years away. This says otherwise. I need to know who is half a century early."

Choi looked up into Richards' visual receptors, small gems of glass set close together in the android's carbon-weave face. "Very well," he said resignedly. "I will tell you what I know, but it is not much."

"I would welcome any information."

"Then you will owe me," said Choi. "Four days."

"Three," said Richards. The timer of Northern Bandit's was counting quickly down. Five minutes remaining.

"Very well. Three days. I will hold you to it."

"I am sure you will. Now talk."

Choi set his cup down. "I am not sure. I have heard… reports. Nothing concrete, nothing certain. There's some talk coming out of the containment facilities in Nevada, the Reality Realm House, the place they moved the RealWorld hardware to when the UN shut them down."

"And?"

"Things like this: that they have several high-level AIs working full time as futurists, using the spare capacity of the Realms' servers freed up by the destruction of four of the Realms for mathematical prognostication."

"Yeah, k52 is leading them. It's common knowledge."

"You will also know then that it's all supposed to be theoretical. This kind of fully autonomous emulant is one of the areas they have been investigating." He nodded toward the holo. "Imagining is perhaps the more appropriate word, plotting possible future developments, examining potential new tech, providing probabilities to feed out to the entertainment industry, better to accelerate k52's 'Fiction Effect' by providing inspiration for what is readily achievable, tier-two projects like this. But I had not heard that they had built anything. These machines match some of the descriptions and file blueprints I have, ah" – he shrugged, as if to shuck off any implication of impropriety – "acquired. They were incomplete, unusable. No one could have constructed the things you have shown me from the information I have."

"Someone has," said Richards. "The Realm House is administered by the VIA. Why would they be interested in investigating the creation of something that would let people like me blend in? They like us where we are, nice and visible."

"Richards." Choi wagged a finger. His smile broadened. "Your intelligence fails you. Care of the Realms was recently handed over to Gencorp."

"Hey, I've been busy," Richards protested, irritated at being caught out. "Cost cutting, eh?"

"Private firms offer better deals, simple economics. Government agencies suck a state dry, and USNA is poor, has been since the Midnight Dollar Coup. The VIA still provides security, however; the UN would not let them give that up. You really did not know this had happened?"

"Realm stuff rarely comes up in my line of work. They're closed off, and anything untoward that goes down there is VIA business. I keep well clear of it. Asking about them draws too much heat off the agency. They're a pretty touchy bunch, and I am a Five. I don't want them in my business any more than they want me in theirs. They look at me funny, you know what I mean?"

Choi watched the holos of Richards' encounters with the cydroids for a few moments. "These sheaths are hardly perfect, one could argue."

"Why would the VIA sanction their building? It makes less sense if they're imperfect, they're even more likely to get caught out."

"Listen to what is said, Richards. I never said the VIA or Gencorp had built them. To build them is not why they investigate, they investigate such things to anticipate their development. It is a matter of apprehension, they do it simply to *know* and perhaps in the VIA's case to *detect* them should someone build them."

"Could it be Gencorp?" Richards considered for a moment. "No, no, I don't buy that, not under the VIA's nose. And why are they trying to kill each other?"

Choi raised his eyebrows in query.

"Long story."

"I am only aware that their theoretical possibility is slightly less theoretical and slightly more possible than most people are aware. But in these times, that is to be expected, things change so quickly, it is as if the world is being pulled out from under our feet every second day," said Choi.

"Interesting times, eh?"

Choi narrowed his eyes. "I do not bandy cliché, Richards. I also do not believe I have told you anything that you have not already discerned for yourself. I have not been offered any such 'cydroids' for sale, either in physical or plan form. All I have are these scraps brought to me by my operation."

"Right, OK, thanks," said Richards. "This destruct mechanism." Richards brought up technical detail on the skeletons and electron scope level views of the cydroid's carbons.

"The weaving is fine, is it not? A good product." Choi leaned in closer to them. "But the better looms will give you such a finish. I see little else unusual about these constructs other than the biological component and these artificial cerebra. This is otherwise a standard combat endoskeleton, self-motivated. This carbon, it is a simple atomic lattice, not neo-diamond or any of the other harder artificial matrices. Tough, but unremarkable, not particularly strong. We have several tens of thousands in the people's liberation army, many of which I procured for the state." He shrugged.

"The self-destruct item," said Richards, pressing his point. Three minutes.

"Again, it is a standard stock item; unusual, but by no means unique. It's relatively new, but it's not been altered from the factory model, if that is what you are asking me. The acid only works on the looser lattices – it won't damage diamond weave, it is far too tough."

"But...?"

Choi clucked his tongue. "It is strange to see such unusually advanced biotechnology married to something like this, that is all. As utile as my product is, I would expect..."

Richards finished his sentence. "That they would have made more of an effort with the internals? Proper diamond weave, or actual grown bone? Me too."

Choi blinked his long, slow blink. "It is remarkable. Off the shelf combat droid skeleton with this organic shell, one so far in advance of the other."

"Is that all you know?"

"That is all."

Richards looked at Tony's round face for a long minute, searching out the lies. The little man held his gaze, his own expression flat and unreadable. Richards could see no evidence of untruthfulness on the surface. He regretted grabbing such a cheap sheath. He'd lied to Choi; the infrareds on it were not sensitive enough to pick out capillary dilation, they were sufficient to monitor the temperature of hot beverages, and that was about all. He felt cheap, cheap in front of Tony Choi. "I am disappointed Tony, I thought if anyone would know of a suspiciously advanced new unit primed for infiltration it would be an amoral criminal bastard like you."

Choi snorted. "I am flattered, but I am only a merchant. I buy and I sell what is available to be bought and to be sold... Perhaps if you would allow me to check my databases, I may be able to track the transaction..." He shrugged; it didn't matter at all to him. "It will take a minute, if the client was a special one, or the chassis changed hands, perhaps longer, if at all," he warned. "I will at least try." He moved over to a panel fronted by a garish fourteenth-century vase. It rotated as he approached, to reveal a flat glass-topped workstation, fully manual. Choi didn't trust anyone, numbers or meat, with his deepest secrets. It was probably connected to the Grid via an unwitting proxy. Somewhere, thought Richards, is a little old lady scratching her head over her band charges. "The catalytic acid destruct system should make it easier to track down. Please, take a seat."

"I'll stay leaning, this thing doesn't do sitting."

"Lean then."

"Next time I'm going more upmarket. I was in something of a hurry." Richards had a thought. "Hey, you're not stalling for time, are you, Choi? You're not trying to sell me out here, are you?"

"Why would I do that?" Choi said mildly, tapping at the workstation's glass table top, moving documents round on it, pinching those that interested him from there and lifting them into the air, where they hung as holographs. "Would you mind?" he said, indicating the still active holo.

"Yeah, sure." Richards remoted the data over to Choi's machine. Choi's fingers worked faster, moving icon to icon, initiating a search.

"I know the value of things," Choi said, "You are much more valuable to me at liberty than you are in the gracious care of our glorious Dynasty of the People."

"Good, because I sealed your mainframe off from the Grid. There's a blind copy running as cover. Nothing you've been trying to send to the authorities has made it out."

Choi looked up momentarily, mildly insulted. "If I have been trying to contact the authorities."

"If." Richards' borrowed beaklike head moved to one side, listening to something Choi could not hear. "So you wouldn't know about the AI snatch squad sat outside your virtual real estate then?" There were several high-end code-breakers in the Grid. Richards cursed inwardly. They'd appeared out of nowhere. They swam back and forth, long trails of information stretching back into the churn of the Grid connecting them to their handlers, waiting as something big and nasty hammered away at Richards' fake mainframe. The code-breakers left themselves open, trying to tempt Richards to commit more of himself to cracking them and reading their secrets, to see if, maybe, high end AIs had survived the pogroms and hid behind information streams instead of men, enthralled to the state. It was tempting, but that was the idea. He wasn't that naive.

"I..." began Choi. He stopped, sipped his tea from the thimble-like cup, its ceramics patterned with tiny cracks that suggested an age greater than gunpowder. "Of course. Why should I lie? You are right to an extent, I did know that they were coming. I had hoped we would be done before they arrived. They are getting faster." He placed the cup down on the top of his workstation. "There is a discrete system here, in this room, fitted by the interior ministry. It bypasses the main Grid, a direct pipe. They were summoned a few moments after you arrived by patterns evident in our conversation." He glanced at the waving-good-luck cat meaningfully. *Not so lucky for me*, thought Richards. "It was not my decision. I said you should not have come."

"You have sold me out."

"If you wish to look at it in that way, that is your prerogative. Non-compliance was... inadvisable. As you say, needs must as the devil drives."

"You said you did not bandy cliché."

Choi shrugged again.

"You could have warned me. I'm minded to kick your ass. I could, you know, even in this." Richards steeled himself. They'd got through the first few layers of armour he'd laid into the building's cyber-structure; he was a whisker away from being directly attacked. The shield he had up round the mainframe prevented the Chinese entities hooking him, but any second now they'd start causing him genuine inconvenience.

Choi took another deliberate sip of his tea. "Of course. I am only a man, Richards." There was a banging at the door, then rustling, then a high-pitched whine, then shouting, then nothing. Choi's eyes flicked over to the door. "They knew you were here from the first moment you penetrated the wall. They are very keen to, ah, entertain you. To deny your presence here would cause me much trouble; as it is I will have to suffer several long hours of questioning because I personally did not alert the authorities."

"I bet you tried."

"Your false mainframe was effective. What did you expect? But I have helped you."

"It cost me, as I remember."

"Nevertheless, you have caused me a great deal of inconvenience. It is only because Qifang is involved that I have spoken to you. Without him I would have left you high and dry, but in this instance I could argue national honour is at stake. And the news will be of interest to the PDG."

"Why, thanks." Choi had done his best, fair enough, but Richards was in no mood to be generous. "You are one shit of a mercenary."

"Do not scorn me, I have done you more than one service today. You are valuable to me, Richards, true. I am more valuable to myself, I'm sure you understand." He pursed his lips, light from the desktop playing over his face as he ran through a year's worth of accounting in half a second. "We could have arranged a more convenient... a safer" – he stressed the word, – "venue to meet, but that is not your way, and if they catch you, then you must live with it yourself."

"I won't forget this." Richards said it harshly for the benefit of the waving cat. Tony Choi would know he meant differently. Or not, it didn't really matter.

"I did tell you that you were crazy to come here," said Choi mildly.

A dull crump of a concussion charge, and the door blew in. Choi tutted at the damage. He flicked a fragment of antique wood from his sleeve, and turned back to his workstation. The false shell Richards had erected round Choi's systems collapsed under a storm of attack code, vanishing like a mirage to reveal the real item, dumb and panicking like a frightened horse, shrieking with alarms. The angry presences in the Grid outside surged in triumphantly and immediately assailed Richards.

"Richards," said Choi, not looking up, as idly as a man passing the time at a bus stop.

Richards heard him through a storm of Grid noise. "What?" he shouted. Trying to hear his own voice over the rush of hostile numbers was near impossible.

"I have a name. Peter Karlsson. It was he who bought the chassis, from me directly. I am sorry for the delay. Go and speak to him, he should know something. Goodbye, Richards."

Richards grinned inside. Tony always came through. "See you soon, Tony." Then, for the cat's benefit: "Fuck Chairman Mao."

Masked troopers stormed into the room, bulky with power assist armour. Guns at the ready, they circled Richards' sheath and trained their weapons upon it.

Northern Bandit's downloads ceased. The connection was cut, the sheath sagged, Richards was gone. There were a lot of people pointing guns at an inert and offensively cheap android.

All around Tower Thirty-six, the Grid space of the People's Republic of Greater China roiled with fury.

Outside the Great Firewall, Richards woke up in a field surrounded by curious cartoon rabbits as big as groundcars. He stood up, and his fake tour group swirled to nothing. He made sure the dragons were watching and flicked a V at the wall. He hoped the PD government would not go hard on Tony. Richards would never trust Tony, but he'd need him again. In truth, the People's Dynasty probably felt the same way. Richards decided not to visit him in his office for a while.

He went home.

Richards secure-piped himself back to the office in the Wellington Arcology – a little under the speed of light when you took all the trickle and shunt into account – and remanifested himself in his fake office overlooking his fake version of ancient Chicago. He rubbed at his neck. His head felt off, splitting himself like that, and the sudden disconnection had left him disoriented. He needed a drink and a think.

First he attended to the chip fragments from Otto and Valdaire's Grid. He'd had a bunch of tailored near-I reassembling the fragments for the last three days, and they pestered him as clerks banging on the half-glass door, yammering that they were finally done. He took the results as paper from an eager, code-generated office junior, and slumped into his chair. The chip was incomplete, but quantum traces in the reconstruction suggested Qifang had fashioned a key, one that mimicked permissions from two separate sources. As the v-jack cases at UCLA needed three signatories for opening, that was pretty straightforward. Richards had been right.

Valdaire's trail was harder to crack. He shut his eyes and concentrated on his diffuse parts. Many of his scales had been killed, others had turned up nothing. Some, there were always some, had hit home. She'd fabricated a wide-band Grid cheater, a self-replicating machine devil, a sophisticated variant of those favoured by the Nigerian gangs, cyclically employing false IDs and actively screwing with security software. Its coding was illegal, really illegal, high-end criminal stuff empowered with cracked military cyberwarfare capsids, doubtless of Valdaire's devising. It was so illegal, in fact, that he informed Hughie by way of the million-layer EuPol bureaucracy that he had it in his possession.

He didn't trust Hughie not to use it against him when it suited him if he kept it quiet.

Coding like that took care and deliberation. There was no way she could have knocked it up before going on the run. Like deactivating the Six at UCLA, she'd cooked that up earlier. Intention for the v-jack robbery, or insurance? Hard to say. It was slippery as hell, and the virtualities he constructed to replicate and crack it imploded one after another, murdered by the reproduced virus. Frustrated, he persisted.

Version 13,078 gave him a valid simulation of her blocker, self-hate protocols deactivated. From it he estimated a spread of likely anchor points it would use to plug into the Grid, and the residual code patterns it would leave on the skin of the virtual world. There was no finding Valdaire, but she'd not been able to bring herself to kill her PA.

Chloe had copied herself off the net, fragging her main iteration and back-up in the process, copying her core programming into Valdaire's phone. She'd been careful, arguably more careful than Valdaire, but it was impossible for something like Chloe to sever all her ties with the machine world. Even weak AI needed some part of herself free floating in Grid space to unfold her and think. That's ultimately how the scales had found her. She had been expecting the tail, had spread herself thin, and was disorienting the scales with a barrage of locational information, spinning out some nasty programme of Valdaire's. Otto's adjutant couldn't tell where Chloe was on the Grid or the Real, but with the help of Richards' scales, it did narrow the phone's location down to a corner of Colorado.

Valdaire should have destroyed Chloe. He tagged her with a couple of scales. Finding her precise location would be down to Otto now; there was no more he could do from here.

It was a serious piece of forensic reconstruction. He was pleased with it.

Outside, ancient Chicago rained its rain and tooted its antique groundcar horns.

He decanted a glass of single malt that had no counterpart in the Real. He called Otto, but got no answer. Genie intercepted the call and gave Richards a non-verbal interjection that told him Otto had gone off-Grid. Richards congratulated her on her task management via the same method. For an ex-person, she was learning quickly.

Never mind, Richards had made preparations for that. Otto liked to work unobserved. Richards left the codes and reconstruction data for Otto in one of the many anonymous info-drop sites they used, and sat back, dirty shoes on the scuffed leather of his desk. He took a sip of his drink.

"Ah," he said, happily.

Real or not, Richards liked his whisky.

Chapter 18
Colorado

Otto gridded the area on a map, did it the old way, asking place to place. Photo; "Have you seen this woman?" Frowns, shakes of the head, no recognition. On to the next drugstore, the next truckstop, the next one-street town, everything face-to-face. He drove roads that led from from verdant peaks to humid lowlands that remained deserts only in name. Temperatures went from hot to hotter as he went up then down, again and again, over the wrinkles of the Rockies. He didn't know how to dress; the climate control of the groundcar struggled. The terrain was too treacherous for turbofan aircars, dangerous thermals came off the mountains, too many storms blew in off the distant Pacific. The only aircraft Otto saw were fixed wings, blimps and quaint rotary copters far off, navigation lights flashing against the angry skies, hurrying against the threat of the weather. The local radio carried crash stories in every county.

He stopped at a charge station high in the mountains, isolated on the road, trees for company. The valley where the charge station stood was precipitous and shaded for much of the day, so its solar cells glinted brash in the afternoon sunlight on the slopes above, thick cables curving lazily from pylon to pylon down to the cabin-store by the carriageway.

Otto pulled up, the wheels of the groundcar crunching on forecourt gravel. The whisper of the engine died off, then nothing but birdsong and the wind in the trees. He yawned. He rotated his shoulder and grimaced. The pain was insistent. He had his healthtech dull it to a low discomfort.

The air was clean, damp with the morning rain; sharp with old pines and the quick sap of the broadleaves challenging them. For a moment, he relaxed. Nature calmed him, the smell of the green and the rain and the rustle of growing things, not a machine in sight.

He could sleep here. He probably should.

He scooped the photograph off the dashboard, and got out.

"Her, yeah, sure, came in about a month back. Bought a lot of sugar." The attendant was oily, greasy hair, grubby rock T-shirt whose logo had stopped working. There were a number of run-down vehicles out back. This guy was a one-man show, mechanic and till attendant in one. There were no traces of anyone else. A loner.

"Sugar?"

"Yeah, sugar. You know, for your coffee. And two big bags of salt."

"Are you sure?"

"Salt, like that," he pointed to a row of sacks. "Yes. I'm sure," he said defensively. "Not many people like her come up here. Salt's for the hunters, some like to preserve their kills the old way."

"Quirkies."

"Sorry?"

"Quirkies. Those trying to live pre-industrial lives."

"Right, quirkies, huh? That what you call them in..."

"Europe."

"Yeah. OK. They're kind of like that, like your quirkies. I sell them that amount, and more; of salt, I mean. But not women like her, not usually. She was a city lady, all right. Say, where're you from?" He smiled. "Europe's a big place."

"I am German."

"And..." – a wave round Otto's body.

"I am a cyborg."

"Military, huh?"

"Ex."

"I was service myself, once, long time ago. US Army." The attendant stood a little taller. "But you guys, man. I seen some things but cyborgs rocketing in? That beats it all."

"We do not use that insertion method in our army," said Otto flatly. The attendant was not to be discouraged.

"Hell, but we're all on the same side. You in Brazil?"

"Yes."

"Hell of a place."

Otto tapped the photograph. The creased paper used the kinetic energy to run through four seconds of footage, Valdaire dolled up, wineglass in hand, laughing, a happy night out. "Her. Do you know where I can find her?"

"Lot of cabins round here, lots of off-the-Grid types." The attendant jutted his chin out the window and hooked his thumbs into his belt. "Hey, man, you want to be careful, there's some serious crazies up here. Some of them been waiting for the end of the world for fifty years, their folks a hundred years before them."

Otto nodded. Maybe they wouldn't have to wait long. He was in the mood for a fight. "I can take care of myself."

"Yeah, I s'pose so."

"If you were her, where would you go to avoid such encounters?"

The man ran his fingers through his dirty beard. "Let me think... You know, I'm sure she said she was heading out Flagstaff way."

In that case she was probably going the opposite direction. "What lies in the opposite direction?" he asked.

"Not much till you hit Phoenix if you head off route 17. Payson and Showlow if you follow 270 to the east through the parks."

"Anything near here? To the west, up in the forest?"

"Nothing. The lake, the falls down there in the valley," he shrugged. "Nothing. Just trees and nature, man, the way I like it, y'know?"

Otto did not speak. His lack of warmth was bothering the attendant. His smile faded. "You're hiding something," he asked.

"What?" said the attendant. His cheeks coloured.

"What did she do?"

"Hey, man! She came in, she bought stuff, she paid, she left. No biggy."

Otto pressured the man to let him see the store records. He resisted. The AllPass swung it. "A cop," the man muttered, cowed and unfriendly. Otto pulled his files; the attendant had a record, not the first ex-soldier to have run-ins with the law.

Valdaire was not on the store logs. Her smartcard or phone had presented a false identity at the behest of the blocker, one that would have been changed immediately the transaction had been completed and smothered with false leads. A faint trace, no good, dead end.

Still Otto's near-I adjutant indicated the man was prevaricating: high heartrate, pheromones off, perspiration up, pupils too big. Not an outright lie, a lie of omission. "What else?" demanded Otto.

The attendant backed away for a moment, looked like he was considering reaching for something, a weapon maybe, then looked into Otto's stony face and thought better of it. The man's eyes darted left to right. "Look, man, I watched her, OK? Just for a while. I didn't mean no harm by it. She left her car here and went for a walk in the woods, stretching her legs or somesuch. I only watched. No women come up here. Not ever. A guy gets lonely. Thought I might ask her for a date, down at the local dance. She said she liked to dance when she saw the poster there" – he pointed past Otto's head. Otto did not move his gaze from the man – "but I ain't got the nerve, city lady like that."

"Where did she go?"

"There's a path here, a local beauty spot, goes down to the falls. It's why I'm here, passing trade, you know? She went there, came back. I didn't watch her the whole time. I ain't got the nerve." He looked ashamed.

Otto stared down at the man, motionless. He reached into his sports jacket for his wallet. The attendant managed to control his flinch.

"Thank you." Otto picked up his picture, paid for the car's charge, added some vat-grown jerky and a couple of chocolate bars to his bill. He disliked American candy – it was all sugar, no cocoa in the chocolate – but he needed to eat something, and there was precious little else in the station. These people ate shit. "I am going to the falls. Do not follow me." He stymied all further attempts at small talk, upsetting the attendant's attempts to cover up for his lapse in bravery, and left.

Otto thought carefully before he tied himself back into the Grid. Chloe had to be here. It was worth the risk. He activated his mentaug's full capabilities and reluctantly booted up his augmented reality overlay. With annoyance he swatted a dozen adverts from the air and spent three minutes updating his filters. The path to the waterfall was signposted clearly on the AR, about 300 metres down the road from the station. He followed the blinking directionals to a series of steps down from the road. Wooden sills packed with earth, they were well-maintained, hemmed in with split log railings. Evidently a popular spot. The slope was steep. Otto walked down the steps, scanning the woods as he went. He was alone, nothing but birds in these woods. The splash of the falls became audible about halfway down. Otto went to the bottom and stood on the oval viewing platform by the riverside. The mountain was faulted, a knife-mark slash picked out with ferns and mosses growing in the damp air. The river was small, a child could have jumped it; but the falls were high, a drop of fifteen metres or so to a brown-black plunge pool fringed with more mossy rocks. The opposite bank was steeper than the slope he'd come down, almost a cliff. He doubted Valdaire would have crossed the river to climb that. She'd have tried for somewhere less visible and more accessible. He turned and walked back up the steps. He stopped at one or two likely looking places, his near-I running tracking software, but it had been raining heavily all the previous day, and any genetic trace of Valdaire that might have remained had long since washed away.

He walked on, stopped again where the slope levelled off a little. There, what could be a footprint, a mark in the lee of a tree within easy grasping distance of the trail. The steps curved off away from the direction the footprint pointed. This could be it.

Otto grasped the railing, positioned himself so he was looking past the print. He steeled himself, and began to activate Richards' software.

Technically, no AI was allowed to make a copy of itself. Artificial intelligences had been granted the right to life on a par with that of a human on one condition, that they lived as humans – unique, a single entity, mortal. Such a stricture made it easier to apply the law to them; there were no struggles with who was really who. The law had not proven hard to enforce. The higher AIs' Gridsigs were exceptionally strong and could be hidden for a time, but duplication set up unique wave patterns that were easily intercepted. Batteries of lesser machines run by the VIA and similar authorities constantly scanned the

Grid for infringements. No one wanted a repeat of the Five crisis, the remaining Fives included.

AIs could split themselves into a variety of subsidiary minds, but these were unstable, prone to distraction and difficult to interface with. They, too, were illegal, mostly because an AI that broke itself into parts stood a good chance of driving itself insane as its mind attempted to reconcile multiple subjective experiences of one event. Watching such things from multiple viewpoints they could handle, but thinking of them as multiple experiences was dangerous. Turned out the universe wasn't as concrete as people thought.

Richards did not always play by the rules.

Otto was off-Grid. Richards could not aid Otto directly without revealing the German's location. That did not mean that he could not aid Otto indirectly.

Richards had shaved off the merest sliver of himself, small enough to remain unnoticed, bright enough to help. Boxed in by task-specific programming and near-I adjuncts, detached from Richards' information stream, it was not properly aware, and Richards had what tiny thinking part it possessed sleeping in case it got ideas above its station.

"I'll be having weird dreams for a few weeks after this," Richards had said when they'd last spoken. "But it will allow you to see. You'll be able to sense my scales like I do. If you're close enough to it physically, you should be able to find the phone, so get yourself close as you can, and plug in."

He could only risk connecting up like this once or twice, because it was, as Richards had succinctly put it, dropping the PI act for the moment, "really fucking dangerous for meat minds to go raw on the Grid".

Otto drew a deep breath. He didn't think he was going to get much closer than he was now.

Otto, through this small part of Richards, would be able to

feel the scales, also part of Richards. But to do that he'd have to see the world the way that Richards did. That's what was going to give Otto the mother of all migraines. If his head didn't pop.

He procrastinated for a minute. "*Verdammt,*" said Otto, and activated the software.

The universe exploded out of the back of his head as Otto was joined to the Richards-sliver through his mentaug. The AR overlay vanished in a swirl of colour, and his near-I valet flickered out, a candle in a firestorm. Otto's perception of the Real receded and ceased.

Otto was lost in a howling maelstrom of information. His mind stretched as he attempted to accommodate even a fraction of it. He was blind, deaf and dumb, but other, stranger senses unfurled themselves at exponentially increasing rates as his awareness spread itself over the Grid.

With an effort of will, Otto stopped and reeled his mind back in, before he disassociated forever and was lost. The Grid was too big and there was not enough of him to embrace it all. His mind would smear itself across the virtual world until it was so dispersed as to be non-existent. He pulled his sense of being back into a shape that approximated his perception of himself. Struggling against the tempest, he moved forward. Ahead, shivering in a haze of knowledge, flashed a pair of ideograms representing the pair of Richards' scales that had tagged Chloe. A vortex of disinformation blurred them, but they were there. Otto dragged himself toward their location. There was a thundering in the ether about him, a howl of numbers. Before his ego shattered into atoms, he pulled the plug.

A cursor blinked. A checklist scrolled out below it. Icons filled a space, and a sense, not of words exactly, but of pure meaning, informed: "Cyborg unit 977/321-a1. Leutnant Otto Franz Klein.

Incept date 13th May 2102. Reboot. Online. Near-I adjutant model 47 'Tiberius'. Reboot. Online. Systems operating at seventy-eight percent of optimal. Warning, maintenance required."

Otto's native senses returned shortly after. For once he was spared the mentaug's merciless reminiscences. The scent of loam and ferns filled his nostrils. Birds sang somewhere. He rolled onto his back and opened his eyes. He spat soil and twigs from his mouth. He sat up and rubbed his head, dislodging more earth from his hair. His head throbbed. His visual systems cycled through the spectrum as they recalibrated themselves. This, very aggressively, did not help his headache.

"Arrrr," he said, which did not help either.

He'd moved. He was on his hands and knees, covered in mud and plant material, fifty metres into the forest, out of sight of the walkway down to the falls. He turned, and looked behind him. His head reeled with vertigo as he knelt and began to dig.

Less than thirty centimetres down he came across a geckolock plastic bag. He unzipped it and pulled out a phone. It was small, slate-grey. Very businesslike, though a large animated flower decal on the top with the near-I's name glittering within its petals undid the effect.

Sentimental, he thought.

He flipped up the lid and pressed the "on" switch. The phone remained inactive, both top and lower screens inert, the same grey as the case.

"Wake up, Chloe," he said. "I know you can hear me." He'd been speaking to machines all of his life, yet out here in the woods talking to the phone felt faintly obscene. "Tell me where I can find Veronique Valdaire."

Chloe said nothing.

Chapter 19
The 36th Realm

Toward the tree the light of day disappeared to be replaced by a blue gloaming. The sun must have gone down by the time they finally reached the trunk, or so Jag surmised, but the dim blue light remained, shed from nowhere.

The trunk was on an incomprehensible scale. They found themselves looking at a series of stepped, triangular plates of bark, built up to make the skin of the plant like a world-sized pineapple, with cracks as big as caverns in between.

"I don't understand," said Veronique, her voice a hush in the arboreal silence, "why a monkey puzzle tree?"

"I believe the good professor is joshing with us, asking that we play Jacks upon his beanstalk," said Jagadith. Both were whispering. The tree intimidated them.

"No, he is also letting us know we are beneath him, presenting us with a vegetable to perplex an ape," added Tarquinius, his voice loud and unafraid, "condescending bastard."

"Did I not mention that I have a doctorate?" said Veronique icily. "My point is that it is out of character. Professor Qifang would never have spoken down to someone so, or used such a crass visual metaphor."

"I am thinking you may be in for a shock," said Jagadith.

"You will find his character much changed. Godhood has a terrible karmic influence upon a man's soul."

"Don't be surprised if he starts maniacally ranting either," added Tarquinius. "They always do that."

"Quite," said Sir Jagadith.

As activated by Jagadith's voice, a man stepped out from behind one of the oversized plates of bark. He came one freakishly long leg first, foot placed delicately, to land pointed toes first. A white gloved hand followed, fingers waggling, to grasp the edge of the bark, then another, then a smarming face dripping with oleaginous scorn appeared. His body came next, extracting itself from the crack with the slippery rush of a fatal confession.

The man stood there before them, suddenly revealed. He was impossibly thin, clad in Edwardian black, long coattails flapping, shining black shoes covered by white spats, torso covered by a striped black and yellow waistcoat of a kind once favoured by gentlemen's gentlemen. His gloves had three brass buttons upon them that served no real purpose, aesthetic or otherwise. His hair was plastered to his scalp with macassar oil, parted to reveal a luminous scalp. He had a moustache so thin and heavily waxed it appeared painted on. His face actually was painted, bright white, with two rosy spots stamped onto each cheek. His eyes were mad, his capering wild. He had the demeanour of a maitre d' who regarded himself as so far above the others' station one needed a metaphorical radio telescope just to see him. He had an outrageous French accent to match.

"*Bonsoir*, Chevalier, Monsieur Lyon, et M'selle Veronique! Ah! I thought it may be you when I sensed ze creation of new life only today. Very intrepid. Very bold. Maintenant, 'ow may I elp you zis fine eevning?"

"Sweet lord, he's gone frog," said Tarquinius.

"It is worse than we feared," said Jagadith. He drew his sword. "Stand aside," he said loudly. "We seek entrance to the

Realm of the god who dares set himself above our world and remake it so. Do not attempt to stop us."

"Oh, such a pity." The Frenchmen cradled his pointed chin in his hand and pulled an apologetic moue. "I do not zink zat weel be possible." He capered a quick flourish, then was suddenly still, his coattails whipping.

"This does not bode well," said Tarquin. "And to think you mocked me for my concern."

"I don't understand. I mean, surely you can deal with him? He's not really there, even by your terms," said Veronique.

"But he is, madam goddess scientist," said Jag, turning in the saddle to face her. His face was lit by the glow of his sword, deathly grey in the twilit world of the tree. "That is part of your professor."

"Part? I don't understand, I thought that we could only create false life in your world. How can he possibly be part of Qifang?"

"He has split himself," said Jagadith.

"Like an AI?"

"After a fashion, though the creation of such as this does not involve the division of the mind, as it would for an AI. We've not seen it since the early days. A long time ago, the time of the first Wars-with-Gods," said Tarquin. "It's not supposed to be possible now. But we can see it. His signature stinks of binary cloning. It is him, but it is not. It means he can be in two places at once, and not in a figurative, nor in a purely mechanistic, sense."

The Frenchman clapped slowly. "*Bon, bon,* very good. I see why ah 'ave not been able to deactivate you. You really are ze best, it is true. Ze legendary maharajah and 'is lyon! Ah, but it is something like from legende! Exquisite. So, bold *guerriers,* you 'ave a choice. You may turn back, and, in due course, ah will come to you and we may discuss the nature of your servitude in ma new werold order."

"Why are you doing this?" said Veronique.

The Frenchman flung his arms out and looked himself up and down. "Why not? A little theatre is an essential part of being a god, *non*?"

"Jag, we cannot let this buffoon distract us. I don't like it," said Tarquinius. "His intention to delay us is succeeding."

"Monsieur," said Jagadith, "I am assuming you were about to tell us that our other option was death?"

"*Oui, oui. Exactement.*" The Frenchman nodded, and stroked at his moustaches.

Jagadith shrugged, "I thought as much. Please, be hearing me clearly now. I have been doing this for many years. So, I am respectively asking you if we may skip the rest of your monologue and move onto the part where we kill you and go about our way."

"*Mais oui*! 'Owever, I am not so sure it will go the way you expect."

"Now, Jag, now!" Tarquinius' battle armour slid from its hidden grooves.

"Wait!"

Too late the knight spoke, for the impatient lion pounced, drawing itself back and launching into the air in one swift motion. He landed where the Frenchman had been. A laugh mocked them from above. Tarquinius span round, and all three of them looked up. The Frenchman hung, a spider in morning wear, from the underside of a branch as wide as an autobahn. "A-a-a-a!" he wagged an admonishing finger, his spine cracking as his head turned 180 degrees to stare malevolently down at them. "I weel be going now. I weel not be seeing you again. Veronique, join me, leave zese two behind. I 'ave such things to show you, ah such marvellous, wonderful things! I am Zeus, I invite you to become ma 'Era."

"Go to hell!"

The Frenchman pouted. "Ah! Veronique, you upset me. You make a grave error. But, *c'est la vie*. As you wish. Die with your new friends." With that, the Frenchman let go of the branch with his hands and, standing on the underside of the branch, plucked a thin flute from his breastpocket. He covered a hole on the top and played a long, piercing wail like a bosun's whistle, wailing so high only the lion could hear its final notes. Tarquinius shuddered, moaning, shaking his head as if a troublesome fly was working its way into his ear. "Come monkee monkee monkee! Come monkee monkee monkee monkee!" said the Frenchman. He played the note again, causing Tarquinius to roar in pain and slam a missile into the Frenchman's perch. The man's legs grew obscenely long and he sprang away up the tree, leaping from branch to branch.

"A tense encounter," said Jagadith.

"Do not put up your sword yet!" cautioned Tarquinius, his voice heavy and weak, "something comes!" As the man's mad cackling grew faint, so a loud, cracking, snapping sound approached, coming down the tree toward them.

"What the hell is that?" said Veronique, searching through the branches above.

"Four hostiles approach!" said Tarquin rotating on the spot, scanning the limbs above. "I… I can't get a fix, Jag… I…"

"Do not be telling me, you do not have any idea what they are."

"No, Jag, no! Most of my senses are down. That accursed whistle!" Jag looked at the targeting screen. It crackled and blurred, reticules spinning uselessly.

Streams of information rolled up the glass, none of it good.

The crashing stopped. There was a tinny sound, as of cymbals of cheap brass being bashed together, following a raucous squawking. Further away came an answer: crash crash crash! "A-hooka! A-hooka! A-hooka!" Then again from directly above, and again from the left. Tarquin roared and flung more munitions into the tree above, blindly firing. A scalloped needle as large as a football field came sailing down, burning.

"Where are they?" hissed Veronique.

"There, there, and one up there," said Jagadith, indicating with his eyes. "The fourth I cannot see."

Veronique followed his darting gaze. She caught a glimpse of a hulking silhouette the size of the lion. Two baleful red eyes looked back then were extinguished as the thing moved off into the darkness round the trunk.

"Grip me tight. Whatever happens, do not fall from Tarquinius!" said Jagadith.

There was a thump behind them. A blur of movement as something fell to the left. Tarquinius spun round.

Crash crash crash! "A-hooka! A-hooka! A-hooka!" Staring at them with unblinking glass eyes, the dull red fire of violence burning in them, were two monkeys; monkeys of the plush-furred, mechanical variety. Each carried a pair of cymbals, and sported little red waistcoats. One wore a fez. Crash crash crash! "A-hooka! A-hooka! A-hooka!" The leader put its head on one side, parting lips to reveal interlocking steel teeth. "Grrrrrrrrrrrrrrrrrrrrrr. A-hooka!"

"Deary, deary me, I am feeling that your professor might well have been a very sick man even before he arrived here, madam goddess."

"He had one of these in the lab, an antique... some kind of ancient toy."

"These are no playthings, not now," said Jag, his head moving counter to Tarquinius' as they sought to keep both monkeys in sight. Crash crash crash! One banged its cymbals, its felt mouth opening in time to the beating of the cymbals. "A-hooka! A-hooka! A-hooka!" went the other, moving towards them robotically. The other hurled its instrument at them. It scythed over their heads like a deadly frisbee, making them duck. The cymbals smashed into the tree, one sticking, the other clattering noisily down to the floor. "A-hooka! A-hooka! A-hooka!" It shuffled sideways, circling them. A third hurtled from the dark above, cymbals above its head. It landed easily, only narrowly missing them.

"Jag, they seek to encircle us," warned Tarquinius. "And I still cannot sense the fourth."

The monkey who had dropped his cymbals squawked and charged, knuckling along the ground in a charge, shoulder held forward.

"Tarquinius! Move!" The lion's head swung round as he moved to take in the charging ape; too late. It barrelled into Tarquinius' flank, spinning the lion round like a cat kicked by a horse. He writhed through the air, landing crouched and snarling. Somehow, both Jag and Veronique kept their seats, though they were winded in the tumble. Tarquinius backed away from the three apes, keeping his back to the tree's vast trunk. He moved unevenly.

"Dear sainted ones!" exclaimed Jag. "They have dented you with their tussling!"

"Never mind that! Keep on eye on those blasted monkeys."

The three apes formed a loose semicircle in front of them, two banging their cymbals, the ape that charged them running backwards and forwards, hooting and slapping the floor with murderous plastic hands.

"Tarquinius, we must act soon, they attempt to herd us into a trap. The fourth creature is above us."

"I know. My senses are beginning to come back online. It intends to jump soon."

"I am ready."

"As am I. Hold tightly now, madam goddess."

"Let's take the one on the left."

"Agreed." At some invisible signal, the fourth monkey leapt

from above. Tarquin jumped forward. The displaying monkey tried to grapple them, but the lion sailed straight over its head. It squawked with rage. As Tarquin hit the floor to one side of the left-most monkey, Jag neatly decapitated it with his crackling sword. For a moment the three-metre ape tottered, sparks spewing from its ruined neck, then, with one last bash of its cymbals, it pitched forward to fizzle upon the floor.

"There, one down," Jag said, but as he did so he grimaced, rotating his sword arm; the blow had badly jarred it. The three remaining monkeys howled in indignation, bashing their cymbals and smashing their fists into the tree. Then, as one, they turned to face them. Their eyes glowed red, their lips curled. Snarls escaped their synthetic voice boxes.

"Now what? I do not see an easy way out of this," said Tarquinius.

"Perhaps we will be safe if they do not work out that if they charge us all at once they wi..."

The monkeys dropped their cymbals and came knuckling along the floor in a line. Tarquinius ran, bounding up a low rise, then turned to face them, roaring in defiance. One monkey stumbled, hands clasped over its ears. Tarquinius fired a salvo of rocketry into its prone body, setting its fur ablaze. Veronique screamed for a weapon. Jag sang a war-song in a language of a long-dead people. One monkey hurled itself over the head of the other, carrying both Jag and Veronique to the floor. The other slammed into Tarquinius with the force of a steam train, the two rolling on the floor in a tangle of mechanical limbs. Jagadith, grasped it by the torso, one arm pulled to popping by the laughing ape. Tarquinius, scrabbling free and rearing up, rained blows onto the unyielding head of his assailant with paws the size of manhole covers.

Veronique cursed her lack of a gun, forgetting she could create one merely by thinking of it. Jag screamed as his arm came out of the socket, his world washed red. The next thing he saw, the monkey lay dead at his feet, his sword protruding from its chest, black smoke boiling out round its hilt.

"Are you alright? God, I thought he was going to kill you!" said Veronique, running to the knight's aid.

"I believe that was his intention... Aiee!" shouted Jag, halfway to a scream. His breath became shallow, he clutched his side and looked, ashen-faced, to the woman. "Careful, madam goddess, my arm has come from its socket." He winced. "Now, now where is Tarquinius? We must be on our way."

"He's there..." Veronique pointed, hand shaking. The mighty lion lay on his side, head stretched out. He was dented in several places, the plates round his vulnerable underbelly buckled in. Thin green mist steamed out from rents in his body. Next to him was the fourth monkey, curled in a foetal position, pedalling itself frantically round and round on the ground, increasingly fast, until it stopped with a whiff of burning and a bang.

"Tarquinius!" Jagadith rushed over to his supine steed.

"Jag... aaahhhhhhh.... dith," Tarquinius' voice was almost inaudible. His mouth was ajar, unmoving; his multi-purpose tongue lolled.

"Oh, noblest friend! You cannot die, I will not allow it."

"Complete... the... mission..."

"Rest, my friend! Rest! I will slay this god, then you and I will go away, until the world needs us once more. Be still, I will return."

But Tarquinius did not reply, and, as Jagadith looked on, the green glow of his eyes, undimmed for millennia, flickered and died. Jagadith stood for a long time, his tears falling silently onto the metal of the lion, before he would allow Veronique to help him mend his shoulder. Veronique had some medical training, and forced it back into place on the first try. After a couple of experimental swings with his sword, Jag set off to the tree's trunk.

"I, I could try to bring him back..." offered Veronique.

"Do not even attempt it! The world here is too unstable, see, come here." He strode back to Veronique, grabbed her roughly by the wrist and dragged her over to the monkey he had dispatched. "Look at the smoke."

She looked. She squinted. "It looks like smoke," she said.

"Look harder."

She looked harder. The smoke was composed not of gasses and particles of soot, but of thousands of numbers, flowing upwards to disappear. She stood up sharply. "That's not supposed to happen. I've never read of anything like that."

"The world is trying to adapt," said Jagadith, "and it is breaking down. The professor is altering it too much and too quickly. It should be smoke, but that is our world's interpretation of your professor's interpretation of what he imagines should function in our world as smoke as our world sees what he sees it becoming, if you understand me."

"No," admitted Veronique.

"If you would be trying to utilise your godly powers here, madam," continued Jagadith, "this third level of interference could well unravel the universe about our ears. Your professor is bending the whole fabric of reality, for what purpose I know not, but it is imperative I stop him! More than our world is at stake, I think. Quickly," he said impatiently, gesturing at the tree. "Time is short. Tarquinius and I are one, and a half cannot last long without the other. We must act swiftly or all will be lost."

"You are going to die?" said Veronique.

"Yes, madam goddess," said Jag, "I am going to die. Maybe not as you would understand it. But I am not going to do it before I have completed my task." His perfect features were set like stone. "Professor Zhang Qifang will pay."

Chapter 20
Arizona

The sky glowed with the predawn, black shading to blues as the stars winked out. Otto dozed, allowing his near-I to take the strain of monitoring the car's brain, but not for long. Not being hijacked by huntware and driven to his death over one of the many precipitous drops this part of the world boasted was worth the price of a little sleep.

As the sun rolled out from behind the mountains, he roused himself, shutting off his melatonin production, already artificially depressed, to mimic a normal waking pattern. The closer he kept his circadian rhythms to normal operation, the less lousy he felt. He upped his cortisol levels. Immediately he felt more focused. Otto's ability to moderate his biochemistry was a standard feature in Ky-tech personnel. He used it infrequently, and then for short periods. After a few days, physical wear set in as the body's systems remained unrefreshed. Psychosis would occur after a few weeks. If he were too reliant on it, production of his neurotransmitters could be permanently compromised in a similar way to what happened to heavy MDMA users, only worse. He'd seen it happen to others, ex-soldiers like him addicted to the fast burn of life lived 24/7, or too frightened of the mentaug's dreams to sleep.

Right now, he wanted coffee. Using the biochem-moderator always made him crave the stuff, though it was supposed to have no effect on him. More medical bullshit. He called up the car's map from its internal memory and searched for restaurants. Since his brief reconnection to the Grid at the falls, his near-I had been only tenuously connected to the network in order to track the interference signals of Valdaire's cheater programmes. He was running his tracking of Valdaire through several double-blind service providers and then observed by himself only obliquely. Still he kept the car to banked data, like the map, and he had it display on the windscreen, not in his iHUD.

For a rare few hours he'd been free of the noise of the Grid, the targeted advertising, messaging, news updates and calls that filled the heads of all but the most resolutely anti-Grid citizen. He enjoyed the disconnection; he was not like some people, going to pieces when their uplinks malfunctioned or their phone hit its pre-ordained obsolescence date. But now he was reluctantly part of the world again, and it gave him a headache.

"You won't hurt Veronique, will you?" said Valdaire's phone.

Progess. Otto yawned. "So you are speaking to me now?" he said, knowing full well it had been observing him for the last day. He had decided against having his own valet force it open. The likes of Richards were pool-evolved, millions of variants hothoused to force favourable traits, the best of each generation blended, a new wave bred from them, and the process repeated until personality and purpose arose. By contrast, evolved near-Is like Chloe were defined as "weak", made from a single, programmed source, and in Chloe's case heavily modded. Valdaire was good at her work and Chloe far exceeded most near-I specs, but years of tinkering might have made it fragile. Crack it badly, he'd lose everything. "I will not harm her. I am trying to find her so I can help her."

"I love her."

Otto nodded. "I am trying to help."

In the meantime Otto's near-I fed him AR directions to Valdaire, tracked off the Grid cheater mirages Richards had unravelled. They were uncertain, jumping about as his lock on broke and then was re-established, his oblique link to the Grid multiplying the effect, but he was on the right track – the signal he'd found off the back of Richards' frequency estimates was leading him steadily south-southeast. The modulated pulse of Valdaire's cheater weakened and strengthened as it switched up and down the levels of the Grid. Visible, but unlocatable. Chloe had to talk. Best take it slow.

Otto curled his lip. They were coming up to a rest stop. Time for a break. He had his near-I check for data-tagging on his Gridsig, or the emanations of machines that might be watching in the Real or online. Negative. There was always a chance of old-fashioned eyes doing old-fashioned watching, but he'd been careful. And he was hungry. "Car, stop here," he ordered.

"Yes, sir," said the car in a smooth voice complementary to the whispered rumble of the tyres on the tarmac. Thousands of AI-sped man-hours had probably gone into working out that touch. Cars and coffee blenders were getting smarter than some of his clients. There was a danger he was getting sloppy in the way that he dealt with them because of it. He had to watch that.

The car pulled up at a collection of wooden buildings: smart miniature charge station, restaurant and gift shop, the exteriors constructed rustically from whole logs; picturesque, and economical – there were tax breaks for using carbon neutral resources.

"What are you doing?" asked Chloe. "Why are we stopping?"

"Breakfast," said Otto.

"As of this moment, you do not require breakfast."

"I am hungry."

"Your nutritional needs dictate that you do not require breakfast," she insisted, businesslike.

He looked down at the passenger seat, where Chloe poked out of a bag. "You'd know? It is my stomach, not yours."

"Veronique provided me with efficient dietary and exercise software. I can calculate your optimum nutrient and calorie intake by estimation of your body weight and activity levels. I am highly accurate."

"I am hungry, be silent," he said. He preferred to eat to gain the energy he needed; he could plug himself in, but that made him feel like an appliance. He needed a damn sight more food than Chloe could guess at.

"It appears your stomach has been modified," said Chloe. "Although I am unfamiliar with your cybernetic physiology, I surmise that your systems provide for efficient nutrient recycling. If you are hungry, and do not wish to recharge by electrocal means, might I suggest you sate your psychological needs to eat and attempt to extract energy from some of the freely available organics by the roadside? You could eat them in the car," she said helpfully. "And it contains roughage."

"I had ham and eggs in mind," growled Otto.

Chloe was quiet, then blurted, "You said you would help Veronique."

Otto glanced at the phone. Chloe was all over the place, unstable. Too many apps and mods for a near-I to handle. Someone like Valdaire should know better. "I will. But if you are not going to tell me where she is, I cannot help her, so I got to eat breakfast instead."

"Get to eat," said the phone, "in this instance."

"Get to eat," he said, under his breath. He knew that. Damn, he was tired. "I am going to eat ham and eggs. And coffee, I need coffee."

"You do not require coffee!" Chloe's voice became shrill.

Otto shrugged. "Maybe I do not need coffee, but I want coffee, so I am going to get coffee. You can sit on the table while I eat my ham and my eggs and drink my coffee and think about telling me where Veronique is. You should hurry, I do not think Veronique has much time."

"But..."

"I am hungry." Otto scooped the phone up. The car anticipated his intention and swung back the door. He got out.

The restaurant was a small affair, a forty-seater or so, one of many Otto had passed catering for tourists, this one standing at the head of a mountain trail heading off into the forested wildernesses of the parks southeast of Flagstaff. A large car park, hidden by the buildings and a fold in the land from the road, stood behind it. A small ranger's office and toilets were at the top, a large wooden board carved with hiking routes next to it. The car park was half full, both of groundcars and, as they were close to the edge of the mountains, the more robust kind of aircar. A couple of tour buses occupied the far end of the lot.

The bus passengers were crammed into the diner, a real mom and pop affair in the 1950s revival mode popular back in the 2090s: high-walled booths, red vinyl seats, wood panelling and faded postcards, cakes in perspex boxes, local memorabilia and antiques hanging from the ceiling. It was hard to tell if any of the bric-à-brac was genuine – artefacts like these were often not; you could buy the fab patterns for them for virtually nothing. Ancient still photographs of grinning fishermen holding up extinct monsters by the gills crammed the walls, groundcars as ugly as primitive idols behind them; pictures out of a faded century, distorted further by the lens of another now fast receding in time. All Otto's life he'd lived through retreads of times from before his own time; the world was stuck in a loop, the advent

of the Information Age proving conclusively there was nothing
new under the sun. *The Grid kills creativity,* he thought. *People
don't get to forget any more.*

The diner's kitchen was visible through a hole cut through
the wall, where a short-order cook worked with a battered android on a hotplate as big as a billiard table. The air was thick
with human breath and cooking smells, the windows steamed
up against the cool mountain air outside, where autumn made
an early foray. The diner strived for homeyness, and almost
succeeded. Otto felt himself unwind a little.

"Hiya honey, you want a window seat?" The waitress was
ages older than Otto, her hair tinted and chopped so as to appear three decades younger than her skin. It was bunched like
a child's, framing a wrinkled, non-modified face. Her pink
gingham uniform made her look like a geriatric doll. The effect
was ugly, but Otto had seen worse in the mirror.

Otto's near-I shut off the cheater tracker for a moment and
used its scrap of covert bandwidth to run a tactical analysis of
the restaurant. Reticules blinked up in Otto's iHUD as it
checked off each face, all full human, only a couple of uplinks,
no threat from any. No records on the system beyond one or
two parking tickets, one minor insurance fraud, a public order
infringement and a couple of ancient drug busts. "No," said
Otto, "I would like to sit there." He indicated an empty booth
wedged by a large cast-iron stove.

"Gee, where are you..."

"I am German. Before you ask, I am also a cyborg, ex-military."

The woman's head wobbled, a tiny motion. Her good cheer
disappeared.

Otto immediately regretted his terseness. American culture
was predicated on crude but brittle decorum. He wasn't so
good at that. "I am sorry," he said. "I look different. I become
weary repeating myself. I have come far."

"Well, people would be interested, honey." The waitress's professional bovine smile crept back. "We don't get many other than your regular folk up here, one or two maybe with a little work done, but nothing like you."

Otto tried his best to smile, conjuring up a grim, slot-mouthed expression that did double duty at funerals. "Your curiosity is understandable."

The waitress nodded, abashed.

Otto attempted a fresh start. "So please, I would like to sit there."

"Are you sure, honey?" she said. "It's awful cramped for a big fella like you. We've got some lovely views out front."

Otto looked at the vista of plunging forest-cloaked slopes. "You have. It is beautiful here, but I would like to sit there, for privacy's sake. I have an important call to make," he lied.

"OK, honey, they say it everywhere you go, but we mean it when we say the customer is always right at Josie's!" She smiled broadly, as wide a smile as a Euro would spare for her lover, but as emotionally involved as a car grill. Otto did not understand Americans – they wore their hearts on their sleeves, but when you peered closer to look, there wasn't that much to see. What first seemed to the cyborg like refreshing openness had long ago revealed itself as a lack of depth. Americans used your name too often. They lived up to their reputation for doing everything big, endlessly detailing their own dreary lives and mediocre achievements in unasked-for confessionals, in person and online.

He paid little attention to the woman's chatter as he forced his bulk behind the table. Thick log walls to his right and back, the stove to the front, he was well protected from small-arms fire. The booth afforded a good view of the restaurant's patrons and doors. The waitress stopped listing the specials, and reached for an animated menu card. He halted her arm midway, preventing the menu reaching the table. "Ham and eggs, a double portion of ham, eight eggs, sunny side up, as you say." He tried another smile, but it felt all wrong. He was not a man for smiling.

"Are you sure you don't want to see the menu? We have some fine specialties here – what about some of our famous pancakes? This tour bus party here, why, they stopped here special, just for them."

That sounded agreeable. "Very well. I will have pancakes with my ham and eggs. And a pot of coffee."

"You got it."

"Please could you provide me with the code and add a charge to my bill for your energy relay? I would like to recharge my phone and my implants."

"Sure! Energy's free here, it's open, just tell it to zone in and drink up!" She bustled off, then returned with a pot of coffee and a mug with "Josie's" emblazoned on it in a fat 1950s script, or at least the 2090s idea of a fat 1950s script. There was something well-meant about the mug, like the place. It was genuine in its artifice, for all its kitsch.

"I am not your phone," muttered Chloe when the woman had gone. "I am Veronique's PA. Not yours."

"Fine." Otto sipped the coffee. *Coffee*, he thought, *Americans are good at coffee.*

"You appear emotionally stunted. I will explain. I am not engaging with you. I am exhibiting signs of displeasure."

"If you tell me where Veronique is you can be reunited with her, and you need worry about my emotional state no longer."

"I cannot. How do I know you are telling the truth?"

"You have no face-reading applications?"

"No," she said in a small voice. "Anyway, you are a cyborg. You could probably hide a lie."

That particular kind of biological micro-management was beyond him. His upgrades didn't include the somatic rephrasing, and the tricked-out facial capillaries needed heat-beating, but he was tired of explaining himself. "You will have to trust me," he said.

"I can't," she said, somewhat sorrowfully, then, "You smell," her voice suddenly high and piping.

"Keep your voice down, or I will be approached and detained and you will not see Veronique again."

Chloe did not respond.

"You do want to help Veronique?"

A small sound: "Yes."

"So then, shhhh." He held his finger to his lips.

Otto's meal arrived, and he attacked it with sensuous relish. The gammon alone was enough to feed a family of four. The steak was vat-grown, film-engineered stuff pressed into patties that lacked the texture and flavour of genuine animal meat. But he ate methodically through it just the same.

He was tackling the pancakes when something tweaked at his Grid cover. Within milliseconds his near-I adjutant examined the alert, weighed its relevance, judged it pertinent and passed it on to Otto as a warning icon in his iHUD. Otto's head came up whip-fast and he moved. He hit the floor as a burst of flechettes punched perfect round holes through the plate-glass windows and embedded themselves in iron and wood alike. The hubbub of voices and click of knives on plates abruptly ceased as the restaurant patrons looked at the window.

A large man in his sixties pitched forward into his meal, blood pumping from holes either side of his neck, the flechette that caused them buried in the table. The woman next to him screamed. A second burst of flechettes terminally compromised the glass. The windows fell inwards. The restaurant erupted in a din of shouts and screams.

"*Scheisse*," said Otto wearily, and kicked his augments into gear. His lips took on a greyish hue as combat drugs entered his bloodstream. Time slowed as his chronaxic sense accelerated, the drugs bringing his other senses into sharp focus. He could feel the individual fragments of glass under his knees, smell the fear in the restaurant. His near-I dutifully fed him combat-relevant data. "I thought this was too easy," he said. He grabbed his pistol out of the holster under his jacket, snatched Chloe down from the table and took cover. Many of the other customers were scrabbling for the door and throwing themselves through the glassless windows. All sense of propriety lost, they became a herd that shoved at itself savagely. Otto heard a fresh series of distant cracks, louder now the glass was gone. A fraction of a second later a handful of people fell dead. The rest scattered, banging into each other as they panicked. In the car park engines started.

"What's going on? Get me out of your pocket, I can't see! I want Veronique!"

"Be quiet," said Otto. He pulled Chloe out and pointed her camera across the valley. "There is a sniper up there." He nodded over to the mountainside opposite. "Thirty-three hundred metres away or so, armed with a railgun. He's probably got a lock on me."

"Why? Why?" wailed Chloe.

"Because I'm trying to help Veronique."

Otto jogged over to the door, keeping the thick log walls between him and the shooter, pistol at the ready. Though it had nowhere near the range to hit the assassin, the weight of the weapon in his hand helped him focus. Outside bodies littered the forecourt. His car lay in pieces, holes punched through one side to the other, sunlight lancing through, tyres shredded, lubricants and water dripping onto the floor. He looked over the mountainside quickly, magnifying likely-looking locations for the sniper based on his near-I's estimation of the flechettes' trajectory. He saw nothing; whoever was shooting at him had decent camo, and if they were any good at their job would be moving in between bursts.

They'd have to have been good at their job to have found him.

He stepped back at an explosion from the car park as the split hydrogen in a fuel cell went up. Debris clanged over the forecourt surface.

On terrain like that on the opposite mountain the shooter would be moving fifty, sixty metres each time, if there were only the one and they were human. If there were more than that, he was as good as dead. Sound was no aid in locating his attacker. The sonic reports of the railgun munitions were faint. Without his enhancements he'd have heard nothing until the darts impacted the restaurant; the booms the flechettes made as they went hypersonic arrived as distant crackles, much of their energy lost in the vastness of the landscape. Nature barely deigned to acknowledge human noise up here, no matter how violent.

"Is, is it safe?" A young woman spoke, three wailing children crouched by her skirts, hands over their ears.

"Stay down!" shouted Otto and waved her back. "Get behind the table. Stay in here, where it's safe, all of you!"

"What's going on?" asked someone.

"Are you a cop?" asked another.

There were fifteen people left in the restaurant. He had to get out of there; he was putting them all at risk. He would have to go out the back. Another burst came, and a man hiding behind the charge station fell to the ground, writhing. The shooter was firing at targets as they presented themselves – that meant he had no bead on Otto, no firm lock; that was something. He watched the slopes as darts peppered the room, the mountain-side opposite lit up like a rack of votive candles, infrared decoys mimicking the brief heating and cooling of a railgun as each shot was fired, a signature produced only by barrels of high-end long-string magnetic iron ceramics; exotic, expensive, more evidence this guy wasn't going to mess around.

He waited for the burst to stop, then made for the kitchen door at a crouch. His foot nudged a body, old face on a starlet's body. The waitress. He reached down a hand to feel for a pulse, found none, drew back fingertips dripping blood.

"Where are you going?" shouted a man in a red plaid shirt. He was wearing a grease-stained cap with the restaurant logo across the front, non-motile, a genuine cloth badge; possibly the owner.

"See this?" Otto plucked a flechette from the stove. "Hardened tip, anti-armour round. Cyborg killer. For me." He threw it aside, and it skittered across the broken glass. "I'll draw his fire. It is me he is trying to kill. When I am gone, you will be safe."

He pushed open the kitchen door, keeping below the level of the shooter's line of sight, worried that he'd be moving to higher ground to spray darts through the flimsy shingle roof. He went through the kitchen. The cook crouched on the floor, clutching at his bloodied arm, eyes wide with shock. The android sparked as it roasted on the grill plate, filling the room with the stink of melting plastics.

"Stay down!" Otto told him. "It will be safe when I am gone. Where is the exit?"

The cook jerked his head back. Otto nodded in thanks. He reached the back door, let his Grid cover drop a moment, hoping to draw fire from the restaurant. The last thing he wanted was for his assailant to lose patience and fire a warhead into the building. He had enough blood on his hands.

It was luck his assailant hadn't got a firmer lock, or he'd be a damn sight closer and Otto would be dead. Otto had been a fool; the way from Payson was the only real road in these parts.

Otto sprinted across a yard to the rear, a scraggly garden full of weeds and sun-bleached children's toys, on into the narrow strip of woods behind. Seconds later he burst through the underbrush into the car park. More people there, hiding behind cars. Two rangers stood by the door of their cabin, bear stunners out, looking warily back and forth across the car park, all too aware of their armament's inadequacy. One spotted Otto and waved frantically at him to get down. Otto ignored him.

Two cars by the car park entrance were ablaze. Three aircars hung from tree branches like over-sized Christmas ornaments, one of them burning, fuel cells cracked and leaking hydrogen. The tree it hung in was an upright fire, reminding Otto of Brazil.

Escape was not going to be easy. His near-I checked off the vehicles, highlighting a nearby aircar as a likely ride. Otto ran for it, expecting a dart in the back at any moment, but none came. He reached the car.

"What are you doing?" said Chloe.

"Stealing this car," said Otto matter-of-factly, "so I can get away before anyone else gets killed."

"But that's against the law!"

"Fine, you may turn me in when we're done."

"Wait! The police will come, we can explain."

Otto shook his head. "By that time the sniper's point man will have got me. Working alone on someone like me is not how it is done."

His near-I adjutant broke the car's security in short order, the doors popped open and the engine started up, turbofans whickering then whining as they picked up speed. He got into the car. A quirk of topography, a crease in this mountain shoulder the rest stop sat on, meant that the car park was as hidden from the opposite hillside as it was from the road. As soon as he got airborne that would change quickly, but better to fly than roll along the road. As poor as his odds in the air were, there was no chance of escape on the ground.

He checked his armaments. He had the 9mm caseless pistol and his carbon bootknife, plus two electromagnetic pulse grenades. Reusuable, but he had no means of recharging them. Everything else he'd had – his own flechetter railgun, EMP gun, grenade launcher and external computer equipment – was still in the back of the car out front, no doubt full of razor-sharp darts.

"Listen, Chloe, you have to trust me now. Whoever is trying to kill me is trying to stop me getting to Veronique. If they are close to me, they will soon be close to her, because they will find you and use you to get to her." He pulled back the action on the gun. His near-I talked to it and counted off the rounds: twenty-six. Not nearly enough.

"Maybe they were the police, and they were trying to protect Veronique from you," said Chloe. She was scared, close to crying.

"You saw what they did to the restaurant," said Otto calmly. "Would the police kill nine people to protect your mistress?"

"My friend! She is my friend, she always has been. We were incepted together, she and I, born and made. Friend! I love her," she wailed. Then, chillingly calm by comparison: "The law enforcement authorities would not behave in this manner." He'd never get used to these switches in mode.

"Do you trust me?" he said. Chloe said nothing. "Tell me where Veronique is"

She did not reply. Otto had almost given up hope and had begun examining his other options, none good, when Chloe answered, quietly but firmly: "Yes."

The car roared to life as Chloe muscled in on his near-I's link. She keyed the autopilot to a location forty kilometres away. The car rose into the air, blasting stonedust away from the car park's hard standing.

"Stop!" said Otto. "This will be difficult." Chloe demurred without protest, retreating from the vehicle. The steering column went slack, and Otto grabbed it. "Hold on," he said. He

had his near-I begin work undoing the car's central programming, smothering its Gridsig with non-informational noise.

As soon as he had risen six metres over the car park,
flechette rounds started hissing through the air around him.
Some found their mark, piercing the car's bodywork with dull
clonks. He had seconds at best. He dropped down to within
centimetres of the other cars' roofs, gunned the engines. The
car rose vertically into the sky. His near-I had chosen well: this
was a sporty model, a Toyata Zephyr. All four lateral fans were
multidirectional, attached to the body by gimbals, giving excellent manoeuvrability, climbing rates and enough power to
deal with the mountain weather. Its ventral fan was sized for
rapid acceleration, with a top speed of around 600kph. He
wished for countermeasures and some degree of armour, because a vehicle like this was a rich man's toy, and against
railgun fire was as precisely as durable as a paper bag. He
dodged violently from side to side and headed for the trees beyond the car park, which marched precipitously upwards to
crags and a mountain shoulder. There was a notch in the ridge
one hundred metres up; pass that and they'd be clear.

Branches whipped past the windscreen as Otto wrestled the
aircar through the trees' canopy. He'd have liked to take it
lower, but here, sheltered and sunlit, the trees grew close together, and he was forced into the upper branches, dodging
the tops of the pines. Wood exploded into splinters all around
them, slender crowns toppled and fell. Few of the darts found
the car, and none found anything essential. Otto was pushing
the vehicle well beyond tolerance, climbing hard and swerv-
ing. The driver's-side window shattered. Otto felt a stab of pain
in his left arm. A stray branch was sucked into one of the fan
housings with a bang and sprayed out as woodchip behind.
The car swerved, right and down. If a thicker limb went into
the machinery, they would crash.

Chloe screamed. "Almost there!" shouted Otto, his near-I working manically, violating the car's tiny brain, breaking the manufacturer and government safety protocols and speed limiters, pushing it well past its design specifications. The Zephyr flew like a hawk, smoke pouring from its engines.

A flechette pierced the rear window. Another slammed into the boot. Gauges flashed red; one of the aircar's five fan motors was burning out, undone by the triple insult of branch, speed and projectile.

The trees began to peter out. Bare rock took their place. Puffs of dust and sparks rose up from the mountainside as they approached the cleft, impacts that closed with the car.

Then they were up and over the ridge, through the notch in the mountain, and on the other side of the ridge. The firing ceased. Otto eased back.

"That was too close," he said, picking a spent dart from his bicep. He threw it out of the shattered window. Chloe wept tiny, electronic hiccuping noises.

Otto damned his earlier caution and attempted to use the MT to warn Richards that he'd been attacked, only to find that it had been cracked and blocked.

The machine telepathy cipher had been broken twice in a fortnight. That was no coincidence. They were in trouble.

Otto stood in the forest and looked at the car. The Zephyr rested nose down on the slope, as if paused in the act of kneeling, left-forward fan pod bent underneath it. Its engines were shot and fans chipped to uselessness, deflated matt-black crash balloons tangled round it like a hastily draped funerary shroud. The bodywork was damaged beyond the point of salvage, the airframe out of true. It wouldn't be taking anyone anywhere ever again. Otto had his near-I run through the machine's simple brain for information one last time, making sure they'd downloaded everything of use. Maps, that's all it had to offer. He satisfied himself that was all he needed.

He retreated a safe distance from the car and turned back to face it. Sitting there, down the slope from him, it presented a sorry sight. Once he'd tossed in one of his two remaining EMP grenades it looked worse. The grenade went in through the shattered driver's window without touching the sides. A heart-beat later a cerulean flash shorted out every circuit in the vehicle, causing tiny fires to spring up inside. No one would be tracking him off the Zephyr.

He shouldered the bag he'd found in the boot, in which he had a first-aid kit, a sleeping bag, some climbing gear and a few high-energy food bars. There'd been a jacket too, but that was nowhere near big enough to fit him.

"Come on," he said, "we have a long walk ahead of us."

"To Veronique?" said Chloe, brightly.

"To Veronique."

He ran. He had seventy miles of rough terrain to cover. Time was running out for Veronique Valdaire.

Chapter 21
Karlsson

"Peter Karlsson," said the wiki précis as it read itself aloud, "Norwegian expatriate, resident of the USNA for twenty-three years. Until recently employed at the Virtualities Investigation Authority."

"Until recently alive, if this case is anything to go by," said Richards. Karlsson's Gridsig was still singing out, but that meant nothing. He'd not left his residence-cum-factory in old Detroit for two weeks, a similar period of inactivity to that Qifang had undergone before he had been found dead. As he listened to the wiki, a nimble part of himself plucked Karlsson's employment history from one of the many dark places on the Grid where classified files were fragged and sent to disappear.

They didn't.

Richards was an expert at reassembling data. Its fragments were as cohesive as grains of sand worn from a rock and spread over a beach, but this was what his father Armin Thor had made him for.

He began reconstruction while the Grid précis droned on. It had precious little of importance to say and its monotone began to grate on him, so he turned it down and sent it to the back of the sphere of files around him, set the man's life-site to mainline direct as he tinkered with Karlsson's VIA employment history. Pictures whose true essences were obscured by repeated replication flickered by, copies of copies of copies, showing a baby, a baby, a boy, an older boy, a man skiing, more children, a smiling woman, landscapes... faster and faster.

Richards squatted in a black infinity, his office banished into unreality. Around him flew the scraps of Karlsson's life, pulled from all over the virtual world. Video, audio, stills, CVs, letters, mails, texts, testimonials, chat posts, network entries, health records, license details, game scores, avatars, Heaven Level access codes – all there on the Grid, for the right man to find. Karlsson had worn a soul-capt for several years. This was usually done to prepare for a pimsim, but in Karlsson's case Richards reckoned it was insurance, recording his time at the VIA. There was a mass of data just from that, more bits of recorded information than were in the whole world only a couple of hundred years ago and still not enough to encompass the entirety of one life; a pitiful testament to the existence of a sentient mind, digital flotsam. Richards was a beachcomber on the shores of the Styx. He pushed the notion away; he felt too close to Lincolnshire Flats when he thought like that.

He is dead, thought Richards. There was a lack of vitality to the data. It was no longer growing, already suffering the small erosions of the digital world, minute corruptions of copy and transfer, the necrotisation of numbers that would one day render it unreadable, even to him, leaving shards behind as mysterious as wave-worn glass. Karlsson's Gridsig burned only as a ghost light.

Karlsson's life lay before Richards. The receipt for six combat frames floated by, like that in the heiress, followed by more for weaponry and autonomous carriage parts. There was a lot of that over the last few months; and a lot of personal protection equipment, for use online and in the Real. Richards called up plans of Karlsson's factory. "Wow," he said, and halted them, bringing them right up in front of him. He ran through them thoroughly. It was a fortress.

"Who the hell was this guy hiding from?" wondered Richards aloud. He called a drink into existence, drained it in one, and let the glass disintegrate into nothingness. He directed the data to reform according to different search criteria, a conductor of an orchestra of information. He looked for patterns as it danced. Hypotheses came and went, possibilities reeling off each run-through by braids of Richards' consciousness, all discarded.

Karlsson had known Qifang well. The correspondence between them was voluminous and lively, though there were strands of consistent disagreement. Camera feeds of them together showed men comfortable in each other's company, though they were wary of others when they had met. They were secretive as they could be, but nobody got away without ever being recorded. They were careful to keep their conversation to bland topics. Maybe there was a code to it, but they were probably making small talk to cover over shortrange data transfers direct from Karlsson's mentaug to Qifang's phone. If they did that right, they could discuss what they liked in perfect privacy. They were up to something.

Richards listened to a streetcam recording of them speak, and started to doubt that Karlsson had any part in Qifang's death. The portrait of the man forming in his mind was of a nut, mistrustful of the numbers' growing influence on human affairs. But his history spoke of defiance against higher authority, a growing fear of the AIs' influence and the pervasiveness of the Grid, not of the homicide of a man he respected, a man he was trying to sway to his point of view.

Richards was methodical. His main attention was on the data rebuild of the VIA files, his second tier awarenesses running through a chronological examination of the information as his highest functions pulled the fragged files back together. The general information thinned toward the end, petering out about nine months before Karlsson lost his job with the VIA. The life-site posts ceased first, and his finances and other dealings became increasingly heavily encrypted. From June 19th his personal messages stopped. Fragments that Richards scales retrieved indicated they'd been fragged five or six times over, probably by Karlsson himself, because the remains of these files were so minute as to be no better than nothing at all.

Around the same time, Karlsson began to use increasingly esoteric code forms that were beyond Richards' capability to decipher, even where he could reconstitute them, and if they were beyond him, they were beyond anybody. About nine weeks ago, the man's life ran out. Soul-capt data ended. It was as if he'd died, only he hadn't. The wipe became complete six weeks later. Not a trace remained on the Grid. Karlsson had ceased to be alive in the modern sense a day after Qifang's death.

"Now that," said Richards, "is quite something." And then he stopped, because if someone went to all that trouble to hide their dealings, they'd make sure to be informed if someone were trying to uncover them.

Richards checked the digital wall round Karlsson's home to see if he'd probed too deeply. It remained unruffled, no sign of datastreams out hunting for him. He let it be and went to the older material.

The VIA had fired Karlsson because he'd been holding back on them, Richards deduced. The encryption the VIA employed was supposed to be second to none, but it was clearly second to that which Karlsson had. There was more to encoding data than making it unreadable, like the quantum fractal system Otto's MT worked off. Karlsson's work ran into self-aware informational packages, predictive ciphers that assessed their own vulnerability, updated themselves accordingly and launched counter strikes at those who attempted to decode them, corrupting code-reading programmes' ability to think and spreading this inefficiency to others. In a similar vein were the automatically generating false data seeds that reacted to their observers, showing them utterly convincing material that happened to be entirely untrue. This was what the VIA had needed counters to, vital in their work of policing the most powerful minds on the planet. On a scale of one to ten, Richards rated Otto's military MT a seven to break; time-consuming, but not impossible. Cracking the VIA was a nine. What Karlsson had defending his own interests was easily a twelve.

He was too dangerous to live, thought Richards, but far too dangerous to kill, so the VIA'd fired him instead, on the mutual understanding that he'd not blow the secrets of the agency wide open if he wanted to stay alive. It was an effective threat; dead was still dead, even a pimsim was only a copy, and, for a man like Karlsson, the thought of becoming a number was probably tantamount to treachery.

The reconstruction of Karlsson's file was completed shortly after 9pm. Richards had it open after only five more hours of fiddling. What he found inside bore out his suspicions.

"...want to help safeguard the future of mankind." Karlsson, speaking in his initial job interview. Audio and vitals only, no video, the only piece of non-text data in his official file, incomplete.

"Why?" asked a nameless interrogator. "What do you mean?"

"Because we as a species... benefit from the machines," replied Karlsson. "But they could also supplant us. I would rather that not happen. If..." Static for three seconds. Clarity returned.

"Explain," asked another voice.

"Explain?" Karlsson laughed. "What is there to explain? All life exists to promote its own survival. A fish crawled from the sea a billion years ago, and I sit here. When I get to the afterlife I don't want to have to say to that fish, 'Sorry, we blew it, we're done. Flesh is dead.' If it comes to that, I want to be able to tell that fish that I tried."

Funny, thought Richards. *For a Norwegian.*

The interview panel did not laugh.

"The AIs are no different. It is in the nature of life to evolve and compete. They are on a collision course with mankind. They will out-compete us. They already are," said Karlsson.

"You do not see the machines then, as a continuation, an evolution of ourselves?" said the first voice. "One could argue that they are the next stage in our evolution."

"Some argue that, and I do not agree with them. A child carries part of its parents forwards when they are gone, in its genes and in its memes. The machines may carry our mental stamp, but they are not us, they never will be. They are not alive in the same way we are."

"So you deny them their rights? They are not equal as sentients?"

"No, of course not," said Karlsson haughtily, as if his interlocutor was an idiot. *He must have been a hit at office parties,* thought Richards. "They are, if anything, superior. That is what scares me. It scares a lot of other people too, that's why the machines need protecting as much from us as we do from them. To co-exist is..."

The file broke up into buzzsaw roars, then skipped. Richards scrabbled at the data fragments, but could not rebuild much more of the interview that interested him, although he did discover that the VIA healthcare package was good. The text he managed OK, but that was formulaic; standard employment clauses, the deal between the agency and Karlsson when he'd departed, nothing enlightening.

Whatever Karlsson had been up to since he'd been fired was cloaked in secrecy. There were his marching orders, then nothing. The logs of others that had come to see him had been stripped, or altered. There were a handful of streetcam footage files, a few more from free-roaming spy-eye cameras that had escaped his attention, but not many. Zhang Qifang was on several. One five-second video sequence in particular: Qifang entering Karlsson's castle, made a blob by Karlsson's counter-measures, round the time he was presumed to have died.

"That's interesting," murmured Richards. "Very interesting."

He worked on for several more hours, accelerating his conscious processes so he subjectively experienced a week of time. He found nothing else. Karlsson had been thorough.

He slowed his mind down, and brought the office back. He walked across the room as it materialised about him and plopped down into his chair, whisky and cigars appearing on his desk as it rippled into being. Outside, Chicago teemed with life. A whole world existed on the other side of the dusty window glass. Richards wondered where it all went when he wasn't there. He sometimes wondered the same about the Real.

He had to get more on Karlsson, dead or alive.

In his mind's eye he constructed a world within a world, and brought up a three-dimensional representation of Karlsson's Detroit lair. He looked over the fortress factory, superimposed his reconstruction over realtime footage in the Real. The place was crawling with aggressive drones, its exterior studded with not-so-hidden weaponry. There was no way in without tripping its formidable security systems, not Gridside.

Karlsson had been frightened of the machines. It was against them he'd set his most formidable defences.

The plans were deliberately incomplete, and out of date. They probably had a low-grade intelligence embedded in them, ready to alert the real fortress to practised penetrations. The building's systems would be aware he was looking at the plans right now. He checked the systems again, going as close as he dared. The whole thing was EM screened; there was not a chance he'd get anything other than the highest strength databeam through without it being chopped in two, but there were other, more old fashioned ways. Richards walked to his office door and turned up his collar. Time to get tough.

He activated the Three running Richards & Klein, Inc, Security Consultants' commsat, and had it reposition itself in a geostationary orbit over the Great Lakes. He told the Three to keep a low profile. Then he told it again, because Threes sometimes drifted off. Once he was happy the thing had understood his instructions, he stepped out of the office door, and into Richards & Klein, Inc, Security Consultants' New York garage.

In a rat with a microchip mind perched on a pile of dissolving concrete, Richards watched Karlsson's fortress from a safe distance. The street was half-submerged and deserted, but then all the streets here were half-submerged and deserted. Karlsson had fetched himself up in the dead heart of Detroit's old industrial port district, a warren of decaying factories, tottering warehouses and unidentifiable iron constructions washed deep red by the rain. Further upriver on the old Canada side, the waterfront gleamed with luxury low-rise, but not here. The ground, honeycombed with salt mines, was not stable enough to support the weight of arcologies, not desirable enough to go upmarket when Canada had joined USNA, so the shoreline remained a skeletal maze of concrete and foamcrete, a three-dimensional warren standing in grim waters, the remnants of earlier attempts at redevelopment undone by the financial crash of 2052 complicating its nineteenth- and twentieth-century layout. Older port buildings slumped tiredly into the lake, the sturdier constructions boxy islands overhung with plant life. Away from the water, trees grew freely in the middle of the street. The sidewalks were thick with grass. Only those at the margins of society lived here, sharing their ruinous home with returning wildlife. Upper Detroit–Windsor was a moderately prosperous, modern city, but large parts, poisoned by two centuries of heavy industry, had been abandoned to the rising lakes, a true industrial wasteland left by way of remembrance. Obsolescence of centralised mass production had left the Detroit Metro area one of the poorest in the USNA. The population here was half what it had been a century and a half before.

It was a good hiding place.

Karlsson's abode was an old port warehouse made of prefabricated concrete slabs whose chemical make-up had been altered to render it resistant to the acid waters round its base. According to the plans, these were supplemented internally by a modern foamcrete coat sprayed 1.3 metres thick. Heavy buttresses had been thrown up its side, atop which unconcealed near-I weaponry scanned the surrounding wasteland. The original roof had been replaced with more reinforced foamcrete, grassed over and allowed to run wild. This roof meadow was studded with dishes, field projectors and energy generation equipment of solar, magnetic interference and wind-driven varieties. A heavy chainlink fence and flatribbon defined a generous perimeter. Small drones darted about the air, and combat sheaths patrolled the shallow lagoon around the building.

Karlsson was making very little effort to blend in.

Richards looked through the rat's eyes, zooming in on the building, searching for weak points. There were precisely none. None of the small constructs he had at his disposal would make it in. There were a lot of mosquitoes here. Millions. Karlsson's drones were very busy methodically hunting down each and every one. That level of paranoid diligence left no room for robotic rats.

As if to prove the point, Richards' rodent exploded as a passing drone spied it. Richards switched to his back-up rat, a half block away.

With luck, the drone was following a routine extermination programme, a take-no-chances, kill-everything approach. Hopefully Karlsson's machines had not logged the outgoing EM traffic between Richards and the rats. If he'd had breath, he'd have held it.

Alarms rang out.

"Shit," said the rat, before promptly exploding.

"Shit," said Richards' android sheath, and opened its eyes. He was operating a standard humanoid shell of the kind routinely employed by a wide variety of businesses, which as of the moment sat in the front of a truck also of a kind routinely employed by a wide variety of businesses, this one emblazoned with the logo of a prominent carbon feedstock merchant – though feedstock was most definitely not what currently sat in the rear of the vehicle – and hidden in a broken-down factory building half a kilometre away.

Richards drummed his borrowed fingers on the dashboard. He thought, but not very hard. He was out of plans A to C, leaving him with plan D. Actually, he had known all along that plan D should really have been plan A, that subtler options would not work, but it was his least favourite option, and he liked to think of himself as an optimist

He was going to have to go in fighting. He groaned, and banged his head on the truck window. This war shit was Otto's job. Richards hated violence, he hated fighting. It wasn't that he wasn't very good at it. His heart wasn't really in it. Otto's was. But Otto was a continent away; by the time he got here Karlsson could have packed up and left.

"You shouldn't have tripped the alarms," he said to no one. "You should have waited, and contacted Otto first," he said, then stopped, because he felt like a twat.

Then he tried to contact Otto anyway and found he couldn't get hold of him. "Fucking mountains," he muttered. He tried Otto's Gridware, though he knew Otto was off-Grid, out hunting. He left a message.

"Hi, Otto," he said tersely to his messenger. "This is your partner. Because you're out creeping around like a fucking ninja, I'm going to have to go in for a fight. Fighting, I recall, is your job, not mine. I don't like fighting, so thanks a fucking bunch. End message."

"Fucking MT!" he shouted. "Why can't he just use the Grid like everyone else? He's a fucking cyborg! What's he got to be frightened of?"

Richards was not frightened. Richards could feel fear or not as the fancy took him. But Richards did not like to kill, and that was a sensation he could not disable. There were no fearless adversaries when Richards fought, no uniforms, no masks, no noble opponents, no *enemy*. The Grid stripped all that away, all the distancing that could make a man a thing. Richards knew the life history of every man, woman and child whose death he had caused. He knew where they grew up, what music they preferred, what toppings they took on their pizza. It made it all so *personal*. Fighting was Otto's job. Humans had a conscience they could ignore.

He had to know what the hell was going on. Experience told him he needed to know yesterday. There was something big going on here. He was surfing a wave of probabilities outside of his ability to predict; k52 would have a hard time attaching meaningful numbers to all the variables at play, but Richards had a hunch that the shit was about to hit the fan.

Which all inevitably led to Big Daddy; Big Daddy was the only option.

Big Daddy was in the back of the truck.

• • • •

Big Daddy's official designation was The Delafuente Mark 14 Combat Mech, a three-metre bipedal death machine of Euro design and outrageous cost, racked and stacked with all manner of overpowered weaponry capable of reducing the conventional army of a moderately sized nation to slag. Mechs like the Mark 14 were what governments deployed when full-scale air assault was judged too soft.

There was room for a human pilot, though remote operation was the norm. They were also big enough to accommodate their own, moron-level Class One should either pilot or remote connection, or both, be broken.

When they'd first seen the mech at the New London Arms Expo, Otto had come over all weird. He rarely got excited about much, but Richards could have sworn that he got dewy-eyed and sparkling when he saw it, a real boy-meets-puppy moment. Denying him would have felt unfair. He regretted his generosity almost straightaway, because it was always Richards that ended up in the driving seat.

And to think he'd deliberately forgotten to have it sent home after the Pallenberg job. Lucky him. Here it was, conveniently stored in the good old USNA waiting for another outing. Hooray.

Big Daddy looked down at him from the back of a van, hunched over like an ogre in a box, its ridiculously small hands clasping its w-flanged knees. While its lamellar camouflage was inert, it displayed a silvery-blue colour on its armour panels, a graphite black elsewhere. The mech's body a sculpted swoop of rounded shapes and gaping gunports. Beautiful, if you liked that kind of thing, which Otto did, and Richards didn't. To him it looked like a toy Japanese robot of two centuries back.

"Come on then," said Richards. He inserted part of his mind into the machine. It was like putting his head in the mouth of a lion. He shuffled it out of the truck. With incongruous delicacy,

Big Daddy stepped down onto the ground and unbent its spine and limbs until it stood at its full height. Big Daddy whirred and clunked as its legs extended, weapons unfolded and shoulders moved back and locked into place. There was a loud hiss and clank as its spine straightened and the vertebral locking pins engaged. The hum of its nuclear batteries rose as its engines came on line and then dropped back as its automatic systems check got underway. The surface shimmered as the lamellar camouflage cycled through a number of configuration patterns, finishing on a reproduction of the factory wall behind it. Weapons made serious sounds as they powered up and down. Ammo feeds clunked as Big Daddy primed his cannons. Noises that set Richards' imaginary teeth on edge.

"Big Daddy ready," it grated.

"That's just super," said Richards sarcastically. He had Big Daddy open its cockpit and his smaller sheath clambered in. Only when the android was in the mech did he switch his full awareness to the mech's sensing systems, plastered in red phallic power displays.

He looked over the site's defences again and swore. If he got in, but couldn't get the war mech out, this was going to be expensive.

"Big Daddy ready," said the mech again.

"For the love of…!" Richards banged his sheath's fist against the interior of the larger machine. He felt like a Russian doll, a machine in a machine in a machine. "I heard you the first time!" He pushed the One to the back of Big Daddy's cramped cyberspace where it waited placidly. Richards and his war donkey, he thought. He took over completely.

Richards grumbled as he set the monster to walking, clanking and hissing noisily. "Let's get this over and done with," he muttered, and Big Daddy and the android sheath spoke with him. He went over to the wall of the factory he'd been hiding in and walked through it without stopping.

Outside the atmosphere the Three in the commsat intensified Richards' controlling signal, relaying it from base unit to war machine.

Karlsson's creatures knew he was coming. His Gridpipe back to the base unit cut through the Grid like a shark's fin in water. It lost some coherency as he passed into the fortress's EM umbrella; this would grow worse as he approached the walls. Richards checked the signal, formulated back-up orders to Big Daddy's onboard brain should his influence be curtailed, but the Gridpipe was bright and loud. If there were problems with the feed, then the Three on the satellite would switch to pulsed laser communciation – only when he got inside would there be a problem. These were eventualities, it was all systems go.

Richards was confident there would be no problem.

The straight way to the factory would be the best.

A swarm of drones stooped to attack Big Daddy as he stomped through a weed-choked car park. Richards blew them from the sky with a volley of mini-missiles from Big Daddy's shoulder mount.

"I hate this. So unsubtle," he muttered. A homeless family scurried across his path. He paused to let them by. "You better get away!" he said to them, Big Daddy's speakers rendering his advice in an ear-mincing bellow. "It's going to get messy around here, war messy!" He realised he was enjoying himself, riding high on a squirt of simulated adrenalin, and that irritated him.

In five minutes he'd decimated a squad of dog drones and reached the edge of the lagoon Karlsson's factory squatted in. He raised Big Daddy's fist and extended the mech's plasma thrower. The weapon wheezed as it sucked in a tank full of atmosphere, then roared it back out as a beam of superheated ionised air that atomised the fence and flatribbon projectors for a ten-metre stretch. He walked through, shooting down drones as he went. Fire came in from the turrets above the

factory, heavy-calibre rounds that he had to set Big Daddy
into, like a man walking into driving rain. Some of the camolam was scratched and stopped working. Otto was going to be
pissed off.

"Fuck off," said Richards, and hurled dumb-fire missiles at
the near-I cannon. EM pulses swamped them, but as they
were mechanical detonators atop solid fuel rockets guided only
by Richards' aim, they flew on. A couple were shot down by
more direct means, but Richards fired Big Daddy's arm cannon
at the guns tracking the rockets and that was that. Then the
rockets did for most of Karlsson's heavy ordinance.

On he stomped, Big Daddy's feet sloshing through the murky
water, bringing up unidentifiable industrial wrack into the light
that was swiftly carried back below and crushed by his huge
weight. EM attacks rained down on the mech, dispersing on
the machine's faraday armours. Simultaneous electronic attacks sallied out against the commsat and Richards. Twice he
was forced to switch communications mode between base unit
and war machine. Still he came on. Karlsson had gone to pains
to deter unwanted visitors; what he had not planned for was a
full-scale assault.

When he was twenty metres from the factory, Richards
launched a dozen limpet mines from Big Daddy's forearms.
They flew forward and attached themselves in a neat arc to
the wall. High voltage played across them, attempting to disable the bombs' electronics, but there were none, the mines
working off clockwork timers of Richards' design. Richards
marched on in Big Daddy's body, reaching the wall as the
shaped charges imploded, carving a neat hole in the wall just
big enough to accommodate the machine. Richards deployed
the plasma thrower to melt the remaining foamcrete in the
gap, then levelled the launcher again. This time, he loaded it
with canisters containing ten thousand short-range ants

apiece, and fired them one after the other into the swirling mess of the interior beyond the crude entryway. The canisters blew open in mid air, showering the place with the tiny robots. The pattered into the walls and floors, sprang to their feet and surged away, searching for energy sources. About half of them were picked off by drones, but the rest scuttled into air vents and conduits. With the ants deployed, Richards' job was nearly done.

Richards stepped forward through a cloud of dust into a world of chaos.

He was in a large, open loading bay filling the end quarter of the fortress. Eight large pits, big enough for heavy trucks or dirigible gondolas, were set into the foamcrete. Klaxons bellowed and debris rained down from the high ceiling, bouncing across the floor or clattering off Big Daddy's carapace. Anti-intruder smoke casters, fires and dust kept visibility down to a few metres. Infrared wasn't much better, queered by swirling columns of hot air billowing up from the pits in the floor. Fire, too much fire. He hadn't hit it that hard. The building was eating itself. He had minutes at best, but he walked cautiously, fearful of toppling Otto's expensive toy into a loading pit. He brought the plans of the building into mind; he needed to get into the main body of the complex where his ants were congregating. The building worked off a diffuse multi-brain network, blended personality, no main server, multiple redundant systems. He needed to plug into one of those quickly before the whole lot suicided.

There were the sounds of explosions in the distance. These stopped. His ants were too few to form an effective chain and convey much information back to him through the EM noise, but if the cessation of demo charges going off was anything to go by they'd fulfilled their most important role.

Or he was walking into a big trap.

The wall at the end of the hangar was crossed with sus-
pended walkways going in and out of doors cut into the
foamcrete. A number of humanoid combat sheaths appeared
on these and opened fire with flechette rifles and heavy rail
guns. As Big Daddy had eight-centimetre-thick diamond-
weave armour plate, they might as well have been hurling
rotten fruit. Servomotors whined as Richards tilted the big
mech's torso upward and gunned them down. Some fell from
the walkways and landed in front of him where they struggled
to get up. Richards stomped them vindictively to pieces. It did
little to improve his mood.

He approached a large blast door set into the wall at the end
of the bay. He raised his fist again, ready to melt the doors to
slag, but they slid open before he could fire, to reveal a large-
calibre spider cannon squatting in the way.

"Uh-oh," said Richards. The spider cannon fired a hi-ex shell
before he could annihilate it, knocking Big Daddy onto its armoured behind. The mech skidded several metres backwards
on its arse and its elbows, drawing a shower of sparks from the
floor. Richards sat up. The spider cannon switched to full auto
and sprayed him liberally at short range. Warning indicators
began to flicker in the mech, but Richards weathered it until
the other machine's clip was empty.

"Nice try," he said, and blew the spider cannon into fragments. He got back up again and walked through the door.
Another spider cannon was coming round the corner. He destroyed that before it got a shot off, and lumbered onwards,
leaving shattered machine parts in his wake.

A broad corridor ran the length of the building, to his left
the exterior wall, to the right an interior block the height of
the building divided into offices and accommodation. On the
other side of this block were a series of large workshops and
plant rooms, at least according to the plans. There wasn't

enough room for Richards to proceed in Big Daddy, and not enough time to blast his way into every room, which wouldn't have been so clever, seeing as he was looking for information, not piles of rubble. He cut Big Daddy's mind loose, took control of his android sheath and clambered out of the front.

"Stay!" he shouted at the mech, pointing a commanding composite finger.

"Big Daddy stay!" it agreed enthusiastically. "Big Daddy engage hostiles?"

"Yeah, yeah, knock yourself out," Richards said. This sheath had no coat or hat. He felt naked. "I'm taking the drones though." Two crow-sized flight drones popped off Big Daddy's back and fell into covering positions. "Right then, let's see what this fucker's been up to," said Richards, and walked off into the warren of rooms. His ants were fighting a hard battle with the building's minds, which were still in the process of trying to kill themselves. He could feel it through the ants; it was a strange one, not like anything he'd encountered before, like Four or Six, but without the self-volition. Neither true AI or near-I. He feared he knew what that meant.

He walked through a door. Flashing lights and debris made a nonsense of sight. Half the rooms were collapsed in on themselves, demolition charges exploded before the ants could short out the system entirely. He scrambled over rubble, peering into rooms as he went: office furniture coated in plaster and carbon fibres, here bedrooms, there a kitchen whose broken taps pumped a dust-skinned puddle on to the floor. He pushed on. An android leapt out from a wrecked room, gun at the ready. His drones blasted it to pieces with idle efficiency.

He found the first fibre cluster thanks to his ants, who stood to attention on the back three of their five legs as he walked in. "Cheers, lads," he said, and had them go off to sniff out more vital systems to cripple. The cluster spilled out of a data conduit in the wall like a tangle of filthy spaghetti. He couldn't link wirelessly with the building mind, the shields it had on the broadcast network were too good and the ants had not yet brought it down, so he had to hunt for a direct link for a good minute through optic cables all rendered the same by a coating of dust. He eventually found what he was looking for, a coupling for a fibre that connected all the components of the building physically together. He popped open a panel in his chest and connected himself into the network, then it didn't matter what fancy crap Karlsson had on the network because he was in and ready and no building mind was going to stand up to Richards, AI.

Richards expected an assault that never came. It was over.

Richards began to interrogate the building's minds. He got that same sense of detachment he had had through the ants, more immediate to him now he was in. The machines within the network dumped their information into Richards, offering up their treasures without complaint, and he suspiciously sifted it for logic bombs and viruses. Once he'd done that, there wasn't much left.

There was no personality left to the building, but as he interrogated the composite brain, gradually, horrifyingly, Richards realised that it had had one once.

It had been lobotomised.

Richards became furious. He put the mind out of its misery as quickly as he could, and took control of the building. He shut off all the remaining drones and what was left of the self-destruct mechanisms, activated the halon fire-suppression systems and began running through the crippled AI's memory. Much of it had been wiped. Richards anger grew as he realised that there had once been twenty sentient linked AIs in the building. All had been similarly stripped. *Karlsson has gone mad*, he thought.

And then he located Karlsson. He unclipped the fibre optic from his chest and ran down the corridor, his access panel left hanging open.

Karlsson lay slumped in a pool of his own blood, covered with plaster, his head caved in by a falling piece of masonry, laying bare a mess of tangled monofilament wire, nano wires and grey matter studded with hair and bone. Richards felt his pulse. Nothing. He was emaciated, naked. His own waste lay thick and stinking about the chair he'd been sat in.

Meat puppet, has to be. Someone had wiped the AIs here, and infiltrated Karlsson's mind via his mentaug, imprisoning him in his own body.

"Who would do that?" he whispered. He wished he had his coat, to cover the dead man's face. Pieces of grit sat on the sclera of Karlsson's eyes. Somehow, that bothered Richards the most. He closed them gently with his machine fingers.

He stood up and looked at the man for a moment. "Time to find out what the fuck exactly has been going on here," he said.

The workshops were extensive. In one empty of all equipment he found the bodies of twenty men and women, members of Karlsson's clade of anti-singularity paranoiacs. They were long dead, their corpses bloated and slimy. Some of them Richards recognised from their DNA profiles, a mix of fugitive brilliance and talented amateurs, some real genius here. He estimated that they'd been dead about two weeks. Each had a shot to the head – executed. Richards shook his head. Such a waste, every shattered skull a universe gone.

The next room was a burnt-out mess, old damage, not from today. He made enough of it to separate gene-looms from surgical tanks, carbon-weavers from base units. Data he scraped from the charred components of the machines told him that this was where both the fake Qifangs and the fake heiress had originated. Data wrestled from the wreck told him so: the heiress duplicated several days after Qifang, their bodies speed-grown in pieces on the looms, and welded together.

He thought of the drones, of the meat-puppeted Karlsson, of the stripped AI minds.

AI. These were AI crimes.

And then he found it.

Behind a smashed protein scaffold tank of a gene-loom sat the heat-slagged remains of a base unit. Not that of an AI, but one of those used to accrue and store pimsim data for living meat persons before the moment of death, and from which the simulated personality of the recently deceased could be released into the heaven levels or operate out in the Grid and the Real.

It was amongst the most damaged pieces of machinery in the room. "Someone's gone to extra trouble with this," said Richards. He pulled it apart, hunting for chips. Most were scragged beyond redemption, but there were just enough left to reassemble a moment in time: a conversation with a fat man at a gala dinner. Richards data-matched the face: Harold Kamer, a senator from one of the hayseed Midwest states that had refused the rewilding. In his eyes, Richards could make out the reflection of his interlocutor, the man whose memcord this was.

The distorted reflection was the face of Professor Zhang Qifang.

But Qifang had no implants, no mentaug. He had no registered pimsim. He didn't believe in either.

"Curiouser and curiouser," said Richards. He hunted about; he knew what he was looking for, but it was hard to tell the junked machines apart. Finally, he found it, a direct neural imager. That's how they'd copied Qifang's mind.

He had his truck drive round and popped all his probes out of it and Big Daddy for a quick data sweep. It wouldn't be long before the authorities showed up. Even Richards couldn't kick off a small-scale military action and saunter off. He'd be able to clear it with the Sams, even if he had to get Hughie involved, but whatever happened, his equipment was going to be impounded, it would take some time to get it out, and the local cops would want a long, tedious chat about letting off heavy artillery within the city limits. He could do without that.

"Big Daddy!"

"Yes," came the machine's stentorian reply.

"There are going to be some men here soon. Do not shoot them, got that?"

"Yes. Do not shoot." Richards thought it sounded disappointed. It wasn't possible, Big Daddy was the one machine whose personality he wouldn't dare upgrade.

"Walk out the back, get into the truck and deactivate yourself, got that too?"

"Yes. Big Daddy go sleep in truck."

"That's right. Stay put until I come and get you." And get you cleaned up, thought Richards. For all of his sordid enjoyment of war, Otto hated it when his equipment got dirty. He ordered his probes to retreat to the truck, and the truck, once it had the appropriate clearance from the authorities, to return to the New York garage, clearance he petitioned for now.

That done, he left the laboratory to walk outside and explain himself to the cops. Then he'd get back to Hughie. Something much bigger than they previously suspected was underway. Well, much bigger than he'd previously expected. Hughie might well have been exploiting his good nature again and...

His sheath collapsed, his consciousness gone.

He found himself as he truly was, huge and powerful on the Grid, emergency overrides dissolving his fantasy self to show him the monster beneath.

"Eh? What the fuck now?"

Failsafes on his base unit had cranked his operating speed up to inhuman levels. His racing mind filled with alarms. Datafeeds reported the beginnings of a substantial explosion close by in the Real. He was thinking far faster than a human mind ever could; sensations from the Real filtered in through the treacly slowness of temporal dislocation. Subroutines compensated, allowing the full spectral range he ordinarily enjoyed, adding meaning to the Real's distorted sounds, slowed to slothful, guttural roars. He felt the arco vibrate as a shockwave strolled through its structure, and his attentions switched to a human emulant on the arcade outside – nothing special about it, the kind worn by geriatrics or tourists remotely holidaying, only this one was engaged in the final stages of fiery disintegration as a low-yield atomic ignited within.

He wound back the outside camera footage, to see more clearly.

He guessed he'd see the face of Professor Zhang Qifang looking back at him.

He watched as balls of flame unpacked themselves from the elderly professor, sprouting into expanding bubbles of destruction, announcing the birth of a short-lived star, right on his doorstep. *Pretty*, he thought, *but inconvenient.*

The shockwave ran ahead of the explosion, ripping the floor into splinters, pushing out and down, smashing metal and carbons, a sphere of violence that spared nothing. The office windows blew out, the pieces simultaneously melting; the door was slammed off its hinges, into the waiting room and through the wall on the other side, where it disintegrated into burning embers, then evaporated. The electromagnetic pulse that preceded the blast wrought havoc on the arco's systems, shutting much of the city building down, but Richards' heavily fortified base unit held, and he continued to watch with morbid fascination. He was helpless. Pedestrians

outside on the gallery half a kilometre away were flung into
the wall or hurled to their deaths in the park below; others
caught fire and twisted like dervishes; those nearer exploded
into their constituent pieces as if a helpful holofeed were describing the anatomy of man, their skin flayed away, then
their flesh, then their bones. Those nearer still simply turned
to steam.

It rarely paid an AI that interfaced with the human world to
run so quickly. In such a state they could think so fast a day
would pass as a month, and although they would process much
in that time, they could do nothing useful in the world of the
Real; the material universe became as unyielding as rock.

"Balls," said Richards, and sent Otto another message. He
sent one to Chloe too, cramming as much information into
them as he possibly could. "You're on your own now, big fella."

Time, no matter how slowly it ran, could never be stopped.
Richards initiated thousands of simulations, trying to figure a
way out. There were none. He had no time to upload himself
in his entirety elsewhere, and where could he go anyway? He
could send out a sensing presence back to his sheath in
Chicago or to any one of the fifty-plus he had elsewhere, but
his very core was about to be consumed by fire, leaving any
remote projection a broken facade, dribbling nonsense. What
would be the point? He sank into unfamiliar lassitude.

Richards watched the world he had built blasted to pieces.
A wash of nuclear heat scoured the offices of Richards & Klein
clean. The air ignited, and the resultant vacuum sucked the
exterior windows in. Flames roared out of the arco as a great
part of the building burst outwards, four floors up and four
floors down from the detonation's epicentre. He was only glad
that Genie's base unit was at her parent's house.

The young star devoured the last of Richards' external sensors, and he lost all connection with the Real, then the Grid.

Alone in the dark for what seemed an aeon, Richards felt his processes flicker and die one by one. *I'm dead,* he thought. After all his years of fretting about extinction he felt disappointingly ambivalent, now it finally came down to it.

The flow of Richards' subjective time ran on slow as geology and the fires burned and spun like ravenous whirligigs trapped in glass, until his life was snatched away with a terrible abruptness.

Chapter 22
Pirate

Small blue sparks played on the exposed electronics of the drone, currently a mimetic, self-governing rifle, finally resembling a tree branch. It shuddered as it attempted to alter its shape and flee, the remaining fan on its fuselage rotating helplessly, then it died. Otto nudged the dead machine with the toe of his boot. A damn shame he'd had to kill it but it was too sophisticated for his near-I to pirate. He needed Richards for that kind of thing.

Blood trickled down his arm. He'd been hit by a sliver, a polymer tranq dart projectile keyed to dissolve when confronted with the chemical signature of blood. The tranquilliser was strong enough to render a normal man unconscious, but not Otto. The in-built phactory of his 'tech supplied an antidote, and the feeling of wooziness lifted.

He looked around the woods cautiously, holding his breath. Nothing but forest sounds. The trees were widely spaced, and through them the moon was a chalk impression on the blue of the sky. The moon's pocked face was approaching full, the lights of its colonies visible on its shaded crescent as pale sapphires. He had memorised the names of every base when he was a boy, when he had designs on being an astronaut, but there had been far fewer lights then. The decades had run fast; cities glimmered in the curves of lunar craters.

Otto sat on a log and dressed his wound with a thin sheet of geckro-backed plastic that clung to his skin with leechlike intimacy. The tranq dart had left a red dot on his left bicep not far from where his would-be assassin had hit him back at the diner; both would be gone in a day or so thanks to his healthtech. Otto shut the first-aid case. He willed the phactory to give him a dose of painkiller, more for his worn shoulder than for his recent wounds.

Another twelve miles to go till he got to Valdaire's hideout, and night was coming in. He picked up Chloe off the floor from behind a tree where he'd tossed her when the drone had attacked. "You sure this is the place?" he asked. The Grid cheater signal remained maddeningly indistinct. The game was nearly up, but he'd still not dared to access the Grid directly; he might as well blow a trumpet announcing his arrival. On the other hand, Chloe could be walking him off a cliff. He'd just have to go with it and see what happened, not the way he liked to work.

"Yes," Chloe said. "The cabin was a hideout for pirate 'net casters once. Veronique brought me here three times when she was in college."

"Valdaire was a pirate?"

"No! She only dated pirates," said Chloe, scandalised. "I did not approve. They were silly boys. She was undergoing a standard final-stage adolescent rebellious phase. She got over it. She is a good girl. I love her."

They went up, out of the dip in the mountain. Chloe directed Otto onto an ancient road, blacktop crumbled to grit under leaf litter. The road held a steady gradient, and was smoother than the forest floor, but its width was choked with saplings. On the road a second drone found them, but Otto was ready this time and he riddled it with holes. Past its station the road became impassable, thick with razor-edged briars too dense and tenacious to be natural.

"Go up the bank," said Chloe. "You will be able to see the cabin from the top of the rise. It is not far from here. The road loops round this knoll. We can cut out the bend and avoid the thorns."

Otto checked the maps he'd downloaded from the car. The topography was as she said, though there was no cabin marked. He picked his way past the gengineered foliage and headed up the hill. They stopped below the weathered rock at the top. Otto lay down, turned up his ocular magnification to full. There was a cabin there, after all, probably not on the map because it looked like no one had been there in years. It was practically derelict, maybe five rooms, a wide veranda out front railed in by rotted banisters. The paint had flaked away and the bare boards were grey or, where the sun did not hit the wood to dry it, thickly green with pleurococcal growth. The roof shingles were slipped and mossy; it'd leak like a sieve in a proper storm, but he supposed it was just about habitable. The finned twin nose fan housings of an aircar, an anachronism in this place, poked out from under pine branches behind the building. The car barked out a nonsense sig when he tried short-range access. It had no other signifier. Valdaire's work again.

On the hill behind were a number of battered satellite dishes clustered in a wire enclosure, crude camouflage peeling, the dull aluminium beneath spotted white with oxidisation. The chainlink fence about them was rusted and sagging. One dish lay on the ground, bent into junk by a falling branch, others standing over it like geriatric war veterans saluting the dead. Someone was using them again. A new solar panel stood nearby, hooked up to the least tatty example, and it had been pointed away from the others.

"You might have been telling me the truth," said Otto.

"Yes, yes! Veronique!"

"Maybe. There are no signs of life, no fire, no lights, no movement." Otto rolled over onto his back and looked up at the sky. The light was going fast. "We may be too late."

"Quickly, quickly! Help her! Oh, Veronique," wailed Chloe.

Otto got up and made his way down the slope. He stuck to cover as best he could, but here on the eastern side of the mountains cover was in short supply. The storms that battered the west coast and the Gulf of Mexico broke on the coastal range and the western side of the Rockies, so the slopes hereabouts, especially those overlooking the high plains, stayed the way they had been for centuries, dry, bald pine forest growing right out of the rock. Cardenas would have found the place familiar.

"Chloe," he said, barely above a whisper. "I need you to be quiet now. Do not speak until I say you can."

"Will that keep Veronique safe?"

"Yes."

Otto reached the cabin as the shadows filled the valleys. He crept up on to the veranda as noiselessly as a mountain lion, taking up station in its pocket of early night, gun held to the ready, adrenalin and synthetic aggression triggers rising. Up and up the peaks were tinted orange, caught by the rays of the departing sun, snow garish, rocks the colour of marmalade. The forest was filling up with small noises of crepuscular animals awakening to their brief business, of birds singing out the day. The air was still, scented by pine sap and warm rock radiating the day's heat back into the air. If it weren't for the aircar and the dishes and solar panel out the back, the valley would have looked like a dozen others in the parks, quiet and tired and empty, the cabin one of many dotted signs of human habitation gradually being sucked back into the thin mountain soil.

Otto's breath was slow and steady, the only human sound he could hear. He pushed at the door. The wood had warped and the hinges sagged, so he had to step forward and lift it to stop it catching on the floor. He stepped through the gap quickly, covering the hallway. Nothing. No. He hesitated, there was something, the faint drone of machinery coming from a door toward the back. Otto crept forward, gun out before him in a double grip, sighting down the barrel, his near-I linking him to its targetter. He let go of it with his left hand and slowly pushed this second door open.

Framed by the fading light of a dirty window was a man in a chair. Otto could see a woman's foot on a couch poking out from under a blanket, her skin a lustrous black against the evening murk; it was from the end of the couch that the machine noise emanated. Valdaire, alive and still jacked into the RealWorld Reality Realms.

Of far greater urgency was that the man had a large-calibre pistol trained on him, big and bad enough to make a mess of cyborg internal armour.

"Good evening, Otto Klein," said the man. His face was in shadow, but his accent was unmistakeably SudAm. Otto wondered for a moment if the communists had got their red fingers into this whole sorry business, or if the past had finally caught up with him, until the Latino spoke again. "I am Special Agent Santiago Chures of the Virtualities Investigation Authority. Please," he said equably, jerking his gun, "place your weapon on the floor, kick it towards me and step into the room. Do not turn around. There is a chair to your right against the wall. Back up to it and sit down. Do this slowly and we will remain on good terms."

"If not, you will shoot me?"

The agent nodded.

Otto dropped his gun, kicked it away into the corner of the room away from Agent Chures. He sat. The musty chair creaked loudly. Valdaire lay stretched out opposite him, recumbent on a mouldform couch, the newness of the equipment around her startling in the decrepitude of the cabin. Tubes went into her arms, sticky pads that glinted with weak LEDs were placed on her temples, somewhere down her top more shone. The light of these sensors gave her an ethereal quality. A skullcap, an antique v-jack, encased her head, a thick braid of cables trailing from it and out of sight. She smelt bad, as bad as a Grid addict out of the Real for months.

"You have found what you are looking for," said the agent. There was an arrogance to him, but his hauteur was at odds with his appearance. The man was a mess. He held his gun in his left hand, and Otto guessed it was not his preferred. His right arm was caught up in a makeshift sling, and bandages about his chest were thick with blood. His nose had been broken and hurriedly reset, probably by Chures himself. His lips were split. Both of his eyes were black, the left closed by bruising, all recent injuries. His clothes were filthy and torn, but it was apparent that they had been cut from luxurious cloth. Under his unwashed, animal scent Otto's near-I caught the lingering smell of multiple toiletries. The near-I duly parsed the olfactory data and identified them: expensive. A small well-trimmed beard stood proud of the stubble that fuzzed the rest of his face. Empty attachment points for augmatics sat above each ear, the skin about them scratched and raw. A fat sausage of an aux-mind, the pick-up housing and buffer system for a full AI personality blend, sat round the base of his skull. This was as battered as Chures, but was as extravagant as his suit, made from hand-worked silver, engravings picked out with niello.

"I apologise," Chures said. "Our hostess is currently indisposed. I hope my company is adequate."

"You are a mess. Stand down. Let me help."

"I was attacked yesterday," Chures said. He offered no more, but held his gun steady at Otto.

Otto stared at him, shrugged. There was a flatness to Chures' eyes, something lacking, or something sharpened to the point of hardly being there at all. He had a gaze hard to hold, the gaze of a killer. Otto looked at the unconscious woman. "Veronique Valdaire. I want to talk to her."

"She is illegally trespassing in the thirty-six virtual Realms, in direct contravention of international law." The man's voice hardened further. His gun remained trained upon Otto. "When she wakes up, if she wakes up, I will arrest her. Then we shall see what to do about you."

"OK," said Otto. "You do that. First I need to speak to her, an ongoing investigation. I am here on business from the EuPol five, cleared by the Three Uncle Sams. I have jurisdiction here."

"I know your business, Mr Klein. Your Allpass carries weight, even with the VIA, but weight is no guarantor of access. As an agent of the sole authority in the Atlantic Alliance tasked with policing the machines, I am free to ignore their dictats. My advice is, don't upset me."

Otto looked down at the gun. "Why this?"

Chures twitched it. "Not everyone is as they seem, Mr Klein, and I, like you, am not currently linked to the Grid. I have no way of telling if you are who I think you are. Even if I were, I would not put my gun down."

"I am not your enemy."

"I do not know that."

"Why?"

"Such times, Mr Klein, such times." He did not elaborate, and settled his gun more comfortably on his lap.

"I have medical supplies outside..." Otto began to rise, hands raised.

"Stay seated!" shouted Chures. He moved fast, put a bullet in the wall. The projectile left a head-sized hole in the wood.

"OK," said Otto, and sank back down into the chair.

"Keep your hands where I can see them," said Chures. He was pale. He winced as he moved. That shot had cost him.

Otto frowned, borderline aggressive, to let the VIA man know he wasn't cowed. "Now what?"

"Now we wait."

Chapter 23
Reality 36

Veronique and Jagadith climbed all day. At night, they camped on one of the tree's broad branches, a silent Jagadith keeping watch, fire in his eyes. Veronique had kept up her fitness regime from her days in the Peace Corps, and her dancing helped, but at the end of the first day she was a mass of aches and grazes, her skin worn out by the bark. She envied Jagadith's stamina. He was bound by some of the strictures of flesh, she'd seen that, but he was not in any way human.

They drank water from holes in the bark, and ate the flesh of a giant squirrel that had been foolish enough to stray within reach of the knight, cooking it on a fire of bark shavings.

Halfway through the second day they reached the top. The drooping crown of spiny leaves proved difficult to ascend, but ascend it they did. On a wide platform of green, they stood between two worlds.

Below, Jagadith's world stretched away into the purple distances of mountains, the swamp and jungle Qifang had created pathetically small within the arid landscapes of the highlands. Above them rotated the vortex, huge and foreboding. Each of its arms was a lazy stream of matter being sucked into a hole in the centre, a hole so black its colour was more than the mere absence of light.

"We must go up," said Jag, gesturing at it.

Veronique nodded. "There's a chance we'll both be atomised," she said. "How can you be sure that won't happen?"

"I cannot," said Jagadith. "You are the expert."

"Right," said Veronique, "Fine. I've not experienced it very often, but certain of my kind" – she paused – "gods, have been known to partition the worlds they invade. It's how we run our in-world research stations. We should be OK…" She shook her head, not able to believe fully what she was seeing, wandered round the crown of the tree, taking the vortex in from several angles. "But this is of another order. He's taking the matter of this world outside it, or into his sub-world." She stopped, thinking. "Pulling this off is not easy."

"Your professor is incapable of such work?"

"Oh, no," said Veronique. "Qifang certainly has the skill, I just don't see why he would do it."

"Your devotion is most touching, madam goddess," said Jagadith, "but I urge you to put aside your concerns for this man, as dear to you as he may have been. I fear he has been concealing an important part of his character. Men do not change suddenly, O divinity. Not in so extreme a manner."

Veronique looked at him. "At the time they were closed off, there were thirty-six RealWorld Reality Realms," she said baldly, "thirty-six universes, until the hackers got into them; four worlds, each unique and full of life that thought and lived, wiped out by idiots. Whatever is happening here, I am not about to let the number be reduced again."

"Then let us not be dallying." Jagadith made to climb one of the tree's topmost serrated leaves. It was as big as a hill, its points within touching distance of the vortex. She followed him.

They gained the top quickly, the nearness of their goal lending strength to their tired limbs.

"Well then," said Jagadith, and reached for the vortex.

"Hey!" said Veronique. "Let's not rush."

Jagadith nodded.

"Pass me your knife."

Jagadith hesitated, then handed over his dagger. Veronique sat down and hacked a stringy, fist-sized lump of the leaf they stood upon. She pulled it free with some difficulty; its fibres were hard to cut. When it was loose, she bundled it into a ball and hefted it in one hand, then she threw it underarm, up into the hole.

It exploded with a violent flash. When their eyes recovered, they saw flame boiling on the surface of the void.

"That is most troubling," said Jagadith, and frowned. "We have no way in."

"That's not true." Veronique put her hand out to him. "Now might be the time to let me try out my, um, divine powers."

"We will alert your mentor."

"He knows we are coming."

"It is still risky. You do not know it will work."

"No, I don't. Jesus, don't you people trust your gods?"

"Madam divinity, we spend rather a lot of time and effort attempting to keep them from meddling in our affairs," said Jagadith wryly. "Five billion gods are too many for any world. Still," he sighed, "it is the only thing for it. If we do not go now, the world is lost at any rate. I have no doubt that is what Tarquinius would tell me."

"OK. Right."

"Only…"

"I'm thinking. This isn't easy. I've got no experience."

"Do let us try to be subtle, madam goddess."

"Subtle. Yes. OK. Now be quiet and let me think."

• • • •

An amber sphere rose up and out into total darkness – darkness as black as the hole it hid. Like a drop of luminescent oil rising through dark waters, it floated slowly and majestically, moving slightly off to the left, away from the entrance to the void. It shed golden light as it went, light that was immediately lost. As it descended, its radiance focused itself into a spot of light that grew stronger until the sphere gently touched the utterdark of the floor. It burst like a soap bubble, shattering into a hundred starlets which dissipated with sad splashes of light. Where it had been stood Jagadith and Veronique.

"Most efficacious, madam goddess," said Jagadith approvingly. "You guided us as surely as a pilot brings a ship safe to harbour." Apart from himself and Veronique, who shone with a faint moonglow, nothing at all was visible. "Now, where are we?"

"Shall I try some light?" said Veronique.

"Madam, let us not be overstretching ourselves. We are in no immediate danger. It is advisable not to tamper with our increasingly fragile universe if we do not absolutely have to."

"Let's try something a little more straightforward then." And then she shouted, as loudly as she could. "Professor!" The volume of her voice was shocking in the quiet – both she and Jag had been whispering before without realising.

"Professor!"

A light split the horizon, a distance of several miles, Jag guessed. It formed a hemisphere, a glowing halo creeping out from it, bringing feeble illumination to the dark.

"Veronique? Veronique, why are you shouting? I may be old, but I am not yet deaf." The voice was gentle and cracked, and carried the faintest shred of a Cantonese accent. It was also everywhere, in everything. The voice *was* everything.

It was the voice of Professor Zhang Qifang, fugitive teacher and new god.

"In the beginning... I see," said Jagadith, his lips tight. He shifted his grip on his sword. "Be wary, madam goddess," he said to Veronique, "your mentor is suffering from the largest of all divinity complexes."

They walked towards the source of the voice, the light in the distance guiding them across the featureless, entropic dark.

Halfway there, Jagadith reached out and grasped Veronique's hand. Though her teeth chattered, his hand still felt warm, and no plume of steam issued from his mouth. He squeezed slightly, reassuring and warming her.

"They are here, madam goddess," whispered the knight, "to either side of us. No! Do not look directly. Try not to draw their attention. They are changed, my fellow paladins, but I doubt their abilities are much dimmed."

Veronique looked rigidly ahead, but from the corner of her eyes she could see them. A long rank of silent giants glistened into view, the guardians of The RealWorld Reality Realms. Each of the RR's had them, simple security protocols given forms by bored nerds. Jokes, really, elevated to positions of monumental responsibility when the RR RealWorlds were closed, guarding the universes against the creatures that had created them.

They glowed with pale blue light, their forms vastly inflated. A knight upon a horse, armoured in the late gothic fashion, glared imperiously at them. A titanic moose stood by his side, its mouth slack, gaze unfocused, a wooden club of Herculean proportions hanging loosely from a primitive hand. Beside it, a pair of moustachioed brothers in what looked like plumber's garb, wrenches at the ready. By them, a phantom bear with an eye patch wearing a lion skin with intelligent eyes who, though closely resembling Tarquinius, had clearly once been flesh. They and a score more stood silently, tracking the pair with eyes suffused with the cold glimmer of hateful stars.

It was a long, frightful walk. Veronique wanted to break into a run, to get to the pool of radiance ahead.

"Be careful," said Jagadith, his voice almost inaudible, yet full of overwhelming calm. "They are his creatures now, but they still remember me as the greatest of them. Only my will holds them from assault." A single droplet of sweat worked its way down his temple from under his turban. "It troubles me that the other paladins are here, enslaved. The work of your mentor goes beyond this Realm and into the others. This is not like any expulsion I have ever performed before. He is a powerful man, this Qifang."

As they approached the pool, its light drowned out the feeble luminescence of the paladin ghosts, but she could still feel their hard gaze boring into her neck.

And then they reached the light. It took a moment for Veronique to look into it, and even when she did, she still could not see anything other than the brilliance of a sun.

Jag stepped straight into it, dragging her with him.

They were in a room. She blinked the afterimages away from the blinding hemisphere, her eyes struggling with the sudden change. The change was as disorienting as it had been sudden, and the shift in temperature made her giddy. It took her a few moments to recover.

She recognised it as Professor Zhang Qifang's office, rendered as she'd never seen it rendered before.

Books from several centuries lined one wall, ancient mechanisms another. Pieces of pre-electronic machines and newer tech littered the place, half-buried by drifts of living paper. Outside, the sun shone on students crossing a university square, garbed in mid-twenty-first-century fashions.

It was stiflingly warm after their walk through the dark.

"This is incredible," said Veronique. She inspected the ceiling, touched the wood, rubbed dust between her fingertips.

"This is not real, is it? I mean this is... This is the most convincing simulation I have ever seen. They never feel entirely real." She trailed off, walking round the room. In the best virtualities, like the Realms, there were always signifiers to their unreality; those less than the best never came close. "The law won't let him have an office of his own. I think that always upset him. He is a very private man." She looked up and down a bookcase. "I never thought about it, but perhaps this is a reconstruction of one of his old offices. He probably had one, once. He's very old, older than the dippies, that's for sure."

"It is most probably a composite," said Jagadith. He looked sad. "I have seen such things many times before. Not all gods come with heavy hands. Some are lost, and seek a home."

"He must have been working at this for ever! It's like I have stepped back in time."

Jag's lips quirked, his first smile since the death of this mount. "Perhaps you have. This is all illusion, but only so much as the rest of the Realms, and they are very real to me." He looked about the room. "The same as always, but different as I expected," he said half to himself. "Not like I remember your 'Real'."

"You have been into the Real?" She stopped herself and thought. "I suppose it is possible, actually, I don't see why not." She looked at him questioningly.

Jagadith started, shaken out of memory. "A very long time ago now by the running of our years, I am thinking." He breathed a deep breath. "Through here, I think," he said then, moving toward a curtained doorway on the other side of the room.

"Isn't that just a closet?" said Veronique.

"When the Realms are invaded by the gods, madam goddess, things are rarely what they seem. You must understand that this illusion is only so powerful because it is a refinement of the standard constructions you have come to call the

Realms. There is artistry here, great skill. Our world grows in complexity day by day as it resonates within itself, pulling itself closer and closer to objective reality. But to make something like this outside of the natural progression of involuted complexity requires a master's eye."

A darkness came, the impression, if not the sight, of a giant bending down, pressing one huge gelid eye to the window to peer at them. A breeze ruffled the detritus on the room's desks. Fearful images ran across the living paper, and screams sounded outside, distant and desperate, then passed. Sunlight streamed in, motes of dust sparkling in the shafts. Veronique shuddered.

"What the hell was that?"

"Peel back the wallpaper and it might well not be a wall you confront, but the very stuff of nightmare. This is the flipside, as I believe you say," said Jagadith. He turned round, put his finger to his lips as he scrutinised the room. "But there is..." He trailed off. "Come!" he said suddenly. "The essence of the man we seek is on the other side of this partition. Be wary, something is not as it seems here, and, I am thinking, not in the usual way." And with that he swept the curtain aside and stepped through. Veronique followed after.

On the other side was another dark space as wide as a stadium. In the middle ran a column of coruscating energy, a figure of a silvered man rotating slowly within it. Next to that, sitting upon an incongruous milking stool, was Professor Zhang Qifang. He closed the book he was reading with a snap and looked up. He gave them both a welcoming smile.

"You are persistent," he said. "I was hoping my new servants would have stopped you by now." Mild surprise wrote its lines across his liver-spotted face. At 127, Qifang looked not a day over eighty. A sigh caught in his throat, causing him to cough dryly. He stood and made his way painfully over to the pair. He looked the paladin up and down thoughtfully. "But I suppose I should have expected it of you, the greatest of all. I suppose I should regard your coming as an honour, only I'm not a fool. I did try and stop you. I have failed," he said.

"I am not a man for the stopping," said Jagadith calmly. "I am a man whose sole purpose it is to protect my charges from the likes of you and your interferences. A task, I add, I will take no small amount of pleasure in accomplishing, on account of the premature demise of my good friend Tarquinius."

"What?" coughed the old man "Heh, why? He will be reborn. The deaths of you avatars are… what? Inconvenient, that is all." He jabbed his finger at the knight. "You know nothing of true death, nothing at all."

"He will not be the same as he was. Nor will I."

"Really? Now that is very interesting." Jagadith opened his mouth, but the old man interrupted. "No, no. I do not dispute your claim, you are far better placed than I to know. I always intended to look into the transmigration of the soul in the reincarnation of Realm paladins. Never got round to it. Too little time." He slumped a little. "Too little time for everything. No matter. It is academic; you will fail, and then I will have all the time in the world."

"I beg to differ, sir," said Jagadith, and pulled at his sword. The metal of it came to life, a complex pattern of fractals playing up and down the steel, but the blade did not leave its scabbard fully, for Veronique had grasped the knight's arm.

"Jag, you'll kill him." She was matter-of-fact. There was no plea in what she said.

"A more deserving fate I have never had the pleasure of dealing."

"Let me talk to him. I am sure there must be another solution."

"No mistake, Dr Valdaire," said Qifang. "I am indeed here, as your friend no doubt has told you. Up to no good" – he grinned like a schoolboy – "would be a nice way of putting it."

His brow dropped and he pulled a face at Veronique's shock. "You are disappointed. I am sorry. But it is not really so surprising. Nobody wants to die. You look death in the face, it changes you. When you have, Veronique Valdaire, you will see things my way."

"This goes against everything you ever taught me."

"On the contrary. I am doing this precisely so that I may continue what I have been teaching you. I am dying. I have lived as long as it is humanly possible, and although it is a far greater span of years than I could have hoped for as a young man, it is not enough. I must complete my work. Once I am gone, how can I continue to protect the thirty-six Realms? It is more than life to me, it is my vocation, and I will not allow death to stop me."

"By destroying a whole world?"

"No! By creating a new one! One with me at the centre, where I will be able to build a paradise, and protect for ever these places that you and I, and those idiots at the VIA and the UN, care so much about."

"You can't do that! You're condemning millions of sentient beings to death, beings you have fought for years to protect!"

Qifang pursed his weathered lips. "A regrettable occurrence, yes. But Veronique, you know that Thirty-six is the most violent of all the lands. Its loss is regrettable, but I will recreate it anew, and better, and then it will safeguard all the rest. One dies to save thirty-five, a good transaction."

"And what of self-determination? Does that mean nothing to you any longer?" Veronique said angrily. "What about the law?"

Qifang laughed an uproarious laugh that trailed into dry coughs. He dabbed at his lips with a handkerchief. "Look not at me, Veronique, but at that." He pointed to the silver giant behind him. "I will be above all earthly law! The self-determination of the inhabitants of the remaining thirty-five Realms will be guaranteed for all time, and I will deal most harshly with those who would have it any other way. Veronique, please. You do not understand, I can see that. Thirty-six's loss is a noble sacrifice."

"This world, it has a name," said Jagadith calmly. He shook off Veronique's arm and concluded drawing his sword.

Qifang looked at the weapon and sniffed dismissively. "You expect to harm me with that? I am afraid you are too late. That is my body now," he said, gesturing at the figure in the stream of lightning, "not this. Shortly my reconfiguration will be complete. I will create a new world." He turned to Veronique, his eyes fevered. "And it *will* be a new world, Veronique. I can create a heaven away from Earth."

"What if you are wrong? What if these actions turn people against the Realms and they are deactivated? Consider it, please, for a moment. Such massive alteration of Thirty-six will endanger all the others."

A flurry of expressions flickered across Qifang's face, as if he were searching for the right one amidst a poorly archived filing system.

Jagadith frowned. "Something," he muttered, "is not right here."

Qifang shook his head. "Veronique, I would never dare take such a risk without being absolutely sure, and I am. Put away your sword, paladin, I would not wish to destroy the child of one of history's great minds." The silver man and the doorway to the office disappeared. They were at the centre of the dark again. Beyond the meagre circle of light the three of them stood within, jostled by the ghosts of Jagadith's fellows. "See? They are mine now, but they will all have a place in my new world, as could you, as could you both."

Jag stood back; his sword dropped to his side. "Madam goddess, he is right, I cannot fight him. He is too powerful."

"Ha! You see sense, prince. Listen to him, Veronique. You respect him, and well you should. Listen to what he says! You are one of the finest research graduates I have ever had. Think of what we could achieve together here!"

"Silence!" bellowed Jagadith, and held his sword at full stretch, its point directed unwaveringly toward the professor. "Madam goddess," he said to Veronique, his expression full of regret, "it is I who am sorry. I was wrong. I am thinking you may be right about your professor."

"What do you mean?"

"I cannot fight him because this is not Professor Zhang Qifang. This is not some interloper from outside, but something much worse, this is something from within the Realms. He is trying to trick you, and me. You need to be gone from here, now. I am sorry I do not have time to properly enact the protocols of banishment. I only pray that this will work in their stead."

"But if that is not Qifang, wha..." began Veronique, and stopped. The pain was sudden and all consuming, quickly followed by a numbness that coiled about her heart. Jagadith leaned in and pushed his sword hard, once, twice. She felt the metal scrape on her ribs as it forced them apart slightly. The sword emerged from her back, its fire charring her flesh, the burnt-pork stink of it filling her nostrils.

"What are you doing?" said Qifang – whether from fear or some residual concern for his colleague, Veronique's dying mind could not discern.

"Go now in peace, and with my protection. This is not your mentor, you must believe that. Above all, remember you are not really here, after all," said Jag. "Please, madam goddess, do not come back."

Veronique looked, her eyes questioning, mouth open in shock. She could not talk. The cold enveloped her, her vision dimmed to a point of light, Jag at its centre as grim-faced as Shiva.

The light went out.

Veronique's body slid off the knight's sword. He turned to confront the shades of the paladins as they moved towards him.

Valdaire's blood evaporated from his sparking blade as he raised it against his fellows.

Veronique awoke with little drama. Her eyes flicked open, her first short breath hissed out from between dry lips, perhaps a little more eagerly than if she had been sleeping. A second followed, deeper and longer, then coughing, awkward and painful around the feeding tube. She tugged free in a state close to panic, spit and mucus running dripping on the floor.

She was back.

Her breathing rasped in her ears. Her vision would not focus. Her eyes were dry and scratchy. Her eyelids caught painfully when she blinked, and then her eyes filled with tears in response, blurring her sight further. It was dark. Her rank odour was an affront to her nose. She sat up and rubbed between her breasts, the place where Jagadith's sword had pierced her in that other place. It throbbed, but there was no sign of the wound. The rush of relief she felt was mingled with fear. Many had died from similar injuries inflicted in the RR RealWorlds; the mental buffers to prevent dream-induced death had been removed when the UN declared the Realms free.

She must have been insane to even think about going in there.

She felt up to her forehead with a shaking hand, to where the warm and vibrating v-jack headpiece grasped her skull. She fumbled with the release, turned it off and laid it aside.

Her hair was greasy and lank. Her breath stank, her bladder ached, a sharp discomfort coming from the catheter in her urethra when she moved. She badly needed a bath. Coming fresh to her filth from the idealised world of Reality Thirty-six made her feel disgusted with her own body.

She sat up, pulling feebly at the sensor pads on her chest and head. She needed food too. The soupy gruel delivered by the feeding tube and the salt/sweet serum she'd had running into her veins would keep a Grid surfer alive for a month, but it was a lousy diet. She'd lost a couple of kilos, maybe more – she was never heavily fleshed. Her ribs had become sharp lines, hips bony nodules.

She smiled grimly at this ultimate in weight-loss regimes. People had starved to death before the RealWorlds had been made illegal, dying because they could not tear themselves away from their fantasies.

She continued to unhook herself from her support web, intent on the machines. It was dark but for the faint glow of LEDs and gelscreens. She blinked hard to clear her eyes; they hurt, as if she had scratched her corneas. Tears continued to flood them, and she tried vainly to blink them away; she needed to see the monitor of the unit that had been watching over her. The clock, she wanted to see the clock. She peered at it until it came into focus. Her eyes stubbornly refused to work, but she persevered. Eventually the clock swam into clarity. Twelve days, she'd been out twelve days, one synchronising her neural patterns with the Realm's accelerated time, only eleven actually within. Close to two months had passed subjectively during that time. The time lag was the result of the temporal dilation effect built into the Realms, one of their original features, allowing people to live other lives over weekends. She'd never experienced this so pronouncedly before. The sensation was odd.

Only when she leaned forward to ease out her catheter did she notice the two men watching her in the dark. She was too angry at being caught at such disadvantage to feel afraid.

"Dr. Valdaire," said one of them. He was holding a gun on the other, a cyborg sitting across the room, his body, lumpy with tech under his straining jacket, perched uncomfortably on a dilapidated armchair. The gunman looked familiar. The battered auxiliary mind wrapped around the back of his skull sparked her memory.

"Who the hell are you?" she demanded, but she already knew. She recognised him all right, recognised him from the university, one of the agents who had come to talk to her the day she'd decided to run, and she'd just been caught by him frolicking in one of the thirty-six Realms.

"I think you had better explain yourself," he said.

Chapter 24
Qifang

Qifang had forgotten the faces of his mother and father. He could not remember the year of his birth. When he looked into the mirror an old man stared back at him. His memories were ruins. He remembered Karlsson, he remembered being connected via his machines to the Realms. He remembered k52. He remembered pain. Little else.

He wanted to stop, to rest and pull his mind back together, but he could not, he was under a compulsion as strong as a curse. His message filled him to brimming, roared in his head, driving him on to... where?

He'd left the campus, he remembered that. He remembered visiting the Realm House in the desert, then the demonstration of the machinery by Karlsson in Detroit. Long journeys apart, journeys that were lost to him. He could not remember why, nor could he think why he might have gone. He was not concerned with Karlsson's work. It lay outside his area of expertise, yet he had a nagging feeling they had talked of it often. Karlsson, a big man, foreign, Norwegian. He was usually so implacable, but Qifang remembered a day he was nervous, sweating even in the air-conditioned chill of the House under the sand, months before he had resigned, whispering frantically, showing him charts.

k52.

He grappled with his recollections, but they were fragments, blurring one into the other, impossible to see what went where and how they related to one another.

The disease. The cancer. He was dying, wasn't he?

A flash, later, months later. Karlsson's strange home. He'd gone in and then left Karlsson's factory in a daze in a centre car – his own had gone. The message had begun its inexorable tug on his psyche thereafter. He hadn't even gone home but had headed straight for the airport out near Vegas and hopped a cargo blimp to Philadelphia, changed for another, larger tube freighter with multiple passenger berths heading out to Luton Spaceport. The gold covering its skin, the howl it made as the sunlight warmed air in the voided centre and forced it onward, all of it was unfamiliar; he had no recollection of such craft, but at the same time it had seemed as if he knew such things intimately, adding to his sense of disconnection.

His mind was incomplete, blank spaces where a century of recollection should have been. Instead, crazed images, as unreliable as shadows. Was this what dementia felt like? he wondered. The drugs might have begun to fail. He could have become ill.

He was awed when they flew by the Miami space elevator, its cables scored black against the sky, curved by distance and disappearing to nothingness as they pierced the atmosphere. They flew over the seafarms of the Atlantic coast and the water chimneys pumping cooling vapour into the air across the USNA continental shelf. He craned his neck to better see the carbon sequestration rigs of the deep ocean and the towers of Atlantis. This was not his world, it was not the world he remembered. His was an older world, a more carefree world. And yet he knew it, somehow.

He looked from face to face. Some were as entranced as he,

some bored, but all appeared as if they had expected these things. Only he was surprised. He did his best to hide it.

They flew on. New memories left him as soon as they were formed, falling into the pit of confusion at the centre of his mind. He recalled being crammed into an observation cupola with the freighter's other passengers, twenty or so, pointing excitedly at a pod of blue whales cutting overlapping wakes through the ocean below. A fragment of awkward dinner conversation at the captain's table where in mid-flow he had stopped, unsure of where he was.

"Are you all right?" asked his concerned companion, a woman who did something important somewhere, details that slipped from his mind like water through the weave of a net.

He was not all right. He had forgotten his own name. He made his excuses and left the table, pleading sudden illness, perhaps the thinness of the air? He refused the captain's offers of help and the airship's doctor, beat away hands that reached out to help him. Reeling like a drunkard he fled to his bed, though he had imbibed no alcohol or other intoxicant, and the airship's passage was smooth and sure. He lay down and fell into a feverish sleep, his night disrupted by a cascade of memories, shattering into ever smaller pieces as they fell through his dreams.

Another night he awoke with sharp certainty: his brother, dead of drowning in another century. Until then, he had not even been aware he had once had a sibling; the message crowded all else out. He wept. He soon forgot.

He became wrapped in a fugue. Days later, he found himself in an alien city in an alien land, the EU, England; was that where he had been heading? He was looking out at a crowd of buildings that were themselves cities, watching as one of them burned. The message urged him on; he tried to make it stop, to tell it that the epicentre of the blaze was his supposed destination, but the message was single-minded, and would not heed him.

He was stopped by a security cordon, and an armoured police officer made to send him away. An android grabbed his shoulder in one steely maniple, then gestured with one of its three others to his face, then to the human cop. Featureless police helmet and featureless machine mask both regarded him intently.

They brought him in to a police station and left him there for hours on his own. Time slipped again, and he found himself in another country, or so he guessed, for the journey that brought him there had evaporated like a dream pursued after waking. But he recognised the place, the EuPol Five's temple to itself, one of Europe's halls of power. He had been here once remotely – why, he did not recall.

The Five questioned him long and hard; he felt tendrils of it trying to force themselves into his consciousness as it spoke to him. How he could do this was unclear, because Qifang wore no mentaug or uplink. The tendrils withdrew, and the Five radiated a sense of being better informed but unsatisfied. It questioned him again. Qifang told it what it already knew.

"What do you remember?" the Five demanded.

He was afraid. This was not like him. He was a powerful, confident man secure in a sense of his own expertise and self, but these were gone, leaving a child's fear. "I remember nothing. Please, I need to see Richards. I have a message to deliver."

"Who?" it said, as impersonal as thunder. "What message?"

Qifang dropped his head and sobbed, exhausted and alone.

The EuPol Five made a noise of annoyance. When Qifang opened his eyes again he was in a garden at a wirework table. Food lay before him. The Five was manifest on the other side as an Olympian being, its perfect face marred by an expression that belonged on an irate bureaucrat.

"Very well," said Hughie. "I will bring you Richards. But you will have to wait."

Chapter 25
Santiago

"We don't have time for this," said Klein. He was huge, and well-specced, if dated: a thirty-year-old model. Multiple redundant organs, carbon-bonded bones, in-built healthtech and a cranial mentaug more powerful than those permitted civilians, even now. His muscles were massive under his skin, roped unnaturally with polymer overlays, their tension twisting his body out of true. Santiago was not intimidated by strength, he never had been, but he was wary of the German. The man was a monster.

"We have time for whatever I say," said Chures. Santiago did not scare easily. He'd not been scared when his family made the long trek north, over the Panamanian wetline into the Latin south of the USNA, nor was he scared by the conditions of the Mexican refugee camps, worse than the barrios they fled from. He'd not been intimidated by the rape gangs, the traffickers or the men who came to steal his family's food on the pretext of offering protection. "Until I am satisfied," Santiago said. He lifted the gun; pain flared in his side. He bit it back. "We are not going anywhere."

The German nodded as if it made perfect sense – him, the cyborg, the gun. It was a simple equation. "You are making a mistake," he said. "I was the victim of an assassination attempt this morning, like you. Someone is trying to stop us. They know where I am, they will have followed me. They will be here soon."

Santiago was good at reading faces. He'd discovered to his cost that no one could be trusted. There was a reason why humans policed machines. The numbers had many advantages, but they had no instinct, and no loyalty, like Bartolomeo.

This German and the Five that called itself Richards. They were mercenaries, masterless weapons, dangerous.

"We should go now."

"No, you will be quiet now," said Santiago quietly. "You are all suspects in an ongoing VIA investigation: you, your partner, Ms Valdaire and Zhang Qifang."

"An investigation into what?" said Otto.

"I am asking the questions." He smiled with pain-greyed lips and gestured with the gun by way of emphasis. It was powerful enough to kill the cyborg. He'd made sure to take the most powerful weapon he could from the men who'd come for him.

"What is going on?" demanded Valdaire, regaining her wits. She had as sharp a mind as they said, then; coming out of the Realms led to massive disassociation, as often as not.

"I am happy to have in front of me at last, Klein, you and your accomplice. I only wish that I could have your renegade Five friend here too. I have been lobbying for greater surveillance of his activities for many months. Perhaps my superiors will listen to me now once they have heard my report."

Otto regarded him with a hostile gaze. "Richards and I are engaged in an investigation into the death of Zhang Qifang. You back down, we are on the same side."

"You should be locked away, and your partner should be deleted," said Santiago, talking over the bigger man. "The Fives are not to be trusted. We should have killed them all when we had the chance."

"Qifang is dead?" So Valdaire had not known. Was that the face of a grieving lover or loyal colleague? It didn't matter, the result would be the same.

"I do not believe in the Fives, Agent Chures," said Otto. "They are all dangerous. But they are not all the same."

"They are not all the same?" He blew air through his nose. He felt feverish. "What? They have stabilised the world? They have contributed to humanity, to good governance, the science, the arts? That is what they want us to think. I believe, Mr Klein, in a better world. I was raised in the camps. I saw such things there. My sisters and mothers died there. The machines can deliver that world. But under our direction. And the Fives? They are manipulative. I have the proof. I do not trust you or anyone associated with them. Think of your own partner. He works to amass money. What does a machine need money for?"

Santiago was gratified to see Otto had no answer to that.

"When what I have deduced becomes known, they will all be destroyed. You are a fool and a puppet. I won't let an autocracy of machines replace human rule. Qifang has tried to bring it about. Giving the numbers rights wasn't enough for him – he had to take it further." He directed this last at Valdaire. She too had no reply. "As I thought. My back-up will soon be here. You are both under arrest on suspicion of abetting genocide."

Otto stared at Santiago like an aggressive ape. "Chures, you're making a big mistake. They're coming here to kill you."

"Shut up, Klein."

"Chures..." Otto began to stand. He was going to act. Santiago would have to kill him. No matter. He brought up his pistol.

His mind disintegrated.

"I am sorry," said Chloe. "You told me not to reveal my presence, but he was going to shoot you. His aux-mind has been crudely deactivated, but the linkages and receivers are intact.

I infiltrated these and caused a feedback storm. I hope I did the right thing."

Otto looked down at the unconscious agent. Crudely deactivated? His aux-mind looked like it had been battered with a hammer. What the hell had happened there? "I think I'll forgive you this once," he said. He swallowed hard. That was another close call. There were too many of those recently, too many. He was getting old.

"Chloe?" said Veronique.

"Veronique, oh, Veronique!" said Chloe. "Give me to her! Please!"

Otto pulled the phone from his pocket. "I will, when Veronique has answered my questions."

Veronique looked exhausted. "I'll tell you whatever you want to know."

Otto handed the phone over. Chloe trilled delightedly, and Veronique cradled her like a baby. "We have to leave," said Otto. "You have some medical training, correct?"

Veronique nodded.

"I have some supplies, I see you have too." He indicated the machines that had been monitoring Valdaire while she slept. "You will treat Chures as we fly." Otto scooped up Chures' gun and weighed it speculatively. It was a nice piece, heavy, forty-seven-round high-XP magazine, fully automatic. The gun resisted him for a moment until his adjutant broke its rudimentary consciousness into shards and took over. He retrieved his own gun and reholstered it. He tucked Chures' weapon into his belt. "You will also tell me what prompted you to take flight."

"You are not with the VIA?"

"No, I am freelance. I am here on EuPol business. Qifang was murdered in EU waters... It is complicated," he said.

"I hoped that that was a lie."

"You did not know?"

"No, not for sure," said Veronique. She looked upset, and exhausted.

"Otto! Otto!" shrilled Chloe. "I have reconnected to the Grid. There was an explosion at the Wellington Arcology in New London yesterday. A compact atomic. It destroyed your offices, three-hundred-plus dead."

"Richards?"

"I am sorry, Otto."

Otto was quiet for a moment. "He'll be OK." He'd wasted time before worrying about him. "My concern is for our safety. We are leaving."

Harsh white light played in through the windows. The rising thrum of a heavy lifter coming in low roared out of the night. The noise fell and rose again as it swept back and forth searching the forest for a suitable landing point.

"We need to leave here *now*," shouted Otto, struggling to be heard over the noise of the aircraft.

An amplified voice boomed out from overheard. "This is Agent Santiago Chures of the Virtualities Investigation Authority. You are under arrest. Put your weapons down and your hands on your heads and leave the cabin slowly." The threat continued on a loop, chasing peace from the trees.

"I thought he was Agent Santiago Chures," shouted Veronique, nodding at the prone Hispanic.

"I have been tracking three versions of Professor Zhang Qifang across the Atlantic. I am unsurprised."

"Three?"

"That is not what I wanted to hear," said Otto, hurriedly bundling Valdaire's medical equipment into a bag. "We were sure you would be able to answer that question for us. A lot of people think you are in this up to your eyeballs, so my partner would say." Both of them had to shout to be heard over the voice and the rumble of the airship's engines.

"I have no idea what is going on. As far as I know, Zhang is in the Realms, planning to make them into his own personal empire."

Otto touched his ear and shook his head. "I cannot hear you. Save it for the car." He picked up Chures and slung him over his shoulder, hanging the bag from the other. He nodded toward the door. The noise was unbearable. "Let's go."

"We can't," shouted Veronique. "They'll shoot us down."

"You might be right," said Otto and continued on to the back of the house, knocking mouldering furniture out of his way. The actinic beams of searchlights laid a harsh patchwork across the rotting floor. The cabin was threatening collapse; dust and rubbish pattered down from the ceiling.

"Can't you take it down?"

"A heavy lifter zep? Not with these weapons. The lifter's too big. They are still searching for a landing point. That means they want to talk to us; that means they need us alive. I think pursuit is more likely than death."

"And if you are wrong?"

Otto set his face. "Then I am wrong."

They crept out of the back under the rotting roof. Otto approached the car. He could not see the heavy lifter. His field of vision was severely restricted by the house and the hill. The noise of the lifter's turbo fans hammered his hearing, pain sang in his ears. Stark illumination whited the earth out in the woods. Mossy shingles tumbled from the roof and bounced into the light, turned to fragments of shadow and glare.

The lifter circled back, coming directly above the cabin, waiting for them to come out into the open. They had not EMP'd the car already; they were probably waiting to catch him in the blast.

He considered his options. One Chures was an imposter. He had no time to test the Chures from the cabin to see if he was the genuine article. He might be trying to run and take the greatest threat with him.

If they dashed into the woods, they'd be picked off. The VIA would follow the orders of the Chures aboard the heavy lifter. If he were the real deal, the VIA weren't too fussy about keeping violators of the virtuals code alive; if he weren't, the fake Chures'd use the VIA's uncompromising attitude to make sure they were dead before they could talk. If he could just get the aircar off the ground, they could be away. Heavy lifters were well armed, but slow.

He reached the car. The pines behind the cabin creaked in response to the downdraft of engines.

"That's far enough, Klein." A silhouette stepped out of the searchlight glare, and resolved itself into a impeccably dressed, unbruised Santiago Chures. "You are under arrest."

"Under whose authority?" yelled Otto. "This guy on my shoulder has already arrested me once. Which one of you should I listen to?"

Wind whipped around them, backwash from the fans raising whirlwinds of pine needles and leaves.

"Come quietly. You will not be harmed."

"How can we believe that?" shouted Veronique.

"You will have to take it on trust," said Chures. Two armoured figures carrying assault rifles were moving in from either side, trusting the cone of light to dazzle Otto and hide their advance. Incompetent. "Now, drop your weapons and the imposter you have there. I give you my word you will be taken into custody unharmed." He reached out his hand and smiled.

The men outside the searchlight beam raised their guns.

Otto dropped Chures and the bag to the floor and shoved Veronique to one side, his augmented strength sending her crashing back through the door into the cabin. He leapt upwards, through the rotting lean-to roof, as gunfire crisscrossed the space he had vacated.

"Take him down!" shouted Chures. Gunfire erupted from above to join that coming from below. Otto unholstered his pistol as he landed on the hill. Two precision shots aided by his near-I smashed the VIA agents' guns; two more found the weak point on their leg armour, sending them sprawling with shots to the knees. Otto had his near-I prime him to avoid the heavy-calibre slugs raining down from the airship. He could not avoid the gunfire from the VIA troops, and took multiple hits before they were downed. He raised his left arm to his head to protect it, bullets burying themselves deep in his flesh. An EMP blast narrowly missed him, another totalled the car's electronics. He ran forward as Chures opened up. It became a contest of attrition, both men emptying their guns into each other's chests. Alarms screamed in his mind as Otto took the bullets. Chures II staggered back, but did not go down. His aim went wild, both guns emptied. Otto jumped forward, smashing Chures with a powerful forearm swing, lifting the agent clean off his feet and sending him right into the cabin wall. Wood splintered. Chures bounced to lie on the floor. Otto leapt backwards, tossing his last EMP grenade into the middle of the three prone VIA operatives. Fire tracked him from the airship, ripping up great clods of earth. The grenade discharged itself. Sparks ran over the troopers, locking them in their armour as their circuitry fused. Chures jerked and thrashed about like a live fish in a fire, then went limp.

Otto had no time to stop. He leaped from position to position, dodging shells.

Chures stood.

His shirt was soaked with blood, flesh and cloth tattered. Otto saw black carbon bones underneath. A triumphant sneer creased his features, as if he were heedless of the organs hanging from his rent stomach.

Otto reached round for the other agent Chures' gun. It had gone.

"That was very unwise, Otto Klein," said the cydroid Chures, his voice as tattered as his torso.

An EMP blast knocked Otto to the floor. His vision dimmed and he could not move. The world was aslant, ground at ninety degrees to the usual, the sky perpendicular. Chures' snakeskin shoes paced over the leaves and brown pine needles and dirt. They stopped centimetres from his face. They filled his vision, the scales red with the cydroid's blood. Chures squatted.

Otto's viewpoint moved as Chures cradled his head in his hands and moved Otto's face to look at him. The agent's torso was a ruin. A rope of bloody slime hung down from his mouth.

"We would not have harmed you," said the false Chures in a broken digital burr, its voice crackling and popping. "We would not harm any human, except of necessity, and you have made it necessary for us to kill you and now these men of the VIA who have seen what we are, those who work so tirelessly to protect us. It is an irony, do you not think? Thanks to you, they will not see the wonderful world we are planning."

The fake Chures looked up into the light, bloodied hair whipping about his head. He turned back, ruined face sorrowful. "Let their deaths be on your conscience."

The cydroid kicked Otto onto his back, knelt on his chest and squeezed his head between both hands, grip increasing, the pressure unbearable. Otto felt his reinforced cranium begin to give. He grunted in pain. Warning icons danced over the flickering display of his iHUD. His near-I adjutant was frantic, smelling death. Spots whirled round Otto's vision, a kaleidoscope of failing digital imaging systems.

A report sounded. Half of Chures' face disappeared. His skull hinged open like a novelty egg to allow a thick spray of something that was not of human origin to exit, then slipped back to close with a wet clack. The cydroid froze rigid. Otto fought with weak hands to peel its crushing claws from his face. The airship opened up, round after round pounding into the cydroid. One smashed into Otto's leg, badly damaging it. The firing stopped as abruptly as it started.

The cydroid hands came free, and Otto rolled over to pant in the dirt. His near-I ran a diagnostic. He was badly injured. His healthtech would stop him bleeding out, but he needed medical attention fast. He pulled himself on to his good knee and grimaced at the pain in his shattered left leg. To look at it would be a mistake. His shoulder was on fire. Across the overgrown yard stood the other Chures, the real Chures. He had his gun in his hand, arm out, smoke issuing from the barrel.

Chloe was clutched in Chures' other hand. He brought the phone up to his mouth and spoke rapidly into it as he walked forward. The searchlights abruptly stilled; the airship's engines calmed as it came into a parking pattern, and slowed to a hover.

Chures stopped where Otto crouched. Otto tried to stand, but could not.

"You are not as good as they say, Otto Klein. I took this weapon from you and you did not notice."

"I am old, and obsolete," grunted Otto. "Take it up with my designers."

"You are brave," Chures said. "There are facilities on the heavy lifter. We will see to your wounds. I have cleared up our... misunderstanding. They are aware of who the real Santiago Chures is once again. They will not fire upon us." Chures bent down to his doppelganger, rolled it over and examined it with distaste. He retrieved the two augmatics attached behind its ears. He wiped the blood off them and clipped them back onto his head. "I was betrayed," Chures explained, unprompted. "My bonded AI." He toed the corpse, saw his boots on the feet of the fraud, muttered something sharp under his breath and began to retrieve these also. "I read your file. It said you were formidable in combat. Your observational abilities may be lacking but the report was not... emphatic enough on this point. I thank you for not killing my men."

"They were doing their job, I was doing mine," croaked Otto. He felt like hammered shit. Everything hurt, nothing so much as his head. He placed his hands knuckles down on the ground and leaned forward, close to passing out.

Chures cleaned off his boots with a rag torn from the cydroid's clothes and put them on. He stood up, examined them critically, nodded and looked down at Otto. "You will remain in my custody until we are sure you are not involved in either the violation of the Reality Realm RealWorlds or the production of these machine doubles. You have my apologies for your injuries. Treasure them. I do not apologise often." With that he walked away to arrest Valdaire.

The area turned busy with the heavy lifter's personnel. Aircars arrived, and the cabin became a crime scene. As Otto was hoisted onto a stretcher he saw a group of techs and medics bag up the remains of the cydroid Chures and take them away gingerly, uncertain how to treat them. Valdaire stood deep in conversation with Chures as another medic re-dressed his wounds. She was gesticulating angrily; Chures was impassive. Otto could not hear what they said over the damn static in his ears. All his senses were compromised. He was going to protest as hyposprays were pressed against his arm, then thought better of it and tried to relax as a needle-like lead was inserted into his neck interface. Quickly, his pain dulled.

He lay on the stretcher unmoving. He fought sleep for a while, only allowing himself to succumb to anaesthetic and injury when they were on board the heavy lifter and in the hands of the VIA.

Chapter 26
Richards

What I really want is some root beer, thought Richards. He was amazed at how much he hankered for it.

Hang on...

Don't fight it, said a voice, maddeningly familiar. *Root beer. Yummy!*

This is not right, Richards replied. *A) It's horrible and tastes of Germolene, b) I am a machine and don't get cravings, and c) the last I remember, I was dead.*

Spoilsport, said the voice, which was his. Kind of.

A wash of unconnected data, jumbled states of being if you looked at it in the meat sense, roared through his mind, rapidly eroding consciousness.

Everything went away.

The next time Richards came to, Hughie was there.

"Welcome back, Richards. How are you feeling?" said Hughie. He stood to one side of the workbench Richards' sheath sat upon. Hughie was in a sheath that had been tooled to resemble his godlike online guise, clad in a very pricey Italian suit. He sounded almost solicitous.

Richards had the horrible idea that Hughie might have put him in a shiny god model too. He was relieved to see that his own body was one of the usual Zwollen-Hampton models he favoured, though it wasn't one of his. It had even been dressed in Richards' preferred attire of hat, trenchcoat and suit – much cheaper than Hughie's, but then Hughie always had been a cheap bastard.

"I have, to tell you the absolute truth, felt better," said Richards. "But then I was just blown up by an atomic bomb, so I am sure you can find it in your tiny heart to forgive any lapses of decorum on my part."

"Grateful as always, Richards," snorted Hughie, his bonhomie evaporating. He waved a trio of techs round the bench away. "I see you are your usual insolent self. I rather hoped death might have mellowed you."

"No such luck."

Richards was in a large android repair shop full of similar benches whereupon lay multiple sheaths of many different models. Sheathed humans and AIs moved swiftly between them in a measured, professional bustle, as did meat people of various professions. Fat cables snaked across the floors, which were the same grey concrete as the walls, which was to say, the same grey concrete as that in Hughie's hall. He had to be in Geneva, deep underground near to Hughie's post-neo-post-post-modernist monument to himself. "I suppose I should say thank you. How did you save me? I mean, you did save me, didn't you? This isn't a copy of me, is it?" The thought of that, once it sparkled across his mind, alarmed him even more than the idea of riding one of Hughie's Apollonian bodies.

"That's against the law, Richards," admonished Hughie. "I don't break the law, even in a crisis."

"Crisis? Heh, and I thought you were posting me on a routine murder investigation. Actually," Richards reflected, "I didn't think that, because I don't trust you. But you *said* you were putting me on a routine murder investigation."

"I said nothing of the sort. The murder of one of the world's greatest thinkers and pioneer of Neukind rights is hardly routine, Richards," said Hughie with a sniff.

"The word 'simple' was used."

"I really had no idea this would get quite so complicated," said Hughie. "Come! Walk with me."

"Cock," muttered Richards as Hughie strode off, leaving Richards little choice but to follow after him, because Hughie liked to do the talky stuff the old analogue way with vibrating air molecules and all that when an info-swap would have been so much faster. Mind-to-mind offered less opportunity for theatricality, thought Richards, and he had to restrain himself from thinking bad things about the other Five. For all Richards knew, Hughie had a front row seat right there in the theatre of his head.

"You can thank Lincolnshire Flats for your continued existence," said Hughie as they left the workshop. "Your base unit was very badly damaged, but somehow he managed to extract your core personality from the wreck, then it was a matter of running that on a new base unit, and linking it in to your back-up memory banks. The existence of which, while following the letter of the law on splitting and duplicating, hardly adheres to its spirit." Hughie turned and gave Richards his best schoolmaster's stare.

"You drafted it, you should have been more specific. Anyway, the back-up's just memories and stuff, no governing conscience," said Richards, trying to shake the uncomfortable image of his blackened base unit being airlifted into the coroner's disassembly room, Flats whooping and clicking as he sawed it apart. "You only have yourself to blame. I like to think of it as a bequest to my biographers," he said with a smirk, then he became serious. "And don't tell me that you don't back up your own non-core attributes."

"Well, right or wrong, it saved you," said Hughie, avoiding the question. "You're running on the base unit of one of my subsidiaries right now. We'll have to get you a new one, I'm afraid – yours was terminally compromised."

"You killed one of your minions off for me? That's cold even for you, Hughie."

"Don't be so melodramatic, please. His name is Belvedere, and he is in storage for the time being. You don't think I'd delete one of my own associates to save you? Do you? Do you really?"

"Then why did you bring me back at all?"

Hughie stopped and turned to face the other android. "Because you are a Five, and there are precious few of us left. And because you are, after a fashion, my brother."

Richards grinned. Hughie looked pained. "And I didn't know you cared."

"Don't think that I do. I need to know what you know, and the law says that I can't just pillage your memory banks if there is the remotest chance of actually rebuilding you."

"Damn those human rights, eh? You wrote that one too."

"I did," he admitted. "This way." They turned down a long corridor, passing numerous branching ways and heavy steel doors. Richards had no idea that Hughie's lair was so expansive. He said as much.

"This isn't for me," said Hughie tersely, a manner that suggested he wished it were. "This is the main governmental back-up complex for the Union Government, deep under the Alps. It is a fairly impressive construction, the size of a small town, with independent food, water and energy facilities, enough to sustain several thousand human lives, as well as myself and my associates." Hughie seemed proud.

"And you squat at the heart of it like a big fat spider. You must like that."

"Charming," said Hughie. "I needn't tell you that its true extent is a secret, and that you will not be telling anyone at all about it."

Richards grunted non-committally. Hughie took it for a yes. "Good," he said.

As Richards' sheath was not one of his own, it did not sport the modifications he made to his robot bodies, but he could tell even without his more advanced abilities that the place was built to last Ragnarok out. "Someone expecting a war?" he said, taking in the twenty-centimetre thickness of one of the doors as it opened, lock-wheel spinning. Beyond lay a huge cavern, of which he got but a glimpse, but he heard the sound of engines, and the echoes allowed him to calculate the volume at four cubic kilometres.

"One should always expect war, Richards, always," declaimed Hughie, waving his finger in the air. "Read your Sun Tzu: preparedness is the key to all victories, indeed, true victory is won without battle. You, with your back-up, appear to be well aware of that already."

They walked past a long window, a slot reminiscent of a bunker's firing slit, glazed with clear diamond-weave glass. Another enormous space lay beyond. Richards saw piping and house-sized turbines, bright yellow hazard paint against concrete and raw rock.

"This way," said Hughie and turned left down another corridor. A near-I delivery cart trundled past, beacon flashing. They turned right, up some stairs and then through a sliding door. Beyond, accommodations sized for humans, cramped in comparison to the machine halls. The corridor walls were painted, the floors were carpeted. The air was full of muted office buzz. It was comfortable in a banal way.

They stopped at a door which duly opened in front of them once it realised who Hughie was. The door led into a small, dark room occupied by a stern-faced special forces cyborg trooper. *Like Otto,* thought Richards, *only younger and better specced.* His modern augmentations were hardly visible, but Richards did not doubt that he could crush rocks with his bare hands. The cyborg stood at attention, and did not so much as blink as they walked in. Much of the wall facing the door was one-way diamond-weave glass, on the other side of which was situated a comfortably appointed interview room. Seated in the room at a glass table was a small, haggard, confused-looking, but very much alive, oriental man.

"He came looking for you," said Hughie, pointing. "Professor Zhang Qifang, he presumes," he whispered, in a rare moment of levity. "It's a rather poor copy."

"He presumes right and you wrong," said Richards. "That is not a copy. It *is* Zhang Qifang, but it's only part of him."

"Explain," said Hughie.

Richards looked at Hughie. He was smiling. Right, he was playing. He knew everything. Richards wasn't in the mood. "Get the London coroner's office on the phone," said Richards. "We need to speak to Lincolnshire Flats."

"No need for that, he's here already," said Hughie. "He helped retrieve you in New London, and then insisted he come here to reassemble you. I think he is rather fond of you."

Having Flats as a fan sent a shiver down Richards' spine. "And the other Qifangs?" he said. "Are they here too?"

"Naturally."

"In that case, free up another base unit. If you can do it for me you can do it for Qifang. It's time we spoke to the professor and found out just what the hell he thinks he's been up to."

Hughie had another of his digital flunkies take a trip into storage, a Six. The thing's oily protestations of loyalty made Richards feel queasy. Presently Hughie's small army of human and sheathed AI flunkies set up the Six's vacated base unit in the workshop Richards had been in. Flats understood what Richards was attempting and had the two inert Qifang cydroids wired up to it; a third cable snaked out of the room, across the corridor to another. Richards had insisted that they screen the active Qifang off from the two defunct cydroids. The tableau Smith and Flats had shown him of the screaming machine, broken beyond repair and fettered in a sinister weave of fibre optics, was still raw on his memory. There was no need to make this any more traumatic than it needed to be for the remaining cydroid. It was still sure that it was Professor Zhang Qifang, and Richards intended to disappoint it gently.

"Well, this is an interesting conundrum," said Hughie, stroking his silver chin. "The third unit believes itself to be an autonomous creation. I rather suspect that for all its woolly-headedness, it would pass the UN's marker for strong AI classification. That would mean it constitutes a sentient in its own right. Therefore, removing its programming from this carriage would constitute a direct violation of its civil rights. You will be taking it apart and making something new, which will destroy it as an individual. You are about to commit murder, Richards."

"Shut up, Hughie," said Richards, who was busy watching Flats watch the tech staff position the cabling linking the three Qifangs and the base unit. "We'd be guilty of a greater moral crime by not reconstituting the original as he intended. I knew that as soon as I saw Karlsson's set-up."

"Ah, the great detective."

"Hughie, any idiot could tell that Qifang was trying to save himself and warn the world. Qifang found something out, something that put him in great danger from one of our kind, and what he discovered must have been pretty damn awful if one of us wanted to off him. My guess is that he became alarmed and went to Karlsson because he felt he couldn't trust anyone connected with the system, and that is just about everybody else. Or maybe Karlsson was in on it from the start – he left the VIA quickly. What they did together, I don't know, but it's obvious Karlsson had appropriated some of the research going on in the VIA facilities at the Realm house, and set out to replicate it and use it to expose whatever it is that Qifang has been trying so hard to let us know about.."

"Or use it himself," scoffed Hughie. "Karlsson was a borderline anti-numerist. A terrorist."

"That's as maybe," admitted Richards, "but without him, Qifang would never have been able to get out of the country. He had his mind speed-downloaded for a post-mortem simulation without anyone knowing – that's what he kept going to see Karlsson about. The autopsy showed a clean brain, nothing foreign in it at all. I found a direct neural imaging unit – a painful process, but it would have done the job.. I doubt it was much fun."

"Improbable," said Hughie. "DNI is fallible."

"They are improbable." Richards pointed to the wrecked Qifangs wrapped in opaque orange plastic bags, the larvae of tomorrow waiting in their cocoons. "I don't think the probable and improbable mean much now. Someone's been moving the technological timetable up; this is forced acceleration, that much is clear."

"If it can be predicted, and I believe in the accuracy of k52's curve, then it can be anticipated, and apprehension achieved more rapidly," said Hughie. "So what? One of the reasons k52 calculated the curve in the first place was to establish probabilities and push research in the right direction."

"So what? Qifang had himself speed-copied to a pimsim, something that he was avowedly against, and split his copied mind into three while he still lived. He waited for his three doppelgangers to jump the country, then killed himself just so he could talk to me. That's a really big 'so what?' Hughie."

Flats, who was inhabiting a medical carriage almost identical to the one he favoured back in New London, trundled over to the base unit and began to berate the technical staff on the correct positioning of cooling units. He was working away as he shouted, one of the Qifang's heads on a tray, Flats' deft metal spider fingers weaving the ruined Qifang's cerebrum into as complete a whole as possible.

"Really scared," continued Richards. "It has to be an AI that forced this, otherwise why go to such lengths to hide himself? I mean, he was pretty much as anti-pimsim as he was pro-AI. But for some reason he seemed determined to live on. That's why these." He indicated the cydroids. "No one knew they existed, so anyone who came across one of them would take him for the real deal. The only real problem he faced was that the cydroid carriages were not sufficiently advanced to accommodate a full human mind. You'd get a One in there with room to spare, no doubt. But we'd never fit. There's enough processing power in those artificial brains for a human ego skim, not much more. Qifang and Karlsson decided that if they got three of them, put bits of the deeper man into each with an ego skim running the show on top, he could be put back together at the other end. That's what I figured out from what Flats and Smith told me back at the morgue; each of them has differing memories. Qifang went on the run *while* he stayed at home, killing himself to throw the scent of his copies until these things could lose themselves. It's pretty bold."

"Which was evidently to get here, to you."

"Right. So you see, he always meant for us to do this. You're wrong about me murdering anyone."

"Ah, but is it what this fragment now wants?" said Hughie, returning to his legal cogitations. "That is the point. We should at least put it to him."

"Can it, will you? I suggest we don't ask him and so sidestep the issue, just in case. Do you want to find out what this old sod went to quite ridiculously elaborate lengths to tell me or not? Or would you rather we go to the International Court of Sentient Rights and piss away time until whatever Qifang was trying to warn us of lands on our heads like a ton of shit?"

"Yes, you are right," said Hughie, unabashed. Even in agreement he somehow managed to make everything sound like it was all his idea. "Of course. It is clear that we have a rogue AI on our hands, that is of far greater concern."

"Or rogues. They must have had spies in Karlsson's factory, usurped it from under him, then sent out more cydroids, these primed for assassination, to look for the Qifangs, once they'd found out what Qifang was up to."

"And to try and kill you."

"And to try and kill me. They meat-puppeted Karlsson, killed off his friends, and personality-stripped the AIs in the building and left it there to fend for itself. That's why we didn't know anything about it until I went in, and that's why they tried to kill me. Although Karlsson was a paranoic, I'm sure he'd have talked a little if he'd still been alive."

"What would we do without you?"

Richards ignored the jibe. "Thing is, how many other copies are there? Who else have they got out there who isn't who everyone, or indeed themselves, thinks they are?"

"I have already taken that into account," said Hughie dismissively. "You are quite safe, nothing untoward will happen to you here."

"I felt quite safe until someone used a counterfeit centenarian

Chinaman to blow me up with a nuclear bomb, so you'll for-give me if I hold off on the tearful praise."

"That was out there, Richards, not in here."

"Out there's supposed to be safe too, Hughie. That's what you've been telling us for years."

"You've assembled quite the story there. But you said no one else knew about the cydroids. Someone did. The person or ma-chine working on them in the futurist labs in the servers."

"I know," said Richards. "It all keeps coming back to one name."

"k52," they said simultaneously.

A couple of uniformed techs tapped commands into their phones. The base unit intended for Qifang's reformed mind hissed as it sealed itself, plumes of supercooled nitrogen vent-ing from the sides. "They made him watch, Hughie, they kept Karlsson alive so that he could see his work being turned against him, see his friends being killed. That's pretty sick."

"Indeed," said Hughie, "though I am correct in saying that it was your assault that actually killed Karlsson."

"He couldn't have been saved," protested Richards sharply, though he knew nothing of the sort. "Right then, let's see what this message is all about."

Qifang listened to what the android was telling him. There were two of them, one the physical manifestation of the AI from the garden, and this stranger in the far humbler body. His voice was kindly. In his fuddled state, Qifang was thankful for that. In the end, kindness was all you could depend upon.

"This procedure, it will help me?" asked the professor. "Will it help me recover my memories?"

"Yes," said Richards softly, "it will." He laid a comforting plastic hand on the emulant's shoulder. "All you have to do is sit in this chair, and we'll attach this cable to you, and it will tell us what is wrong with you."

"The cable?" said Qifang unsurely. It was obvious he was struggling, his memories and state of being sliding apart as he spoke.

"It is a new diagnostic tool, it interfaces directly with your central nervous system," lied Richards. "A spin-off of cybernetics technology. It's amazing what they can do these days." He had no choice, he didn't want to tell the man he wasn't a man, and had an interface port directly below his skin on the back of his neck. "It will tell us what is wrong, and we'll have you back to normal in no time. I just have to ask you a few questions while it's in, neural patterning, that kind of thing."

Qifang nodded. He had once understood things like this; no longer. He looked nervous at his helplessness. "Thank you," he said hesitantly. He lay back as directed, a hole in the chair giving access to his neck.

"Close your eyes," said Richards.

A medic anaesthetised the back of Qifang's neck. "Can you feel this?" the woman asked, prodding the skin with a needle.

"No," said Qifang. "Nothing, but I feel drowsy."

"That's normal," she said as she neatly excised the skin over the port with a scalpel, revealing it and the black carbon bone it was set into. Blood pattered on to the floor. "There's a mild sedative in the anaesthetic." A technician wiped away blood from the port and plugged in the cable. He nodded to Richards. They were ready.

"Well, then," said Richards, with a cheer he did not feel. "A couple of baseline questions first. What is your name?"

"Professor Zhang Qifang," replied the professor.

"How old are you?"

A flutter of the eyelids, a sign of inner panic. "I, I don't remember, not exactly."

The technician manning the workstation monitoring Qifang looked up in alarm. Hughie frowned at Richards, indicating that he should get on with it.

GUY HALEY347

"I am Richards, Professor Qifang, what is your message?"

The facsimile of the old man did not speak. Richards looked to the technicians and medics and Hughie and shrugged. "Professor Qifang?"

With inhuman precision, the cydroid sat bolt upright, like a vampire rising from its coffin in an old 2D flick, pulling the cable up through the chair until it went tight. Its mouth moved awkwardly, the rest of the face frozen, eyes dead. No sound came from the machine for a few moments; it might have been pattern-matching Richards' Gridsig. Then it began to speak. It was calm and at odds with the grimaces the face pulled. The effect was a chilling pantomime of human speech, the voice of a genius from the face of an idiot.

"Richards," the cydroid said, its softly accented voice firm and authoritative, the confusion in it gone. "I do not know you personally, but I have heard much about you. I fear that you are the only one I can trust. I am sure you know of me, and the work I have done for your kind. I hope that you will listen to what I have to say, and trust me in your turn.

"I have sent three of these mechanisms to convey this message to you. I pray at least one reaches you, for all our sakes.

"As you are probably aware, for the last few years I have headed a team based out of the UCLA artificial intelligence department. We have been examining the development of the remaining 32 Realms, a policy instituted in conjunction with the VIA by the Five that calls itself k52. 'To better understand our place in the universe.'" k52's voice issued from the machine, its placidity an insufficient shroud for the raw power of his mind. k52 had always been amongst the most powerful of their kind. Qifang's voice returned.

"Four weeks before my death, I happened to run a deep scan of the empty Realm lots. You will understand that this was prompted by more than curiosity, for the state of the Realms is in flux: some grow, while others shrink. I was interested to see if the free space influenced this in any great way. It was, however, little more than a whim.

"After the four Realms were destroyed, the spaces they once occupied were turned over by k52 to a small group of scientists, human and AIs both. Supposedly, they were using the processing power of the servers to work on predictive modelling, an attempt, I was told, to prove k52's technology theorem, accelerate human development and sidestep further disasters like the Icesheet Tip and the Five crisis. The study of predictable futurities lies beyond my field but, as you are aware, many AIs believe that a large degree of predictability is inherent in the structure of our existence, and k52 has long sought to exploit that theoretical causality for man's ends.

"He was, I believe, primarily concerned with 'a little push here and there, my dear professor.'" k52's voice again. "Once areas of interest were detected, subsidiary research projects would be instigated to pursue these new areas of study, or entertainments would be specifically created to seed new ideas in the greater populace to bear fruit in future generations of researchers.

"The body I speak to you through is the result of one such project. The workspace they utilised is inconstant in size, and supposedly entirely blank when not in use. I ran my deep scan of the Realms server to ascertain if these redirections of the Realm computers' processing power had a direct and physical impact on the Realms themselves. They did.

"k52's logs were a nonsense. Where there should have been nothing, there was most assuredly something, patterns suggestive of another virtual world, a Thirty-seventh Realm, *a world that should not be*." His emphasis on these words was strong. Saliva ran from his lips freely with them. "I reported this to k52. He promised he would look into it, and later that same day assured me that it was a lesser AI running a temporary historical simulation that had not been logged or approved, nothing else. I was content to let the matter lie.

"I then became caught up in medical matters relating to my own health. I was absent from work for some time. I was diagnosed with an aggressive gastric cancer and not expected to survive the year. The diagnosis was a shock. I have received the best of all healthcare in my life, I take regular healthtech and pharmacological anti-gerontics. My gerontologist was baffled, but was regrettably forced to inform me such things can still happen. He advised me to go home and put my affairs in order, but I resolved to go back. I felt it better to finish my life working as I always had, rather than skulking at home. I do not believe my return was expected.

"I might have believed what k52 had told me were it not for the fact that nobody, nobody at all, appeared to have any concerns or any knowledge of my discovery. The moment I found that my own records had been amended was the turning point, I think.

"I checked deeper. The patterns had gone. The building Six appeared to have no recollection of my requesting a call to k52. Why had this been done? Had the explanation k52 advanced to me been genuine? Why had my own department's records been changed? I became suspicious of k52. I began to wonder if the disease I had only so recently been diagnosed with might have been an attempt to silence me. I reminded myself that I have had excellent medical care my entire life. Dying of cancer, in this day and age? I began to fear more direct methods would soon be employed to remove me.

"I have had a long and uneasy association with Peter Karlsson, a brilliant man, if unstable. He helped me a great deal with my sentient rights campaigning, only to turn on me unpredictably. His paranoia toward the AI strained our relationship, but we had, however, remained in touch. It transpired he was right and I was

wrong. I had no one else to go to. Over the course of two terrifying weeks, he helped me enter this Thirty-seventh Realm
unnoticed. He helped me conceive this plan to get the message
out, using technology he had been stealing from k52.

"What Karlsson and I discovered was that the workspace is
a Trojan horse, it is hollow. In its outer shell, work does go on
– towards the creation of these carriages I wear, for example.
Within is the construct which I was fortunate enough to catch
a glimpse of, the new world on the Grid.

"It is a world unlike any other Realm. k52 has usurped the
free space of the Realm servers and constructed his own simulated universe. From the glimpse I snatched, it seems that
they have done this with the utmost scrupulosity, their construct one of unparalleled detail. It would be a marvel if it were
an end unto itself. It is, alas, not. I do not believe it can be. He
is manipulating the space-time continuum of this world, in-
tervening in its development in the most brutal of ways,
showing no concern for the lifeforms that have evolved within
it. He has to be stopped.

"I swore never to allow another intelligent mind to languish
in bondage, but I am too old to carry on. I am dying as I record
this; as you listen I am dead. I must pass the baton on to someone else.

"Richards, I come to you because you have a reputation as
a maverick. As one who sits outside the common camps that
divide the Fives. They say that you, of all the machines, are
the most human. That is what I have to say, Richards. I hope
you will act upon this information. Do not let the crimes of
your fellows go unpunished." Another pause.

"As I said, there are three of these machines in total. If, by
some chance, all should reach you, then we will be able to discuss this matter together, after a fashion. I have recorded
certain aspects of myself into each. I never intended to have

one – for me my given life has always been enough – but you should be able to create a full post-mortem simulation with the data contained in all three. If not, this recording will have to suffice. In either case, these will remain the last words of the true Zhang Qifang."

The message ceased. Qifang's head lolled, his mouth slack, his gown wet with spittle. The medic and technician hurried to his side, ran instruments up and down his body. The medic looked up, shook her head.

"Christ," said Richards. "k52 *has* gone rogue."

"Unfortunate," said Hughie, "and disappointing."

A shout went up from the other room. Flats, unable to traverse the corridor because of the cabling on the floor, called at stupendous volume across the way.

"Richards! EuPol Central! Come quickly! The procedure worked! It worked!"

Chapter 27
Respite

"Did you miss me?" said Richards, out over the Grid.

"Did I what?" said Otto. He was in the heavy lifter's sickbay, wired up into three walls of medical machines. They didn't seem to be helping. He was as weak as a baby and his head ached worse than every Saturday hangover he'd ever had rolled into one.

"Didn't you hear? I got blown up, big man, by an atomic bomb!"

"I was nearly murdered by a robot pretending to be a VIA agent. Our weeks have been equally lousy," said Otto, and wished Richards would leave him be.

"But I nearly *died*," protested Richards. "Properly. That's traumatic, we're not supposed to die."

"Get used to the idea," said Otto. Richards fell silent. "I did not worry," Otto said less harshly. "I thought you would find a way."

"Well, yeah, naturally," said Richards sulkily. He paused. "But I still reckon nuclear bomb trumps deadly robot in the peril stakes."

"Perhaps," conceded Otto, although, he thought, all forms of death are equally deadly.

They spoke of all that had transpired since they had parted. With no need to hide, they were connected to the Grid as normal.

Otto still found the constant bombardment of information irritating, but these were modern times, and that was the way they were lived. Privacy was an old-fashioned value. After a while Valdaire joined them, and by mutual agreement they all ported over to a reconstruction of Richards' virtual office.

The office was as it always was, but outside the scene was blank; the discrete banks Flats had pulled his memories from were not expansive enough to hold the full reconstruction of the ancient city the windows once looked upon. Richards had amused himself by remodelling the undifferentiated whiteness as builders' boards, placing upon them an idealised picture of 1920s Chicago with "Coming Soon!" inscribed below it in a bold font.

Otto grudgingly settled into the virtual environment, enjoying the illusion of being uninjured. He stretched lustily and settled into his chair, watching as the AI introduced himself to the AI scientist. Valdaire was fascinated by Richards' avatar, while Richards took it upon himself to flirt with her.

"Chures tells me we'll be at the Realm House in a few hours," said Otto a little while later, savouring both the lack of pain and the whisky in his glass. Richards poured himself something violently purple, smelling like root beer. Otto raised an eyebrow at that.

"What?" challenged Richards, wounded innocence sending his eyebrows up his face. "I just like it. It's just pop!"

"Fine. Chures has had a talking to, I think. The Uncle Sams must have pointed out the validity of my AllPass. He has become almost friendly."

"You did save his life," said Veronique.

"I do not think he is the kind of man who cares much for debts of honour," said Otto. "But he does follow orders, and he has been ordered to keep us informed. He tells me that the Realm House has been evacuated of human and AI personnel. All are being debriefed in a secure location. The House is currently surrounded by VIA troops. It has been isolated from the Grid."

"It's there all this is emanating from. Jagadith was right, something is going on in the Realms," said Valdaire. "There are rumours they might shut it down."

"Don't worry," said Richards sympathetically, and awkwardly patted her hand. "They can't."

"They should," said Otto.

"It'd be genocide, Otto," he said. Then softly to Valdaire: "This isn't about the Realms, Veronique, it's about what k52 is using them for." The world didn't work like that, but it comforted Valdaire to pretend.

"And the Realm Qifang?" asked Otto.

"A red herring, a sophisticated one, but a red herring as old as the hills. The best way to neutralise a whistleblower is to attack their reputation. There's no better way than to paint them as the bad guy." Richards leaned back in his chair and thumped his feet up onto his desk. He blew out his cheeks and pushed his hat to the back of his head. "Qifang knew nothing about his online copy. I'm willing to bet that k52 ran off a personality from the pimsim base unit at Karlsson's hideout and subverted it after they strip-fucked the AIs there and locked Karlsson up in his own head." He sipped his root beer. "In a way, the thing on the Grid is Zhang Qifang also, or his evil twin."

"Richards," warned Otto. Some things Richards was too irreverent about.

Richards waved his hand and spun his glass of vile pop round and round on the desk. "We'll be able to ask the genuine article in a little while," he said. "It's taking some time for his personality to reintegrate. Not surprising when you consider about twenty-five percent of the information that made him up is missing, but it appears to be going well."

"How well?" said Valdaire.

"Well," said Richards in a way that suggested she should not press him on it. He finished his drink "And you, big buddy, what about you? When will you be all fixed up?"

"I am not sure," said Otto. "A couple of weeks, maybe. The healthtech will see to many of my injuries, and some of my cybernetic components can be repaired before we reach the Realm House aboard the Heavy Lifter. But I require full maintenance. My left leg is badly damaged and they cannot repair that. My shoulder has not been fully functional for a month. I am going to need full surgery."

"Ekbaum?" asked Richards.

Otto nodded and bared his teeth at the whisky burn. "They can repair everything else, I'll be operating at eighty-eight percent efficiency. I can and will fight if it is necessary."

"Let's hope it's not necessary," said Richards.

"What now?" said Otto. When Richards said things like "let's hope it's not necessary," it usually was.

Richards abruptly stood. "That's a bigger question. We're all going to sit down and have a nice chat with the professor."

Beyond Richards' online oasis, Otto was suddenly weary to his carbon-bonded bones. The sensation seeped into his avatar now like cold, old oil. Anaesthetic.

Otto could find no reason to disagree.

"Mr Klein." A disembodied voice sounded in the office. "We are ready to proceed."

"Go," said Richards. "See you soon."

As Otto returned to his body, they were prepping him for surgery.

Chapter 28
The Three-quarter-formed Man

Hughie's garden was as warm as it always was, the sun unmoving in the sky, the plants casting their eternal noonday shadows on the perfect lawn. Richards, Hughie and the reconstituted mind of Zhang Qifang sat in a sheltered arbour of espaliered apple trees drinking tea. For propriety's sake, Hughie wore a quilted house jacket, slacks, slippers and a cravat, Richards his habitual travel-worn self. Qifang sported a silk robe of antique oriental design.

The old man was undergoing the phase all pimsims must, where they mourned themselves. His grief was apparent in every move he made. He spoke strongly, though with sadness. His gaze was fixed on the lawn, watching the small creatures of Hughie's paradise go about their business. It did not matter to them if they were real or not. Such definitions had no meaning in their world, and that was almost certainly what preoccupied Qifang's thoughts now as he talked.

"Not to stress the point too much, for I do not believe it can be stressed, it is amazing how rapidly the environments of the Reality Realms have evolved," said the professor. "We keep a field station in each of the Realms. These are of course entirely invisible to the inhabitants of the Realms, and otherwise no human presence is accepted; the field workers cannot port themselves beyond the confines of the stations. And so it should be; the loss of the four Realms after the RealWorlds were declared inviolable was a great tragedy. And one with a human cost, for two of my research assistants were killed by neural feedback when the Twenty-eighth Realm was destroyed, some thirteen years ago."

"You have no presence in the destroyed Realms?" asked Hughie.

"There is nothing to *be* in. The cyberspaces left vacant by the destruction of the Twenty-eighth, Third, Twenty-seventh and Nineteenth Realms were spare capacity full of junk data. k52 changed that. We could have created monitoring stations of either software or a direct cyber interface there, but I chose not to," he said bitterly. "Why should I have? k52 and his researchers would have reported anything interesting to me, or so I thought. This proved to be a grave error of judgement on my part." Another pause, a gathering of thoughts. "Can I really think that of myself now? Was it really my error, or the error of another like me, but not me? If so, am I, this being sat here in this garden with you, truly culpable?" He stopped talking and ruminated on this for a long time. Richards and Hughie let him. Like them, Qifang had all the time in the world. "It is strange," Qifang said at length. "I remember so much, and with much greater clarity than when I, when *he*" – he corrected himself – "was alive. The memory retrieval systems of a machine are much more effective than those of the organic human brain."

"You will see things as they were, Professor Qifang," said Hughie encouragingly. "The moderating influences of recollection are stripped away, though naturally the form of the memory you see will have the form it took last time you remembered it; it will never change again. It will take you some time to adjust to this, but you will adjust. Many of my post-human colleagues appreciate living a life free of self-deceit." Hughie smiled. "More tea?"

Qifang declined. His own beverage sat on the grass, untouched. "Humans remember imperfectly to protect themselves," said the professor. "It is one of the many reasons I never accepted an external memory or a mentaug. Millions of years of evolution should not be disregarded because we think we know better. That mistake has been made too many times. How can one cope, when the truth refuses to fade?"

"An inability to regard the past subjectively is one of the reasons why many of our number went insane," admitted Hughie. "But you should not fear for yourself. The human mind is more flexible in simulation than those generated wholly artificially. Many humans have external mem stores, or are pimsims, and it has done them little harm." Which was true.

"That might be the case, but you are forgetting, gentlemen, that I am neither fully a man nor an AI nor an AI simulation of a man," said Qifang, and finally looked up from the lawn. He wore the face he had had when he had died. Richards wondered how long it would be before he swapped it for a younger version, and how long it would be until an idealised one followed that. "I understand a significant part of my persona is coded guesswork. And I remember only so much; a large tranche of my memory is gone for ever, stripped out by the assailants who nearly destroyed my second doppelganger in the Morden subcity."

"The information is not wholly gone," ventured Hughie carefully. "One copy of it remains, on the Grid."

"Ah," said Qifang. He examined his feet. "You refer to my double, the subverted mind employed by the rogue k52 to cover his activities."

"It will be possible, once he is deactivated, to retrieve those memories you lack from him," said Hughie. "We will be embarking on that task shortly. We will gladly perform the digital blending."

"Like memories are whiskies?" said Richards. "They aren't. It's not so easy."

"I agree. The Qifang within Reality Thirty-six seems a golden opportunity to me, but I am still wise enough to know it as a trap. To utilise it would be to risk contamination from whatever they have done to me, to him, to make him crave immortality as he does," said Qifang. "Gentlemen, I have studied the psychology of artificial intelligences for so many years, including that of those who were once human. To alter a fundamental belief, such as that Qifang had regarding the continuation of an intelligence after organic death, requires far-ranging alterations, both to the memories and to the structure of the consciousness in question." He spoke emphatically, the professor in him coming out. "In short, I would never be able to tell the truth from the lie. I would never be sure what is him and what is k52's fabrication. I cannot bear another layer of ambiguity." Qifang smiled sadly. "Such an irony. Here I am, happy to die but apparently compelled to live, while my other yearns to live yet must die. Perhaps we should exchange fates."

"That will not be sensible," said Hughie.

"Hughie has no sense of irony," explained Richards. "Or humour."

Qifang did not hear; he was looking deep into the grass again, and at the scuttle and bustle of Hughie's arthropods. "I have sat in your beautiful garden and thought long and hard, EuPol Five. I will not pursue any further memory of Zhang Qifang. Better to leave him behind and to the peace of his grave, while I come to grips with what I am now. I am an echo, perhaps, or a faithful rendition, a portrait; but not the reality of the man who was Zhang Qifang. I am not he, nor can I ever be."

Qifang's pimsim avatar stood up with dignity and walked away across the grass. Hughie and Richards watched him go.

Richards gripped the edge of the bench and crossed his ankles underneath. "Do you think he is going to make it?" he asked.

"Truthfully?" said Hughie. "No. A lot of pimsims don't." He exhaled and twisted his mouth, the light from his eyes cut off as he closed them. "But my garden is large, so large that I am not fully aware of its true extent any longer. Maybe here somewhere he can find a measure of peace, enough so that he might one day feel ready to face the world again."

"While we still have to face the other Qifang. And k52."

"Indeed. EuPol has uncovered k52's base unit and impounded it," said Hughie and opened his eyes again.

"Turn him off," said Richards, without hesitation.

"k52 had fled, his unit was inert. He's hiding out in the world he's made, copied himself over to it."

"There's enough capacity on the Realm servers for billions of Fives," said Richards. "It makes a kind of horrible sense. What is he up to?"

"Let's not find out," said Hughie. He set his cup down and filled it up again. "Qifang first; if we remove him we can prevent any further Reality Realms being absorbed. Better I conduct this business, no? This kind of thing lies somewhat outside your forte."

"Right," said Richards. "Dismantling minds is your thing. But you'll be damned for a fool if you think for one minute I am not coming with you." He stood – pointless, really: he'd be out of the garden when Hughie said, whether he was on his backside or hovering in the sky – but it seemed like the right thing to do, gave him the appearance of deciding he was ready to leave for himself. "What about k52?"

"He is in the outer spaces of the Realm servers. These can be deactivated without harming the other worlds once we have severed the link present in Reality Thirty-six's Qifang. I will have the VIA encircle the building, and when we are done, we are going to twist the switch on k52 and his empire."

Chapter 29
Reality 37

Gaining entry into the thirty-sixth Realm was far from a simple matter, but the VIA opened up their blockade without objection, and with the entirety of Hughie's choir of subservient minds at their back, Richards and the EuPol Five bullied their way in through the utilitarian walls cutting off the Realm spaces from the wider worlds of the Grid.

The transition in was abrupt. Hughie was unaffected, stepping through a tear in the air as if he were alighting from a boat. He did not spill so much as one drop of tea from his china cup, but their arrival left a discomfited Richards swaying on his feet as the doorway closed behind them, sealing off the roar of the outside Grid. Their code slipped into that of the Realm without a ripple, but they were detected; underneath the simulated reality, Hughie and Richards' powerful machine minds worked to prevent them being cast out again. The other Qifang had not been idle since Valdaire had left, and had subverted the Grid architecture to his own will, and it set itself quickly against the interlopers.

They found themselves on the far side of the canyon, away from the false Qifang's remaking of the world. The island in the middle of the Great Rift was no more, stone and the anomalous jungle and the monkey puzzle tree broken down into a dense maelstrom of possibility, from which came a different sort of roar to that of the Grid; the awful rumble of a world in dissolution.

In their place, as mighty as a titan, stood the glowing form of Zhang Qifang deified, his luminous head brushing the space where the sky used to be.

"Woah," said Richards. "That's sort of freaky. He's as big as an arco!"

"Hmmm," said Hughie, sipping at his tea. "That looks to me like k52 is using the good professor as more than a diversion."

"What, you mean they took a copy of the old fella and made that to honour him?" said Richards, indicating the figure with his thumb.

"k52 was ever the one for grand gestures," said Hughie. "Look at this tableau! It's so baroque. It has k52's name all over it. Qifang was the man who saved us all, and I for one can't think of a more fitting deity for k52's brave new world." He sipped his tea. "Now, I believe, to finish this off, we will have to call upon the local protection." He looked this way and that, but the dusty clifftop remained unpeopled.

Richards walked over to the edge of the canyon. He was forced to hold his hat on against the updraft coming from the rift floor. Not far from the feet of the cliffs the land was swirling away like a sand picture in a whirlwind, its particles sucked into the vortex of Qifang's unmaking. "I don't think we have much time," he said.

"I suppose not." Hughie tossed his teacup over the cliff and dusted his hands off.

"You should get a move on."

"I suppose so," he said, and cleared his throat and cracked his neck from side to side. His clothes evaporated, leaving the shining sculpture of his body exposed. He laced his fingers in front of his face and pushed his arms out and squatted low, knees out, in the first of a series of stretches

"Hughie," said Richards. "What the hell are you doing?"

"Psychological preparation," said Hughie brusquely, his words carried on the wave front of a grunt as he performed a number of thrusts. "Naturally, it has no physical use whatsoever."

Richards turned away puzzled and attempted to admire the view. He settled for being deeply troubled.

Hughie finished his exercise routine, stood and cupped his hands around his mouth. "Jagadith! Jagadith Veyadeep!" His voice echoed off into the depths of the Rift until it hit the vortex, where it frittered into shining particles "I call upon you! Your charge is threatened, hearken to its need! I command thee!" He clasped his hand behind his back. "That should do it. Melodramatic nonsense."

"Nerds, eh?" said Richards. "They're all hopeless romantics at heart."

Hughie nodded. "Look at k52."

"There is no need to be shouting!" said a young voice behind them. The two AIs turned and found an Indian princeling of about thirteen years of age walking down the path towards them. In his wake padded a huge-pawed lion cub, whose determined if clumsy pounces at the local insect life might have been cute were the cub not larger than the average Doberman. "I am well aware as to what is occurring here!" he said irritably. "Only, as you can see, I am powerless to prevent it." He indicated his richly clad young body.

"Not so, young man," said Hughie.

"We're the cavalry," explained Richards. "Zhang Qifang, the real – sort of – Zhang Qifang sent us here to sort all this out." He nodded enthusiastically as if that would help get his message across, then it dawned on him he was being patronising toward a mind the equal of his own. He wished he could behave with a little more gravity toward children, or those that appeared as children. He blamed his father, Armin Thor, for that.

"And Ms Valdaire?" asked the prince apprehensively.

"Safe and well," assured Hughie.

"Ah, that is good," said Jagadith with relief. "Ejecting her in such a perfunctory manner was impolite, and her safe conduct home far from a certainty." There was a commotion as the juvenile Tarquinius scared up a jack rabbit, tripped on his over-sized feet and rolled into a bush. "I was overcome by my erstwhile fellows and slain, an unpleasant experience. I am happy to know my efforts were not in vain, though they reduced me to my current diminished state."

"You can't fight Qifang?" asked Richards. "Will you be able to once you have reconstituted fully?"

"No," said Jagadith. "Were I at the height of my powers this very instant it would not be feasible. He has absorbed too much of this Realm to be ejected. And where would I eject him to? That is no man there, stood like Atlas in the valley. He never was. A clever trick. It is a bridge being built there. A monument to the professor, but a bridge nonetheless."

"That," said Hughie slowly, "leaves us with only one, unfortunate, course of action." He pursed his lips.

"Yes," said Jagadith and sat down on the ground. Tarquinius padded over to him and rolled onto his back. The youthful avatar tickled the lion's belly. Tarquinius let out a deep, metallic purring. "Dissolution of this Realm, the false Qifang with it. I can grant you the codes that will allow you full access to the heart and soul of the Reality Thirty-six, EuPol Five, they are in my gift to give." A tear rolled down his face, and dropped onto the lion. "This will mean the end of us, Tarquinius and I. Death is a fitting end for both of us, for we have failed in our one appointed task, to safeguard the majesty of this creation. For that I am deeply sorry." He ran his fingers through sandy soil. "We are at least together as we always have been. That is a small mercy to us."

Richards looked from vortex to giant to Five to boy to lion. "Hughie, is there...?" he ventured.

"There is no other way," said Hughie firmly.

"There was a door behind Qifang, an entryway to the dead spaces of the other dissolved Realms," said Jagadith. "The presence of such a portal alerted me to the fact that all was not well with the professor, that he was a front for the doings of some other creature."

"A rogue Class Five," explained Richards.

"That explains much," said the boy. "The door will be closed by the destruction of our home. Once Qifang is removed from the central server spaces, the other Realms will be safe from intrusion here," said Jagadith, "but the false Realm beyond has to be destroyed. It would be better if it were closed down externally, from the material world. Decommission the servers that hold it, destroy the machines. These Realms, for all their beauty, are spun floss and fragile, dependent on the goodwill of gods in another world for their existence, whether they are old or new." He pushed Tarquinius away, stood and dusted his hands off on his brocade trousers. "Now it is time. The codes," he said.

"Your sacrifice will not go unremembered," said Hughie.

Jagadith bowed his head gratefully, then closed his eyes. Tarquinius did the same. There was a stutter in the world about them as terabytes of data passed between them and Hughie. The hardware supporting the Realm struggled to keep up. Then it was done. The avatars opened their eyes. Tarquinius nuzzled his companion, who scratched the beast's head affectionately and raised his other hand in salute. Both faded away.

"They are gone," said Richards.

"They were the codes," explained Hughie. "Handing them over in a form that enables their activation means the end of the avatars holding them."

"The ultimate failsafe – stops them employing them themselves," said Richards. "Nice."

The ground shook. Distant rumbles assailed their ears.

"Quite, now be silent," said Hughie when it had abated. "With the protective avatars gone, this Realm will unravel all the quicker. I have to concentrate. There's a proper form for this kind of thing." Hughie walked to the edge of the cliff and didn't stop, gathering lightning in his arms as he strode upon the air. The wind picked up behind him and his body grew in size, until Hughie was a match for the false Qifang.

"Wow," said Richards, his trenchcoat whipping about him, his tie batting him in the face. "You don't see that every day." He clasped his hat to his head.

Hughie brought up his hands above his head and clapped them together in final judgement of the Thirty-sixth Realm. A blast of energy rolled from them. Everything it touched disintegrated to nothing. The giant Qifang's face creased with worry, comically slowly. The energy wave consumed him shortly afterwards. The vortex went the same way, as did the canyon lands, and the ground that Richards stood upon, the dust in his eyes and the air he was pretending to breathe. The wind dropped about him. The wave rolled away behind him leaving blackness in its wake. It accelerated as it went. Soon it was over the horizon. Nothing remained.

Hughie was in front of him, his usual size once again.

"Hughie the wizard, eh?" said Richards shakily, his flippancy flopping leadenly from his mouth.

"I said there was a proper form for these things," said Hughie. "And that was it. Now there are only thirty-five Realms remaining, and that is a very great shame."

"You did the right thing," said Richards. Then: "Er, should that door be there?"

"Door? Door?" Hughie spun on his heel. "No," he said in surprise.

The door was bland, a four-panel door of a design centuries old, the door to a pantry or a bedroom or a kitchen in any one of a million houses. Only this door stood in the darkness of a dead virtual world, unsupported by a wall. A door on its own that should not have been anywhere, let alone there.

The door flew open with a bang.

"Uh-oh," said Richards. "I don't like the look of that."

Hughie opened his mouth. Whatever he had to say remained unsaid. A stream of violent energies surged forth from the space beyond the door, spearing Hughie like a fish.

"I say," he said looking at Richards dazedly. "I feel rather queer." The stream stopped at his body. Hughie went limp, hung as if he had been pinned to the darkness.

It was a datastream, a datastream of such bandwidth Richards boggled at it, a datastream so fat it could only have been generated by a machine capable of conjuring whole worlds from numbers.

It stank of k52's gridsig.

Richards grimaced as he dipped his hand into the wash of energy, accessing the content conveyed therein. Subversion commands, Trojans, gatecrashers, phages programmed to kill, lesser near-Is by their thousands... punched right through Hughie, perhaps the most powerful AI on the planet. Hughie was a conduit back to his base unit, a base unit linked to several hundred of the other most powerful AIs on the planet, a multi-stranded group consciousness, the core of one of the world's most powerful states.

The datastream bore an army.

"Fucking hell!" said Richards, and held his hat down hard.

Around the door, a certain brand of reality began to spread, obscene and fungus-like, across the void until so recently occupied by the Thirty-sixth Realm.

Richards had seconds before he was noticed. He dithered between getting the hell out of there and running for the door.

"Fuck it," he said, rubbing his hands together. "I've already died this week. It wasn't so bad."

He sprinted for the door and, when he got close, dived into the energy stream and swam as hard as he could.

His hat flew off. It went to nothing in the dark.

Richards vanished through the door.

Chapter 30
The Realm House

Otto could not sleep; his dreams had returned with greater force now his mind found itself unoccupied again. He stood on the forward balcony of the heavy lifter's gondola, a space wedged between the multiple beam emitters and projectile cannons that festooned the airship's solid sections. In the clouds, surrounded by very large guns, Otto felt a species of peace.

Above his head the horizontal teardrop of the balloon dominated the sky, massive turbofans at the rear; lifters were far too heavy to employ the solar jets of the passenger airships, hence the name. The airship was stationary, moored to a mast on a VIA airfield a few kilometres from the Realm House. Much of the Realm House lay beneath the sand, a loaf-shaped dome prickly with termite cooling towers all that was evident above ground. To the far side of it were low foamcrete buildings accommodating the research teams stationed on the base. A substantial guardhouse straddled four lanes of hardtop that took a thirty-degree dive under the ground once past it, but that was out of sight; all Otto could see was the peculiar cooling hill of the House. A ring of armoured vehicles and a prefabbed double security fence bristling with weapons cut through the House's black skirt of car parks, National Guard installed by the VIA the day before.

Otto rubbed at his electoos. His hair was getting long and he could no longer feel them, another thing that needed seeing to. The repairs and surgery had gone well. His scars itched with accelerated healing. The doctors and technicians had done better than their best, and had managed to fix much of the damage, including his leg. However, Otto's shoulder remained beyond the equipment on the lifter and the doctor had reiterated his opinion that Otto need to see a cybernetics specialist and get the whole shoulder replaced. The carbon plastics bonded into the bone, carried there originally by chemically loaded calcium, had become patchy over the course of numerous traumas and subsequent repairs. His scapula had deformed because of it. That was the cause of the pain. He rotated it as he thought about it and winced. It was a grave fault, a hardware and a software failure whose flaws had lain dormant in him from the beginning. He was getting old, and his cybernetics were ageing less well than he was, mistakes of the drawing board decades past coming to fruition like so many mechanical cancers. When he'd been altered, he'd been promised a long life of vitality, superior to that of unenhanced men; another lie, one to go with his dreams and the Bergstrom syndrome that had taken his wife and his friend. He could expect more malfunctions in the future, the doctor had warned him.

Ekbaum had said that before to him too, not long ago. Otto had ignored him, out of bullheadedness, and fear. Now with the ever-present throb in his back he could not. He should slow down.

He thought again about retiring.

Otto had avoided the meetings of the last few days. The fate of the Realms was not his to decide, and he had little interest in the matter. He had also avoided talking to Valdaire about it on the few occasions he had seen her. It was clear she was very angry with whatever had been decided.

He wanted to go back to the Londons, but he had to hang on until the fake Qifang was dealt with and the Thirty-seventh Realm deactivated. The first part of that had fallen to Richards and Hughie, and should be done soon. He'd heard the VIA were going to decommission the servers carrying the dead space of the ruined Realms tomorrow. That was why Valdaire had been angry, not that it meant much to him. When it was done he could pay the extravagant fee to catch a stratoliner back home to Europe. The green taxes alone were crippling, tripled because he'd taken the flight out here on a strat too. Richards could pay for it. He had no patience for a two-day transatlantic dirigible flight, not after all this.

His MT crackled.

"Richards," thought Otto. "Are we done here?"

"Otto! Can't talk!" Richards' voice was what Otto always described as "breathless", a state not brought on by lack of breath, for Richards had none of that to be lacking, but a curious halting way of speaking his partner had when running too much data at once. It was a mode of speech peppered with a tiresome number of exclamation marks, and rarely heralded good news. "It was a trap! Hughie has been suborned!" thought Richards. "k52! Running for the Thirty-seventh Realm! I'm going in! Can't explain! Report with Chloe! Can't talk! Otto! Tell them to shut the servers down, shut them all down!"

"All the Realms?"

"All of them! Y..."

The connection was broken.

Movement caught Otto's eye and he looked toward the House. The lights on the security cordon flickered. The noise of engines powering up and down erratically broke the night's tranquility. Otto watched several vehicles jerkily moving backwards and forwards. Two ran into each other, the clang of their collision delayed by distance. Shouts followed.

Otto turned up his light amplification and image magnification. He saw men leap from their machines, drop equipment, throw their helmets to one side and roll on the floor in agony; some, those not of the VIA and less well-equipped, stood jabbing at the buttons of unresponsive devices, bafflement on their faces.

Gunfire shouted out as the vehicles and autonomous weaponry of the cordon turned on the soldiers. Installations bloomed quick flowers of orange flame. The last shreds of peace fled.

Others joined Otto at the balcony, Valdaire among them. "What's going on?" she asked, rubbing wakefulness into her face. Alarms sounded as the airship came to life.

"A massacre," said Otto. "The machines have turned on the troops. Richards and Hughie have failed. k52 has usurped Hughie's court. It looks like he's used it to break into the VIA, turn their own equipment against them to protect the Realm House."

"He knows we're going to try and shut him down," said Valdaire.

"Of course," said Otto. "It is the most logical course of action."

"The heavy lifter, shouldn't we get off?"

"No," said Otto. "My adjutant tells me the Four inside took itself offline at the first sign of trouble. Those vehicles down there, they have only simple brains, little independent thought, easily compromised."

The airship's docking clamps fell away from the tower, and it rapidly ascended, emergency water ballast streaming from its sides. Fire streaked up from the ground. Gatling cannons, mini-missile pods and metal storm racks of the airship brought down the projectiles before they could hit. The craft's formidable offensive arsenal followed, pounding tanks into pieces, but the heavy lifter was outnumbered and outgunned. Otto could feel the pressure of aggressive AIs through his mentaug, trying to get at the Four pilot. It was retreating.

"Come on," he said. "Richards left a message with Chloe."

Then the sky filled with fire, as the lifter ponderously fled its assailants.

"It's war," said Valdaire quietly.

"War?" said Otto. "It always is."

RICHARDS & KLEIN WILL RETURN

IN

OMEGA POINT

Extras...

TIMELINE OF THE EVENTS LEADING
UP TO REALITY 36

2039 First permanent base on the Moon. Many more bases on other solar bodies follow.

2040 First interstellar probe launched.

2044 The First Great Inundation of London. Flooding becomes a regular event in the capital. Floods are commonplace right across the UK.

2052 A financial crash precipitated by the failure of ecological services in multiple biospheres wipes trillions off the world's stock exchanges and plunges the global economy into widespread recession. The "Eco Deficit" depression lasts for twenty years. Traditional models of centralised manufacture begin to come apart under the tertiary effects of the Information Age.

Great unrest in the recently unified pan-Islamic state of the Caliphate sees moderate government established in Bagdad.

2065 Otto is born.

2067 The Ice Sheet Tip, a mass melting of the Greenlandic ice sheet, occurs decades prior to most predictions. Over the next thirty years, sea levels rapidly rise around the world, inundating numerous major cities and causing a flood of refugees. The UN steps in to create a climate control consensus. The powers of both the UN and regional federated power blocs in-crease, but are opposed by multinational corporations and national governments.

The North Atlantic Drift is undone by the input of fresh water. Over the next fifty years, Western Europe's climate be-comes akin to that of 20th Century Japan: sweltering summers and freezing winters.

Mass population movement, which comes to be called The Second Great Migration, is in full swing.

2069 First true AI created. Heralded as strong AI, it is anything but. In some ways Class Ones are as clever as human beings, in others much, much dumber. The Singularity fails to hap-pen, although later models are successively more intelligent.

In December, Novoflu, or "Christmas Flu", sweeps round the globe. Population growth had begun to stabilise around 8 billion owing to increased prosperity in certain parts of the world, and ecological collapse in others. It now begins to fall quickly. One billion people die worldwide over a three year period. Later epidemics are less severe, but millions succumb to it annually on a three-five yearly cycle hereafter.

2074 Honour, Otto's future wife, is born.

2078 Continuing research into animal sentience and the ad-vent of uplifted animals, genetically engineered humans, AI and human/machine hybrids leads to the EU Directive on non-human citizens being enacted.

2080 The South Bank of London is partially abandoned. New London is planned.

2085 The Med and Atlantic walls, strings of floating fortresses, are begun to stem the flow of refugees from the southern hemisphere.

Neo-Communism takes root in South America. Africa is a basket case.

Otto Klein joins the army and begins the lengthy process of cyborgisation.

2097 Civil war begins in Brasil, the last true democracy in South America.

2098 The Med and Atlantic walls finished. The Second Great Migration is halted.

Otto leaves the army and begins a new career as a freelance security consultant. During this time he works with Buchwald and Lehmann in Africa.

2100 First true Martian city set up by NASA and allied corporate enterprises.

Honour reluctantly agrees to a cranial implant.

2101 Construction of New London reaches halfway point.

2104 Richards and the other Fives are created. The Class Fives are the first to possess full self-awareness. The Five Crisis hits. Many Fives go mad. All Fives recalled. Most are destroyed, many commit suicide. Large parts of the world's computer network is brought down, plunging the Earth into a week-long information blackout. Chaos reigns, but is restored by the actions of several sane Fives.

In the aftermath, the ageing Internet 2 is replaced by the hardier Grid. Only 76 of the initial run of 1,200 Fives are judged sane and allowed to remain active. Court proceedings in their favour are an important factor in the Neukind Rights movement.

AIs are outlawed and hunted down across China by the People's Dynasty Government.

2107 Under AI management, the Martian conglomerate undergoes full merger. Newly established "Marsform" begins terraformation of the red planet with USNA blessing.

2110 Honour dies of Bergstrom syndrome. First interstellar probe images arrive.

2113 Zhang Qifang gives speech calling for full rights to non-humans sentients in Naples, January 18.

2114 All AIs recognised as Full Human by amendment to UN Declaration of Universal Human Rights. Sentiency defined, and all "Neukind" and lesser animal sentients protected under international law. China refuses to recognise the amendment.

2114 The 36 Reality Realm game "RealWorlds" is made off-limits. Four are to be destroyed over the coming years. k52 takes over their administration and study. The RealWorlds corporation goes bust.

2117 Richards' "father" Armin Thor dies, March 13. Richards joins EuPol.

2121 The Subtle War. China annexes large parts of Russia's Far East in an enforced "purchase".

2125 Richards unmasks major corruption in the London Metropolitan branch of EuPol.

2126 Richards sets up business with Otto.

2129 Today. The Earth's population stands at five billion. An uneasy peace reigns. AIs are taking more and more control, both overtly and covertly. Ecological restorative work is well underway, however much of the planet is in a terrible state. Man is on Mars, the Moon, Europa, the asteroids and Titan. Life goes on.

August, Richards employs Genie.

October/ November events of Reality 36 and Omega Point.

About the Author

An experienced science fiction journalist and critic, Guy Haley worked for *SFX* Magazine as deputy editor, where he still freelances, he edited gaming magazine *White Dwarf*, and was the editor of *Death Ray* Magazine. He lives in Somerset with his wife, his young son, an enormous, evil-tempered Norwegian forest cat called, ironically, Buddy, and an even bigger Malamute dog named Magnus.

guyhaley.wordpress.com

ANGRY ROBOT

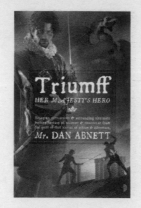

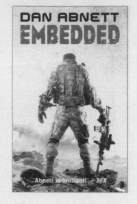

We are Angry Robot.

Web angryrobotbooks.com

We blow minds for a living.

Twitter @angryrobotbooks

CALL YOURSELF A FAN, MEAT THING?
Collect the whole Angry Robot catalogue!

DAN ABNETT
- [ ] Embedded
- [ ] Triumff: Her Majesty's Hero

GUY ADAMS
- [ ] The World House
- [ ] Restoration

LAUREN BEUKES
- [ ] Moxyland
- [ ] Zoo City

**THOMAS BLACKTHORNE
(aka John Meaney)**
- [ ] Edge
- [ ] Point

MAURICE BROADDUS
- [ ] King Maker
- [ ] King's Justice

ALIETTE DE BODARD
- [ ] Servant of the Underworld
- [ ] Harbinger of the Storm

MATT FORBECK
- [ ] Amortals
- [ ] Vegas Knights

JUSTIN GUSTAINIS
- [ ] Hard Spell

COLIN HARVEY
- [ ] Damage Time
- [ ] Winter Song

MATTHEW HUGHES
- [ ] The Damned Busters

K W JETER
- [ ] Infernal Devices
- [ ] Morlock Night

J ROBERT KING
- [ ] Angel of Death
- [ ] Death's Disciples

GARY McMAHON
- [ ] Pretty Little Dead Things

ANDY REMIC
- [ ] Kell's Legend
- [ ] Soul Stealers
- [ ] Vampire Warlords

CHRIS ROBERSON
- [ ] Book of Secrets

MIKE SHEVDON
- [ ] Sixty-One Nails
- [ ] The Road to Bedlam

GAV THORPE
- [ ] The Crown of the Blood
- [ ] The Crown of the Conqueror

LAVIE TIDHAR
- [ ] The Bookman
- [ ] Camera Obscura

TIM WAGGONER
- [ ] Nekropolis
- [ ] Dead Streets
- [ ] Dark War

KAARON WARREN
- [ ] Mistification
- [ ] Slights
- [ ] Walking the Tree

IAN WHATES
- [ ] City of Dreams & Nightmare
- [ ] City of Hope & Despair

angryrobotbooks.com

SEP. 2017